THE COMPLEX VISION

THE COMPLEX VISION
A COLLECTION OF SHORT STORIES

Edited by

RAY KYTLE
Central Michigan University

and

ANNETTE PETERSON KYTLE
Central Michigan University

HARCOURT BRACE JOVANOVICH, INC.
New York   Chicago   San Francisco   Atlanta

ISBN: 0-15-512615-6

Library of Congress Catalog Card Number: 70-187854

Printed in the United States of America

Contents

Introduction   *1*

Coming to terms with oneself   7

BARN BURNING
William Faulkner   *9*
GOLD COAST
James Alan McPherson   *26*
THE SHORT HAPPY LIFE OF FRANCIS MACOMBER
Ernest Hemingway   *42*

Understanding others   *71*

THE EIGHTY-YARD RUN
Irwin Shaw   *73*
HAIRCUT
Ring Lardner   *86*
RAIN
W. Somerset Maugham   *97*
THE BLUE HOTEL
Stephen Crane   *133*

Man and nature   *159*

TO BUILD A FIRE
Jack London   *161*
THE LEDGE
Lawrence Sargent Hall   *176*

The way life is

191

THE PATENTED GATE AND THE MEAN HAMBURGER
Robert Penn Warren   193

THE LANGUAGE OF MEN
Norman Mailer   205

THE WALL
Jean-Paul Sartre   216

THE PORTABLE PHONOGRAPH
Walter Van Tilburg Clark   234

Plumbing the depths

241

LA LUPA
Giovanni Verga   243

THE WORLD THE CHILDREN MADE
Ray Bradbury   248

THE COVE
Gina Berriault   261

Just for fun—and sanity

269

HEARTBURN
Hortense Calisher   271

THE OPEN WINDOW
"Saki" (H. H. Munro)   281

THE CATBIRD SEAT
James Thurber   285

For Discussion   295

A Selected Bibliography   305

THE COMPLEX VISION

Introduction

At a time when the rhetoric of confrontation often seems the only rhetoric left to us, we might profitably examine the old Hellenic rhetoric of balance. For the Greek philosophers, Plato as well as Aristotle, balance was the goal and the finest achievement of humanity. One of the best ways to achieve this balance was through a recognition of the complexity of man's universe and an acceptance of that complexity, that is, through the development of a sense of *irony*. For the Greeks, achieving this recognition and this acceptance was a humanizing experience; we believe that it continues to be so for all men.

The nature of irony in literature is the same as in life; the vision, the stance, and the techniques are the same. The literary ironist is more than anything else a man of complex vision, a man who sees the universe (and himself) as an incredibly complicated and paradoxical system—if a system at all. Unlike the romantic who is hungry for absolutes, the ironist is afraid of absolute-poisoning. He is Heraclitean in his conviction that the only certainty is uncertainty, that only change abides. He is a skeptic who is skeptical even of his skepticism; a relativist who nevertheless takes sides, though always tentatively; a Faust hungry for all knowledge and experience and equally an anti-Faust who derides knowledge, and sometimes life itself, as meaningless. He is more Apollonian than Dionysian, but he mocks the god of reason and moderation even as he invokes his blessing.

A brief and partial glance at the development of literary irony may be helpful before we turn to the modern concept of irony and its literary use today. In the Greek "old comedy" two of the stock characters were the *alazon* and the *eiron*. The *alazon* was a "boastful imposter"; the *eiron,* though apparently simple-minded and vulnerable, was in reality a sly and canny dissembler. The cunning *eiron* always got the best of the braggart *alazon;* his method was to pose as the ignorant, innocent, and ingenuous fool. When the *alazon* took the bait, the trap snapped shut, and the *eiron* (irony) won again. Both dramatic characters were rogues and pretenders; but, for the Greek lovers of comedy, understatement was more appealing and more effective than hyperbole.

Not only in comedy did the Greek dramatists reveal their love of irony. Their tragedies too were often based on a kind of dissembling Fate who made great promises to proud men and then kept those promises in tragically unexpected ways. In *Oedipus Rex,* for example, Oedipus becomes almost the tragic equivalent of the comic *alazon,* boasting that he will find the truth and punish the transgressor. The gods (or Fate) allow him to discover the truth he seeks, but irony is again triumphant. Oedipus himself is the transgressor, and it is he who must mete out the punishment to himself. In most Greek tragedy (and, some would argue, in all tragedy), the tragic hero is punished both for his pride (*hubris*) and for the concomitant failure of his reason to distinguish between the appearances of his world and its reality.

The Greek philosophers and poets, as well as the Greek dramatists, were often ironists. Socrates feigned ignorance so that his students might find their own way to "truth"; today we use the phrase "Socratic irony" to indicate this philosophic method. Homer, the Greek epic poet, created one of the archetypal ironic characters. His hero Odysseus survived because of his "resourcefulness" and adaptability, that is, because he could change from boastful warrior (*alazon*) to sly and canny dissembler (*eiron*) at a moment's notice. Homer's hero had many masks, and it was his use of masks which allowed him to survive, survival being the ironist's ultimate goal.

III

From the age of the Greeks to modern times, the ironic temper in literature has opposed itself to man's tendency to take things at face value; has been consistently wary of deception (especially self-deception); and has taken the perhaps defensive stance of assumed modesty and ignorance in preference to the romantic, Byronic attitude of arrogance and defiance. The ironic vision does not belong to one age or culture. It has, however, been especially pervasive in twentieth-century literature. In this century the most notable English and American writers have been ironists. Few of the great poets or novelists of modern times have been without "the complex vision" of the ironic perspective. In this century of rapid change, in which disillusion steps on the heels of illusion, in which one decade's truths become the next decade's lies, in which powerful men—and nations—are threatened and destroyed almost casually, in which all of the old faiths—political, religious, psychological—are being challenged, how could it possibly be otherwise? Today a man who sees his life and his universe as simple and uncomplicated may be content, but he is unlikely to be a writer or an artist of any kind.

Obviously there are some writers—and good ones—who are not primarily ironic in their vision. Several modern writers of great power have agreed with the post-conversion Tolstoi that simple truths, simple morality, and simple literature are needed to take us out of our incredibly complex world and back to times and ideas more gentle than our own. Among these writers and artists are the nostalgic, the primitive, the heroic, and the saintly; all of whom appeal to and assault our feelings and emotions. But the wary readers of the twentieth century are likely to be suspicious of emotional calls to arms; of simple truths which, on examination, often turn out to be not-so-simple lies; of promises which are not always kept; of righteousness which sometimes becomes complacency, hypocrisy, or brutality. Believers who have been robbed of their beliefs are likely to become skeptics, cynics, or nihilists. Thomas Mann wrote in the middle of this century that modern man's only choice is "radicalism or irony." As we approach the century's final quarter, many social critics tend to agree with Mann.

IV

The essence of irony is tension. Not the emotional tenseness created by a suspense story, but an intellectual tension created by incongruity—by the contrast between what appears to be and what really is, between what is intended and what is achieved, between the way a person views himself and the way others view him, between what is said and what is meant, between what is attempted and what is achieved, between what is and what should be. This cartoon is ironic:

As is this poem:

> A man said to the universe:
> "Sir, I exist!"
> "However," replied the universe,
> "The fact has not created in me
>   a sense of obligation."

Stephen Crane

The person who cultivates an ability to recognize and appreciate irony cultivates a sense of proportion. He gains the ability to view others, himself, and life itself from multiple perspectives. And in doing so, he inevitably acquires a sense of objectivity, a philosophical balance and steadfastness. The ironist is equally unlikely to try to save society by bombing a building or by lynching the bomber. He sees the irony inherent in each extreme and is stayed. Neither could an ironist state, in solemn uncomprehending rationalization, "We had to destroy the village to save it." He could never make such a statement in seriousness because he would perceive the ironic contradiction it entails. Unable to make such a statement, he would be equally unable to commit the action that statement attempts to justify. To cultivate one's ability to recognize and appreciate irony is, ultimately, to cultivate one's essential humanity.

And that is the reason for this book. We attempt to take the reader on an imaginative journey that parallels the stages of emotional and intellectual growth postulated by some psychologists. First, the focus is on the self, the "I," the need for an established identity. In Section Two, the focus broadens to include "significant others," the people immediately around us. Expanding the complex vision still further, the stories in Section Three explore man's relationship to nature. The terrible complexities and ambiguities of the societies in which men live are demonstrated in Sections Four and Five. Finally, in Section Six, the reader is invited to conclude his journey with three imaginative stories offered just for fun and, perchance, for sanity.

Coming to terms with oneself

Barn Burning

William Faulkner
(1897–1962)

Faulkner grew up in Oxford, Mississippi (the "Jefferson" of his novels). As a teenager, he demonstrated a strong interest in literature, but never completed high school. During World War I, Faulkner enlisted in the Canadian Royal Flying Corps; when the war ended he returned to Oxford and studied briefly at the University of Mississippi. In 1922 Faulkner took a position as postmaster at the University; he thought that the job would allow him time to write but, instead, found himself "at the beck and call of every son-of-a-bitch who happened to have two cents." He resigned and moved in 1924 to New Orleans, where he became associated with members of the literary community. While in New Orleans, Faulkner wrote his first novel, Soldier's Pay *(1926), and* Mosquitoes *(1927), a satire on contemporary writers. But not until Faulkner returned to Oxford and began to write about his home county was his creative genius realized.*

Beginning in 1929 with Sartoris *and* The Sound and the Fury, *Faulkner wrote novels and short stories about the South that soon made him one of America's most celebrated authors and the winner in 1950 of the Nobel Prize for literature. Faulkner's major works include* As I Lay Dying *(1930);* Absalom, Absalom! *(1936);* The Unvanquished *(1938);* The Hamlet *(1940);* Go Down, Moses and Other Stories *(1942);* Intruder in the Dust *(1948);* Collected Stories *(1950);* Requiem for a Nun *(1951);* The Town *(1957);* The Mansion *(1959); and* The Reivers *(1962).*

Lhe store in which the justice of the peace's court was sitting smelled of cheese. The boy, crouched on his nail keg at the back of the crowded room, knew he smelled cheese, and more: from where he sat he could see the ranked shelves close-packed with the solid, squat, dynamic shapes of tin cans whose labels his stomach read, not from the lettering which meant nothing to his mind but from the scarlet devils and the silver curve of fish—this, the cheese which he knew he smelled and the hermetic meat which his intestines believed he smelled coming in intermittent gusts momentary and brief between the other constant one, the smell and sense just a little of fear because mostly of despair and grief, the old fierce pull of blood. He could not see the table where the Justice sat and before which his father and his father's enemy (*our enemy* he thought in that despair; *ourn! mine and hisn both! He's my father!*) stood, but he could hear them, the two of them that is, because his father had said no word yet:

"But what proof have you, Mr. Harris?"

"I told you. The hog got into my corn. I caught it up and sent it back to him. He had no fence that would hold it. I told him so, warned him. The next time I put the hog in my pen. When he came to get it I gave him enough wire to patch up his pen. The next time I put the hog up and kept it. I rode down to his house and saw the wire I gave him still rolled on to the spool in his yard. I told him he could have the hog when he paid me a dollar pound fee. That evening a nigger came with the dollar and got the hog. He was a strange nigger. He said, 'He say to tell you wood and hay kin burn.' I said, 'What?' 'That whut he say to tell you,' the nigger said. 'Wood and hay kin burn.' That night my barn burned. I got the stock out but I lost the barn."

"Where is the nigger? Have you got him?"

"He was a strange nigger, I tell you. I don't know what became of him."

"But that's not proof. Don't you see that's not proof?"

"Get that boy up here. He knows." For a moment the boy thought too that the man meant his older brother until Harris said, "Not him. The little one. The boy," and, crouching, small for his age, small and wiry like his father, in patched and faded jeans even too small for him, with straight, uncombed, brown hair and eyes gray and wild as storm scud, he saw the men between himself and the table part and become a lane of grim faces, at the end of which he saw the Justice, a shabby, collarless, graying man in spectacles, beckoning him. He felt no floor under his bare feet; he seemed to walk beneath the palpable weight of the grim turning faces. His father, stiff in his black Sunday coat donned not for the trial but for the moving, did not even look at him. *He aims for me to lie,* he thought, again with that frantic grief and despair. *And I will have to do hit.*

"What's your name, boy?" the Justice said.

"Colonel Sartoris Snopes," the boy whispered.

"Hey?" the Justice said. "Talk louder. Colonel Sartoris? I reckon anybody named for Colonel Sartoris in this country can't help but tell the truth, can they?" The boy said nothing. *Enemy! Enemy!* he thought; for a moment he could not even see, could not see that the Justice's face was kindly nor discern that his voice was troubled when he spoke to the man named Harris: "Do you want me to question this boy?" But he could hear, and during those subsequent long seconds while there was absolutely no sound in the crowded little room save that of quiet and intent breathing it was as if he had swung outward at the end of a grape vine, over a ravine, and at the top of the swing had been caught in a prolonged instant of mesmerized gravity, weightless in time.

"No!" Harris said violently, explosively. "Damnation! Send him out of here!" Now time, the fluid world, rushed beneath him again, the voices coming to him again through the smell of cheese and sealed meat, the fear and despair and the old grief of blood:

"This case is closed. I can't find against you, Snopes, but I can give you advice. Leave this country and don't come back to it."

His father spoke for the first time, his voice cold and harsh, level, without emphasis: "I aim to. I don't figure to stay in a country among people who. . . ," he said something unprintable and vile, addressed to no one.

"That'll do," the Justice said. "Take your wagon and get out of this country before dark. Case dismissed."

His father turned, and he followed the stiff black coat, the wiry figure walking a little stiffly from where a Confederate provost's man's musket ball had taken him in the heel on a stolen horse thirty years ago, followed the two backs now, since his older brother had appeared from somewhere in the crowd, no taller than the father but thicker, chewing tobacco steadily, between the two lines of grim-faced men and out of the store and across the worn gallery and down the sagging steps and among the dogs and half-grown boys in the mild May dust, where as he passed a voice hissed:

"Barn burner!"

Again he could not see, whirling; there was a face in a red haze, moonlike, bigger than the full moon, the owner of it half again his size, he leaping in the red haze toward the face, feeling no blow, feeling no shock when his head struck the earth, scrabbling up and leaping again, feeling no blow this time either and tasting no blood, scrabbling up to see the other boy in full flight and himself already leaping into pursuit as his father's hand jerked him back, the harsh, cold voice speaking above him: "Go get in the wagon."

It stood in a grove of locusts and mulberries across the road. His two hulking sisters in their Sunday dresses and his mother and her sister in calico and sunbonnets were already in it, sitting on and among the sorry residue of the dozen and more movings which even the boy could remember—the battered stove, the broken beds and chairs, the clock inlaid with mother-of-pearl, which would not run, stopped at some fourteen minutes past two o'clock of a dead and forgotten day and time, which had been his mother's dowry. She was crying, though when she saw him she drew her sleeve across her face and began to descend from the wagon. "Get back," the father said.

"He's hurt. I got to get some water and wash his. . . ."

"Get back in the wagon," his father said. He got in too, over the tail-gate. His father mounted to the seat where the older brother already sat and struck the gaunt mules two savage blows with the peeled willow, but without heat. It was not even sadistic; it was exactly that same quality which in later years would cause his descendants to overrun the engine before putting a motor car into motion, striking and reining back in the same movement. The wagon went on, the store with its quiet crowd of grimly watching men dropped behind; a curve in the road hid it. *Forever* he thought. *Maybe he's done satisfied now, now that he has . . .* stopping himself, not to say it aloud even to himself. His mother's hand touched his shoulder.

"Does it hurt?" she said.

"Naw," he said. "Hit don't hurt. Lemme be."

"Can't you wipe some of the blood off before hit dries?"

"I'll wash tonight," he said. "Lemme be, I tell you."

The wagon went on. He did not know where they were going. None of them ever did or ever asked, because it was always somewhere, always a house of sorts waiting for them a day or two days or even three days away. Likely his father had already arranged to make a crop on another farm before he. . . . Again he had to stop himself. He (the father) always did. There was something about his wolf-like independence and even courage when the advantage was at least neutral which impressed strangers, as if they got from his latent ravening ferocity not so much a sense of dependability as a feeling that his ferocious conviction in the rightness of his own actions would be of advantage to all whose interest lay with his.

That night they camped, in a grove of oaks and beeches where a spring ran. The nights were still cool and they had a fire against it, of a rail lifted from a nearby fence and cut into lengths—a small fire, neat, niggard almost, a shrewd fire; such fires were his father's habit and custom always, even in freezing weather. Older, the boy might have remarked this and wondered why not a big one; why should not a man who had not only seen the waste and extravagance of war, but who had in his blood an inherent voracious prodigality with material not his own, have burned everything in sight? Then he might have gone a step farther and thought that that was the reason: that niggard blaze was the living fruit of nights passed during those four years in the woods hiding from all men, blue or gray, with his strings of horses (captured horses, he called them). And older still, he might have divined the true reason: that the element of fire spoke to some deep main-spring of his father's being, as the element of steel or of power spoke to other men, as the one weapon for the preservation of in-tegrity, else breath were not worth the breathing, and hence to be regarded with respect and used with discretion.

But he did not think this now and he had seen those same niggard blazes all his life. He merely ate his supper beside it and was already half asleep over his iron plate when his father called him, and once more he followed the stiff back, the stiff and ruthless limp, up the slope and on to the starlit road where, turn-ing, he could see his father against the stars but without face or depth—a shape black, flat, and bloodless as though cut from tin in the iron folds of the frockcoat which had not been made for him, the voice harsh like tin and without heat like tin:

"You were fixing to tell them. You would have told him." He didn't answer. His father struck him with the flat of his hand on the side of the head, hard but without heat, exactly as he had struck the two mules at the store, exactly as he would strike either of them with any stick in order to kill a horse fly, his voice still without fear or anger: "You're getting to be a man. You got to learn. You got to stick to your own blood or you ain't going to have any blood to stick to you. Do you think either of them, any man there this morning would? Don't you know all they wanted was a chance to get at me because they knew I had them beat? Eh?" Later, twenty years later, he was to tell himself, "If I had

said they wanted only truth, justice, he would have hit me again."
But now he said nothing. He was not crying. He just stood there.
"Answer me," his father said.

"Yes," he whispered. His father turned.

"Get on to bed. We'll be there tomorrow."

Tomorrow they were there. In the early afternoon the wagon stopped before a paintless two-room house identical almost with the dozen others it had stopped before even in the boy's ten years, and again, as on the other dozen occasions, his mother and aunt got down and began to unload the wagon, although his two sisters and his father and brother had not moved.

"Likely hit ain't fitten for hawgs," one of the sisters said.

"Nevertheless, fit it will and you'll hog it and like it," his father said. "Get out them chairs and help your Ma unload."

The two sisters got down, big, bovine, in a flutter of cheap ribbons; one of them drew from the jumbled wagon bed a battered lantern, the other a worn broom. His father handed the reins to the older son and began to climb stiffly over the wheel. "When they get unloaded, take the team to the barn and feed them." Then he said, and at first the boy thought he was still speaking to his brother: "Come with me."

"Me?" he said.

"Yes," his father said. "You."

"Abner," his mother said. His father paused and looked back —the harsh level stare beneath the shaggy, graying, irascible brows.

"I reckon I'll have a word with the man that aims to begin tomorrow owning me body and soul for the next eight months."

They went back up the road. A week ago—or before last night, that is—he would have asked where they were going, but not now. His father had struck him before last night but never before had he paused afterward to explain why; it was as if the blow and the following calm, outrageous voice still rang, repercussed, divulging nothing to him save the terrible handicap of being young, the light weight of his few years, just heavy enough to prevent his soaring free of the world as it seemed to be ordered but not heavy enough to keep him footed solid in it, to resist it and try to change the course of its events.

Presently he could see the grove of oaks and cedars and the other flowering trees and shrubs where the house would be, though not the house yet. They walked beside a fence massed with honeysuckle and Cherokee roses and came to a gate swinging open between two brick pillars, and now, beyond a sweep of drive, he saw the house for the first time and at that instant he forgot his father and the terror and despair both, and even when he remembered his father again (who had not stopped) the terror and despair did not return. Because, for all the twelve mornings, they had sojourned until now in a poor country, a land of small farms and fields and houses, and he had never seen a house like this before. *Hit's big as a courthouse* he thought quietly, with a surge of peace and joy whose reason he could not have thought into words, being too young for that: *They are safe from him. People whose lives are a part of this peace and dignity are beyond his touch, he no more to them than a buzzing wasp: capable of stinging for a little moment but that's all; the spell of this peace and dignity rendering even the barns and stable and cribs which belong to it impervious to the puny flames he might contrive* . . . this, the peace and joy, ebbing for an instant as he looked again at the stiff black back, the stiff and implacable limp of the figure which was not dwarfed by the house, for the reason that it had never looked big anywhere and which now, against the serene columned backdrop, had more than ever that impervious quality of something cut ruthlessly from tin, depthless, as though, sidewise to the sun, it would cast no shadow. Watching him, the boy remarked the absolutely undeviating course which his father held and saw the stiff foot come squarely down in a pile of fresh droppings where a horse had stood in the drive and which his father could have avoided by a simple change of stride. But it ebbed only for a moment, though he could not have thought this into words either, walking on in the spell of the house, which he could even want but without envy, without sorrow, certainly never with that ravening and jealous rage which unknown to him walked in the ironlike black coat before him: *Maybe he will feel it too. Maybe it will even change him now from what maybe he couldn't help but be.*

They crossed the portico. Now he could hear his father's stiff foot as it came down on the boards with clocklike finality, a sound out of all proportion to the displacement of the body it bore and which was not dwarfed either by the white door before it, as though it had attained to a sort of vicious and ravening minimum not to be dwarfed by anything—the flat, wide, black hat, the formal coat of broadcloth which had once been black but which had now that friction-glazed greenish cast of the bodies of old house flies, the lifted sleeve which was too large, the lifted hand like a curled claw. The door opened so promptly that the boy knew the Negro must have been watching them all the time, an old man with neat grizzled hair, in a linen jacket, who stood barring the door with his body, saying, "Wipe yo foots, white man, fo you come in here. Major ain't home nowhow."

"Get out of my way, nigger," his father said, without heat too, flinging the door back and the Negro also and entering, his hat still on his head. And now the boy saw the prints of the stiff foot on the doorjamb and saw them appear on the pale rug behind the machinelike deliberation of the foot which seemed to bear (or transmit) twice the weight which the body compassed. The Negro was shouting "Miss Lula! Miss Lula!" somewhere behind them, then the boy, deluged as though by a warm wave by a suave turn of carpeted stair and a pendant glitter of chandeliers and a mute gleam of gold frames, heard the swift feet and saw her too, a lady —perhaps he had never seen her like before either—in a gray, smooth gown with lace at the throat and an apron tied at the waist and the sleeves turned back, wiping cake or biscuit dough from her hands with a towel as she came up the hall, looking not at his father at all but the tracks on the blond rug with an expression of incredulous amazement.

"I tried," the Negro cried. "I tole him to. . . ."

"Will you please go away?" she said in a shaking voice. "Major de Spain is not at home. Will you please go away?"

His father had not spoken again. He did not speak again. He did not even look at her. He just stood stiff in the center of the rug, in his hat, the shaggy iron-gray brows twitching slightly above the pebble-colored eyes as he appeared to examine the house with brief deliberation. Then with the same deliberation he turned; the boy watched him pivot on the good leg and saw the stiff foot drag round the arc of the turning, leaving a final long and fading smear. His father never looked at it, he never once looked down at the rug. The Negro held the door. It closed behind them, upon the hysteric and indistinguishable woman-wail. His father stopped at the top of the steps and scraped his boot clean on the edge of it. At the gate he stopped again. He stood for a moment, planted stiffly on the stiff foot, looking back at the house. "Pretty and white ain't it?" he said. "That's sweat. Nigger sweat. Maybe it ain't white enough yet to suit him. Maybe he wants to mix some white sweat with it."

Two hours later the boy was chopping wood behind the house within which his mother and aunt and the two sisters (the mother and aunt, not the two girls, he knew that; even at this distance and muffled by walls the flat loud voices of the two girls emanated an incorrigible idle inertia) were setting up the stove to prepare a meal, when he heard the hooves and saw the linen-clad man on a fine sorrel mare, whom he recognized even before he saw the rolled rug in front of the Negro youth following on a flat bay carriage horse—a suffused, angry face vanishing, still at full gallop, beyond the corner of the house where his father and brother were sitting in the two tilted chairs; and a moment later, almost before he could have put the axe down, he heard the hooves again and watched the sorrel mare go back out of the yard, already galloping again. Then his father began to shout one of the sisters' names, who presently emerged backward from the kitchen door dragging the rolled rug along the ground by one end while the other sister walked behind it.

"If you ain't going to tote, go on and set up the wash pot," the first said.

"You Sarty!" the second shouted. "Set up the wash pot!" His father appeared at the door, framed against that shabbiness, as he had been against that other bland perfection, impervious to either, the mother's anxious face at his shoulder.

"Go on," the father said. "Pick it up." The two sisters stooped, broad, lethargic; stooping, they presented an incredible expanse of pale cloth and a flutter of tawdry ribbons.

"If I thought enough of a rug to have to git hit all the way from France I wouldn't keep hit where folks coming in would have to tromp on hit," the first said. They raised the rug.

"Abner," the mother said. "Let me do it."

"You go back and git dinner," his father said. "I'll tend to this."

From the woodpile through the rest of the afternoon the boy watched them, the rug spread flat in the dust beside the bubbling wash-pot, the two sisters stooping over it with that profound and lethargic reluctance, while the father stood over them in turn, implacable and grim, driving them though never raising his voice again. He could smell the harsh homemade lye they were using; he saw his mother come to the door once and look toward them with an expression not anxious now but very like despair; he saw his father turn, and he fell to with the axe and saw from the corner of his eye his father raise from the ground a flattish fragment of field stone and examine it and return to the pot, and this time his mother actually spoke: "Abner. Abner. Please don't. Please Abner."

Then he was done too. It was dusk; the whippoorwills had already begun. He could smell coffee from the room where they would presently eat the cold food remaining from the mid-afternoon meal, though when he entered the house he realized they were having coffee again probably because there was a fire on the hearth, before which the rug now lay spread over the backs of the two chairs. The tracks of his father's foot were gone. Where they had been were now long, water-cloudy scoriations resembling the sporadic course of a Lilliputian mowing machine.

It still hung there while they ate the cold food and then went to bed, scattered without order or claim up and down the two rooms, his mother in one bed, where his father would later lie, the older brother in the other, himself, the aunt, and the two sisters on pallets on the floor. But his father was not in bed yet. The last thing the boy remembered was the depthless, harsh silhouette of the hat and coat bending over the rug and it seemed to him that he had not even closed his eyes when the silhouette was standing over him, and the fire was almost dead behind it, the stiff foot prodding him awake. "Catch up the mule," his father said.

When he returned with the mule his father was standing in the back door the rolled rug over his shoulder. "Ain't you going to ride?" he said.

"No. Give me your foot."

He bent his knee into his father's hand, the wiry, surprising power flowed smoothly, rising, he rising with it, on to the mule's bare back (they had owned a saddle once; the boy could remember it though not when or where) and with the same effortlessness his father swung the rug up in front of him. Now in the starlight they retraced the afternoon's path, up the dusty road rife with honeysuckle, through the gate and up the black tunnel of the drive to the lightless house, where he sat on the mule and felt the rough warp of the rug drag across his thighs and vanish.

"Don't you want me to help?" he whispered. His father did not answer and now he heard again that stiff foot striking the hollow portico with that wooden and clocklike deliberation, that outrageous overstatement of the weight it carried. The rug, hunched, not flung (the boy could tell that even in the darkness) from his father's shoulder struck the angle of wall and floor with a sound unbelievably loud, thunderous, then the foot again, unhurried and enormous; a light came on in the house and the boy sat, tense, breathing steadily and quietly and just a little fast, though the foot itself did not increase its beat at all, descending the steps now; now the boy could see him.

"Don't you want to ride now?" he whispered. "We kin both ride now," the light within the house altering now, flaring up and sinking. *He's coming down the stairs now,* he thought. He had already ridden the mule up beside the horse block; presently his father was up behind him and he doubled the reins over and slashed the mule across the neck, but before the animal could begin to trot the hard thin arm came round him, the hard, knotted hand jerked the mule back to a walk.

In the first red rays of the sun they were in the lot, putting plow gear on the mules. This time the sorrel mare was in the lot before he heard it at all, the rider collarless and even bareheaded, trembling, speaking in a shaking voice as the woman in the house had done, his father merely looking up once before stooping again to the hame he was buckling, so that the man on the mare spoke to his stooping back:

"You must realize you have ruined that rug. Wasn't there anybody here, any of your women. . . ." he ceased, shaking, the boy watching him, the older brother leaning now in the stable door, chewing, blinking slowly and steadily at nothing apparently. "It cost a hundred dollars. But you never had a hundred dollars. You never will. So I'm going to charge you twenty bushels of corn against your crop. I'll add it in your contract and when you come to the commissary you can sign it. That won't keep Mrs. de Spain quiet but maybe it will teach you to wipe your feet off before you enter her house again."

Then he was gone. The boy looked at his father, who still had not spoken or even looked up again, who was now adjusting the logger-head in the hame.

"Pap," he said. His father looked at him—the inscrutable face, the shaggy brows beneath which the gray eyes glinted coldly. Suddenly the boy went toward him, fast, stopping as suddenly. "You done the best you could!" he cried. "If he wanted hit done different why didn't he wait and tell you how? He won't git no twenty bushels! He won't git none! We'll gather hit and hide hit! I kin watch. . . ."

"Did you put the cutter back in that straight stock like I told you?"

"No, sir," he said.

"Then go do it."

That was Wednesday. During the rest of that week he worked steadily, at what was within his scope and some which was beyond it, with an industry that did not need to be driven nor even commanded twice; he had this from his mother, with the difference that some at least of what he did he liked to do, such as splitting wood with the half-size axe which his mother and aunt had earned, or saved money somehow, to present him with at Christmas. In company with the two older women (and on one afternoon even one of the sisters), he built pens for the shoat and the cow which were a part of his father's contract with the landlord, and one afternoon, his father being absent, gone somewhere on one of the mules, he went to the field.

They were running a middle buster now, his brother holding the plow straight while he handled the reins, and walking beside the straining mule, the rich black soil shearing cool and damp against his bare ankles, he thought *Maybe this is the end of it. Maybe even that twenty bushels that seems hard to have to pay for just a rug will be a cheap price for him to stop forever and always from being what he used to be;* thinking, dreaming now, so that his brother had to speak sharply to him to mind the mule: *Maybe he won't collect the twenty bushels. Maybe it will all add up and balance and vanish—corn, rug, fire; the terror and grief, the being pulled two ways like between two teams of horses—gone, done with for ever and ever.*

Then it was Saturday; he looked up from beneath the mule he was harnessing and saw his father in the black coat and hat. "Not that," his father said. "The wagon gear." And then, two hours later, sitting in the wagon bed behind his father and brother on the seat, the wagon accomplished a final curve, and he saw the weathered paintless store with its tattered tobacco- and patent-medicine posters and the tethered wagons and saddle animals below the gallery. He mounted the gnawed steps behind his father and his brother, and there again was the lane of quiet, watching faces for the three of them to walk through. He saw the man in spectacles sitting at the plank table and he did not need to be told this was a Justice of the Peace; he sent one glare of fierce, exultant, partisan defiance at the man in collar and cravat now, whom he had seen but twice before in his life, and that on a galloping horse, who now wore on his face an expression not of rage but of amazed unbelief which the boy could not have known was at the incredible circumstances of being sued by one of his own tenants, and came and stood against his father and cried at the Justice: "He ain't done it! He ain't burnt. . . ."

"Go back to the wagon," his father said.

"Burnt?" the Justice said. "Do I understand this rug was burned too?"

"Does anybody here claim it was?" his father said. "Go back to the wagon." But he did not, he merely retreated to the rear of the room, crowded as that other had been, but not to sit down this time, instead, to stand pressing among the motionless bodies, listening to the voices:

"And you claim twenty bushels of corn is too high for the damage you did to the rug?"

"He brought the rug to me and said he wanted the tracks washed out of it. I washed the tracks out and took the rug back to him."

"But you didn't carry the rug back to him in the same condition it was in before you made the tracks on it."

His father did not answer, and now for perhaps half a minute there was no sound at all save that of breathing, the faint, steady suspiration of complete and intent listening.

"You decline to answer that, Mr. Snopes?" Again his father did not answer. "I'm going to find against you, Mr. Snopes. I'm going to find that you were responsible for the injury to Major de Spain's rug and hold you liable for it. But twenty bushels of corn seems a little high for a man in your circumstances to have to pay. Major de Spain claims it cost a hundred dollars. October corn will be worth about fifty cents. I figure that if Major de Spain can stand a ninety-five dollar loss on something he paid cash for, you can stand a five-dollar loss you haven't earned yet. I hold you in damages to Major de Spain to the amount of ten bushels of corn over and above your contract with him, to be paid to him out of your crop at gathering time. Court adjourned."

It had taken no time hardly, the morning was but half begun. He thought they would return home and perhaps back to the field, since they were late, far behind all other farmers. But instead his father passed on behind the wagon, merely indicating with his hand for the older brother to follow with it, and crossed the road toward the blacksmith shop opposite, pressing on after his father, overtaking him, speaking, whispering up at the harsh, calm face beneath the weathered hat: "He won't git no ten bushels neither. He won't git one. We'll . . ." until his father glanced for an instant down at him, the face absolutely calm, the grizzled eyebrows tangled above the cold eyes, the voice almost pleasant, almost gentle:

"You think so? Well, we'll wait till October anyway."

The matter of the wagon—the setting of a spoke or two and the tightening of the tires—did not take long either, the business of the tires accomplished by driving the wagon into the spring branch behind the shop and letting it stand there, the mules nuzzling into the water from time to time, and the boy on the seat with the idle reigns, looking up the slope and through the sooty tunnel of the shed where the slow hammer rang and where his father sat on an upended cypress bolt, easily, either talking or listening, still sitting there when the boy brought the dripping wagon up out of the branch and halted it before the door.

"Take them on to the shade and hitch," his father said. He did so and returned. His father and the smith and a third man squatting on his heels inside the door were talking, about crops and animals; the boy, squatting too in the ammoniac dust and hoof-parings and scales of rust, heard his father tell a long and unhurried story out of the time before the birth of the older brother even when he had been a professional horsetrader. And then his father came up beside him where he stood before a tattered last year's circus poster on the other side of the store, gazing rapt and quiet at the scarlet horses, the incredible poisings and convolutions of tulle and tights and the painted leers of comedians, and said, "It's time to eat."

But not at home. Squatting beside his brother against the front wall, he watched his father emerge from the store and produce from a paper sack a segment of cheese and divide it carefully and deliberately into three with his pocket knife and produce crackers from the same sack. They all three squatted on the gallery and ate, slowly, without talking; then in the store again, they drank from a tin dipper tepid water smelling of the cedar bucket and of living beech trees. And still they did not go home. It was a horse lot this time, a tall rail fence upon and along which men stood and sat and out of which one by one horses were led, to be walked and trotted and then cantered back and forth along the road while the slow swapping and buying went on and the sun began to slant westward, they—the three of them—watching and listening, the older brother with his muddy eyes and his steady, inevitable tobacco, the father commenting now and then on certain of the animals, to no one in particular.

It was after sundown when they reached home. They ate supper by lamplight, then, sitting on the doorstep, the boy watched the night fully accomplish, listening to the whippoorwills and the frogs, when he heard his mother's voice: "Abner! No! No! Oh, God. Oh, God, Abner!" and he rose, whirled, and saw the altered light through the door where a candle stub now burned in a bottle neck on the table and his father, still in the hat and coat, at once formal and burlesque as though dressed carefully for some shabby and ceremonial violence, emptying the reservoir of the lamp back into the five-gallon kerosene can from which it had been filled, while the mother tugged at his arm until he shifted the lamp to the other hand and flung her back, not savagely or viciously, just hard, into the wall, her hands flung out against the wall for balance, her mouth open and in her face the same quality of hopeless despair as had been in her voice. Then his father saw him standing in the door.

"Go to the barn and get that can of oil we were oiling the wagon with," he said. The boy did not move. Then he could speak.

"What. . . ," he cried. "what are you. . . ."

"Go get that oil," his father said. "Go."

Then he was moving, running, outside the house, toward the stable: this the old habit, the old blood which he had not been permitted to choose for himself, which had been bequeathed him willy nilly and which had run for so long (and who knew where, battening on what of outrage and savagery and lust) before it came to him. *I could keep on,* he thought. *I could run on and on and never look back, never need to see his face again. Only I can't. I can't,* the rusted can in his hand now, the liquid splashing in it as he ran back to the house and into it, into the sound of his mother's weeping in the next room, and handed the can to his father.

"Ain't you going to even send a nigger?" he cried. "At least you sent a nigger before!"

This time his father didn't strike him. The hand came even faster than the blow had, the same hand which had set the can on the table with almost excruciating care flashing from the can toward him too quick for him to follow it, gripping him by the back of his shirt and on to tiptoe before he had seen it quit the can, the face stooping at him in breathless and frozen ferocity, the cold, dead voice speaking over him to the older brother who leaned against the table, chewing with that steady, curious, sidewise motion of cows:

"Empty the can into the big one and go on. I'll catch up with you."

"Better tie him up to the bedpost," the brother said.

"Do like I told you," the father said. Then the boy was moving, his bunched shirt and the hard, bony hand between his shoulderblades, his toes just touching the floor, across the room and into the other one, past the sisters sitting with spread heavy thighs in the two chairs over the cold hearth, and to where his mother and aunt sat side by side on the bed, the aunt's arms about his mother's shoulders.

"Hold him," the father said. The aunt made a startled movement. "Not you," the father said. "Lennie. Take hold of him. I want to see you do it." His mother took him by the wrist. "You'll hold him better than that. If he gets loose don't you know what he is going to do? He will go up yonder." He jerked his head toward the road. "Maybe I'd better tie him."

"I'll hold him," his mother whispered.

"See you do then." Then his father was gone, the stiff foot heavy and measured upon the boards, ceasing at last.

Then he began to struggle. His mother caught him in both arms, he jerking and wrenching at them. He would be stronger in the end, he knew that. But he had no time to wait for it. "Lemme go!"

"I don't want to have to hit you!"

"Let him go!" the aunt said. "If he don't go, before God, I am going up there myself!"

"Don't you see I can't?" his mother cried. "Sarty! Sarty! No! No! Help me, Lizzie!"

Then he was free. His aunt grasped at him but it was too late. He whirled, running, his mother stumbled forward on to her knees behind him, crying to the nearer sister: "Catch him, Net! Catch him!" But that was too late too, the sister (the sisters were twins, born at the same time, yet either of them now gave the impression of being, encompassing as much living meat and volume of weight as any other two of the family) not yet having begun to rise from the chair, her head, face, alone merely turned, presenting to him in the flying instant an astonishing expanse of young female features untroubled by any surprise even, wearing only an expression of bovine interest. Then he was out of the room, out of the house, in the mild dust of the starlit road and the heavy rifeness of honeysuckle, the pale ribbon unspooling with terrific slowness under his running feet, reaching the gate at last and turning in, running, his heart and lungs drumming, on up the drive toward the lighted house, the lighted door. He did not knock, he burst in, sobbing for breath, incapable for the moment of speech; he saw the astonished face of the Negro in the linen jacket without knowing when the Negro had appeared.

"De Spain!" he cried, panted. "Where's . . ." then he saw the white man too emerging from a white door down the hall. "Barn!" he cried. "Barn!"

"What?" the white man said. "Barn?"

"Yes!" the boy cried. "Barn!"

"Catch him!" the white man shouted.

But it was too late this time too. The Negro grasped his shirt, but the entire sleeve, rotten with washing, carried away, and he was out of that door too and in the drive again, and had actually never ceased to run even while he was screaming into the white man's face.

Behind him the white man was shouting, "My horse! Fetch my horse!" and he thought for an instant of cutting across the park and climbing the fence into the road, but he did not know the park nor how high the vine-massed fence might be and he dared not risk it. So he ran on down the drive, blood and breath roaring; presently he was in the road again though he could not see it. He could not hear either: the galloping mare was almost upon him before he heard her, and even then he held his course, as if the very urgency of his wild grief and need must in a moment more find him wings, waiting until the ultimate instant to hurl himself aside and into the weed-choked roadside ditch as the horse thundered past and on, for an instant in furious silhouette against the stars, the tranquil early summer night sky which, even before the shape of the horse and rider vanished, stained abruptly and violently upward: a long, swirling roar incredible and soundless, blotting the stars, and he springing up and into the road again, running again, knowing it was too late yet still running even after he heard the shot and, an instant later, two shots, pausing now without knowing he had ceased to run, crying "Pap! Pap!", running again before he knew he had begun to run, stumbling, tripping over something and scrabbling up again without ceasing to run, looking backward over his shoulder at the glare as he got up, running on among the invisible trees, panting, sobbing, "Father! Father!"

At midnight he was sitting on the crest of a hill. He did not know it was midnight and he did not know how far he had come. But there was no glare behind him now and he sat now, his back toward what he had called home for four days anyhow, his face toward the dark woods which he would enter when breath was strong again, small, shaking steadily in the chill darkness, hugging himself into the remainder of his thin, rotten shirt, the grief and despair now no longer terror and fear but just grief and despair. *Father. My father,* he thought. "He was brave!" he cried suddenly, aloud but not loud, no more than a whisper: "He was! He was in the war! He was in Colonel Sartoris' cav'ry!" not knowing that his father had gone to that war a private in the fine old European sense, wearing no uniform, admitting the authority of and giving fidelity to no man or army or flag, going to war as Malbrouck himself did: for booty—it meant nothing and less than nothing to him if it were enemy booty or his own.

The slow constellations wheeled on. It would be dawn and then sun-up after a while and he would be hungry. But that would be tomorrow and now he was only cold, and walking would cure that. His breathing was easier now and he decided to get up and go on, and then he found that he had been asleep because he knew it was almost dawn, the night almost over. He could tell that from the whippoorwills. They were everywhere now among the dark trees below him, constant and inflectioned and ceaseless, so that, as the instant for giving over to the day birds drew nearer and nearer and nearer, there was no interval at all between them. He got up. He was a little stiff, but walking would cure that too as it would the cold, and soon there would be the sun. He went on down the hill, toward the dark woods within which the liquid silver voices of the birds called unceasing—the rapid and urgent beating of the urgent and quiring heart of the late spring night. He did not look back.

Gold Coast

James Alan McPherson
(b. 1943)

James Alan McPherson was born and grew up in Savannah, Georgia. As an undergraduate, he attended Morgan State College in Baltimore and Morris Brown College in Atlanta; in 1968 he graduated from Harvard Law School. At various times during his years in college, McPherson worked as a janitor, a waiter, a community organizer in a Settlement House, and a research assistant in the Harvard Business School. In the summer of 1968 he was a reporter for the Bay State Banner, *a black newspaper in Roxbury, Massachusetts. He is now teaching English and Afro-American literature at the University of Iowa and has become a contributing editor to the* Atlantic. *McPherson's first collection of short stories,* Hue and Cry, *was published in 1969.*

That spring, when I had a great deal of potential and no money at all, I took a job as a janitor. That was when I was still very young and spent money very freely, and when, almost every night, I drifted off to sleep lulled by sweet anticipation of that time when my potential would suddenly be realized and there would be capsule biographies of my life on dust jackets of many books, all proclaiming: ". . . He knew life on many levels. From shoeshine boy, free-lance waiter, 3rd cook, janitor, he rose to. . . ." I had never been a janitor before, and I did not really have to be one, and that is why I did it. But now, much later, I think it might have been because it is possible to be a janitor without becoming one, and at parties or at mixers, when asked what it was I did for a living, it was pretty good to hook my thumbs in my vest pockets and say comfortably: "Why, I am an apprentice janitor." The hippies would think it degenerate and really dig me and people in Philosophy and Law and Business would feel uncomfortable trying to make me feel better about my station while wondering how the hell I had managed to crash the party.

"What's an apprentice janitor?" they would ask.

"I haven't got my card yet," I would reply. "Right now I'm just taking lessons. There's lots of complicated stuff you have to learn before you get your own card and your own building."

"What kind of stuff?"

"Human nature, for one thing. *Race* nature, for another."

"Why race?"

"Because," I would say in a low voice, looking around lest someone else should overhear, "you have to be able to spot Jews and Negroes who are passing."

"That's terrible," would surely be said then with a hint of indignation.

"It's an art," I would add masterfully.

After a good pause I would invariably be asked: "But you're a Negro yourself, how can you keep your own people out?"

At which point I would look terribly disappointed and say: "*I* don't keep them out. But if they get in it's my job to make their stay just as miserable as possible. Things are changing."

Now the speaker would just look at me in disbelief.

"It's Janitorial Objectivity," I would say to finish the thing as the speaker began to edge away. "Don't hate me," I would call after him to his considerable embarrassment. "Somebody has to do it."

It was an old building near Harvard Square. Conrad Aiken had once lived there, and in the days of the Gold Coast, before Harvard built its great houses, it had been a very fine haven for the rich; but that was a world ago, and this building was one of the few monuments of that era which had survived. The lobby had a high ceiling with thick redwood beams, and it was replete with marble floor, fancy ironwork, and an old-fashioned house telephone which no longer worked. Each apartment had a small fireplace, and even the large bathtubs and chain toilets, when I was having my touch of nature, made me wonder what prominent personage of the past had worn away all the newness. And, being there, I felt a certain affinity toward the rich.

It was a funny building, because the people who lived there made it old. Conveniently placed as it was between the Houses and Harvard Yard, I expected to find it occupied by a company of hippies, hopeful working girls, and assorted graduate students. Instead, there was a majority of old maids, dowagers, asexual middle-aged men, homosexual young men, a few married couples, and a teacher. No one was shacking up there, and walking through the quiet halls in the early evening, I sometimes had the urge to knock on a door and expose myself just to hear someone breathe hard for once.

It was a Cambridge spring: down by the Charles happy students were making love while sad-eyed middle-aged men watched them from the bridge. It was a time of activity: Law students were busy sublimating, Business School people were making records of the money they would make, the Harvard Houses were clearing out, and in the Square bearded pot-pushers were setting up their restaurant tables in anticipation of the Summer School faithfuls. There was a change of season in the air, and to comply with its urgings, James Sullivan, the old superintendent, passed his three beaten garbage cans on to me with the charge that I should take up his daily rounds of the six floors, and with unflinching humility, gather whatever scraps the old-maid tenants had refused to husband.

I then became very rich, with my own apartment, a sensitive girl, a stereo, two speakers, one tattered chair, one fork, a job, and the urge to acquire. Having all this and youth besides made me pity Sullivan: he had been in that building thirty years and had its whole history recorded in the little folds of his mind, as his own life was recorded in the wrinkles of his face. All he had to show for his time there was a berserk dog, a wife almost as mad as the dog, three cats, bursitis, acute myopia, and a drinking problem. He was well over seventy and could hardly walk, and his weekly check of twenty-two dollars from the company that managed the building would not support anything. So, out of compromise, he was retired to superintendent of my labor.

My first day as janitor, while I skillfully lugged my three overflowing cans of garbage out of the building, he sat on his bench in the lobby, faded and old and smoking, in patched, loose blue pants. He watched me. He was a chain smoker, and I noticed right away that he very carefully dropped all of the ashes and butts on the floor and crushed them under his feet until there was a yellow and gray smear. Then he laboriously pushed the mess under the bench with his shoe, all the while eyeing me like a cat in silence as I hauled the many cans of muck out to the big disposal unit next to the building. When I had finished, he gave me two old plates to help stock my kitchen and his first piece of advice.

"Sit down, for Chrisake, and take a load off your feet," he told me.

I sat on the red bench next to him and accepted the wilted cigarette he offered me from the crushed package he kept in his sweater pocket.

"Now, I'll tell you something to help you get along in the building," he said.

I listened attentively.

"If any of these sons of bitches ever ask you to do something extra, be sure to charge them for it."

I assured him that I absolutely would.

"If they can afford to live here, they can afford to pay. The bastards."

"Undoubtedly," I assured him again.

"And another thing," he added. "Don't let any of these girls shove any cat shit under your nose. That ain't your job. You tell them to put it in a bag and take it out themselves."

I reminded him that I knew very well my station in life, and that I was not about to haul cat shit or anything of that nature. He looked at me through his thick-lensed glasses for a long time. He looked like a cat himself. "That's right," he said at last. "And if they still try to sneak it in the trash be sure to make the bastards pay. They can afford it." He crushed his seventh butt on the floor and scattered the mess some more while he lit up another. "I never hauled out no cat shit in the thirty years I been here, and you don't do it either."

"I'm going up to wash my hands," I said.

"Remember," he called after me, "don't take no shit from any of them."

I protested once more that, upon my life, I would never, never do it, not even for the prettiest girl in the building. Going up in the elevator, I felt comfortably resolved that I would never do it. There were no pretty girls in the building.

I never found out what he had done before he came there, but I do know that being a janitor in that building was as high as he ever got in life. He had watched two generations of the rich pass the building on their way to the Yard, and he had seen many governors ride white horses into that same Yard to send sons and daughters of the rich out into life to produce, to acquire, to procreate, and to send back sons and daughters so that the cycle would continue. He had watched the cycle from when he had been able to haul the cans out for himself, and now he could not, and he was bitter.

He was Irish, of course, and he took pride in Irish accomplishments when he could have none of his own. He had known Frank O'Connor when that writer had been at Harvard. He told me on many occasions how O'Connor had stopped to talk every day on his way to the Yard. He had also known James Michael Curley, and his most colorful memory of the man was a long-ago day when he and James Curley sat in a Boston bar and one of Curley's runners had come in and said: "Hey, Jim, Sol Bernstein the Jew wants to see you." And Curley, in his deep, memorial voice, had said to James Sullivan: "Let us go forth and meet this Israelite Prince." These were his memories, and I would obediently put aside my garbage cans and laugh with him over the hundred or so colorful, insignificant little details which made up a whole lifetime of living in the basement of Harvard. And although they were of little value to me then, I knew that they were the reflections of a lifetime and the happiest moments he would ever have, being sold to me cheap, as youthful time is cheap, for as little time and interest as I wanted to spend. It was a buyer's market.

In those days I believed myself gifted with a boundless perception and attacked my daily garbage route with a gusto superenforced by the happy knowledge that behind each of the fifty or so doors in our building lived a story which could, if I chose to grace it with the magic of my pen, become immortal. I watched my tenants fanatically, noting their perversions, their visitors, and their eating habits. So intense was my search for material that I had to restrain myself from going through their refuse scrap by scrap; but at the topmost layers of muck, without too much hand soiling in the process, I set my perception to work. By late June, however, I had discovered only enough to put together a skimpy, rather naive Henry Miller novel, the most colorful discoveries being:

1. The lady in #24 was an alumnus of Paducah College
2. The couple in #55 made love at least 500 times a week, and the wife had not yet discovered the pill
3. The old lady in #36 was still having monthly inconvenience
4. The two fatsos in #56 consumed nightly an extraordinary amount of chili
5. The fat man in #54 had two dogs that were married to each other, but he was not married to anyone at all
6. The middle-aged single man in #63 threw out an awful lot of flowers.

Disturbed by the snail's progress I was making, I confessed my futility to James one day as he sat on his bench chain-smoking and smearing butts on my newly waxed lobby floor. "So you want to know about the tenants?" he said, his cat's eyes flickering over me. I nodded.

"Well, the first thing to notice is how many Jews there are."

"I haven't noticed any Jews," I said.

He eyed me in amazement.

"Well, a few," I said quickly to prevent my treasured perception from being dulled any further.

"A few, hell," he said. "There's more Jews here than anybody."

"How can you tell?"

He gave me that undecided look again. "Where do you think all that garbage comes from?" He nodded feebly toward my bulging cans. I looked just in time to prevent a stray noodle from slipping over the brim. "That's right," he continued. "Jews are the biggest eaters in the world. They eat the best too."

I confessed then that I was of the chicken-soup generation and believed that Jews ate only enough to muster strength for their daily trips to the bank.

"Not so!" he replied emphatically. "You never heard the expression: 'Let's get to the restaurant before the Jews get there'?"

I shook my head sadly.

"You don't know that in certain restaurants they take the free onions and pickles off the tables when they see Jews coming?"

I held my head down in shame over the bounteous heap.

He trudged over to my can and began to turn back the leaves of noodles and crumpled tissues from #47 with his hand. After a few seconds of digging, he unmucked an empty pâté can. "Look at that," he said triumphantly. "Gourmet stuff, no less."

"That's from #44," I said.

"What else?" he said, all-knowingly. "In 1946 a Swedish girl moved in up there and took a Jewish girl for her roommate. Then the Swedish girl moved out and there's been a Jewish Dynasty up there ever since."

I recalled that #44 was occupied by a couple that threw out a good number of S. S. Pierce cans, Chivas Regal bottles, assorted broken records, and back issues of *Evergreen* and the *Realist*.

"You're right," I said.

"Of course," he replied, as if there were never any doubt. "I can spot them anywhere, even when they think they're passing." He leaned closer and said in a you-and-me voice: "But don't ever say anything bad about them in public. The Anti-Defamation League will get you."

Just then his wife screamed for him from the second floor, and the dog joined her and beat against the door. He got into the elevator painfully and said: "Don't ever talk about them in public.

You don't know who they are, and that Defamation League will take everything you got."

Sullivan did not really dislike Jews. He was just bitter toward anyone better off than himself. He lived with his wife on the second floor, and his apartment was very dirty because both of them were sick and old, and neither could move very well. His wife swept dirt out into the hall, and two hours after I had mopped and waxed their section of the floor, there was sure to be a layer of dirt, grease, and crushed-scattered tobacco from their door to the end of the hall. There was a smell of dogs and cats and age and death about their door, and I did not ever want to have to go in there for any reason because I feared something about it I cannot name.

Mrs. Sullivan, I found out, was from South Africa. She loved animals much more than people, and there was a great deal of pain in her face. She kept little cans of meat posted at strategic points about the building, and I often came across her in the early morning or late at night throwing scraps out of the second-floor window to stray cats. Once, when James was about to throttle a stray mouse in their apartment, she had screamed at him to give the mouse a sporting chance. Whenever she attempted to walk she had to balance herself against a wall or a rail, and she hated the building because it confined her. She also hated James and most of the tenants. On the other hand, she loved the "Johnny Carson Show," she loved to sit outside on the front steps (because she could go no further unassisted), and she loved to talk to anyone who would stop to listen. She never spoke coherently except when she was cursing James, and then she had a vocabulary like a drunken sailor. She had great, shrill lungs, and her screams, accompanied by the rabid barks of the dog, could be heard all over the building. She was never really clean, her teeth were bad, and the first most pathetic thing in the world was to see her sitting on the steps in the morning watching the world pass, in a stained smock and a fresh summer blue hat she kept just to wear downstairs, with no place in the world to go. James told me, on the many occasions of her screaming, that she was mentally disturbed and could not help herself. The admirable thing about him was that he never lost his temper with her, no matter how rough her curses became and no matter who heard them. And the second most pathetic thing in the world was to see them slowly making their way in Harvard Square, he supporting her, through the hurrying crowds of miniskirted summer girls, J-Pressed Ivy Leaguers, beatniks, and bused Japanese tourists, decked in cameras, who would take pictures of every inch of Harvard Square except them. Once a hippie had brushed past them and called back over his shoulder: "Don't break any track records, Mr. and Mrs. Speedy Molasses."

Also on the second floor lived Miss O'Hara, a spinster who hated Sullivan as only an old maid can hate an old man. Across from her lived a very nice, gentle celibate named Murphy, who had once served with Montgomery in North Africa and who was now spending the rest of his life cleaning his little apartment and gossiping with Miss O'Hara. It was an Irish floor.

I never found out just why Miss O'Hara hated the Sullivans with such a passion. Perhaps it was because they were so unkempt and she was so superciliously clean. Perhaps it was because Miss O'Hara had a great deal of Irish pride, and they were stereotyped Irish. Perhaps it was because she merely had no reason to like them. She was a fanatic about cleanliness and put out her little bit of garbage wrapped very neatly in yesterday's *Christian Science Monitor* and tied in a bow with a fresh piece of string. Collecting all those little neat packages, I would wonder where she got the string and imagined her at night breaking meat market locks with a hairpin and hobbling off with yards and yards of white cord concealed under the gray sweater she always wore. I could even imagine her back in her little apartment chuckling and rolling the cord into a great white ball by candlelight. Then she would stash it away in her bread box. Miss O'Hara kept her door slightly open until late at night, and I suspected that she heard everything that went on in the building. I had the feeling that I should never dare to make love with gusto for fear that she would overhear and write down all my happy-time phrases, to be maliciously recounted to me if she were ever provoked.

She had been in the building longer than Sullivan, and I suppose that her greatest ambition in life was to outlive him and then attend his wake with a knitting ball and needle. She had been trying to get him fired for twenty-five years or so, and did not know when to quit. On summer nights when I painfully mopped the second floor, she would offer me root beer, apples, or cupcakes while trying to pump me for evidence against him.

"He's just a filthy old man, Robert," she would declare in a little-old-lady whisper. "And don't think you have to clean up those dirty old butts of his. Just report him to the Company."

"Oh, I don't mind," I would tell her, gulping the root beer as fast as possible.

"Well, they're both a couple of lushes, if you ask me. They haven't been sober a day in twenty-five years."

"Well, she's sick too, you know."

"Ha!" She would throw up her hands in disgust. "She's only sick when he doesn't give her the booze."

I fought to keep down a burp. "How long have *you* been here?" She motioned for me to step out of the hall and into her dark apartment. "Don't tell him"—she nodded toward Sullivan's door —"but I've been here thirty-four years." She waited for me to be taken aback. Then she added: "And it was a better building before those two lushes came."

She then offered me an apple, asked five times if the dog's barking bothered me, forced me to take a fudge brownie, said that the cats had wet the floor again last night, got me to dust the top of a large chest too high for her to reach, had me pick up the minute specks of dust which fell from my dustcloth, pressed another root beer on me, and then showed me her family album. As an afterthought, she had me take down a big old picture of her great-grandfather, also too high for her to reach, so that I could dust that too. Then together we picked up the dust from it which might have fallen to the floor. "He's really a filthy old man, Robert," she said in closing, "and don't be afraid to report him to the Property Manager anytime you want."

I assured her that I would do it at the slightest provocation from Sullivan, finally accepted an apple but refused the money she offered, and escaped back to my mopping. Even then she watched me, smiling, from her half-opened door.

"Why does Miss O'Hara hate you?" I asked James once.

He lifted his cigaretted hand and let the long ash fall elegantly to the floor. "That old bitch has been an albatross around my neck ever since I got here," he said. "Don't trust her, Robert. It was her kind that sat around singing hymns and watching them burn saints in this state."

In those days I had forgotten that I was first of all a black and I had a very lovely girl, who was not first of all a black. It is quite possible that my ancestors rowed her ancestors across on the *May-flower,* and she was very rich in that alone. We were both very young and optimistic then, and she believed with me in my potential and liked me partly because of it; and I was happy because she belonged to me and not to the race, which made her special. It made me special too because I did not have to wear a beard or hate or be especially hip or ultra Ivy Leagueish. I did not have to smoke pot or supply her with it, or be for any cause at all except myself. I only had to be myself, which pleased me; and I only had to produce, which pleased both of us. Like many of the artistically inclined rich, she wanted to own in someone else what she could not own in herself. But this I did not mind, and I forgave her for it because she forgave my moods and the constant smell of garbage and a great deal of latent hostility. She only minded James Sullivan, and all the valuable time I was wasting listening to him rattle on and on. His conversations, she thought, were useless, repetitious, and promised nothing of value to me. She was accustomed to the old-rich, whose conversations meandered around a leitmotiv of how well off they were and how much they would leave behind very soon. She was not at all cold, but she had been taught how to tolerate the old-poor and perhaps toss them a greeting in passing. But nothing more.

Sullivan did not like her when I first introduced them because he saw that she was not a beatnik and could not be dismissed. It is in the nature of things that liberal people will tolerate two interracial beatniks more than they will an intelligent, serious-minded mixed couple. The former liaison is easy to dismiss as the dregs of both races, deserving of each other and the contempt of both races; but the latter poses a threat because there is no immediacy of overpowering sensuality or "you-pick-my-fleas-I'll-pick-yours" apparent on the surface of things, and people, even the most publicly liberal, cannot dismiss it so easily.

"That girl is Irish, isn't she?" he had asked one day in my apartment soon after I had introduced them.

"No," I said definitely.

"What's her name?"

"Judy Smith," I said, which was not her name at all.

"Well, I can spot it," he said. "She's got Irish blood all right."

"Everybody's got a little Irish blood," I told him.

He looked at me cattily and craftily from behind his thick lenses. "Well, she's from a good family, I suppose."

"I suppose," I said.

He paused to let some ashes fall to the rug. "They say the Colonel's Lady and Nelly O'Grady are sisters under the skin." Then he added: "Rudyard Kipling."

"That's true," I said with equal innuendo, "that's why you have to maintain a distinction by marrying the Colonel's Lady."

An understanding passed between us then, and we never spoke more on the subject.

Almost every night the cats wet the second floor while Meg Sullivan watched the "Johnny Carson Show" and the dog howled and clawed the door. During commercials Meg would curse James to get out and stop dropping ashes on the floor or to take the dog out or something else, totally unintelligible to those of us on the fourth, fifth, and sixth floors. Even after the Carson show she would still curse him to get out, until finally he would go down to the basement and put away a bottle or two of wine. There was a steady stench of cat functions in the basement, and with all the grease and dirt, discarded trunks, beer bottles, chairs, old tools, and the filthy sofa on which he sometimes slept, seeing him there made me want to cry. He drank the cheapest sherry, the wino kind, straight from the bottle: and on many nights that summer at 2:00 A.M. my phone would ring me out of bed.

"Rob? Jimmy Sullivan here. What are you doing?"

There was nothing suitable to say.

"Come on down to the basement for a drink."

"I have to be at work at 8:30," I would protest.

"Can't you have just one drink?" he would say pathetically.

I would carry down my own glass so that I would not have to drink out of the bottle. Looking at him on the sofa, I could not be mad because now I had many records for my stereo, a story that was going well, a girl who believed in me and who belonged to me and not to the race, a new set of dishes, and a tomorrow morning with younger people.

"I don't want to burden you unduly," he would always preface.

I would force myself not to look at my watch and say: "Of course not."

"My Meg is not in the best health, you know," he would say, handing the bottle to me.

"She's just old."

"The doctors say she should be in an institution."

"That's no place to be."

"I'm a sick man myself, Rob. I can't take much more. She's crazy."

"Anybody who loves animals can't be crazy."

He took another long draw from the bottle. "I won't live another year. I'll be dead in a year."

"You don't know that."

He looked at me closely, without his glasses, so that I could see the desperation in his eyes. "I just hope Meg goes before I do. I don't want them to put her in an institution after I'm gone."

At 2:00 A.M., with the cat stench in my nose and a glass of bad sherry standing still in my hand because I refuse in my mind to touch it, and all my dreams of greatness are above him and the basement and the building itself, I did not know what to say. The only way I could keep from hating myself was to start him talking about the AMA or the Medicare program or beatniks. He was pure hell on all three. To him, the Medical Profession was "morally bankrupt," Medicare was a great farce which deprived oldsters like himself of their "rainy-day dollars," and beatniks were "dropouts from the human race." He could rage on and on in perfect phrases about all three of his major dislikes, and I had the feeling that because the sentences were so well constructed and well turned, he might have memorized them from something he had read. But then he was extremely well read, and it did not matter if he had borrowed a phrase or two from someone else. The ideas were still his own.

It would be 3:00 A.M. before I knew it, and then 3:30, and still he would go on. He hated politicians in general and liked to recount, at these times, his private catalog of political observations. By the time he got around to Civil Rights it would be 4:00 A.M., and I could not feel responsible for him at that hour. I would begin to yawn, and at first he would just ignore it. Then I would start to edge toward the door, and he would see that he could hold me no longer, not even by declaring that he wanted to be an honorary Negro because he loved the race so much.

"I hope I haven't burdened you unduly," he would say again.

"Of course not," I would say, because it was over then, and I could leave him and the smell of the cats there, and sometimes I would go out in the cool night and walk around the Yard and be thankful that I was only an assistant janitor, and a transient one at that. Walking in the early dawn and seeing the Summer School fellows sneak out of the girls' dormitories in the Yard gave me a good feeling, and I thought that tomorrow night it would be good to make love myself so that I could be busy when he called.

"Why don't you tell that old man your job doesn't include baby-sitting with him," Jean told me many times when she came over to visit during the day and found me sleeping.

I would look at her and think to myself about social forces and the pressures massing and poised, waiting to attack us. It was still July then. It was hot, and I was working good.

"He's just an old man," I said. "Who else would listen to him."

"You're too soft. As long as you do your work you don't have to be bothered with him."

"He could be a story if I listened long enough."

"There are too many stories about old people."

"No," I said, thinking about us again, "there are just too many people who have no stories."

Sometimes he would come up and she would be there, but I would let him come in anyway, and he would stand there looking dirty and uncomfortable, offering some invented reason for having intruded. At these times something silent would pass between them, something I cannot name, which would reduce him to exactly what he was: an old man, come out of his basement to intrude where he was not wanted. But all the time this was being communicated, there would be a surface, friendly conversation between them. And after five minutes or so of being unwelcome, he would apologize for having come, drop a few ashes on the rug, and back out the door. Downstairs we could hear his wife screaming.

We endured the aged and August was almost over. Inside the building the cats were still wetting, Meg was still screaming, the dog was getting madder, and Sullivan began to drink during the day. Outside it was hot and lush and green, and the Summer girls were wearing shorter miniskirts and no panties and the middle-aged men down by the Charles were going wild on their bridge. Everyone was restless for change, for August is the month when undone summer things must be finished or regretted all through the winter.

Being imaginative people, Jean and I played a number of original games. One of them we called "Social Forces," the object of which was to see which side could break us first. We played it with the unknown night riders who screamed obscenities from passing cars. And because that was her side I would look at her expectantly, but she would laugh and say: "No." We played it at parties with unaware blacks who attempted to enchant her with skillful dances and hip vocabularies, believing her to be community property. She would be polite and aloof, and much later, it then being my turn, she would look at me expectantly. And I would force a smile and say: "No." The last round was played while taking her home in a subway car, on a hot August night, when one side of the car was black and tense and hating and the other side was white and of the same mind. There was not enough room on either side for the two of us to sit and we would not separate; so we stood, holding on to a steel post through all the stops, feeling all of the eyes, between the two sides of the car and the two sides of the world. We aged. And getting off finally at the stop which was no longer ours, we looked at each other, again expectantly, and there was nothing left to say.

I began to avoid the old man, would not answer the door when I knew it was he who was knocking, and waited until very late at night, when he could not possibly be awake, to haul the trash down. I hated the building then; and I was really a janitor for the first time. I slept a lot and wrote very little. And I did not give a damn about Medicare, the AMA, the building, Meg, or the crazy dog. I began to consider moving out.

In that same week, Miss O'Hara finally succeeded in badgering Murphy, the celibate Irishman, and a few other tenants into signing a complaint about the dog. No doubt Murphy signed because he was a nice fellow and women like Miss O'Hara had always dominated him. He did not really mind the dog: he did not really mind anything. She called him "Frank Dear," and I had the feeling that when he came to that place, fresh from Montgomery's Campaign, he must have had a will of his own; but she had drained it all away, year by year, so that now he would do anything just to be agreeable.

One day soon after the complaint, the little chubby Property Manager came around to tell Sullivan that the dog had to be taken away. Miss O'Hara told me the good news later, when she finally got round to my door.

"Well, that crazy dog is gone now, Robert. Those two are enough."

"Where is the dog?" I asked.

"I don't know, but Albert Rustin made them get him out. You should have seen the old drunk's face," she said. "That dirty old useless man."

"You should be at peace now," I said.

"Almost," was her reply. "The best thing is to get rid of those two old boozers along with the dog."

I congratulated Miss O'Hara and went out. I knew that the old man would be drinking and would want to talk. But very late that evening he called on the telephone and caught me in.

"Rob?" he said. "James Sullivan here. Would you come down to my apartment like a good fellow? I want to ask you something important."

I had never been in his apartment before and did not want to go then. But I went down anyway.

They had three rooms, all grimy from corner to corner. There was a peculiar odor in that place I did not ever want to smell again, and his wife was dragging herself around the room talking in mumbles. When she saw me come in the door, she said: "I can't clean it up. I just can't. Look at that window. I can't reach it. I can't keep it clean." She threw up both her hands and held her head down and to the side. "The whole place is dirty, and I can't clean it up."

"What do you want?" I said to Sullivan.

"Sit down." He motioned me to a kitchen chair. "Have you changed that bulb on the fifth floor?"

"It's done."

He was silent for a while, drinking from a bottle of sherry, and he gave me some and a dirty glass. "You're the first person who's been in here in years," he said. "We couldn't have company because of the dog."

Somewhere in my mind was a note that I should never go into his apartment. But the dog had never been the reason. "Well, he's gone now," I said, fingering the dirty glass of sherry.

He began to cry. "They took my dog away," he said. "It was all I had. How can they take a man's dog away from him?"

There was nothing I could say.

"I couldn't do nothing," he continued. After a while he added: "But I know who it was. It was that old bitch O'Hara. Don't ever trust her, Rob. She smiles in your face, but it was her kind that laughed when they burned Joan of Arc in this state."

Seeing him there, crying and making me feel unmanly because I wanted to touch him or say something warm, also made me eager to be far away and running hard.

"Everybody's got problems," I said. "I don't have a girl now."

He brightened immediately, and for a while he looked almost happy in his old cat's eyes. Then he staggered over to my chair and held out his hand. I did not touch it, and he finally pulled it back. "I know how you feel," he said. "I know just how you feel."

"Sure," I said.

"But you're a young man, you have a future. But not me. I'll be dead inside of a year."

Just then his wife dragged herself in to offer me a cigar. They were being hospitable, and I forced myself to drink a little of the sherry.

"They took my dog away today," she mumbled. "That's all I had in the world, my dog."

I looked at the old man. He was drinking from the bottle.

During the first week of September one of the middle-aged men down by the Charles got tired of looking and tried to take a necking girl away from her boyfriend. The police hauled him off to jail, and the girl pulled down her dress tearfully. A few days later another man exposed himself near the same spot. And that same week a dead body was found on the banks of the Charles.

The miniskirted brigade had moved out of the Yard, and it was quiet and green and peaceful there. In our building another Jewish couple moved into #44. They did not eat gourmet stuff, and on occasion, threw out pork-and-beans cans. But I had lost interest in perception. I now had many records for my stereo, loads of S. S. Pierce stuff, and a small bottle of Chivas Regal which I never opened. I was working good again, and I did not miss other things as much; or at least I told myself that.

The old man was coming up steadily now, at least three times a day, and I had resigned myself to it. If I refused to let him in, he would always come back later with a missing bulb on the fifth floor. We had taken to buying cases of beer together, and when he had finished his half, which was very frequently, he would come up to polish off mine. I began to enjoy talking politics, the AMA,

Medicare, beatniks, and listening to him recite from books he had read. I discovered that he was very well read in history, philosophy, literature, and law. He was extraordinarily fond of saying: "I am really a cut above being a building superintendent. Circumstances made me what I am." And even though he was drunk and dirty and it was very late at night, I believed him and liked him anyway because having him there was much better than being alone. After he had gone I could sleep, and I was not lonely in sleep; and it did not really matter how late I was at work the next morning because when I thought about it all, I discovered that nothing really matters except not being old and being alive and having potential to dream about, and not being alone.

The Short Happy Life of Francis Macomber

Ernest Hemingway

(1899–1961)

Hemingway was born and raised in Oak Park, Illinois, where in high school, he played football, boxed, and wrote for the school newspaper. Throughout his youth he frequently went hunting and fishing with his father at Walloon Lake in the northern Michigan woods, which Hemingway later used as the setting for his Nick Adams collection, In Our Time *(1925). After graduating from high school in 1917, Hemingway worked as a cub reporter for the* Kansas City Star *but, eager to participate in World War I, soon left to join a volunteer American ambulance unit in France. Transferred into combat on the Italian front, he was badly wounded in a mortar attack and spent several months hospitalized in Milan. After the war he became a foreign correspondent. Writing for the Hearst papers, he eventually settled in Paris where he became a close friend of such expatriates as Gertrude Stein and Ezra Pound.* The Sun Also Rises *(1926), Hemingway's first major novel, reflects the spiritual defeat and moral confusion he saw in most expatriates during his years in Paris.*

Hemingway traveled all over the world, and many of his writings parallel his own adventures in foreign lands. The protagonist of A Farewell to Arms *(1929) is an American who, as Hemingway had done, fights with the Italians in World War I.* Green Hills of Africa *(1935) and "The Short Happy Life of Francis Macomber" (1940) reflect Hemingway's big-game hunting expeditions in Africa.* For Whom the Bell Tolls *(1940) concerns an American volunteer guerrilla in the Spanish Civil War, a war in which Hemingway took part.* The Old Man and the Sea *(1952), which won for him both the Nobel Prize for literature and the Pulitzer Prize, is set in Cuba, a country Hemingway loved and in which he made his home for many years.*

———————————————

It was now lunch time and they were all sitting under the double green fly of the dining tent pretending that nothing had happened.

"Will you have lime juice or lemon squash?" Macomber asked.

"I'll have a gimlet," Robert Wilson told him.

"I'll have a gimlet too. I need something," Macomber's wife said.

"I suppose it's the thing to do," Macomber agreed. "Tell him to make three gimlets."

The mess boy had started them already, lifting the bottles out of the canvas cooling bags that sweated wet in the wind that blew through the trees that shaded the tents.

"What had I ought to give them?" Macomber asked.

"A quid would be plenty," Wilson told him. "You don't want to spoil them."

"Will the headman distribute it?"

"Absolutely."

Francis Macomber had, half an hour before, been carried to his tent from the edge of the camp in triumph on the arms and shoulders of the cook, the personal boys, the skinner and the porters. The gun-bearers had taken no part in the demonstration. When the native boys put him down at the door of his tent, he had shaken all their hands, received their congratulations, and then gone into the tent and sat on the bed until his wife came in. She did not speak to him when she came in and he left the tent at once to wash his face and hands in the portable wash basin outside and go over to the dining tent to sit in a comfortable canvas chair in the breeze and the shade.

"You've got your lion," Robert Wilson said to him, "and a damned fine one too."

ERNEST HEMINGWAY   **43**

Mrs. Macomber looked at Wilson quickly. She was an extremely handsome and well-kept woman of the beauty and social position which had, five years before, commanded five thousand dollars as the price of endorsing, with photographs, a beauty product which she had never used. She had been married to Francis Macomber for eleven years.

"He is a good lion, isn't he?" Macomber said. His wife looked at him now. She looked at both these men as though she had never seen them before.

One, Wilson, the white hunter, she knew she had never truly seen before. He was about middle height with sandy hair, a stubby mustache, a very red face and extremely cold blue eyes with faint white wrinkles at the corners that grooved merrily when he smiled. He smiled at her now and she looked away from his face at the way his shoulders sloped in the loose tunic he wore with the four big cartridges held in loops where the left breast pocket should have been, at his big brown hands, his old slacks, his very dirty boots and back to his red face again. She noticed where the baked red of his face stopped in a white line that marked the circle left by his Stetson hat that hung now from one of the pegs of the tent pole.

"Well, here's to the lion," Robert Wilson said. He smiled at her again and, not smiling, she looked curiously at her husband.

Francis Macomber was very tall, very well built if you did not mind that length of bone, dark, his hair cropped like an oarsman, rather thin-lipped, and was considered handsome. He was dressed in the same sort of safari clothes that Wilson wore except that his were new, he was thirty-five years old, kept himself very fit, was good at court games, had a number of big-game fishing records, and had just shown himself, very publicly, to be a coward.

"Here's to the lion," he said. "I can't ever thank you for what you did."

Margaret, his wife, looked away from him and back to Wilson. "Let's not talk about the lion," she said.

Wilson looked over at her without smiling and now she smiled at him.

"It's been a very strange day," she said. "Hadn't you ought to put your hat on even under the canvas at noon? You told me that, you know."

"Might put it on," said Wilson.

"You know you have a very red face, Mr. Wilson," she told him and smiled again.

"Drink," said Wilson.

"I don't think so," she said. "Francis drinks a great deal, but his face is never red."

"It's red today," Macomber tried a joke.

"No," said Margaret. "It's mine that's red today. But Mr. Wilson's is always red."

"Must be racial," said Wilson. "I say, you wouldn't like to drop my beauty as a topic, would you?"

"I've just started on it."

"Let's chuck it," said Wilson.

"Conversation is going to be so difficult," Margaret said.

"Don't be silly, Margot," her husband said.

"No difficulty," Wilson said. "Got a damn fine lion."

Margot looked at them both and they both saw that she was going to cry. Wilson had seen it coming for a long time and he dreaded it. Macomber was past dreading it.

"I wish it hadn't happened. Oh, I wish it hadn't happened," she said and started for her tent. She made no noise of crying but they could see that her shoulders were shaking under the rose-colored, sun-proofed shirt she wore.

"Women upset," said Wilson to the tall man. "Amounts to nothing. Strain on the nerves and one thing'n another."

"No," said Macomber. "I suppose that I rate that for the rest of my life now."

"Nonsense. Let's have a spot of the giant killer," said Wilson. "Forget the whole thing. Nothing to it anyway."

"We might try," said Macomber. "I won't forget what you did for me though."

"Nothing," said Wilson. "All nonsense."

So they sat there in the shade where the camp was pitched under some wide-topped acacia trees with a boulder-strewn cliff behind them, and a stretch of grass that ran to the bank of a boulder-filled stream in front with the forest beyond it, and drank their just-cool lime drinks and avoided one another's eyes while the boys set the table for lunch. Wilson could tell that the boys all knew about it now and when he saw Macomber's personal boy looking curiously at his master while he was putting dishes on the table he snapped at him in Swahili. The boy turned away with his face blank.

"What were you telling him?" Macomber asked.

"Nothing. Told him to look alive or I'd see he got fifteen of the best."

"What's that? Lashes?"

"It's quite illegal," Wilson said. "You're supposed to fine them."

"Do you still have them whipped?"

"Oh, yes. They could raise a row if they chose to complain. But they don't. They prefer it to the fines."

"How strange!" said Macomber.

"Not strange, really," Wilson said. "Which would you rather do? Take a good birching or lose your pay?"

Then he felt embarrassed at asking it and before Macomber could answer he went on, "We all take a beating every day, you know, one way or another."

This was no better. "Good God," he thought. "I am a diplomat, aren't I?"

"Yes, we take a beating," said Macomber, still not looking at him. "I'm awfully sorry about that lion business. It doesn't have to go any further, does it? I mean no one will hear about it, will they?"

"You mean will I tell it at the Mathaiga Club?" Wilson looked at him now coldly. He had not expected this. So he's a bloody four-letter man as well as a bloody coward, he thought. I rather liked him too until today. But how is one to know about an American?

"No," said Wilson. "I'm a professional hunter. We never talk about our clients. You can be quite easy on that. It's supposed to be bad form to ask us not to talk though."

He had decided now that to break would be much easier. He would eat, then, by himself and could read a book with his meals. They would eat by themselves. He would see them through the safari on a very formal basis—what was it the French called it? Distinguished consideration—and it would be a damn sight easier than having to go through this emotional trash. He'd insult him and make a good clean break. Then he could read a book with his meals and he'd still be drinking their whisky. That was the phrase for it when a safari went bad. You ran into another white hunter and you asked, "How is everything going?" and he answered, "Oh, I'm still drinking their whisky," and you knew everything had gone to pot.

"I'm sorry," Macomber said and looked at him with his American face that would stay adolescent until it became middle-aged, and Wilson noted his crew-cropped hair, fine eyes only faintly shifty, good nose, thin lips and handsome jaw. "I'm sorry I didn't realize that. There are lots of things I don't know."

So what could he do, Wilson thought. He was all ready to break it off quickly and neatly and here the beggar was apologizing after he had just insulted him. He made one more attempt. "Don't worry about me talking," he said. "I have a living to make. You know in Africa no woman ever misses her lion and no white man ever bolts."

"I bolted like a rabbit," Macomber said.

Now what in hell were you going to do about a man who talked like that, Wilson wondered.

Wilson looked at Macomber with his flat, blue, machine-gunner's eyes and the other smiled back at him. He had a pleasant smile if you did not notice how his eyes showed when he was hurt.

"Maybe I can fix it up on buffalo," he said. "We're after them next, aren't we?"

"In the morning if you like," Wilson told him. Perhaps he had been wrong. This was certainly the way to take it. You most certainly could not tell a damned thing about an American. He was all for Macomber again. If you could forget the morning. But, of course, you couldn't. The morning had been about as bad as they come.

"Here comes the Memsahib," he said. She was walking over from her tent looking refreshed and cheerful and quite lovely. She had a very perfect oval face, so perfect that you expected her to be stupid. But she wasn't stupid, Wilson thought, no, not stupid.

"How is the beautiful red-faced Mr. Wilson? Are you feeling better, Francis, my pearl?"

"Oh, much," said Macomber.

"I've dropped the whole thing," she said, sitting down at the table. "What importance is there to whether Francis is any good at killing lions? That's not his trade. That's Mr. Wilson's trade. Mr. Wilson is really very impressive killing anything. You do kill anything, don't you?"

"Oh, anything," said Wilson. "Simply anything." They are, he thought, the hardest in the world; the hardest, the cruelest, the most predatory and the most attractive and their men have softened or gone to pieces nervously as they have hardened. Or is it that they pick men they can handle? They can't know that much at the age they marry, he thought. He was grateful that he had gone through his education on American women before now because this was a very attractive one.

"We're going after buff in the morning," he told her.

"I'm coming," she said.

"No, you're not."

"Oh, yes, I am. Mayn't I, Francis?"

"Why not stay in camp?"

"Not for anything," she said. "I wouldn't miss something like today for anything."

When she left, Wilson was thinking, when she went off to cry, she seemed a hell of a fine woman. She seemed to understand, to realize, to be hurt for him and for herself and to know how things really stood. She is away for twenty minutes and now she is back, simply enamelled in that American female cruelty. They are the damnedest women. Really the damnedest.

"We'll put on another show for you tomorrow," Francis Macomber said.

"You're not coming," Wilson said.

"You're very mistaken," she told him. "And I want *so* to see you perform again. You were lovely this morning. That is if blowing things' heads off is lovely."

"Here's the lunch," said Wilson. "You're very merry, aren't you?"

"Why not? I didn't come here to be dull."

"Well, it hasn't been dull," Wilson said. He could see the boulders in the river and the high bank beyond with the trees and he remembered the morning.

"Oh, no," she said. "It's been charming. And tomorrow. You don't know how I look forward to tomorrow."

"That's the eland he's offering you," Wilson said.

"They're the big cowy things that jump like hares, aren't they?"

"I suppose that describes them," Wilson said.

"It's very good meat," Macomber said.

"Did you shoot it, Francis?" she asked.

"Yes."

"They're not dangerous, are they?"

"Only if they fall on you," Wilson told her.

"I'm so glad."

"Why not let up on the bitchery just a little, Margot," Macomber said, cutting the eland steak and putting some mashed potato, gravy and carrot on the down-turned fork that tined through the piece of meat.

"I suppose I could," she said, "since you put it so prettily."

"Tonight we'll have champagne for the lion," Wilson said. "It's a bit too hot at noon."

"Oh, the lion," Margot said. "I'd forgotten the lion!"

So, Robert Wilson thought to himself, she *is* giving him a ride, isn't she? Or do you suppose that's her idea of putting up a good show? How should a woman act when she discovers her husband is a bloody coward? She's damn cruel but they're all cruel. They govern, of course, and to govern one has to be cruel sometimes. Still, I've seen enough of their damn terrorism.

"Have some more eland," he said to her politely.

That afternoon, late, Wilson and Macomber went out in the motor car with the native driver and the two gun-bearers. Mrs. Macomber stayed in the camp. It was too hot to go out, she said, and she was going with them in the early morning. As they drove off Wilson saw her standing under the big tree, looking pretty rather than beautiful in her faintly rosy khaki, her dark hair drawn back off her forehead and gathered in a knot low on her neck, her face as fresh, he thought, as though she were in England. She waved to them as the car went off through the swale of high grass and curved around through the trees into the small hills of orchard bush.

In the orchard bush they found a herd of impala, and leaving the car they stalked one old ram with long, wide-spread horns and Macomber killed it with a very creditable shot that knocked the buck down at a good two hundred yards and sent the herd off bounding wildly and leaping over one another's backs in long, leg-drawn-up leaps as unbelievable and as floating as those one makes sometimes in dreams.

"That was a good shot," Wilson said. "They're a small target."

"Is it a worth-while head?" Macomber asked.

"It's excellent," Wilson told him. "You shoot like that and you'll have no trouble."

"Do you think we'll find buffalo tomorrow?"

"There's a good chance of it. They feed out early in the morning and with luck we may catch them in the open."

"I'd like to clear away that lion business," Macomber said. "It's not very pleasant to have your wife see you do something like that."

I should think it would be even more unpleasant to do it, Wilson thought, wife or no wife, or to talk about it having done it. But he said, "I wouldn't think about that any more. Any one could be upset by his first lion. That's all over."

But that night after dinner and a whisky and soda by the fire before going to bed, as Francis Macomber lay on his cot with the mosquito bar over him and listened to the night noises it was not all over. It was neither all over nor was it beginning. It was there exactly as it happened with some parts of it indelibly emphasized and he was miserably ashamed of it. But more than shame he felt cold, hollow fear in him. The fear was still there like a cold slimy hollow in all the emptiness where once his confidence had been and it made him feel sick. It was still there with him now.

It had started the night before when he had wakened and heard the lion roaring somewhere up along the river. It was a deep sound and at the end there were sort of coughing grunts that made him seem just outside the tent, and when Francis Macomber woke in the night to hear it he was afraid. He could hear his wife breathing quietly, asleep. There was no one to tell he was afraid, nor to be afraid with him, and, lying alone, he did not know the Somali proverb that says a brave man is always frightened three times by a lion; when he first sees his track, when he first hears him roar and when he first confronts him. Then while they were eating breakfast by lantern light out in the dining tent, before the sun was up, the lion roared again and Francis thought he was just at the edge of camp.

"Sounds like an old-timer," Robert Wilson said, looking up from his kippers and coffee. "Listen to him cough."

"Is he very close?"

"A mile or so up the stream."

"Will we see him?"

"We'll have a look."

"Does his roaring carry that far? It sounds as though he were right in camp."

"Carries a hell of a long way," said Robert Wilson. "It's strange the way it carries. Hope he's a shootable cat. The boys said there was a very big one about here."

"If I get a shot, where should I hit him," Macomber asked, "to stop him?"

"In the shoulders," Wilson said. "In the neck if you can make it. Shoot for bone. Break him down."

"I hope I can place it properly," Macomber said.

"You shoot very well," Wilson told him. "Take your time. Make sure of him. The first one in is the one that counts."

"What range will it be?"

"Can't tell. Lion has something to say about that. Don't shoot unless it's close enough so you can make sure."

"At under a hundred yards?" Macomber asked.

Wilson looked at him quickly.

"Hundred's about right. Might have to take him a bit under. Shouldn't chance a shot at much over that. A hundred's a decent range. You can hit him wherever you want at that. Here comes the Memsahib."

"Good morning," she said. "Are you going after that lion?"

"As soon as you deal with your breakfast," Wilson said. "How are you feeling?"

"Marvellous," she said. "I'm very excited."

"I'll just go and see that everything is ready," Wilson went off. As he left the lion roared again.

"Noisy beggar," Wilson said. "We'll put a stop to that."

"What's the matter, Francis?" his wife asked him.

"Nothing," Macomber said.

"Yes, there is," she said. "What are you upset about?"

"Nothing," he said.

"Tell me," she looked at him. "Don't you feel well?"

"It's that damned roaring," he said. "It's been going on all night, you know."

"Why didn't you wake me," she said. "I'd love to have heard it."

"I've got to kill the damned thing," Macomber said, miserably.

"Well, that's what you're out here for, isn't it?"

"Yes. But I'm nervous. Hearing the thing roar gets on my nerves."

"Well then, as Wilson said, kill him and stop his roaring."

"Yes, darling," said Francis Macomber. "It sounds easy, doesn't it?"

"You're not afraid, are you?"

"Of course not. But I'm nervous from hearing him roar all night."

"You'll kill him marvellously," she said. "I know you will. I'm awfully anxious to see it."

"Finish your breakfast and we'll be starting."

"It's not light yet," she said. "This is a ridiculous hour."

Just then the lion roared in a deep-chested moaning, suddenly guttural, ascending vibration that seemed to shake the air and ended in a sigh and a heavy, deep-chested grunt.

"He sounds almost here," Macomber's wife said.

"My God," said Macomber. "I hate that damned noise."

"It's very impressive."

"Impressive. It's frightful."

Robert Wilson came up then carrying his short, ugly, shockingly big-bored .505 Gibbs and grinning.

"Come on," he said. "Your gun-bearer has your Springfield and the big gun. Everything's in the car. Have you solids?"

"Yes."

"I'm ready," Mrs. Macomber said.

"Must make him stop that racket," Wilson said. "You get in front. The Memsahib can sit back here with me."

They climbed into the motor car and, in the gray first daylight, moved off up the river through the trees. Macomber opened the breech of his rifle and saw he had metal-cased bullets, shut the bolt and put the rifle on safety. He saw his hand was trembling. He felt in his pocket for more cartridges and moved his fingers over the cartridges in the loops of his tunic front. He turned back to where Wilson sat in the rear seat of the doorless, box-bodied motor car beside his wife, them both grinning with excitement, and Wilson leaned forward and whispered,

"See the birds dropping. Means the old boy has left his kill."

On the far bank of the stream Macomber could see, above the trees, vultures circling and plummeting down.

"Chances are he'll come to drink along here," Wilson whispered. "Before he goes to lay up. Keep an eye out."

They were driving slowly along the high bank of the stream which here cut deeply to its boulder-filled bed, and they wound in and out through big trees as they drove. Macomber was watching the opposite bank when he felt Wilson take hold of his arm. The car stopped.

"There he is," he heard the whisper. "Ahead and to the right. Get out and take him. He's a marvellous lion."

Macomber saw the lion now. He was standing almost broadside, his great head up and turned toward them. The early morning breeze that blew toward them was just stirring up his dark mane, and the lion looked huge, silhouetted on the rise of the bank in the gray morning light, his shoulders heavy, his barrel of a body bulking smoothly.

"How far is he?" asked Macomber, raising his rifle.

"About seventy-five. Get out and take him."

"Why not shoot from where I am?"

"You don't shoot them from cars," he heard Wilson saying in his ear. "Get out. He's not going to stay there all day."

Macomber stepped out of the curved opening at the side of the front seat, onto the step and down to the ground. The lion still stood looking majestically and coolly toward this object that his eyes only showed in silhouette, bulking like some super-rhino. There was no man smell carried toward him and he watched the object, moving his great head a little from side to side. Then watching the object, not afraid, but hesitating before going down the bank to drink with such a thing opposite him, he saw a man figure detach itself from it and he turned his heavy head and swung away toward the cover of the trees as he heard a cracking crash and felt the slam of a .30–06 220-grain solid bullet that bit his flank and ripped in sudden hot scalding nausea through his stomach. He trotted, heavy, big-footed, swinging wounded full-bellied, through the trees toward the tall grass and cover, and the crash came again to go past him ripping the air apart. Then it crashed again and he felt the blow as it hit his lower ribs and ripped on through, blood sudden hot and frothy in his mouth, and he galloped toward the high grass where he could crouch and not be seen and make them bring the crashing thing close enough so he could make a rush and get the man that held it.

Macomber had not thought how the lion felt as he got out of the car. He only knew his hands were shaking and as he walked away from the car it was almost impossible for him to make his legs move. They were stiff in the thighs, but he could feel the muscles fluttering. He raised the rifle, sighted on the junction of the lion's head and shoulders and pulled the trigger. Nothing happened though he pulled until he thought his finger would break. Then he knew he had the safety on and as he lowered the rifle to move the safety over he moved another frozen pace forward, and the lion seeing his silhouette now clear of the silhouette of the car, turned and started off at a trot, and, as Macomber fired, he heard a whunk that meant that the bullet was home; but the lion kept on going. Macomber shot again and everyone saw the bullet throw a spout of dirt beyond the trotting lion. He shot again, remembering to lower his aim, and they all heard the bullet hit, and the lion went into a gallop and was in the tall grass before he had the bolt pushed forward.

Macomber stood there feeling sick at his stomach, his hands that held the Springfield still cocked, shaking, and his wife and Robert Wilson were standing by him. Beside him were the two gun-bearers chattering in Wakamba.

"I hit him," Macomber said. "I hit him twice."

"You gut-shot him and you hit him somewhere forward," Wilson said without enthusiasm. The gun-bearers looked very grave. They were silent now.

"You may have killed him," Wilson went on. "We'll have to wait a while before we go in to find out."

"What do you mean?"

"Let him get sick before we follow him up."

"Oh," said Macomber.

"He's a hell of a fine lion," Wilson said cheerfully. "He's gotten into a bad place though."

"Why is it bad?"

"Can't see him until you're on him."

"Oh," said Macomber.

"Come on," said Wilson. "The Memsahib can stay here in the car. We'll go to have a look at the blood spoor."

"Stay here, Margot," Macomber said to his wife. His mouth was very dry and it was hard for him to talk.

"Why?" she asked.

"Wilson says to."

"We're going to have a look," Wilson said. "You stay here. You can see even better from here."

"All right."

Wilson spoke in Swahili to the driver. He nodded and said, "Yes, Bwana."

Then they went down the steep bank and across the stream, climbing over and around the boulders and up the other bank, pulling up by some projecting roots, and along it until they found where the lion had been trotting when Macomber first shot. There was dark blood on the short grass that the gun-bearers pointed out with grass stems, and that ran away behind the river bank trees.

"What do we do?" asked Macomber.

"Not much choice," said Wilson. "We can't bring the car over. Bank's too steep. We'll let him stiffen up a bit and then you and I'll go in and have a look for him."

"Can't we set the grass on fire?" Macomber asked.

"Too green."

"Can't we send beaters?"

Wilson looked at him appraisingly. "Of course we can," he said. "But it's just a touch murderous. You see we know the lion's wounded. You can drive an unwounded lion—he'll move on ahead of a noise—but a wounded lion's going to charge. You can't see him until you're right on him. He'll make himself perfectly flat in cover you wouldn't think would hide a hare. You can't very well send boys in there to that sort of a show. Somebody bound to get mauled."

"What about the gun-bearers?"

"Oh, they'll go with us. It's their *shauri*. You see, they signed on for it. They don't look too happy though, do they?"

"I don't want to go in there," said Macomber. It was out before he knew he'd said it.

"Neither do I," said Wilson very cheerily. "Really no choice though." Then, as an afterthought, he glanced at Macomber and saw suddenly how he was trembling and the pitiful look on his face.

"You don't have to go in, of course," he said. "That's what I'm hired for, you know. That's why I'm so expensive."

"You mean you'd go in by yourself? Why not leave him there?"

Robert Wilson, whose entire occupation had been with the lion and the problem he presented, and who had not been thinking about Macomber except to note that he was rather windy, suddenly felt as though he had opened the wrong door in a hotel and seen something shameful.

"What do you mean?"

"Why not just leave him?"

"You mean to pretend to ourselves he hasn't been hit?"

"No. Just drop it."

"It isn't done."

"Why not?"

"For one thing, he's certain to be suffering. For another, some one else might run onto him."

"I see."

"But you don't have to have anything to do with it."

"I'd like to," Macomber said. "I'm just scared, you know."

"I'll go ahead when we go in," Wilson said, "with Kongoni tracking. You keep behind me and a little to one side. Chances are we'll hear him growl. If we see him we'll both shoot. Don't worry about anything. I'll keep you backed up. As a matter of fact, you know, perhaps you'd better not go. It might be much better. Why don't you go over and join the Memsahib while I just get it over with?"

"No, I want to go."

"All right," said Wilson. "But don't go in if you don't want to. This is my *shauri* now, you know."

"I want to go," said Macomber.

They sat under a tree and smoked.

"Want to go back and speak to the Memsahib while we're waiting?" Wilson asked.

"No."

"I'll just step back and tell her to be patient."

"Good," said Macomber. He sat there, sweating under his arms, his mouth dry, his stomach hollow feeling, wanting to find courage to tell Wilson to go on and finish off the lion without him. He could not know that Wilson was furious because he had not noticed the state he was in earlier and sent him back to his wife. While he sat there Wilson came up. "I have your big gun," he said. "Take it. We've given him time, I think. Come on."

Macomber took the big gun and Wilson said:

"Keep behind me and about five yards to the right and do exactly as I tell you." Then he spoke in Swahili to the two gun-bearers who looked the picture of gloom.

"Let's go," he said.

"Could I have a drink of water?" Macomber asked. Wilson spoke to the older gun-bearer, who wore a canteen on his belt, and the man unbuckled it, unscrewed the top and handed it to Macomber, who took it noticing how heavy it seemed and how hairy and shoddy the felt covering was in his hand. He raised it to drink and looked ahead at the high grass with the flat-topped trees behind it. A breeze was blowing toward them and the grass rippled gently in the wind. He looked at the gun-bearer and he could see the gun-bearer was suffering too with fear.

Thirty-five yards into the grass the big lion lay flattened out along the ground. His ears were back and his only movement was a slight twitching up and down of his long, black-tufted tail. He had turned at bay as soon as he had reached this cover and he was sick with the wound through his full belly, and weakening with the wound through his lungs that brought a thin foamy red to his mouth each time he breathed. His flanks were wet and hot and flies were on the little openings the solid bullets had made in his tawny hide, and his big yellow eyes, narrowed with hate, looked straight ahead, only blinking when the pain came as he breathed, and his claws dug in the soft baked earth. All of him, pain, sickness, hatred and all of his remaining strength, was tightening into an absolute concentration for a rush. He could hear the men talking and he waited, gathering all of himself into this preparation for a charge as soon as the men would come into the grass. As he heard their voices his tail stiffened to twitch up and down, and, as they came into the edge of the grass, he made a coughing grunt and charged.

Kongoni, the gun-bearer, in the lead watching the blood spoor, Wilson watching the grass for any movement, his big gun ready, the second gun-bearer looking ahead and listening, Macomber close to Wilson, his rifle cocked, they had just moved into the grass when Macomber heard the blood-choked coughing grunt, and saw the swishing rush in the grass. The next thing he knew he was running wildly, in panic in the open, running toward the stream.

He heard the *ca-ra-wong!* of Wilson's big rifle, and again in a second crashing *carawong!* and turning saw the lion, horrible-looking now, with half his head seeming to be gone, crawling toward Wilson in the edge of the tall grass while the red-faced man worked the bolt on the short ugly rifle and aimed carefully as another blasting *carawong!* came from the muzzle, and the crawling, heavy, yellow bulk of the lion stiffened and the huge, mutilated head slid forward and Macomber, standing by himself in the clearing where he had run, holding a loaded rifle, while two black men and a white man looked back at him in contempt, knew the lion was dead. He came toward Wilson, his tallness all seeming a naked reproach, and Wilson looked at him and said:

"Want to take pictures?"

"No," he said.

That was all any one had said until they reached the motor car. Then Wilson had said:

"Hell of a fine lion. Boys will skin him out. We might as well stay here in the shade."

Macomber's wife had not looked at him nor he at her and he had sat by her in the back seat with Wilson sitting in the front seat. Once he had reached over and taken his wife's hand without looking at her and she had removed her hand from his. Looking across the stream where the gun-bearers were skinning out the lion he could see that she had been able to see the whole thing. While they sat there his wife had reached forward and put her hand on Wilson's shoulder. He turned and she leaned forward over the low seat and kissed him on the mouth.

"Oh, I say," said Wilson, going redder than his natural baked color.

"Mr. Robert Wilson," she said. "The beautiful red-faced Mr. Robert Wilson."

Then she sat down beside Macomber again and looked away across the stream to where the lion lay, with uplifted, white-muscled, tendon-marked naked forearms, and white bloating belly, as the black men fleshed away the skin. Finally the gun-bearers brought the skin over, wet and heavy, and climbed in behind with it, rolling it up before they got in, and the motor car started. No one had said anything more until they were back in camp.

That was the story of the lion. Macomber did not know how the lion had felt before he started his rush, nor during it when the unbelievable smash of the .505 with a muzzle velocity of two tons had hit him in the mouth, nor what kept him coming after that, when the second ripping crash had smashed his hind quarters and he had come crawling on toward the crashing, blasting thing that had destroyed him. Wilson knew something about it and only expressed it by saying, "Damned fine lion," but Macomber did not know how Wilson felt about things either. He did not know how his wife felt except that she was through with him.

His wife had been through with him before but it never lasted. He was very wealthy, and would be much wealthier, and he knew she would not leave him ever now. That was one of the few things that he really knew. He knew about that, about motor cycles— that was earliest—about motor cars, about duck-shooting, about fishing, trout, salmon and big-sea, about sex in books, many books, too many books, about all court games, about dogs, not much about horses, about hanging on to his money, about most of the other things his world dealt in, and about his wife not leaving him. His wife had been a great beauty and she was still a great beauty in Africa, but she was not a great enough beauty any more at home to be able to leave him and better herself and she knew it and he knew it. She had missed the chance to leave him and he knew it. If he had been better with women she would probably have started to worry about him getting another new, beautiful wife; but she knew too much about him to worry about him either. Also, he had always had a great tolerance which seemed the nicest thing about him if it were not the most sinister.

All in all they were known as a comparatively happily married couple, one of those whose disruption is often rumored but never occurs, and as the society columnist put it, they were adding more than a spice of *adventure* to their much envied and ever-enduring *Romance* by a *Safari* on what was known as *Darkest Africa* until the Martin Johnsons lighted it on so many silver screens where they were pursuing *Old Simba* the lion, the buffalo, *Tembo* the elephant and as well collecting specimens for the Museum of Natural History. This same columnist had reported them *on the verge* at least three times in the past and they had been. But they always made it up. They had a sound basis of union. Margot was too beautiful for Macomber to divorce her and Macomber had too much money for Margot ever to leave him.

It was now about three o'clock in the morning and Francis Macomber, who had been asleep a little while after he had stopped thinking about the lion, wakened and then slept again, woke suddenly, frightened in a dream of the bloody-headed lion standing over him, and listening while his heart pounded, he realized that his wife was not in the other cot in the tent. He lay awake with that knowledge for two hours.

At the end of that time his wife came into the tent, lifted her mosquito bar and crawled cozily into bed.

"Where have you been?" Macomber asked in the darkness.

"Hello," she said. "Are you awake?"

"Where have you been?"

"I just went out to get a breath of air."

"You did, like hell."

"What do you want me to say, darling?"

"Where have you been?"

"Out to get a breath of air."

"That's a new name for it. You *are* a bitch."

"Well, you're a coward."

"All right," he said. "What of it?"

"Nothing as far as I'm concerned. But please let's not talk, darling, because I'm very sleepy."

"You think that I'll take anything."

"I know you will, sweet."

"Well, I won't."

"Please, darling, let's not talk. I'm so very sleepy."

"There wasn't going to be any of that. You promised there wouldn't be."

"Well, there is now," she said sweetly.

"You said if we made this trip that there would be none of that. You promised."

"Yes, darling. That's the way I meant it to be. But the trip was spoiled yesterday. We don't have to talk about it, do we?"

"You don't wait long when you have an advantage, do you?"

"Please let's not talk. I'm so sleepy, darling."

"I'm going to talk."

"Don't mind me then, because I'm going to sleep." And she did.

At breakfast they were all three at the table before daylight and Francis Macomber found that, of all the many men that he had hated, he hated Robert Wilson the most.

"Sleep well?" Wilson asked in his throaty voice, filling a pipe.

"Did you?"

"Topping," the white hunter told him.

You bastard, thought Macomber, you insolent bastard.

So she woke him when she came in, Wilson thought, looking

at them both with his flat, cold eyes. Well, why doesn't he keep his wife where she belongs? What does he think I am, a bloody plaster saint? Let him keep her where she belongs. It's his own fault.

"Do you think we'll find buffalo?" Margot asked, pushing away a dish of apricots.

"Chance of it," Wilson said and he smiled at her "Why don't you stay in camp?"

"Not for anything," she told him

"Why not order her to stay in camp?" Wilson said to Macomber.

"You order her," said Macomber coldly.

"Let's not have any ordering, nor," turning to Macomber, "any silliness, Francis," Margot said quite pleasantly.

"Are you ready to start?" Macomber asked.

"Any time," Wilson told him. "Do you want the Memsahib to go?"

"Does it make any difference whether I do or not?"

The hell with it, thought Robert Wilson. The utter complete hell with it. So this is what it's going to be like. Well this is what it's going to be like, then.

"Makes no difference," he said

"You're sure you wouldn't like to stay in camp with her yourself and let me go out and hunt the buffalo?" Macomber asked.

"Can't do that," said Wilson. "Wouldn't talk rot if I were you."

"I'm not talking rot. I'm disgusted."

"Bad word, disgusted."

"Francis, will you please try to speak sensibly?" his wife said.

"I speak too damned sensibly," Macomber said. "Did you ever eat such filthy food?"

"Something wrong with the food?" asked Wilson quietly.

"No more than with everything else."

"I'd pull yourself together, laddybuck," Wilson said very quietly. "There's a boy waits at table that understands a little English."

"The hell with him."

Wilson stood up and puffing on his pipe strolled away, speaking a few words in Swahili to one of the gun-bearers who was standing waiting for him. Macomber and his wife sat on at the table. He was staring at his coffee cup.

"If you make a scene I'll leave you, darling," Margot said quietly.

"No, you won't."

"You can try it and see."

"You won't leave me."

"No," she said. "I won't leave you and you'll behave yourself."

"Behave myself? That's a way to talk. Behave myself."

"Yes. Behave yourself."

"Why don't *you* try behaving?"

"I've tried it so long. So very long."

"I hate that red-faced swine," Macomber said. "I loathe the sight of him."

"He's really *very* nice."

"Oh, *shut up*," Macomber almost shouted. Just then the car came up and stopped in front of the dining tent and the driver and the two gun-bearers got out. Wilson walked over and looked at the husband and wife sitting there at the table.

"Going shooting?" he asked.

"Yes," said Macomber, standing up. "Yes."

"Better bring a woolly. It will be cool in the car," Wilson said.

"I'll get my leather jacket," Margot said.

"The boy has it," Wilson told her. He climbed into the front with the driver and Francis Macomber and his wife sat, not speaking, in the back seat.

Hope the silly beggar doesn't take a notion to blow the back of my head off, Wilson thought to himself. Women *are* a nuisance on safari.

The car was grinding down to cross the river at a pebbly ford in the gray daylight and then climbed, angling up the steep bank, where Wilson had ordered a way shovelled out the day before so they could reach the parklike wooded rolling country on the far side.

It was a good morning, Wilson thought. There was a heavy dew and as the wheels went through the grass and low bushes he could smell the odor of the crushed fronds. It was an odor like verbena and he liked this early morning smell of the dew, the crushed bracken and the look of the tree trunks showing black through the early morning mist, as the car made its way through the untracked, parklike country. He had put the two in the back seat out of his mind now and was thinking about buffalo. The buffalo that he was after stayed in the daytime in a thick swamp where it was impossible to get a shot, but in the night they fed out into an open stretch of country and if he could come between them and their swamp with the car, Macomber would have a good chance at them in the open. He did not want to hunt buff with Macomber in thick cover. He did not want to hunt buff or anything else with Macomber at all, but he was a professional hunter and he hunted with some rare ones in his time. If they got buff today there would only be rhino to come and the poor man would have gone through his dangerous game and things might pick up. He'd have nothing more to do with the woman and Macomber would get over that too. He must have gone through plenty of that before by the look of things. Poor beggar. He must have a way of getting over it. Well, it was the poor sod's own bloody fault.

He, Robert Wilson, carried a double size cot on safari to accommodate any windfalls he might receive. He had hunted for a certain clientele, the international, fast, sporting set, where the women did not feel they were getting their money's worth unless they had shared that cot with the white hunter. He despised them when he was away from them although he liked some of them well enough at the time, but he made his living by them; and their standards were his standards as long as they were hiring him.

They were his standards in all except the shooting. He had his own standards about the killing and they could live up to them or get some one else to hunt them. He knew, too, that they all respected him for this. This Macomber was an odd one though. Damned if he wasn't. Now the wife. Well, the wife. Yes, the wife. Hm, the wife. Well he'd dropped all that. He looked around at them. Macomber sat grim and furious. Margot smiled at him. She looked younger today, more innocent and fresher and not so professionally beautiful. What's in her heart God knows, Wilson thought. She hadn't talked much last night. At that it was a pleasure to see her.

The motor car climbed up a slight rise and went on through the trees and then out into a grassy prairie-like opening and kept in the shelter of the trees along the edge, the driver going slowly and Wilson looking carefully out across the prairie and all along its far side. He stopped the car and studied the opening with his field glasses. Then he motioned to the driver to go on and the car moved slowly along, the driver avoiding wart-hog holes and driving around the mud castles ants had built. Then, looking across the opening, Wilson suddenly turned and said,

"By God, there they are!"

And looking where he pointed, while the car jumped forward and Wilson spoke in rapid Swahili to the driver, Macomber saw three huge, black animals looking almost cylindrical in their long heaviness, like big black tank cars, moving at a gallop across the far edge of the open prairie. They moved at a stiff-necked, stiff bodied gallop and he could see the upswept wide black horns on their heads as they galloped heads out; the heads not moving.

"They're three old bulls," Wilson said. "We'll cut them off before they get to the swamp."

The car was going a wild forty-five miles an hour across the open and as Macomber watched, the buffalo got bigger and bigger until he could see the gray, hairless, scabby look of one huge bull and how his neck was a part of his shoulders and the shiny black of his horns as he galloped a little behind the others that were strung out in that steady plunging gait; and then, the car swaying as though it had just jumped a road, they drew up close and he could see the plunging hugeness of the bull, and the dust in his sparsely haired hide, the wide boss of horn and his outstretched, wide-nostrilled muzzle, and he was raising his rifle when Wilson shouted, "Not from the car, you fool!" and he had no fear, only hatred of Wilson, while the brakes clamped on and the car skidded, plowing sideways to an almost stop and Wilson was out on one side and he on the other, stumbling as his feet hit the still speeding-by of the earth, and then he was shooting at the bull as he moved away, hearing the bullets whunk into him, emptying his rifle at him as he moved steadily away, finally remembering to get his shots forward into the shoulder, and as he fumbled to re-load, he saw the bull was down. Down on his knees, his big head tossing, and seeing the other two still galloping he shot at the leader and hit him. He shot again and missed and he heard the *carawonging* roar as Wilson shot and saw the leading bull slide forward onto his nose.

"Get that other," Wilson said. "Now you're shooting!"

But the other bull was moving steadily at the same gallop and he missed, throwing a spout of dirt, and Wilson missed and the dust rose in a cloud and Wilson shouted, "Come on. He's too far!" and grabbed his arm and they were in the car again, Macomber and Wilson hanging on the sides and rocketing swayingly over the uneven ground, drawing up on the steady, plunging, heavy-necked, straight-moving gallop of the bull.

They were behind him and Macomber was filling his rifle, dropping shells onto the ground, jamming it, clearing the jam, then they were almost up with the bull when Wilson yelled "Stop," and the car skidded so that it almost swung over and Macomber fell forward onto his feet, slammed his bolt forward and fired as far forward as he could aim into the galloping, rounded black back, aimed and shot again, then again, then again, and the bullets, all of them hitting, had no effect on the buffalo that he could see. Then Wilson shot, the roar deafening him, and he could see the bull stagger. Macomber shot again, aiming carefully, and down he came, onto his knees.

"All right," Wilson said. "Nice work. That's the three."

Macomber felt a drunken elation.

"How many times did you shoot?" he asked.

"Just three," Wilson said. "You killed the first bull. The biggest one. I helped you finish the other two. Afraid they might have got into cover. You had them killed. I was just mopping up a little. You shot damn well."

"Let's go to the car," said Macomber. "I want a drink."

"Got to finish off that buff first," Wilson told him. The buffalo was on his knees and he jerked his head furiously and bellowed in pig-eyed, roaring rage as they came toward him.

"Watch he doesn't get up," Wilson said. Then, "Get a little broadside and take him in the neck just behind the ear."

Macomber aimed carefully at the center of the huge, jerking, rage-driven neck and shot. At the shot the head dropped forward.

"That does it," said Wilson. "Got the spine. They're a hell of a looking thing, aren't they?"

"Let's get the drink," said Macomber. In his life he had never felt so good.

In the car Macomber's wife sat very white faced. "You were marvellous, darling," she said to Macomber. "What a ride."

"Was it rough?" Wilson asked.

"It was frightful. I've never been more frightened in my life."

"Let's all have a drink," Macomber said.

"By all means," said Wilson. "Give it to the Memsahib." She drank the neat whisky from the flask and shuddered a little when she swallowed. She handed the flask to Macomber who handed it to Wilson.

"It was frightfully exciting," she said. "It's given me a dreadful headache. I didn't know you were allowed to shoot them from cars though."

"No one shot from cars," said Wilson coldly.

"I mean chase them from cars."

"Wouldn't ordinarily," Wilson said. "Seemed sporting enough to me though while we were doing it. Taking more chance driving that way across the plain full of holes and one thing and another than hunting on foot. Buffalo could have charged us each time we shot if he liked. Gave him every chance. Wouldn't mention it to anyone though. It's illegal if that's what you mean."

"It seemed very unfair to me," Margot said, "chasing those big helpless things in a motor car."

"Did it?" said Wilson.

"What would happen if they heard about it in Nairobi?"

"I'd lose my license for one thing. Other unpleasantness," Wilson said, taking a drink from the flask. "I'd be out of business."

"Really?"

"Yes, really."

"Well," said Macomber, and he smiled for the first time all day. "Now she has something on you."

"You have such a pretty way of putting things, Francis," Margot Macomber said. Wilson looked at them both. If a four-letter man marries a five-letter woman, he was thinking, what number of letters would their children be? What he said was, "We lost a gun-bearer. Did you notice it?"

"My God, no," Macomber said.

"Here he comes," Wilson said. "He's all right. He must have fallen off when we left the first bull."

Approaching them was the middle-aged gun-bearer, limping along in his knitted cap, khaki tunic, shorts and rubber sandals, gloomy-faced and disgusted looking. As he came up he called out to Wilson in Swahili and they all saw the change in the white hunter's face.

"What does he say?" asked Margot.

"He says the first bull got up and went into the bush," Wilson said with no expression in his voice.

"Oh," said Macomber blankly.

"Then it's going to be just like the lion," said Margot, full of anticipation.

"It's not going to be a damned bit like the lion," Wilson told her. "Did you want another drink, Macomber?"

"Thanks, yes," Macomber said. He expected the feeling he had had about the lion to come back but it did not. For the first time in his life he really felt wholly without fear. Instead of fear he had a feeling of definite elation.

"We'll go and have a look at the second bull," Wilson said. "I'll tell the driver to put the car in the shade."

"What are you going to do?" asked Margaret Macomber.

"Take a look at the buff," Wilson said.

"I'll come."

"Come along."

The three of them walked over to where the second buffalo bulked blackly in the open, head forward on the grass, the massive horns swung wide.

"He's a very good head," Wilson said. "That's close to a fifty-inch spread."

Macomber was looking at him with delight.

"He's hateful looking," said Margot. "Can't we go into the shade?"

"Of course," Wilson said. "Look," he said to Macomber, and pointed. "See that patch of bush?"

"Yes."

"That's where the first bull went in. The gun-bearer said when he fell off the bull was down. He was watching us helling along and the other two buff galloping. When he looked up there was the bull up and looking at him. Gun-bearer ran like hell and the bull went off slowly into that bush."

"Can we go in after him now?" asked Macomber eagerly.

Wilson looked at him appraisingly. Damned if this isn't a strange one, he thought. Yesterday he's scared sick and today he's a ruddy fire eater.

"No, we'll give him a while."

"Let's please go into the shade," Margot said. Her face was white and she looked ill.

They made their way to the car where it stood under a single, wide-spreading tree and all climbed in.

"Chances are he's dead in there," Wilson remarked. "After a little we'll have a look."

Macomber felt a wild unreasonable happiness that he had never known before.

"By God, that was a chase," he said. "I've never felt any such feeling. Wasn't it marvellous, Margot?"

"I hated it."

"Why?"

"I hated it," she said bitterly. "I loathed it."

"You know I don't think I'd ever be afraid of anything again," Macomber said to Wilson. "Something happened in me after we first saw the buff and started after him. Like a dam bursting. It was pure excitement."

"Cleans out your liver," said Wilson. "Damn funny things happen to people."

Macomber's face was shining. "You know something did happen to me," he said. "I feel absolutely different."

His wife said nothing and eyed him strangely. She was sitting far back in the seat and Macomber was sitting forward talking to Wilson who turned sideways talking over the back of the front seat.

"You know, I'd like to try another lion," Macomber said. "I'm really not afraid of them now. After all, what can they do to you?"

"That's it," said Wilson. "Worst one can do is kill you. How does it go? Shakespeare. Damned good. See if I can remember. Oh, damned good. Used to quote it to myself at one time. Let's see. 'By my troth, I care not; a man can die but once; we owe God a death and let it go which way it will he that dies this year is quit for the next.' Damned fine, eh?"

He was very embarrassed, having brought out this thing he had lived by, but he had seen men come of age before and it always moved him. It was not a matter of their twenty-first birthday.

It had taken a strange chance of hunting, a sudden precipitation into action without opportunity for worrying beforehand, to bring this about with Macomber, but regardless of how it had happened it had most certainly happened. Look at the beggar now, Wilson thought. It's that some of them stay little boys so long, Wilson thought. Sometimes all their lives. Their figures stay boyish when they're fifty. The great American boy-men. Damned strange people. But he liked this Macomber now. Damned strange fellow. Probably meant the end of cuckoldry too. Well, that would be a damned good thing. Damned good thing. Beggar had probably been afraid all his life. Don't know what started it. But over now. Hadn't had time to be afraid with the buff. That and being angry too. Motor car too. Motor cars made it familiar. Be a damn fire eater now. He'd seen it in the war work the same way. More of a change than any loss of virginity. Fear gone like an operation. Something else grew in its place. Main thing a man had. Made him into a man. Women knew it too. No bloody fear.

From the far corner of the seat Margaret Macomber looked at the two of them. There was no change in Wilson. She saw Wilson as she had seen him the day before when she had first realized what his great talent was. But she saw the change in Francis Macomber now.

"Do you have that feeling of happiness about what's going to happen?" Macomber asked, still exploring his new wealth.

"You're not supposed to mention it," Wilson said, looking in the other's face. "Much more fashionable to say you're scared. Mind you, you'll be scared too, plenty of times."

"But you *have* a feeling of happiness about action to come?"

"Yes," said Wilson. "There's that. Doesn't do to talk too much about all this. Talk the whole thing away. No pleasure in anything if you mouth it up too much."

"You're both talking rot," said Margot. "Just because you've chased some helpless animals in a motor car you talk like heroes."

"Sorry," said Wilson. "I have been gassing too much." She's worried about it already, he thought.

"If you don't know what we're talking about why not keep out of it?" Macomber asked his wife.

"You've gotten awfully brave, awfully suddenly," his wife said contemptuously, but her contempt was not secure. She was very afraid of something.

Macomber laughed, a very natural hearty laugh. "You know I *have*," he said. "I really have."

"Isn't it sort of late?" Margot said bitterly. Because she had done the best she could for many years back and the way they were together now was no one person's fault.

"Not for me," said Macomber.

Margot said nothing but sat back in the corner of the seat.

"Do you think we've given him time enough?" Macomber asked Wilson cheerfully.

"We might have a look," Wilson said. "Have you any solids left?"

"The gun-bearer has some."

Wilson called in Swahili and the older gun-bearer, who was skinning out one of the heads, straightened up, pulled a box of solids out of his pocket and brought them over to Macomber, who filled his magazine and put the remaining shells in his pocket.

"You might as well shoot the Springfield," Wilson said. "You're used to it. We'll leave the Mannlicher in the car with the Memsahib. Your gun-bearer can carry your heavy gun. I've this damned cannon. Now let me tell you about them." He had saved this until the last because he did not want to worry Macomber. "When a buff comes he comes with his head high and thrust straight out. The boss of the horns covers any sort of a brain shot. The only shot is straight into the nose. The only other shot is into his chest or, if you're to one side, into the neck or the shoulders. After they've been hit once they take a hell of a lot of killing. Don't try anything fancy. Take the easiest shot there is. They've finished skinning out that head now. Should we get started?"

He called to the gun-bearers, who came up wiping their hands, and the older one got into the back.

"I'll only take Kongoni," Wilson said. "The other can watch to keep the birds away."

As the car moved slowly across the open space toward the island of brushy trees that ran in a tongue of foliage along a dry water course that cut the open swale, Macomber felt his heart pounding and his mouth was dry again, but it was excitement, not fear.

"Here's where he went in," Wilson said. Then to the gun-bearer in Swahili, "Take the blood spoor."

The car was parallel to the patch of bush. Macomber, Wilson and the gun-bearer got down. Macomber, looking back, saw his wife, with the rifle by her side, looking at him. He waved to her and she did not wave back.

The brush was very thick ahead and the ground was dry. The middle-aged gun-bearer was sweating heavily and Wilson had his hat down over his eyes and his red neck showed just ahead of Macomber. Suddenly the gun-bearer said something in Swahili to Wilson and ran forward.

"He's dead in there," Wilson said. "Good work," and he turned to grip Macomber's hand and as they shook hands, grinning at each other, the gun-bearer shouted wildly and they saw him coming out of the brush sideways, fast as a crab, and the bull coming, nose out, mouth tight closed, blood dripping, massive head straight out, coming in a charge, his little pig eyes bloodshot as he looked at them. Wilson, who was ahead was kneeling shooting, and Macomber, as he fired, unhearing his shot in the roaring of Wilson's gun, saw fragments like slate burst from the huge boss of the horns, and the head jerked, he shot again at the wide nostrils and saw the horns jolt again and fragments fly, and he did not see Wilson now and, aiming carefully, shot again with the buffalo's huge hulk almost on him and his rifle almost level with the oncoming head, nose out, and he could see the little wicked eyes and the head started to lower and he felt a sudden white-hot, blinding flash explode inside his head and that was all he ever felt.

Wilson had ducked to one side to get in a shoulder shot. Macomber had stood solid and shot for the nose, shooting a touch high each time and hitting the heavy horns, splintering and chipping them like hitting a slate roof, and Mrs. Macomber, in the car, had shot at the buffalo with the 6.5 Mannlicher as it seemed about to gore Macomber and had hit her husband about two inches up and a little to one side of the base of his skull.

Francis Macomber lay now face down, not two yards from where the buffalo lay on his side and his wife knelt over him with Wilson beside her.

"I wouldn't turn him over," Wilson said.

The woman was crying hysterically.

"I'd get back in the car," Wilson said. "Where's the rifle?"

She shook her head, her face contorted. The gun-bearer picked up the rifle.

"Leave it as it is," said Wilson. Then, "Go get Abdulla so that he may witness the manner of the accident."

He knelt down, took a handkerchief from his pocket, and spread it over Francis Macomber's crew-cropped head where it lay. The blood sank into the dry, loose earth.

Wilson stood up and saw the buffalo on his side, his legs out, his thinly-haired belly crawling with ticks. "Hell of a good bull," his brain registered automatically. "A good fifty inches, or better. Better." He called to the driver and told him to spread a blanket over the body and stay by it. Then he walked over to the motor car where the woman sat crying in the corner.

"That was a pretty thing to do," he said in a toneless voice. "He *would* have left you too."

"Stop it," she said.

"Of course it's an accident," he said. "I know that."

"Stop it," she said.

"Don't worry," he said. "There will be a certain amount of unpleasantness but I will have some photographs taken that will be very useful at the inquest. There's the testimony of the gun-bearers and the driver too. You're perfectly all right."

"Stop it," she said.

"There's a hell of a lot to be done," he said. "And I'll have to send a truck off to the lake to wireless for a plane to take the three of us into Nairobi. Why didn't you poison him? That's what they do in England."

"Stop it. Stop it. Stop it," the woman cried.

Wilson looked at her with his flat blue eyes.

"I'm through now," he said. "I was a little angry. I'd begun to like your husband."

"Oh, please stop it," she said. "Please, please stop it."

"That's better," Wilson said. "Please is much better. Now I'll stop."

Understanding others

The Eighty-Yard Run

Irwin Shaw
(b. 1913)

Irwin Shaw was born and educated in New York City. After graduating from Brooklyn College in 1934, Shaw worked for two years as a writer of the radio serials "The Gumps" and "Dick Tracy." During this time he also wrote his first play, Bury the Dead *(1936), in which dead soldiers refuse to be buried. The immediate success of this play has been duplicated by his many subsequent plays, novels, short stories, and Hollywood screenplays.*

Noted for his eloquence, dramatic intensity, and social awareness, Shaw is probably best known for his book The Young Lions *(1948), one of the most important American novels written about World War II. His other major works include* The Gentle People *(1939), and* Sons and Soldiers *(1944), both plays;* The Troubled Air *(1951),* Lucy Crown *(1956),* Two Weeks in Another Town *(1959), and* Voices of a Summer's Day *(1965), all novels; and* Sailor Off the Bremen and Other Stories *(1939),* Welcome to the City *(1942),* Act of Faith and Other Stories *(1946),* Mixed Company *(1950), and* Love on a Dark Street *(1965), all short-story collections. His latest novel is* Rich Man, Poor Man *(1970).*

The pass was high and wide and he jumped for it, feeling it slap flatly against his hands, as he shook his hips to throw off the halfback who was diving at him. The center floated by, his hands desperately brushing Darling's knee as Darling picked his feet up high and delicately ran over a blocker and an opposing linesman in a jumble on the ground near the scrimmage line. He had ten yards in the clear and picked up speed, breathing easily, feeling his thigh pads rising and falling against his legs, listening to the sound of cleats behind him, pulling away from them, watching the other backs heading him off toward the sideline, the whole picture, the men closing in on him, the blockers fighting for position, the ground he had to cross, all suddenly clear in his head, for the first time in his life not a meaningless confusion of men, sounds, speed. He smiled a little to himself as he ran, holding the ball lightly in front of him with his two hands, his knees pumping high, his hips twisting in the almost girlish run of a back in a broken field. The first halfback came at him and he fed him his leg, then swung at the last moment, took the shock of the man's shoulder without breaking stride, ran right through him, his cleats biting securely into the turf. There was only the safety man now, coming warily at him, his arms crooked, hands spread. Darling tucked the ball in, spurted at him, driving hard, hurling himself along, his legs pounding, knees high, all two hundred pounds bunched into controlled attack. He was sure he was going to get past the safety man. Without thought, his arms and legs working beautifully together, he headed right for the safety man, stiff-armed him, feeling blood spurt instantaneously from the man's nose onto his hand, seeing his face go awry, head turned, mouth pulled to one side. He pivoted away, keeping the arm locked, dropping the safety man as he ran easily toward the goal line, with the drumming of cleats diminishing behind him.

How long ago? It was autumn then, and the ground was getting hard because the nights were cold and leaves from the maples around the stadium blew across the practice fields in gusts of wind, and the girls were beginning to put polo coats over their sweaters when they came to watch practice in the afternoons. . . . Fifteen years. Darling walked slowly over the same ground in the spring twilight, in his neat shoes, a man of thirty-five dressed in a double-breasted suit, ten pounds heavier in the fifteen years, but not fat, with the years between 1925 and 1940 showing in his face.

The coach was smiling quietly to himself and the assistant coaches were looking at each other with pleasure the way they always did when one of the second stringers suddenly did something fine, bringing credit to them, making their $2,000 a year a tiny bit more secure.

Darling trotted back, smiling, breathing deeply but easily, feeling wonderful, not tired, though this was the tail end of practice and he'd run eighty yards. The sweat poured off his face and soaked his jersey and he liked the feeling, the warm moistness lubricating his skin like oil. Off in a corner of the field some players were punting and the smack of leather against the ball came pleasantly through the afternoon air. The freshmen were running signals on the next field and the quarterback's sharp voice, the pound of the eleven pairs of cleats, the "Dig, now *dig!*" of the coaches, the laughter of the players all somehow made him feel happy as he trotted back to midfield, listening to the applause and shouts of the students along the sidelines, knowing that after that run the coach would have to start him Saturday against Illinois.

Fifteen years, Darling thought, remembering the shower after the workout, the hot water steaming off his skin and the deep soapsuds and all the young voices singing with the water streaming down and towels going and managers running in and out and the sharp sweet smell of oil of wintergreen and everybody clapping him on the back as he dressed and Packard, the captain, who took being captain very seriously, coming over to him and shaking his hand and saying, "Darling, you're going to go places in the next two years."

The assistant manager fussed over him, wiping a cut on his leg with alcohol and iodine, the little sting making him realize suddenly how fresh and whole and solid his body felt. The manager slapped a piece of adhesive tape over the cut, and Darling noticed the sharp clean white of the tape against the ruddiness of the skin, fresh from the shower.

He dressed slowly, the softness of his shirt and the soft warmth of his wool socks and his flannel trousers a reward against his skin after the harsh pressure of the shoulder harness and thigh and hip pads. He drank three glasses of cold water, the liquid reaching down coldly inside of him, soothing the harsh dry places in his throat and belly left by the sweat and running and shouting of practice.

Fifteen years.

The sun had gone down and the sky was green behind the stadium and he laughed quietly to himself as he looked at the stadium, rearing above the trees, and knew that on Saturday when the 70,000 voices roared as the team came running out onto the field, part of that enormous salute would be for him. He walked slowly, listening to the gravel crunch satisfactorily under his shoes in the still twilight, feeling his clothes swing lightly against his skin, breathing the thin evening air, feeling the wind move softly in his damp hair, wonderfully cool behind his ears and at the nape of his neck.

Louise was waiting for him at the road, in her car. The top was down and he noticed all over again, as he always did when he saw her, how pretty she was, the rough blonde hair and the large, inquiring eyes and the bright mouth, smiling now.

She threw the door open. "Were you good today?" she asked.

"Pretty good," he said. He climbed in, sank luxuriously into the soft leather, stretched his legs far out. He smiled, thinking of the eighty yards. "Pretty damn good."

She looked at him seriously for a moment, then scrambled around, like a little girl, kneeling on the seat next to him, grabbed him, her hands along his ears, and kissed him as he sprawled, head back, on the seat cushion. She let go of him, but kept her head close to his, over his. Darling reached up slowly and rubbed the back of his hand against her cheek, lit softly by a street lamp a hundred feet away. They looked at each other, smiling.

Louise drove down to the lake and they sat there silently, watching the moon rise behind the hills on the other side. Finally he reached over, pulled her gently to him, kissed her. Her lips grew soft, her body sank into his, tears formed slowly in her eyes. He knew, for the first time, that he could do whatever he wanted with her.

"Tonight," he said. "I'll call for you at seven-thirty. Can you get out?"

She looked at him. She was smiling, but the tears were still full in her eyes. "All right," she said. "I'll get out. How about you? Won't the coach raise hell?"

Darling grinned. "I got the coach in the palm of my hand," he said. "Can you wait till seven-thirty?"

She grinned back at him. "No," she said.

They kissed and she started the car and they went back to town for dinner. He sang on the way home.

Christian Darling, thirty-five years old, sat on the frail spring grass, greener now than it ever would be again on the practice field, looked thoughtfully up at the stadium, a deserted ruin in the twilight. He had started on the first team that Saturday and every Saturday after that for the next two years, but it had never been as satisfactory as it should have been. He never had broken away, the longest run he'd ever made was thirty-five yards, and that in a game that was already won, and then that kid had come up from the third team, Diederich, a blank-faced German kid from Wisconsin, who ran like a bull, ripping lines to pieces Saturday after Saturday, plowing through, never getting hurt, never changing his expression, scoring more points, gaining more ground than all the rest of the team put together, making everybody's All-American, carrying the ball three times out of four, keeping everybody else out of the headlines. Darling was a good blocker and he spent his Saturday afternoons working on the big Swedes and Polacks who played tackle and end for Michigan, Illinois, Purdue, hurling into huge pile-ups, bobbing his head wildly to elude the great raw hands swinging like meat-cleavers at him as he went charging in to open up holes for Diederich coming through like a locomotive behind him. Still, it wasn't so bad. Everybody liked him and he did his job and he was pointed out on the campus and boys always felt important when they introduced their girls to him at their proms, and Louise loved him and watched him faithfully in the games, even in the mud, when your own mother wouldn't know you, and drove him around in her car keeping the top down because she was proud of him and wanted to show everybody that she was Christian Darling's girl. She bought him crazy presents because her father was rich, watches, pipes, humidors, an icebox for beer for his room, curtains, wallets, a fifty-dollar dictionary.

"You'll spend every cent your old man owns," Darling protested once when she showed up at his rooms with seven different packages in her arms and tossed them onto the couch.

"Kiss me," Louise said, "and shut up."

"Do you want to break your poor old man?"

"I don't mind. I want to buy you presents."

"Why?"

"It makes me feel good. Kiss me. I don't know why. Did you know that you're an important figure?"

"Yes," Darling said gravely.

"When I was waiting for you at the library yesterday two girls saw you coming and one of them said to the other, 'That's Christian Darling. He's an important figure.' "

"You're a liar."

"I'm in love with an important figure."

"Still, why the hell did you have to give me a forty-pound dictionary?"

"I wanted to make sure," Louise said, "that you had a token of my esteem. I want to smother you in tokens of my esteem."

Fifteen years ago.

They'd married when they got out of college. There'd been

other women for him, but all casual and secret, more for curiosity's sake, and vanity, women who'd thrown themselves at him and flattered him, a pretty mother at a summer camp for boys, an old girl from his home town who'd suddenly blossomed into a coquette, a friend of Louise's who had dogged him grimly for six months and had taken advantage of the two weeks that Louise went home when her mother died. Perhaps Louise had known, but she'd kept quiet, loving him completely, filling his rooms with presents, religiously watching him battling with the big Swedes and Polacks on the line of scrimmage on Saturday afternoons, making plans for marrying him and living with him in New York and going with him there to the night clubs, the theaters, the good restaurants, being proud of him in advance, tall, white-teethed, smiling, large, yet moving lightly, with an athlete's grace, dressed in evening clothes, approvingly eyed by magnificently dressed and famous women in theater lobbies, with Louise adoringly at his side.

Her father, who manufactured inks, set up a New York office for Darling to manage and presented him with three hundred accounts, and they lived on Beekman Place with a view of the river with fifteen thousand dollars a year between them, because everybody was buying everything in those days, including ink. They saw all the shows and went to all the speakeasies and spent their fifteen thousand dollars a year and in the afternoons Louise went to the art galleries and the matinees of the more serious plays that Darling didn't like to sit through and Darling slept with a girl who danced in the chorus of *Rosalie* and with the wife of a man who owned three copper mines. Darling played squash three times a week and remained as solid as a stone barn and Louise never took her eyes off him when they were in the same room together, watching him with a secret, miser's smile, with a trick of coming over to him in the middle of a crowded room and saying gravely, in a low voice, "You're the handsomest man I've ever seen in my whole life. Want a drink?"

Nineteen twenty-nine came to Darling and to his wife and father-in-law, the maker of inks, just as it came to everyone else. The father-in-law waited until 1933 and then blew his brains out and when Darling went to Chicago to see what the books of the firm looked like he found out all that was left were debts and three or four gallons of unbought ink.

"Please, Christian," Louise said, sitting in their neat Beekman Place apartment, with a view of the river and prints of paintings by Dufy and Braque and Picasso on the wall, "please, why do you want to start drinking at two o'clock in the afternoon?"

"I have nothing else to do," Darling said, putting down his glass, emptied of its fourth drink. "Please pass the whisky."

Louise filled his glass. "Come take a walk with me," she said. "We'll walk along the river."

"I don't want to walk along the river," Darling said, squinting intensely at the prints of paintings by Dufy, Braque and Picasso. "We'll walk along Fifth Avenue."

"I don't want to walk along Fifth Avenue."

"Maybe," Louise said gently, "you'd like to come with me to some art galleries. There's an exhibition by a man named Klee. . . ."

"I don't want to go to any art galleries. I want to sit here and drink Scotch whisky," Darling said. "Who the hell hung those goddam pictures up on the wall?"

"I did," Louise said.

"I hate them."

"I'll take them down," Louise said.

"Leave them there. It gives me something to do in the afternoon. I can hate them." Darling took a long swallow. "Is that the way people paint these days?"

"Yes, Christian. Please don't drink any more."

"Do you like painting like that?"

"Yes, dear."

"Really?"

"Really."

Darling looked carefully at the prints once more. "Little Louise Tucker. The middle-western beauty. I like pictures with horses in them. Why should you like pictures like that?"

"I just happen to have gone to a lot of galleries in the last few years. . . ."

"Is that what you do in the afternoon?"

"That's what I do in the afternoon," Louise said.

"I drink in the afternoon."

Louise kissed him lightly on the top of his head as he sat there squinting at the pictures on the wall, the glass of whisky held firmly in his hand. She put on her coat and went out without saying another word. When she came back in the early evening, she had a job on a woman's fashion magazine.

They moved downtown and Louise went out to work every morning and Darling sat home and drank and Louise paid the bills as they came up. She made believe she was going to quit work as soon as Darling found a job, even though she was taking over more responsibility day by day at the magazine, interviewing authors, picking painters for the illustrations and covers, getting actresses to pose for pictures, going out for drinks with the right people, making a thousand new friends whom she loyally introduced to Darling.

"I don't like your hat," Darling said, once, when she came in in the evening and kissed him, her breath rich with Martinis.

"What's the matter with my hat, Baby?" she asked, running her fingers through his hair. "Everybody says it's very smart."

"It's too damned smart," he said. "It's not for you. It's for a rich, sophisticated woman of thirty-five with admirers."

Louise laughed. "I'm practicing to be a rich, sophisticated woman of thirty-five with admirers," she said. He stared soberly at her. "Now, don't look so grim, Baby. It's still the same simple little wife under the hat." She took the hat off, threw it into a corner, sat on his lap. "See? Homebody Number One."

"Your breath could run a train," Darling said, not wanting to be mean, but talking out of boredom, and sudden shock at seeing his wife curiously a stranger in a new hat, with a new expression in her eyes under the little brim, secret, confident, knowing.

Louise tucked her head under his chin so he couldn't smell her breath. "I had to take an author out for cocktails," she said. "He's a boy from the Ozark Mountains and he drinks like a fish. He's a Communist."

"What the hell is a Communist from the Ozarks doing writing for a woman's fashion magazine?"

Louise chuckled. "The magazine business is getting all mixed up these days. The publishers want to have a foot in every camp. And anyway, you can't find an author under seventy these days who isn't a Communist."

"I don't think I like you to associate with all those people, Louise," Darling said. "Drinking with them."

"He's a very nice, gentle boy," Louise said. "He reads Ernest Dowson."

"Who's Ernest Dowson?"

Louise patted his arm, stood up, fixed her hair. "He's an English poet."

Darling felt that somehow he had disappointed her. "Am I supposed to know who Ernest Dowson is?"

"No, dear. I'd better go in and take a bath."

After she had gone, Darling went over to the corner where the hat was lying and picked it up. It was nothing, a scrap of straw, a red flower, a veil, meaningless on his big hand, but on his wife's head a signal of something . . . big city, smart and knowing women drinking and dining with men other than their husbands, conversation about things a normal man wouldn't know much about, Frenchmen who painted as though they used their elbows instead of brushes, composers who wrote whole symphonies without a single melody in them, writers who knew all about politics and women who knew all about writers, the movement of the proletariat, Marx, somehow mixed up with five-dollar dinners and the best-looking women in America and fairies who made them laugh and half-sentences immediately understood and secretly hilarious and wives who called their husbands "Baby." He put the hat down, a scrap of straw and a red flower, and a little veil. He drank some whisky straight and went into the bathroom where his wife was lying deep in her bath, singing to herself and smiling from time to time like a little girl, paddling the water gently with her hands, sending up a slight spicy fragrance from the bath salts she used.

He stood over her, looking down at her. She smiled up at him, her eyes half closed, her body pink and shimmering in the warm, scented water. All over again, with all the old suddenness, he was hit deep inside him with the knowledge of how beautiful she was, how much he needed her.

"I came in here," he said, "to tell you I wish you wouldn't call me 'Baby.' "

She looked up at him from the bath, her eyes quickly full of sorrow, half-understanding what he meant. He knelt and put his arms around her, his sleeves plunged heedlessly in the water, his shirt and jacket soaking wet as he clutched her wordlessly, holding her crazily tight, crushing her breath from her, kissing her desperately, searchingly, regretfully.

He got jobs after that, selling real estate and automobiles, but somehow, although he had a desk with his name on a wooden wedge on it, and he went to the office religiously at nine each morning, he never managed to sell anything and he never made any money.

Louise was made assistant editor, and the house was always full of strange men and women who talked fast and got angry on abstract subjects like mural painting, novelists, labor unions. Negro short-story writers drank Louise's liquor, and a lot of Jews, and big solemn men with scarred faces and knotted hands who talked slowly but clearly about picket lines and battles with guns and leadpipe at mine-shaft-heads and in front of factory gates. And Louise moved among them all, confidently, knowing what they were talking about, with opinions that they listened to and argued about just as though she were a man. She knew everybody, condescended to no one, devoured books that Darling had never heard of, walked along the streets of the city, excited, at home, soaking in all the million tides of New York without fear, with constant wonder.

Her friends liked Darling and sometimes he found a man who wanted to get off in the corner and talk about the new boy who played fullback for Princeton, and the decline of the double wing-back, or even the state of the stock market, but for the most part he sat on the edge of things, solid and quiet in the high storm of words. "The dialectics of the situation. . . . The theater has been given over to expert jugglers. . . . Picasso? What man has a right to paint old bones and collect ten thousand dollars for them? . . . I stand firmly behind Trotsky. . . . Poe was the last American critic. When he died they put lilies on the grave of American criticism. I don't say this because they panned my last book but. . . ."

Once in a while he caught Louise looking soberly and consideringly at him through the cigarette smoke and the noise and he avoided her eyes and found an excuse to get up and go into the kitchen for more ice or to open another bottle.

"Come on," Cathal Flaherty was saying, standing at the door with a girl, "you've got to come down and see this. It's down on Fourteenth Street, in the old Civic Repertory, and you can only see it on Sunday nights and I guarantee you'll come out of the theater singing." Flaherty was a big young Irishman with a broken nose who was the lawyer for a longshoreman's union, and he had been hanging around the house for six months on and off, roaring and shutting everybody else up when he got in an argument. "It's a new play, *Waiting for Lefty;* it's about taxi-drivers."

"Odets," the girl with Flaherty said. "It's by a guy named Odets."

"I never heard of him," Darling said.

"He's a new one," the girl said.

"It's like watching a bombardment," Flaherty said. "I saw it last Sunday night. You've got to see it."

"Come on, Baby," Louise said to Darling, excitement in her eyes already. "We've been sitting in the Sunday *Times* all day, this'll be a great change."

"I see enough taxi-drivers every day," Darling said, not because he meant that, but because he didn't like to be around Flaherty, who said things that made Louise laugh a lot and whose judgment she accepted on almost every subject. "Let's go to the movies."

"You've never seen anything like this before," Flaherty said. "He wrote this play with a baseball bat."

"Come on," Louise coaxed, "I bet it's wonderful."

"He has long hair," the girl with Flaherty said. "Odets. I met him at a party. He's an actor. He didn't say a goddam thing all night."

"I don't feel like going down to Fourteenth Street," Darling said, wishing Flaherty and his girl would get out. "It's gloomy."

"Oh, hell!" Louise said loudly. She looked coolly at Darling, as though she'd just been introduced to him and was making up her mind about him, and not very favorably. He saw her looking at him, knowing there was something new and dangerous in her face and he wanted to say something, but Flaherty was there and his damned girl, and anyway, he didn't know what to say.

"I'm going," Louise said, getting her coat. "I don't think Fourteenth Street is gloomy."

"I'm telling you," Flaherty was saying, helping her on with her coat, "it's the Battle of Gettysburg, in Brooklynese."

"Nobody could get a word out of him," Flaherty's girl was saying as they went through the door. "He just sat there all night."

The door closed. Louise hadn't said good night to him. Darling walked around the room four times, then sprawled out on the sofa, on top of the Sunday *Times*. He lay there for five minutes looking at the ceiling, thinking of Flaherty walking down the street talking in that booming voice, between the girls, holding their arms.

Louise had looked wonderful. She'd washed her hair in the afternoon and it had been very soft and light and clung close to her head as she stood there angrily putting her coat on. Louise was getting prettier every year, partly because she knew by now how pretty she was, and made the most of it.

"Nuts," Darling said, standing up. "Oh, nuts."

He put on his coat and went down to the nearest bar and had five drinks off by himself in a corner before his money ran out.

The years since then had been foggy and downhill. Louise had been nice to him, and in a way, loving and kind, and they'd fought only once, when he said he was going to vote for Landon. ("Oh, Christ," she'd said, "doesn't *anything* happen inside your head? Don't you read the papers? The penniless Republican!") She'd been sorry later and apologized for hurting him, but apologized as she might to a child. He'd tried hard, had gone grimly to the art galleries, the concert halls, the bookshops, trying to gain on the trail of his wife, but it was no use. He was bored, and none of what he saw or heard or dutifully read made much sense to him and finally he gave it up. He had thought, many nights as he ate dinner alone, knowing that Louise would come home late and drop silently into bed without explanation, of getting a divorce, but he knew the loneliness, the hopelessness, of not seeing her again would be too much to take. So he was good, completely devoted, ready at all times to go any place with her, do anything she wanted. He even got a small job, in a broker's office and paid his own way, bought his own liquor.

Then he'd been offered the job of going from college to college as a tailor's representative. "We want a man," Mr. Rosenberg had said, "who as soon as you look at him, you say, 'There's a university man.' " Rosenberg had looked approvingly at Darling's broad shoulders and well-kept waist, at his carefully brushed hair and his honest, wrinkle-less face. "Frankly, Mr. Darling, I am willing to make you a proposition. I have inquired about you, you are favorably known on your old campus, I understand you were in the backfield with Alfred Diederich."

Darling nodded. "Whatever happened to him?"

"He is walking around in a cast for seven years now. An iron brace. He played professional football and they broke his neck for him."

Darling smiled. That, at least, had turned out well.

"Our suits are an easy product to sell, Mr. Darling," Rosenberg said. "We have a handsome, custom-made garment. What has Brooks Brothers got that we haven't got? A name. No more."

"I can make fifty, sixty dollars a week," Darling said to Louise that night. "And expenses. I can save some money and then come back to New York and really get started here."

"Yes, Baby," Louise said.

"As it is," Darling said carefully, "I can make it back here once a month, and holidays and the summer. We can see each other often."

"Yes, Baby." He looked at her face, lovelier now at thirty-five than it had ever been before, but fogged over now as it had been for five years with a kind of patient, kindly, remote boredom.

"What do you say?" he asked. "Should I take it?" Deep within him he hoped fiercely, longingly, for her to say, "No, Baby, you stay right here," but she said, as he knew she'd say, "I think you'd better take it."

He nodded. He had to get up and stand with his back to her, looking out the window, because there were things plain on his face that she had never seen in the fifteen years she'd known him. "Fifty dollars is a lot of money," he said. "I never thought I'd ever see fifty dollars again." He laughed. Louise laughed, too.

Christian Darling sat on the frail green grass of the practice field. The shadow of the stadium had reached out and covered him. In the distance the light of the university shone a little mistily in the light haze of evening. Fifteen years. Flaherty even now was calling for his wife, buying her a drink, filling whatever bar they were in with that voice of his and that easy laugh. Darling half-closed his eyes, almost saw the boy fifteen years ago reach for the pass, slip the halfback, go skittering lightly down the field, his knees high and fast and graceful, smiling to himself because he knew he was going to get past the safety man. That was the high point, Darling thought, fifteen years ago, on an autumn afternoon, twenty years old and far from death, with the air coming easily into his lungs, and a deep feeling inside him that he could do anything, knock over anybody, outrun whatever had to be outrun. And the shower after and the three glasses of water and the cool night air on his damp head and Louise sitting hatless in the open car with a smile and the first kiss she ever really meant. The high point, an eighty-yard run in the practice, and a girl's kiss and everything after that a decline. Darling laughed. He had practiced the wrong thing, perhaps. He hadn't practiced for 1929 and New York City and a girl who would turn into a woman. Somewhere, he thought, there must have been a point where she moved up to me, was even with me for a moment, when I would have held her hand, if I'd known, held tight, gone with her. Well, he'd never known. Here he was on a playing field that was fifteen years away and his wife was in another city having dinner with another and better man, speaking with him a different, new language, a language nobody had ever taught him.

Darling stood up, smiled a little, because if he didn't smile he knew the tears would come. He looked around him. This was the spot. O'Connor's pass had come sliding out just to here . . . the high point. Darling put up his hands, felt all over again the flat slap of the ball. He shook his hips to throw off the halfback, cut back inside the center, picked his knees high as he ran gracefully over two men jumbled on the ground at the line of scrimmage, ran easily, gaining speed, for ten yards, holding the ball lightly in his two hands, swung away from the halfback diving at him, ran, swinging his hips in the almost girlish manner of a back in a broken field, tore into the safety man, his shoes drumming heavily on the turf, stiff-armed, elbow locked, pivoted, raced lightly and exultantly for the goal line.

It was only after he had sped over the goal line and slowed to a trot that he saw the boy and girl sitting together on the turf, looking at him wonderingly.

He stopped short, dropping his arms. "I. . . ," he said, gasping a little, though his condition was fine and the run hadn't winded him. "I—once I played here."

The boy and the girl said nothing. Darling laughed embarrassedly, looked hard at them sitting there, close to each other, shrugged, turned and went toward his hotel, the sweat breaking out on his face and running down into his collar.

Haircut

Ring Lardner
(*1885–1933*)

Ringgold Wilmer Lardner was the youngest of nine chil-
dren born to a wealthy couple in Niles, Michigan. The
year of Lardner's high school graduation, the family lost
its fortune, and Lardner went to Chicago to live with
friends and find work. During the next few years he held
various odd jobs until, at twenty, he became a reporter for
the South Bend Times. *Lardner subsequently worked for*
papers in Chicago, St. Louis, Boston, and New York, and
was already well known as a sports writer and columnist
when he achieved fame with his short stories.

In 1914 The Saturday Evening Post *began carrying his*
series about a rookie player on a professional baseball
team. The collected series was published in 1916 as You
Know Me, Al, *and its success made Ring Lardner a na-*
tional literary figure. In the years that followed, Lardner
produced several more collections of short stories and an
incredible number of magazine articles. His best-known
books include How to Write Short Stories (*1924*), The
Love Nest and Other Stories (*1926*), Round Up (*1929*),
June Moon (*1929*), *a farce about Tin Pan Alley written*
in collaboration with George S. Kaufman, and The Story
of a Wonder Man (*1927*), *a satirical autobiography.*

■ got another barber that comes over from Carterville and helps me out Saturdays, but the rest of the time I can get along all right alone. You can see for yourself that this ain't no New York City and besides that, the most of the boys works all day and don't have no leisure to drop in here and get themselves prettied up.

You're a newcomer, ain't you? I thought I hadn't seen you round before. I hope you like it good enough to stay. As I say, we ain't no New York City or Chicago, but we have pretty good times. Not as good, though, since Jim Kendall got killed. When he was alive, him and Hod Meyers used to keep this town in an uproar. I bet they was more laughin' done here than any town its size in America.

Jim was comical, and Hod was pretty near a match for him. Since Jim's gone, Hod tries to hold his end up just the same as ever, but it's tough goin' when you ain't got nobody to kind of work with.

They used to be plenty fun in here Saturdays. This place is jam-packed Saturdays, from four o'clock on. Jim and Hod would show up right after their supper, round six o'clock. Jim would set himself down in that big chair, nearest the blue spittoon. Whoever had been settin' in that chair, why they'd get up when Jim come in and give it to him.

You'd of thought it was a reserved seat like they have sometimes in a theayter. Hod would generally always stand or walk up and down, or some Saturdays, of course, he'd be settin' in this chair part of the time, gettin' a haircut.

Well, Jim would set there a w'ile without openin' his mouth only to spit, and then finally he'd say to me, "Whitey,"—my right name, that is, my right first name, is Dick, but everybody round here calls me Whitey—Jim would say, "Whitey, your nose looks like a rosebud tonight. You must of been drinkin' some of your aw de cologne."

So I'd say, "No, Jim, but you look like you'd been drinkin' somethin' of that kind or somethin' worse."

Jim would have to laugh at that, but then he'd speak up and say, "No, I ain't had nothin' to drink, but that ain't sayin' I wouldn't like somethin'. I wouldn't even mind if it was wood alcohol."

Then Hod Meyers would say, "Neither would your wife." That

would set everybody to laughin' because Jim and his wife wasn't on very good terms. She'd of divorced him only they wasn't no chance to get alimony and she didn't have no way to take care of herself and the kids. She couldn't never understand Jim. He *was* kind of rough, but a good fella at heart.

Him and Hod had all kinds of sport with Milt Sheppard. I don't suppose you've seen Milt. Well, he's got an Adam's apple that looks more like a mushmelon. So I'd be shavin' Milt and when I'd start to shave down here on his neck, Hod would holler, "Hey, Whitey, wait a minute! Before you cut into it, let's make up a pool and see who can guess closest to the number of seeds."

And Jim would say, "If Milt hadn't of been so hoggish, he'd of ordered a half a cantaloupe instead of a whole one and it might not of stuck in his throat."

All the boys would roar at this and Milt himself would force a smile, though the joke was on him. Jim certainly was a card!

There's his shavin' mug, settin' on the shelf, right next to Charley Vail's. "Charles M. Vail." That's the druggist. He comes in regular for his shave, three times a week. And Jim's is the cup next to Charley's. "James H. Kendall." Jim won't need no shavin' mug no more, but I'll leave it there just the same for old time's sake. Jim certainly was a character!

Years ago, Jim used to travel for a canned goods concern over in Carterville. They sold canned goods. Jim had the whole northern half of the State and was on the road five days out of every week. He'd drop in here Saturdays and tell his experiences for that week. It was rich.

I guess he paid more attention to playin' jokes than makin' sales. Finally the concern let him out and he come right home here and told everybody he'd been fired instead of sayin' he resigned like most fellas would of.

It was a Saturday and the shop was full and Jim got up out of that chair and says, "Gentlemen, I got an important announcement to make. I been fired from my job."

Well, they asked him if he was in earnest and he said he was and nobody could think of nothin' to say till Jim finally broke the ice himself. He says, "I been sellin' canned goods and now I'm canned goods myself."

You see, the concern he'd been workin' for was a factory that made canned goods. Over in Carterville. And now Jim said he was canned himself. He was certainly a card!

Jim had a great trick that he used to play w'ile he was travelin'. For instance, he'd be ridin' on a train and they'd come to some little town like, well, like, we'll say, like Benton. Jim would look out the train window and read the signs on the stores.

For instance, they'd be a sign, "Henry Smith, Dry Goods." Well, Jim would write down the name and the name of the town and when he got to wherever he was goin' he'd mail back a postal card to Henry Smith at Benton and not sign no name to it, but he'd write on the card, well, somethin' like "Ask your wife about that book agent that spent the afternoon last week," or "Ask your Missus who kept her from gettin' lonesome that last time you was in Carterville." And he'd sign the card, "A Friend."

Of course, he never knew what really come of none of these jokes, but he could picture what *probably* happened and that was enough.

Jim didn't work very steady after he lost his position with the Carterville people. What he did earn, doin' odd jobs round town, why he spent pretty near all of it on gin and his family might of starved if the stores hadn't of carried them along. Jim's wife tried her hand at dressmakin', but they ain't nobody goin' to get rich makin' dresses in this town.

As I say, she'd of divorced Jim, only she seen that she couldn't support herself and the kids and she was always hopin' that some day Jim would cut out his habits and give her more than two or three dollars a week.

They was a time when she would go to whoever he was workin' for and ask them to give her his wages, but after she done this once or twice, he beat her to it by borrowin' most of his pay in advance. He told it all round town, how he had outfoxed his Missus. He certainly was a caution!

But he wasn't satisfied with just outwittin' her. He was sore the way she had acted, tryin' to grab off his pay. And he made up his mind he'd get even. Well, he waited till Evans's Circus was advertised to come to town. Then he told his wife and two kiddies that he was goin' to take them to the circus. The day of the circus, he told them he would get the tickets and meet them outside the entrance to the tent.

Well, he didn't have no intentions of bein' there or buyin' tickets or nothin'. He got full of gin and laid round Wright's poolroom all day. His wife and the kids waited and waited and of course he didn't show up. His wife didn't have a dime with her, or nowhere else, I guess. So she finally had to tell the kids it was all off and they cried like they wasn't never goin' to stop.

Well, it seems, w'ile they was cryin', Doc Stair came along and he asked what was the matter, but Mrs. Kendall was stubborn and wouldn't tell him, but the kids told him and he insisted on takin' them and their mother in the show. Jim found this out afterwards and it was one reason why he had it in for Doc Stair.

Doc Stair come here about a year and a half ago. He's a mighty handsome young fella and his clothes always look like he has them made to order. He goes to Detroit two or three times a year and w'ile he's there he must have a tailor take his measure and then make him a suit to order. They cost pretty near twice as much, but they fit a whole lot better than if you just bought them in a store.

For a w'ile everybody was wonderin' why a young doctor like Doc Stair should come to a town like this where we already got old Doc Gamble and Doc Foote that's both been here for years and all the practice in town was always divided between the two of them.

Then they was a story got round that Doc Stair's gal had throwed him over, a gal up in the Northern Peninsula somewheres, and the reason he come here was to hide himself away and forget it. He said himself that he thought they wasn't nothin' like general practice in a place like ours to fit a man to be a good all round doctor. And that's why he'd came.

Anyways, it wasn't long before he was makin' enough to live on, though they tell me that he never dunned nobody for what they owed him, and the folks here certainly has got the owin' habit, even in my business. If I had all that was comin' to me for just shaves alone, I could go to Carterville and put up at the Mercer for a week and see a different picture every night. For instance, they's old George Purdy—but I guess I shouldn't ought to be gossipin'.

Well, last year, our coroner died, died of the flu. Ken Beatty, that was his name. He was the coroner. So they had to choose another man to be coroner in his place and they picked Doc Stair. He laughed at first and said he didn't want it, but they made him take it. It ain't no job that anybody would fight for and what a man makes out of it in a year would just about buy seeds for their garden. Doc's the kind, though, that can't say no to nothin' if you keep at him long enough.

But I was goin' to tell you about a poor boy we got here in town—Paul Dickson. He fell out of a tree when he was about ten years old. Lit on his head and it done somethin' to him and he ain't never been right. No harm in him, but just silly. Jim Kendall used to call him cuckoo; that's a name Jim had for anybody that was off their head, only he called people's head their bean. That was another of his gags, callin' head bean and callin' crazy people cuckoo. Only poor Paul ain't crazy, but just silly.

You can imagine that Jim used to have all kinds of fun with Paul. He'd send him to the White Front Garage for a left-handed monkey wrench. Of course they ain't no such a thing as a left-handed monkey wrench.

And once we had a kind of a fair here and they was a baseball game between the fats and the leans and before the game started Jim called Paul over and sent him way down to Schrader's hardware store to get a key for the pitcher's box.

They wasn't nothin' in the way of gags that Jim couldn't think up, when he put his mind to it.

Poor Paul was always kind of suspicious of people, maybe on account of how Jim had kept foolin' him. Paul wouldn't have much to do with anybody only his own mother and Doc Stair and a girl here in town named Julie Gregg. That is,¹ she ain't a girl no more, but pretty near thirty or over.

When Doc first come to town, Paul seemed to feel like here was a real friend and he hung round Doc's office most of the w'ile; the only time he wasn't there was when he'd go home to eat or sleep or when he seen Julie Gregg doin' her shoppin'.

When he looked out Doc's window and seen her, he'd run downstairs and join her and tag along with her to the different stores. The poor boy was crazy about Julie and she always treated him mighty nice and made him feel like he was welcome, though of course it wasn't nothin' but pity on her side.

Doc done all he could to improve Paul's mind and he told me once that he really thought the boy was gettin' better, that they was times when he was as bright and sensible as anybody else.

But I was goin' to tell you about Julie Gregg. Old Man Gregg was in the lumber business, but got to drinkin' and lost the most of his money and when he died, he didn't leave nothin' but the house and just enough insurance for the girl to skimp along on.

Her mother was a kind of a half invalid and didn't hardly ever leave the house. Julie wanted to sell the place and move somewheres else after the old man died, but the mother said she was born here and would die here. It was tough on Julie, as the young people round this town—well, she's too good for them.

She's been away to school and Chicago and New York and different places and they ain't no subject she can't talk on, where you take the rest of the young folks here and you mention anything to them outside of Gloria Swanson or Tommy Meighan and they think you're delirious. Did you see Gloria in Wages of Virtue? You missed somethin'!

Well, Doc Stair hadn't been here more than a week when he come in one day to get shaved and I recognized who he was as he had been pointed out to me, so I told him about my old lady. She's been ailin' for a couple years and either Doc Gamble or Doc Foote, neither one, seemed to be helpin' her. So he said he would come out and see her, but if she was able to get out herself, it would be better to bring her to his office where he could make a completer examination.

So I took her to his office and w'ile I was waitin' for her in the reception room, in come Julie Gregg. When somebody comes in Doc Stair's office, they's a bell that rings in his inside office so as he can tell they's somebody to see him. So he left my old lady inside and come out to the front office and that's the first time him and Julie met and I guess it was what they call love at first sight. But it wasn't fifty-fifty. This young fella was the slickest lookin' fella she'd ever seen in this town and she went wild over him. To him she was just a young lady that wanted to see the doctor.

She'd come on about the same business I had. Her mother had been doctorin' for years with Doc Gamble and Doc Foote and without no results. So she'd heard they was a new doc in town and decided to give him a try. He promised to call and see her mother that same day.

I said a minute ago that it was love at first sight on her part. I'm not only judgin' by how she acted afterward but how she looked at him that first day in his office. I ain't no mind reader, but it was wrote all over her face that she was gone.

Now Jim Kendall, besides bein' a jokesmith and a pretty good drinker, well, Jim was quite a lady-killer. I guess he run pretty wild durin' the time he was on the road for them Carterville people, and besides that, he'd had a couple little affairs of the heart right here in town. As I say, his wife could of divorced him, only she couldn't.

But Jim was like the majority of men, and women, too, I guess. He wanted what he couldn't get. He wanted Julie Gregg and worked his head off tryin' to land her. Only he'd of said bean instead of head.

Well, Jim's habits and his jokes didn't appeal to Julie and. of course he was a married man, so he didn't have no more chance than, well, than a rabbit. That's an expression of Jim's himself. When somebody didn't have no chance to get elected or somethin', Jim would always say they didn't have no more chance than a rabbit.

He didn't make no bones about how he felt. Right in here, more than once, in front of the whole crowd, he said he was stuck on Julie and anybody that could get her for him was welcome to his house and his wife and kids included. But she wouldn't have nothin' to do with him; wouldn't even speak to him on the street. He finally seen he wasn't gettin' nowheres with his usual line so he decided to try the rough stuff. He went right up to her house one evenin' and when she opened the door he forced his way in and grabbed her. But she broke loose and before he could stop her, she run in the next room and locked the door and phoned to Joe

Barnes. Joe's the marshal. Jim could hear who she was phonin' to and he beat it before Joe got there.

Joe was an old friend of Julie's pa. Joe went to Jim the next day and told him what would happen if he ever done it again.

I don't know how the news of this little affair leaked out. Chances is that Joe Barnes told his wife and she told somebody else's wife and they told their husband. Anyways, it did leak out and Hod Meyers had the nerve to kid Jim about it, right here in this shop. Jim didn't deny nothin' and kind of laughed it off and said for us all to wait; that lots of people had tried to make a monkey out of him, but he always got even.

Meanw'ile everybody in town was wise to Julie's bein' wild mad over the Doc. I don't suppose she had any idear how her face changed when him and her was together; of course she couldn't of, or she'd of kept away from him. And she didn't know that we was all noticin' how many times she made excuses to go to his office or pass it on the other side of the street and look up in his window to see if he was there. I felt sorry for her and so did most other people.

Hod Meyers kept rubbin' it into Jim about how the Doc had cut him out. Jim didn't pay no attention to the kiddin' and you could see he was plannin' one of his jokes.

One trick Jim had was the knack of changin' his voice. He could make you think he was a girl talkin' and he could mimic any man's voice. To show you how good he was along this line, I'll tell you the joke he played on me once.

You know, in most towns of any size, when a man is dead and needs a shave, why the barber that shaves him soaks him five dollars for the job, that is, he don't soak *him,* but whoever ordered the shave. I just charge three dollars because personally I don't mind much shavin' a dead person. They lay a whole lot stiller than live customers. The only thing is that you don't feel like talkin' to them and you get kind of lonesome.

Well, about the coldest day we ever had here, two years ago last winter, the phone rung at the house w'ile I was home to dinner and I answered the phone and it was a woman's voice and she said she was Mrs. John Scott and her husband was dead and would I come out and shave him.

Old John had always been a good customer of mine. But they live seven miles out in the country, on the Streeter road. Still I didn't see how I could say no.

So I said I would be there, but would have to come in a jitney and it might cost three or four dollars besides the price of the shave. So she, or the voice, it said that was all right, so I got Frank Abbott to drive me out to the place and when I got there, who should open the door but old John himself! He wasn't no more dead than, well, than a rabbit.

It didn't take no private detective to figure out who had played me this little joke. Nobody could of thought it up but Jim Kendall. He certainly was a card!

I tell you this incident just to show you how he could disguise his voice and make you believe it was somebody else talkin'. I'd of swore it was Mrs. Scott had called me. Anyways, some woman.

Well, Jim waited till he had Doc Stair's voice down pat; then he went after revenge.

He called Julie up on a night when he knew Doc was over in Carterville. She never questioned but what it was Doc's voice. Jim said he must see her that night; he couldn't wait no longer to tell her somethin'. She was all excited and told him to come to the house. But he said he was expectin' an important long distance call and wouldn't she please forget her manners for once and come to his office. He said they couldn't nothin' hurt her and nobody would see her and he just *must* talk to her a little w'ile. Well, poor Julie fell for it.

Doc always keeps a night light in his office, so it looked to Julie like they was somebody there.

Meanw'ile Jim Kendall had went to Wright's poolroom, where they was a whole gang amusin' themselves. The most of them had drank plenty of gin, and they was a rough bunch even when sober. They was always strong for Jim's jokes and when he told them to come with him and see some fun they give up their card games and pool games and followed along.

Doc's office is on the second floor. Right outside his door they's a flight of stairs leadin' to the floor above. Jim and his gang hid in the dark behind these stairs.

Well, Julie come up to Doc's door and rung the bell and they was nothin' doin'. She rung it again and she rung it seven or eight times. Then she tried the door and found it locked. Then Jim made some kind of a noise and she heard it and waited a minute, and then she says, "Is that you, Ralph?" Ralph is Doc's first name.

They was no answer and it must of came to her all of a sudden that she'd been bunked. She pretty near fell downstairs and the whole gang after her. They chased her all the way home, hollerin', "Is that you, Ralph?" and "Oh, Ralphie, dear, is that you?" Jim says he couldn't holler it himself, as he was laughin' too hard.

Poor Julie! She didn't show up here on Main Street for a long, long time afterward.

And of course Jim and his gang told everybody in town, everybody but Doc Stair. They was scared to tell him, and he might of never knowed only for Paul Dickson. The poor cuckoo, as Jim called him, he was here in the shop one night when Jim was still gloatin' yet over what he'd done to Julie. And Paul took in as much of it as he could understand and he run to Doc with the story.

It's a cinch Doc went up in the air and swore he'd make Jim suffer. But it was a kind of a delicate thing, because if it got out that he had beat Jim up, Julie was bound to hear of it and then she'd know that Doc knew and of course knowin' that he knew would make it worse for her than ever. He was goin' to do somethin', but it took a lot of figurin'.

Well, it was a couple days later when Jim was here in the shop again, and so was the cuckoo. Jim was goin' duck-shootin' the next day and had come in lookin' for Hod Meyers to go with him. I happened to know that Hod had went over to Carterville and wouldn't be home till the end of the week. So Jim said he hated to go alone and he guessed he would call it off. Then poor Paul spoke up and said if Jim would take him he would go along. Jim thought a w'ile and then he said, well, he guessed a half-wit was better than nothin'.

I suppose he was plottin' to get Paul out in the boat and play some joke on him, like pushin' him in the water. Anyways, he said Paul could go. He asked him had he ever shot a duck and Paul said no, he'd never even had a gun in his hands. So Jim said he could set in the boat and watch him and if he behaved himself, he might lend him his gun for a couple of shots. They made a date to meet in the mornin' and that's the last I seen of Jim alive.

Next mornin', I hadn't been open more than ten minutes when Doc Stair come in. He looked kind of nervous. He asked me had I seen Paul Dickson. I said no, but I knew where he was, out duck-shootin' with Jim Kendall. So Doc says that's what he had heard, and he couldn't understand it because Paul had told him he wouldn't never have no more to do with Jim as long as he lived.

He said Paul had told him about the joke Jim had played on Julie. He said Paul had asked him what he thought of the joke and the Doc had told him that anybody that would do a thing like that ought not to be let live.

I said it had been a kind of a raw thing, but Jim just couldn't resist no kind of a joke, no matter how raw. I said I thought he was all right at heart, but just bubblin' over with mischief. Doc turned and walked out.

At noon he got a phone call from old John Scott. The lake where Jim and Paul had went shootin' is on John's place. Paul had come runnin' up to the house a few minutes before and said they'd been an accident. Jim had shot a few ducks and then give the gun to Paul and told him to try his luck. Paul hadn't never handled a gun and he was nervous. He was shakin' so hard that he couldn't control the gun. He let fire and Jim sunk back in the boat, dead.

Doc Stair, bein' the coroner, jumped in Frank Abbott's flivver and rushed out to Scott's farm. Paul and old John was down on the shore of the lake. Paul had rowed the boat to shore, but they'd left the body in it, waitin' for Doc to come.

Doc examined the body and said they might as well fetch it back to town. They was no use leavin' it there or callin' a jury, as it was a plain case of accidental shootin'.

Personally I wouldn't never leave a person shoot a gun in the same boat I was in unless I was sure they knew somethin' about guns. Jim was a sucker to leave a new beginner have his gun, let alone a half-wit. It probably served Jim right, what he got. But still we miss him round here. He certainly was a card!

Comb it wet or dry?

Rain

W. Somerset Maugham
(*1874–1965*)

Maugham's mother and father both died when Maugham was a youngster, and he was placed in the care of his uncle, vicar of Whitstable in Kent, England; the vicar later became the Reverend William Carey in Of Human Bondage (*1915*), *Maugham's autobiographical masterpiece. Like Philip Carey in his novel, Maugham grew up unloved, unhappy, and without companionship. His tendency toward isolation was also encouraged by the embarrassment he suffered due to a pronounced stammer. Having decided to become a physician, he was just completing his medical studies when his first novel,* Liza of Lambeth, *was published in 1897. The novel was a success, and Maugham chose to devote himself to writing rather than to practicing medicine. This decision resulted in "the lean years," a period of semi-poverty and struggle that lasted until October, 1907, when the production of his play* Lady Frederick *introduced him to a life of wealth and literary fame.*

His many novels include The Merry-Go-Round (*1904*), The Moon and Sixpence (*1919*), Cakes and Ale (*1930*), *and* The Razor's Edge (*1944*). *Representative collections of his short stories are* The Trembling of a Leaf (*1921*), The Casuarina Tree (*1926*), *and* First Person Singular (*1931*). *And among the plays that followed* Lady Frederick *are* Penelope (*1909*), Home and Beauty (*1919*), The Circle (*1921*), Our Betters (*1923*), *and* For Services Rendered (*1932*). *Maugham also wrote a number of nonfiction works, including* The Gentleman in the Parlour (*1930*), *a travel book, and* The Summing Up (*1938*), *a series of essays about himself, the nature of the universe, and the art of writing. Excerpts from his journals have been published in* A Writer's Notebook (*1949*).

It was nearly bed-time and when they awoke next morning land would be in sight. Dr. Macphail lit his pipe and, leaning over the rail, searched the heavens for the Southern Cross. After two years at the front and a wound that had taken longer to heal than it should, he was glad to settle down quietly at Apia for twelve months at least, and he felt already better for the journey. Since some of the passengers were leaving the ship next day at Pago-Pago they had a little dance that evening and his ears hammered still the harsh notes of the mechanical piano. But the deck was quiet at last. A little way off he saw his wife in a long chair talking with the Davidsons, and he strolled over to her. When he sat down under the light and took off his hat you saw that he had very red hair, with a bald patch on the crown, and the red, freckled skin which accompanies red hair; he was a man of forty, thin, with a pinched face, precise and rather pedantic; and he spoke with a Scots accent in a very low, quiet voice.

Between the Macphails and the Davidsons, who were missionaries, there had arisen the intimacy of shipboard, which is due to propinquity rather than to any community of taste. Their chief tie was the disapproval they shared of the men who spent their days and nights in the smoking-room playing poker or bridge or drinking. Mrs. Macphail was not a little flattered to think that she and her husband were the only people on board with whom the Davidsons were willing to associate, and even the doctor, shy but no fool, half unconsciously acknowledged the compliment. It was only because he was of an argumentative mind that in their cabin at night he permitted himself to carp.

"Mrs. Davidson was saying she didn't know how they'd have got through the journey if it hadn't been for us," said Mrs. Macphail, as she neatly brushed out her transformation. "She said we were really the only people on the ship they cared to know."

"I shouldn't have thought a missionary was such a big bug that he could afford to put on frills."

"It's not frills. I quite understand what she means. It wouldn't have been very nice for the Davidsons to have to mix with all that rough lot in the smoking-room."

"The founder of their religion wasn't so exclusive," said Dr. Macphail with a chuckle.

"I've asked you over and over again not to joke about religion," answered his wife. "I shouldn't like to have a nature like yours, Alec. You never look for the best in people."

He gave her a sidelong glance with his pale, blue eyes, but did not reply. After many years of married life he had learned that it was more conducive to peace to leave his wife with the last word. He was undressed before she was, and climbing into the upper bunk he settled down to read himself to sleep.

When he came on deck next morning they were close to land. He looked at it with greedy eyes. There was a thin strip of silver beach rising quickly to hills covered to the top with luxuriant vegetation. The coconut trees, thick and green, came nearly to the water's edge, and among them you saw the grass houses of the Samoans; here and there, gleaming white, a little church. Mrs. Davidson came and stood beside him. She was dressed in black and wore round her neck a gold chain, from which dangled a small cross. She was a little woman, with brown, dull hair very elaborately arranged, and she had prominent blue eyes behind invisible *pince-nez*. Her face was long, like a sheep's, but she gave no impression of foolishness, rather of extreme alertness; she had the quick movements of a bird. The most remarkable thing about her was her voice, high, metallic, and without inflection; it fell on the ear with a hard monotony, irritating to the nerves like the pitiless clamour of the pneumatic drill.

"This must seem like home to you," said Dr. Macphail, with his thin, difficult smile.

"Ours are low islands, you know, not like these. Coral. These are volcanic. We've got another ten days' journey to reach them."

"In these parts that's almost like being in the next street at home," said Dr. Macphail facetiously.

"Well, that's rather an exaggerated way of putting it, but one does look at distances differently in the South Seas. So far you're right."

Dr. Macphail sighed faintly.

"I'm glad we're not stationed here," she went on. "They say this is a terribly difficult place to work in. The steamers' touching makes the people unsettled; and then there's the naval station; that's bad for the natives. In our district we don't have difficulties like that to contend with. There are one or two traders, of course, but we take care to make them behave, and if they don't we make the place so hot for them they're glad to go."

Fixing the glasses on her nose she looked at the green island with a ruthless stare.

"It's almost a hopeless task for the missionaries here. I can never be sufficiently thankful to God that we are at least spared that."

Davidson's district consisted of a group of islands to the North of Samoa; they were widely separated and he had frequently to go long distances by canoe. At these times his wife remained at their headquarters and managed the mission. Dr. Macphail felt his heart sink when he considered the efficiency with which she certainly managed it. She spoke of the depravity of the natives in a voice which nothing could hush, but with a vehemently unctuous horror. Her sense of delicacy was singular. Early in their acquaintance she had said to him:

"You know, their marriage customs when we first settled in the islands were so shocking that I couldn't possibly describe them to you. But I'll tell Mrs. Macphail and she'll tell you."

Then he had seen his wife and Mrs. Davidson, their deck-chairs close together, in earnest conversation for about two hours. As he walked past them backwards and forwards for the sake of exercise, he had heard Mrs. Davidson's agitated whisper, like the distant flow of a mountain torrent, and he saw by his wife's open mouth and pale face that she was enjoying an alarming experience. At night in their cabin she repeated to him with bated breath all she had heard.

"Well, what did I say to you?" cried Mrs. Davidson, exultant, next morning. "Did you ever hear anything more dreadful? You don't wonder that I couldn't tell you myself, do you? Even though you are a doctor."

Mrs. Davidson scanned his face. She had a dramatic eagerness to see that she had achieved the desired effect.

"Can you wonder that when we first went there our hearts sank? You'll hardly believe me when I tell you it was impossible to find a single good girl in any of the villages."

She used the word *good* in a severely technical manner.

"Mr. Davidson and I talked it over, and we made up our minds the first thing to do was to put down the dancing. The natives were crazy about dancing."

"I was not adverse to it myself when I was a young man," said Dr. Macphail.

"I guessed so much when I heard you ask Mrs. Macphail to have a turn with you last night. I don't think there's any real harm if a man dances with his wife, but I was relieved that she wouldn't. Under the circumstances I thought it better that we should keep ourselves to ourselves."

"Under what circumstances?"

Mrs. Davidson gave him a quick look through her *pince-nez,* but did not answer his question.

"But among white people it's not quite the same," she went on, "though I must agree with Mr. Davidson, who says he can't understand how a husband can stand by and see his wife in another man's arms, and as far as I'm concerned I've never danced a step since I married. But the native dancing is quite another matter. It's not only immoral in itself, but it distinctly leads to immorality. However, I'm thankful to God that we stamped it out, and I don't think I'm wrong in saying that no one has danced in our district for eight years."

But now they came to the mouth of the harbour and Mrs. Macphail joined them. The ship turned sharply and steamed slowly in. It was a great landlocked harbour big enough to hold a fleet of battleships; and all around it rose, high and steep, the green hills. Near the entrance, getting such breeze as blew from the sea, stood the governor's house in a garden. The Stars and Stripes dangled languidly from a flagstaff. They passed two or three trim bungalows, and a tennis court, and then came to the quay with its warehouses. Mrs. Davidson pointed out the schooner, moored two or three hundred yards from the side, which was to take them to Apia. There was a crowd of eager, noisy, and good-humoured natives come from all parts of the island, some from curiosity, others to barter with the travellers on their way to Sydney; and they brought pineapples and huge bunches of bananas, *tapa* cloths, necklaces of shells or shark's teeth, *kava*-bowls, and models of war canoes. American sailors, neat and trim, clean-shaven and frank of face, sauntered among them, and there was a little group of officials. While their luggage was being landed the Macphails and Mrs. Davidson watched the crowd. Dr. Macphail looked at the yaws from which most of the children and the young boys seemed to suffer, disfiguring sores like torpid ulcers, and his professional eyes glistened when he saw for the first time in his experience cases of elephantiasis, men going about with a huge, heavy arm or dragging along a grossly disfigured leg. Men and women wore the *lava-lava*.

"It's a very indecent costume," said Mrs. Davidson. "Mr. Davidson thinks it should be prohibited by law. How can you expect people to be moral when they wear nothing but a strip of red cotton round their loins?"

"It's suitable enough to the climate," said the doctor, wiping the sweat off his head.

Now that they were on land the heat, though it was so early in the morning, was already oppressive. Closed in by its hills, not a breath of air came in to Pago-Pago.

"In our islands," Mrs. Davidson went on in her high-pitched tones, "we've practically eradicated the *lava-lava*. A few old men still continue to wear it, but that's all. The women have all taken to the Mother Hubbard, and the men wear trousers and singlets.

At the very beginning of our stay Mr. Davidson said in one of his reports: the inhabitants of these islands will never be thoroughly Christianised till every boy of more than ten years is made to wear a pair of trousers."

But Mrs. Davidson had given two or three of her bird-like glances at heavy grey clouds that came floating over the mouth of the harbour. A few drops began to fall.

"We'd better take shelter," she said.

They made their way with all the crowd to a great shed of corrugated iron, and the rain began to fall in torrents. They stood there for some time and then were joined by Mr. Davidson. He had been polite enough to the Macphails during the journey, but he had not his wife's sociability, and had spent much of his time reading. He was a silent, rather sullen man, and you felt that his affability was a duty that he had imposed upon himself Christianly; he was by nature reserved and even morose. His appearance was singular. He was very tall and thin, with long limbs loosely jointed; hollow cheeks and curiously high cheek-bones; he had so cadaverous an air that it surprised you to notice how full and sensual were his lips. He wore his hair very long. His dark eyes, set deep in their sockets, were large and tragic; and his hands with their big, long fingers, were finely shaped; they gave him a look of great strength. But the most striking thing about him was the feeling he gave you of suppressed fire. It was impressive and vaguely troubling. He was not a man with whom any intimacy was possible.

He brought now unwelcome news. There was an epidemic of measles, a serious and often fatal disease among the Kanakas, on the island, and a case had developed among the crew of the schooner which was to take them on their journey. The sick man had been brought ashore and put in hospital on the quarantine station, but telegraphic instructions had been sent from Apia to say that the schooner would not be allowed to enter the harbour till it was certain no other member of the crew was affected.

"It means we shall have to stay here for ten days at least."

"But I'm urgently needed at Apia," said Dr. Macphail.

"That can't be helped. If no more cases develop on board, the schooner will be allowed to sail with white passengers, but all native traffic is prohibited for three months."

"Is there a hotel here?" asked Mrs. Macphail.

Davidson gave a low chuckle.

"There's not."

"What shall we do then?"

"I've been talking to the governor. There's a trader along the front who has rooms that he rents, and my proposition is that as soon as the rain lets up we should go along there and see what we can do. Don't expect comfort. You've just got to be thankful if we get a bed to sleep on and a roof over our heads."

But the rain showed no sign of stopping, and at length with umbrellas and waterproofs they set out. There was no town, but merely a group of official buildings, a store or two, and at the back, among the coconut trees and plantains, a few native dwellings. The house they sought was about five minutes' walk from the wharf. It was a frame house of two storeys, with broad verandahs on both floors and a roof of corrugated iron. The owner was a half-caste named Horn, with a native wife surrounded by little brown children, and on the ground-floor he had a store where he sold canned goods and cottons. The rooms he showed them were almost bare of furniture. In the Macphails' there was nothing but a poor, worn bed with a ragged mosquito net, a rickety chair, and a washstand. They looked round with dismay. The rain poured down without ceasing.

"I'm not going to unpack more than we actually need," said Mrs. Macphail.

Mrs. Davidson came into the room as she was unlocking a portmanteau. She was very brisk and alert. The cheerless surroundings had no effect on her.

"If you'll take my advice you'll get a needle and cotton and start right in to mend the mosquito net," she said, "or you'll not be able to get a wink of sleep to-night."

"Will they be very bad?" asked Dr. Macphail.

"This is the season for them. When you're asked to a party at Government House at Apia you'll notice that all the ladies are given a pillowslip to put their—their lower extremities in."

"I wish the rain would stop for a moment," said Mrs. Macphail. "I could try to make the place comfortable with more heart if the sun were shining."

"Oh, if you wait for that, you'll wait a long time. Pago-Pago is about the rainiest place in the Pacific. You see, the hills, and that bay, they attract the water, and one expects rain at this time of year anyway."

She looked from Macphail to his wife, standing helplessly in different parts of the room, like lost souls, and she pursed her lips. She saw that she must take them in hand. Feckless people like that made her impatient, but her hands itched to put everything in the order which came so naturally to her.

"Here, you give me a needle and cotton and I'll mend that net of yours, while you go on with your unpacking. Dinner's at one. Dr. Macphail, you'd better go down to the wharf and see that your heavy luggage has been put in a dry place. You know what these natives are, they're quite capable of storing it where the rain will beat in on it all the time."

The doctor put on his waterproof again and went downstairs. At the door Mr. Horn was standing in conversation with the quartermaster of the ship they had just arrived in and a second-class passenger whom Dr. Macphail had seen several times on board. The quartermaster, a little, shrivelled man, extremely dirty, nodded to him as he passed.

"This is a bad job about the measles, doc," he said. "I see you've fixed yourself up already."

Dr. Macphail thought he was rather familiar, but he was a timid man and he did not take offence easily.

"Yes, we've got a room upstairs."

"Miss Thompson was sailing with you to Apia, so I've brought her along here."

The quartermaster pointed with his thumb to the woman standing by his side. She was twenty-seven perhaps, plump, and in a coarse fashion pretty. She wore a white dress and a large white hat. Her fat calves in the white cotton stockings bulged over the tops of long white boots in glacé kid. She gave Macphail an ingratiating smile.

"The feller's tryin' to soak me a dollar and a half a day for the meanest sized room," she said in a hoarse voice.

"I tell you she's a friend of mine, Jo," said the quartermaster. "She can't pay more than a dollar, and you've sure got to take her for that."

The trader was fat and smooth and quietly smiling.

"Well, if you put it like that, Mr. Swan, I'll see what I can do about it. I'll talk to Mrs. Horn and if we think we can make a reduction we will."

"Don't try to pull that stuff with me," said Miss Thompson. "We'll settle this right now. You get a dollar a day for the room and not one bean more."

Dr. Macphail smiled. He admired the effrontery with which she bargained. He was the sort of man who always paid what he was asked. He preferred to be over-charged than to haggle. The trader sighed.

"Well, to oblige Mr. Swan I'll take it."

"That's the goods," said Miss Thompson. "Come right in and have a shot of hooch. I've got some real good rye in that grip if you'll bring it along, Mr. Swan. You come along too, doctor."

"Oh, I don't think I will, thank you," he answered. "I'm just going down to see that our luggage is all right."

He stepped out into the rain. It swept in from the opening of the harbour in sheets and the opposite shore was all blurred. He passed two or three natives clad in nothing but the *lava-lava,* with huge umbrellas over them. They walked finely, with leisurely movements, very upright; and they smiled and greeted him in a strange tongue as they went by.

It was nearly dinner-time when he got back, and their meal was laid in the trader's parlour. It was a room designed not to live in but for purposes of prestige, and it had a musty, melancholy air. A suite of stamped plush was arranged neatly round the walls, and from the middle of the ceiling, protected from the flies by yellow tissue paper, hung a gilt chandelier. Davidson did not come.

"I know he went to call on the governor," said Mrs. Davidson, "and I guess he's kept him to dinner."

A little native girl brought them a dish of Hamburger steak, and after a while the trader came up to see that they had everything they wanted.

"I see we have a fellow lodger, Mr. Horn," said Dr. Macphail.

"She's taken a room, that's all," answered the trader. "She's getting her own board."

He looked at the two ladies with an obsequious air.

"I put her downstairs so she wouldn't be in the way. She won't be any trouble to you."

"Is it someone who was on the boat?" asked Mrs. Macphail.

"Yes, ma'am, she was in the second cabin. She was going to Apia. She has a position as cashier waiting for her."

"Oh!"

When the trader was gone Macphail said:

"I shouldn't think she'd find it exactly cheerful having her meals in her room."

"If she was in the second cabin I guess she'd rather," answered Mrs. Davidson. "I don't exactly know who it can be."

"I happened to be there when the quartermaster brought her along. Her name's Thompson."

"It's not the woman who was dancing with the quartermaster last night?" asked Mrs. Davidson.

"That's who it must be," said Mrs. Macphail. "I wondered at the time what she was. She looked rather fast to me."

"Not good style at all," said Mrs. Davidson.

They began to talk of other things, and after dinner, tired with their early rise, they separated and slept. When they awoke, though the sky was still grey and the clouds hung low, it was not raining and they went for a walk on the high road which the Americans had built along the bay.

On their return they found that Davidson had just come in.

"We may be here for a fortnight," he said irritably. "I've argued it out with the governor, but he says there is nothing to be done."

"Mr. Davidson's just longing to get back to his work," said his wife, with an anxious glance at him.

"We've been away for a year," he said, walking up and down the verandah. "The mission has been in charge of native missionaries and I'm terribly nervous that they've let things slide. They're good men, I'm not saying a word against them, God-fearing, devout, and truly Christian men—their Christianity would put many so-called Christians at home to the blush—but they're pitifully lacking in energy. They can make a stand once, they can make a stand twice, but they can't make a stand all the time. If you leave a mission in charge of a native missionary, no matter how trustworthy he seems, in course of time you'll find he's let abuses creep in."

Mr. Davidson stood still. With his tall, spare form, and his great eyes flashing out of his pale face, he was an impressive figure. His sincerity was obvious in the fire of his gestures and in his deep, ringing voice.

"I expect to have my work cut out for me. I shall act and I shall act promptly. If the tree is rotten it shall be cut down and cast into the flames."

And in the evening after the high tea which was their last meal, while they sat in the stiff parlour, the ladies working and Dr. Macphail smoking his pipe, the missionary told them of his work in the islands.

"When we went there they had no sense of sin at all," he said. "They broke the commandments one after the other and never knew they were doing wrong. And I think that was the most difficult part of my work, to instil into the natives the sense of sin."

The Macphails knew already that Davidson had worked in the Solomons for five years before he met his wife. She had been a missionary in China, and they had become acquainted in Boston, where they were both spending part of their leave to attend a missionary congress. On their marriage they had been appointed to the islands in which they had laboured ever since.

In the course of all the conversations they had had with Mr. Davidson one thing had shone out clearly and that was the man's unflinching courage. He was a medical missionary, and he was liable to be called at any time to one or other of the islands in the group. Even the whaleboat is not so very safe a conveyance in the stormy Pacific of the wet season, but often he would be sent for in a canoe, and then the danger was great. In cases of illness or accident he never hesitated. A dozen times he had spent the whole night bailing for his life, and more than once Mrs. Davidson had given him up for lost.

"I'd beg him not to go sometimes," she said, "or at least to wait till the weather was more settled, but he'd never listen. He's obstinate, and when he's once made up his mind, nothing can move him."

"How can I ask the natives to put their trust in the Lord if I am afraid to do so myself?" cried Davidson. "And I'm not, I'm not. They know that if they send for me in their trouble I'll come if it's humanly possible. And do you think the Lord is going to abandon me when I am on his business? The wind blows at his bidding and the waves toss and rage at his word."

Dr. Macphail was a timid man. He had never been able to get used to the hurtling of the shells over the trenches, and when he was operating in an advanced dressing-station the sweat poured from his brow and dimmed his spectacles in the effort he made to control his unsteady hand. He shuddered a little as he looked at the missionary.

"I wish I could say that I've never been afraid," he said.

"I wish you could say that you believed in God," retorted the other.

But for some reason, that evening the missionary's thoughts travelled back to the early days he and his wife had spent on the islands.

"Sometimes Mrs. Davidson and I would look at one another and the tears would stream down our cheeks. We worked without ceasing, day and night, and we seemed to make no progress. I don't know what I should have done without her then. When I felt my heart sink, when I was very near despair, she gave me courage and hope."

Mrs. Davidson looked down at her work, and a slight colour rose to her thin cheeks. Her hands trembled a little. She did not trust herself to speak.

"We had no one to help us. We were alone, thousands of miles from any of our own people, surrounded by darkness. When I was broken and weary she would put her work aside and take the Bible and read to me till peace came and settled upon me like sleep upon the eyelids of a child, and when at last she closed the book she'd say: 'We'll save them in spite of themselves.' And I felt strong again in the Lord, and I answered: 'Yes, with God's help I'll save them. I must save them'."

He came over to the table and stood in front of it as though it were a lectern.

"You see, they were so naturally depraved that they couldn't be brought to see their wickedness. We had to make sins out of what they thought were natural actions. We had to make it a sin, not only to commit adultery and to lie and thieve, but to expose their bodies, and to dance and not to come to church. I made it a sin for a girl to show her bosom and a sin for a man not to wear trousers."

"How?" asked Dr. Macphail, not without surprise.

"I instituted fines. Obviously the only way to make people realise that an action is sinful is to punish them if they commit it. I fined them if they didn't come to church, and I fined them if they danced. I fined them if they were improperly dressed. I had a tariff, and every sin had to be paid for either in money or work. And at last I made them understand."

"But did they never refuse to pay?"

"How could they?" asked the missionary.

"It would be a brave man who tried to stand up against Mr. Davidson," said his wife, tightening her lips.

Dr. Macphail looked at Davidson with troubled eyes. What he heard shocked him, but he hesitated to express his disapproval.

"You must remember that in the last resort I could expel them from their church membership."

"Did they mind that?"

Davidson smiled a little and gently rubbed his hands.

"They couldn't sell their copra. When the men fished they got no share of the catch. It meant something very like starvation. Yes, they minded quite a lot."

"Tell him about Fred Ohlson," said Mrs. Davidson.

The missionary fixed his fiery eyes on Dr. Macphail.

"Fred Ohlson was a Danish trader who had been in the islands a good many years. He was a pretty rich man as traders go and he wasn't very pleased when we came. You see, he'd had things very much his own way. He paid the natives what he liked for their copra, and he paid in goods and whiskey. He had a native wife, but he was flagrantly unfaithful to her. He was a drunkard. I gave him a chance to mend his ways, but he wouldn't take it. He laughed at me."

Davidson's voice fell to a deep bass as he said the last words, and he was silent for a minute or two. The silence was heavy with menace.

"In two years he was a ruined man. He'd lost everything he'd saved in a quarter of a century. I broke him, and at last he was forced to come to me like a beggar and beseech me to give him a passage back to Sydney."

"I wish you could have seen him when he came to see Mr. Davidson," said the missionary's wife. "He had been a fine, powerful man, with a lot of fat on him, and he had a great big voice, but now he was half the size, and he was shaking all over. He'd suddenly become an old man."

With abstracted gaze Davidson looked out into the night. The rain was falling again.

Suddenly from below came a sound, and Davidson turned and looked questioningly at his wife. It was the sound of a gramophone, harsh and loud, wheezing out a syncopated tune.

"What's that?" he asked.

Mrs. Davidson fixed her *pince-nez* more firmly on her nose.

"One of the second-class passengers has a room in the house. I guess it comes from there."

They listened in silence, and presently they heard the sound of dancing. Then the music stopped, and they heard the popping of corks and voices raised in animated conversation.

"I daresay she's giving a farewell party to her friends on board," said Dr. Macphail. "The ship sails at twelve, doesn't it?"

Davidson made no remark, but he looked at his watch.

"Are you ready?" he asked his wife.

She got up and folded her work.

"Yes, I guess I am," she answered.

"It's early to go to bed yet, isn't it?" said the doctor.

"We have a good deal of reading to do," explained Mrs. Davidson. "Wherever we are, we read a chapter of the Bible before retiring for the night and we study it with the commentaries, you know, and discuss it thoroughly. It's a wonderful training for the mind."

The two couples bade one another good night. Dr. and Mrs. Macphail were left alone. For two or three minutes they did not speak.

"I think I'll go and fetch the cards," the doctor said at last.

Mrs. Macphail looked at him doubtfully. Her conversation with the Davidsons had left her a little uneasy, but she did not like to say that she thought they had better not play cards when the Davidsons might come in at any moment. Dr. Macphail brought them and she watched him, though with a vague sense of guilt, while he laid out his patience. Below, the sound of revelry continued.

It was fine enough next day, and the Macphails, condemned to spend a fortnight of idleness at Pago-Pago, set about making the best of things. They went down to the quay and got out of their boxes a number of books. The doctor called on the chief surgeon of the naval hospital and went round the beds with him. They left cards on the governor. They passed Miss Thompson on the road. The doctor took off his hat, and she gave him a "Good morning, doc," in a loud, cheerful voice. She was dressed as on the day before, in a white frock, and her shiny white boots with their high heels, her fat legs bulging over the tops of them, were strange things on that exotic scene.

"I don't think she's very suitably dressed, I must say," said Mrs. Macphail. "She looks extremely common to me."

When they got back to their house, she was on the verandah playing with one of the trader's dark children.

"Say a word to her," Dr. Macphail whispered to his wife. "She's all alone here, and it seems rather unkind to ignore her."

Mrs. Macphail was shy, but she was in the habit of doing what her husband bade her.

"I think we're fellow lodgers here," she said, rather foolishly.

"Terrible, ain't it, bein' cooped up in a one-horse burg like this?" answered Miss Thompson. "And they tell me I'm lucky to have gotten a room. I don't see myself livin' in a native house, and that's what some have to do. I don't know why they don't have a hotel."

They exchanged a few more words. Miss Thompson, loud-voiced and garrulous, was evidently quite willing to gossip, but Mrs. Macphail had a poor stock of small talk and presently she said:

"Well, I think we must go upstairs."

In the evening when they sat down to their high tea Davidson on coming in said:

"I see that woman downstairs has a couple of sailors sitting there. I wonder how she's gotten acquainted with them."

"She can't be very particular," said Mrs. Davidson.

They were all rather tired after the idle, aimless day.

"If there's going to be a fortnight of this I don't know what we shall feel like at the end of it," said Dr. Macphail.

"The only thing to do is to portion out the day to different activities," answered the missionary. "I shall set aside a certain number of hours to study and a certain number to exercise, rain or fine—in the wet season you can't afford to pay any attention to the rain—and a certain number to recreation."

Dr. Macphail looked at his companion with misgiving. Davidson's programme oppressed him. They were eating Hamburger steak again. It seemed the only dish the cook knew how to make. Then below the gramophone began. Davidson started nervously when he heard it, but said nothing. Men's voices floated up. Miss Thompson's guests were joining in a well-known song and presently they heard her voice too, hoarse and loud. There was a good deal of shouting and laughing. The four people upstairs, trying to make conversation, listened despite themselves to the clink of glasses and the scrape of chairs. More people had evidently come. Miss Thompson was giving a party.

"I wonder how she gets them all in," said Mrs. Macphail, suddenly breaking into a medical conversation between the missionary and her husband.

It showed whither her thoughts were wandering. The twitch of Davidson's face proved that, though he spoke of scientific things, his mind was busy in the same direction. Suddenly, while the doctor was giving some experience of practice on the Flanders front, rather prosily, he sprang to his feet with a cry.

"What's the matter, Alfred?" asked Mrs. Davidson.

"Of course! It never occurred to me. She's out of Iwelei."

"She can't be."

"She came on board at Honolulu. It's obvious. And she's carrying on her trade here. Here."

He uttered the last word with a passion of indignation.

"What's Iwelei?" asked Mrs. Macphail.

He turned his gloomy eyes on her and his voice trembled with horror.

"The plague spot of Honolulu. The Red Light district. It was a blot on our civilisation."

Iwelei was on the edge of the city. You went down side streets by the harbour, in the darkness, across a rickety bridge, till you came to a deserted road, all ruts and holes, and then suddenly you came out into the light. There was parking room for motors on each side of the road, and there were saloons, tawdry and bright, each one noisy with its mechanical piano, and there were barbers' shops and tobacconists. There was a stir in the air and a sense of expectant gaiety. You turned down a narrow alley, either to the right or to the left, for the road divided Iwelei into two parts, and you found yourself in the district. There were rows of little bungalows, trim and neatly painted in green, and the pathway between them was broad and straight. It was laid out like a garden-city. In its respectable regularity, its order and spruceness, it gave an impression of sardonic horror; for never can the search for love have been so systematised and ordered. The pathways were lit by a rare lamp, but they would have been dark except for the lights that came from the open windows of the bungalows. Men wandered about, looking at the women who sat at their windows, reading or sewing, for the most part taking no notice of the passers-by; and like the women they were of all nationalities. There were Americans, sailors from the ships in port, enlisted men off the gunboats, sombrely drunk, and soldiers from the regiments, white and black, quartered on the island; there were Japanese, walking in twos and

threes; Hawaiians, Chinese in long robes, and Filipinos in prepos-
terous hats. They were silent and as it were oppressed. Desire is
sad.

"It was the most crying scandal of the Pacific," exclaimed
Davidson vehemently. "The missionaries had been agitating against
it for years, and at last the local press took it up. The police refused to stir. You know their argument. They say that vice is inevitable and consequently the best thing is to localise and control
it. The truth is, they were paid. Paid. They were paid by the
saloon-keepers, paid by the bullies, paid by the women themselves.
At last they were forced to move."

"I read about it in the papers that came on board in Honolulu,"
said Dr. Macphail.

"Iwelei, with its sin and shame, ceased to exist on the very day
we arrived. The whole population was brought before the justices.
I don't know why I didn't understand at once what that woman
was."

"Now you come to speak of it," said Mrs. Macphail, "I remember seeing her come on board only a few minutes before the boat
sailed. I remember thinking at the time she was cutting it rather
fine."

"How dare she come here!" cried Davidson indignantly. "I'm
not going to allow it."

He strode towards the door.

"What are you going to do?" asked Macphail.

"What do you expect me to do? I'm going to stop it. I'm not
going to have this house turned into—into . . ."

He sought for a word that should not offend the ladies' ears. His
eyes were flashing and his pale face was paler still in his emotion.

"It sounds as though there were three or four men down there,"
said the doctor. "Don't you think it's rather rash to go in just
now?"

The missionary gave him a contemptuous look and without a
word flung out of the room.

"You know Mr. Davidson very little if you think the fear of
personal danger can stop him in the performance of his duty," said
his wife.

She sat with her hands nervously clasped, a spot of colour on
her high cheek bones, listening to what was about to happen below. They all listened. They heard him clatter down the wooden
stairs and throw open the door. The singing stopped suddenly,
but the gramophone continued to bray out its vulgar tune. They
heard Davidson's voice and then the noise of something heavy
falling. The music stopped. He had hurled the gramophone on the
floor. Then again they heard Davidson's voice, they could not

make out the words, then Miss Thompson's, loud and shrill, then a confused clamor as though several people were shouting together at the top of their lungs. Mrs. Davidson gave a little gasp, and she clenched her hands more tightly. Dr. Macphail looked uncertainly from her to his wife. He did not want to go down, but he wondered if they expected him to. Then there was something that sounded like a scuffle. The noise now was more distinct. It might be that Davidson was being thrown out of the room. The door was slammed. There was a moment's silence and they heard Davidson come up the stairs again. He went to his room.

"I think I'll go to him," said Mrs. Davidson.

She got up and went out.

"If you want me, just call," said Mrs. Macphail, and then when the other was gone: "I hope he isn't hurt."

"Why couldn't he mind his own business?" said Dr. Macphail.

They sat in silence for a minute or two and then they both started, for the gramophone began to play once more, defiantly, and mocking voices shouted hoarsely the words of an obscene song.

Next day Mrs. Davidson was pale and tired. She complained of headache, and she looked old and wizened. She told Mrs. Macphail that the missionary had not slept at all; he had passed the night in a state of frightful agitation and at five had got up and gone out. A glass of beer had been thrown over him and his clothes were stained and stinking. But a sombre fire glowed in Mrs. Davidson's eyes when she spoke of Miss Thompson.

"She'll bitterly rue the day when she flouted Mr. Davidson," she said. "Mr. Davidson has a wonderful heart and no one who is in trouble has ever gone to him without being comforted, but he has no mercy for sin, and when his righteous wrath is excited he's terrible."

"Why, what will he do?" asked Mrs. Macphail.

"I don't know, but I wouldn't stand in that creature's shoes for anything in the world."

Mrs. Macphail shuddered. There was something positively alarming in the triumphant assurance of the little woman's manner. They were going out together that morning, and they went down the stairs side by side. Miss Thompson's door was open, and they saw her in a bedraggled dressing-gown, cooking something in a chafing-dish.

"Good morning," she called. "Is Mr. Davidson better this morning?"

They passed her in silence, with their noses in the air, as if she did not exist. They flushed, however, when she burst into a shout of derisive laughter. Mrs. Davidson turned on her suddenly.

"Don't you dare to speak to me," she screamed. "If you insult me I shall have you turned out of here."

"Say, did I ask Mr. Davidson to visit with me?"

"Don't answer her," whispered Mrs. Macphail hurriedly.

They walked on till they were out of earshot.

"She's brazen, brazen," burst from Mrs. Davidson.

Her anger almost suffocated her.

And on their way home they met her strolling towards the quay. She had all her finery on. Her great white hat with its vulgar, showy flowers was an affront. She called out cheerily to them as she went by, and a couple of American sailors who were standing there grinned as the ladies set their faces to an icy stare. They got in just before the rain began to fall again.

"I guess she'll get her fine clothes spoilt," said Mrs. Davidson with a bitter sneer.

Davidson did not come in till they were half way through dinner. He was wet through, but he would not change. He sat, morose and silent, refusing to eat more than a mouthful, and he stared at the slanting rain. When Mrs. Davidson told him of their two encounters with Miss Thompson he did not answer. His deepening frown alone showed that he had heard.

"Don't you think we ought to make Mr. Horn turn her out of here?" asked Mrs. Davidson. "We can't allow her to insult us."

"There doesn't seem to be any other place for her to go," said Macphail.

"She can live with one of the natives."

"In weather like this a native hut must be a rather uncomfortable place to live in."

"I lived in one for years," said the missionary.

When the little native girl brought in the fried bananas which formed the sweet they had every day, Davidson turned to her.

"Ask Miss Thompson when it would be convenient for me to see her," he said.

The girl nodded shyly and went out.

"What do you want to see her for, Alfred?" asked his wife.

"It's my duty to see her. I won't act till I've given her every chance."

"You don't know what she is. She'll insult you."

"Let her insult me. Let her spit on me. She has an immortal soul, and I must do all that is in my power to save it."

Mrs. Davidson's ears rang still with the harlot's mocking laughter.

"She's gone too far."

"Too far for the mercy of God?" His eyes lit up suddenly and his voice grew mellow and soft. "Never. The sinner may be deeper in sin than the depth of hell itself, but the love of the Lord Jesus can reach him still."

The girl came back with the message.

"Miss Thompson's compliments and as long as Rev. Davidson didn't come in business hours she'll be glad to see him any time."

The party received it in stony silence, and Dr. Macphail quickly effaced from his lips the smile which had come upon them. He knew his wife would be vexed with him if he found Miss Thompson's effrontery amusing.

They finished the meal in silence. When it was over the two ladies got up and took their work, Mrs. Macphail was making another of the innumerable comforters which she had turned out since the beginning of the war, and the doctor lit his pipe. But Davidson remained in his chair and with abstracted eyes stared at the table. At last he got up and without a word went out of the room. They heard him go down and they heard Miss Thompson's defiant "Come in" when he knocked at the door. He remained with her for an hour. And Dr. Macphail watched the rain. It was beginning to get on his nerves. It was not like our soft English rain that drops gently on the earth; it was unmerciful and somehow terrible; you felt in it the malignancy of the primitive powers of nature. It did not pour, it flowed. It was like a deluge from heaven, and it rattled on the roof of corrugated iron with a steady persistence that was maddening. It seemed to have a fury of its own. And sometimes you felt that you must scream if it did not stop, and then suddenly you felt powerless, as though your bones had suddenly become soft; and you were miserable and hopeless.

Macphail turned his head when the missionary came back. The two women looked up.

"I've given her every chance. I have exhorted her to repent. She is an evil woman."

He paused, and Dr. Macphail saw his eyes darken and his pale face grow hard and stern.

"Now I shall take the whips with which the Lord Jesus drove the usurers and the money changers out of the Temple of the Most High."

He walked up and down the room. His mouth was close set, and his black brows were frowning.

"If she fled to the uttermost parts of the earth I should pursue her."

With a sudden movment he turned round and strode out of the room. They heard him go downstairs again.

"What is he going to do?" asked Mrs. Macphail.

"I don't know." Mrs. Davidson took off her *pince-nez* and wiped them. "When he is on the Lord's work I never ask him questions."

She sighed a little.

"What is the matter?"

"He'll wear himself out. He doesn't know what it is to spare himself."

Dr. Macphail learnt the first results of the missionary's activity from the half-caste trader in whose house they lodged. He stopped the doctor when he passed the store and came out to speak to him on the stoop. His fat face was worried.

"The Rev. Davidson has been at me for letting Miss Thompson have a room here," he said, "but I didn't know what she was when I rented it to her. When people come and ask if I can rent them a room all I want to know is if they've the money to pay for it. And she paid me for hers a week in advance."

Dr. Macphail did not want to commit himself.

"When all's said and done it's your house. We're very much obliged to you for taking us in at all."

Horn looked at him doubtfully. He was not certain yet how definitely Macphail stood on the missionary's side.

"The missionaries are in with one another," he said, hesitatingly. "If they get it in for a trader he may just as well shut up his store and quit."

"Did he want you to turn her out?"

"No, he said so long as she behaved herself he couldn't ask me to do that. He said he wanted to be just to me. I promised she shouldn't have no more visitors. I've just been and told her."

"How did she take it?"

"She gave me Hell."

The trader squirmed in his old ducks. He had found Miss Thompson a rough customer.

"Oh, well, I daresay she'll get out. I don't suppose she wants to stay here if she can't have anyone in."

"There's nowhere she can go, only a native house, and no native'll take her now, not now that the missionaries have got their knife in her."

Dr. Macphail looked at the falling rain.

"Well, I don't suppose it's any good waiting for it to clear up."

In the evening when they sat in the parlour Davidson talked to them of his early days at college. He had had no means and had worked his way through by doing odd jobs during the vacations. There was silence downstairs. Miss Thompson was sitting in her little room alone. But suddenly the gramophone began to play. She had set it on in defiance, to cheat her loneliness, but there was no one to sing, and it had a melancholy note. It was like a cry for help. Davidson took no notice. He was in the middle of a long anecdote and without change of expression went on. The gramophone continued. Miss Thompson put on one reel after another. It looked as though the silence of the night were getting on her nerves. It was breathless and sultry. When the Macphails went to bed they could not sleep. They lay side by side with their eyes wide open, listening to the cruel singing of the mosquitoes outside their curtain.

"What's that?" whispered Mrs. Macphail at last.

They heard a voice, Davidson's voice, through the wooden partition. It went on with a monotonous, earnest insistence. He was praying aloud. He was praying for the soul of Miss Thompson.

Two or three days went by. Now when they passed Miss Thompson on the road she did not greet them with ironic cordiality or smile; she passed with her nose in the air, a sulky look on her painted face, frowning, as though she did not see them. The trader told Macphail that she had tried to get lodging elsewhere, but had failed. In the evening she played through the various reels of her gramophone, but the pretence of mirth was obvious now. The ragtime had a cracked, heart-broken rhythm as though it were a one-step of despair. When she began to play on Sunday Davidson sent Horn to beg her to stop at once since it was the Lord's day. The reel was taken off and the house was silent except for the steady pattering of the rain on the iron roof.

"I think she's getting a bit worked up," said the trader next day to Macphail. "She don't know what Mr. Davidson's up to and it makes her scared."

Macphail had caught a glimpse of her that morning and it struck him that her arrogant expression had changed. There was in her face a hunted look. The half-caste gave him a sidelong glance.

"I suppose you don't know what Mr. Davidson is doing about it?" he hazarded.

"No, I don't."

It was singular that Horn should ask him that question, for he also had the idea that the missionary was mysteriously at work. He had an impression that he was weaving a net around the woman, carefully, systematically, and suddenly, when everything was ready would pull the strings tight.

"He told me to tell her," said the trader, "that if at any time she wanted him she only had to send and he'd come."

"What did she say when you told her that?"

"She didn't say nothing. I didn't stop. I just said what he said I was to and then I beat it. I thought she might be going to start weepin'."

"I have no doubt the loneliness is getting on her nerves," said the doctor. "And the rain—that's enough to make anyone jumpy," he continued irritably. "Doesn't it ever stop in this confounded place?"

"It goes on pretty steady in the rainy season. We have three hundred inches in the year. You see, it's the shape of the bay. It seems to attract the rain from all over the Pacific."

"Damn the shape of the bay," said the doctor.

He scratched his mosquito bites. He felt very short-tempered. When the rain stopped and the sun shone, it was like a hot-house, seething, humid, sultry, breathless, and you had a strange feeling that everything was growing with a savage violence. The natives, blithe and childlike by reputation, seemed then, with their tattooing and their dyed hair, to have something sinister in their appearance; and when they pattered along at your heels with their naked feet you looked back instinctively. You felt they might at any moment come behind you swiftly and thrust a long knife between your shoulder blades. You could not tell what dark thoughts lurked behind their wide-set eyes. They had a little the look of ancient Egyptians painted on a temple wall, and there was about them the terror of what is immeasurably old.

The missionary came and went. He was busy, but the Macphails did not know what he was doing. Horn told the doctor that he saw the governor every day, and once Davidson mentioned him.

"He looks as if he had plenty of determination," he said, "but when you come down to brass tacks he has no backbone."

"I suppose that means he won't do exactly what you want," suggested the doctor facetiously.

The missionary did not smile.

"I want him to do what's right. It shouldn't be necessary to persuade a man to do that."

"But there may be differences of opinion about what is right."

"If a man had a gangrenous foot would you have patience with anyone who hesitated to amputate it?"

"Gangrene is a matter of fact."

"And Evil?"

What Davidson had done soon appeared. The four of them had just finished their midday meal, and they had not yet separated for the siesta which the heat imposed on the ladies and on the doctor. Davidson had little patience with the slothful habit. The door was suddenly flung open and Miss Thompson came in. She looked round the room and then went up to Davidson.

"You low-down skunk, what have you been saying about me to the governor?"

She was spluttering with rage. There was a moment's pause. Then the missionary drew forward a chair.

"Won't you be seated, Miss Thompson? I've been hoping to have another talk with you."

"You poor low-life bastard."

She burst into a torrent of insult, foul and insolent. Davidson kept his grave eyes on her.

"I'm indifferent to the abuse you think fit to heap on me, Miss Thompson," he said, "but I must beg you to remember that ladies are present."

Tears by now were struggling with her anger. Her face was red and swollen as though she were choking.

"What has happened?" asked Dr. Macphail.

"A feller's just been in here and he says I gotter beat it on the next boat."

Was there a gleam in the missionary's eyes? His face remained impassive.

"You could hardly expect the governor to let you stay here under the circumstances."

"You done it," she shrieked. "You can't kid me. You done it."

"I don't want to deceive you. I urged the governor to take the only possible step consistent with his obligations."

"Why couldn't you leave me be? I wasn't doin' you no harm."

"You may be sure that if you had I should be the last man to resent it."

"Do you think I want to stay on in this poor imitation of a burg? I don't look no busher, do I?"

"In that case I don't see what cause of complaint you have," he answered.

She gave an inarticulate cry of rage and flung out of the room. There was a short silence.

"It's a relief to know that the governor has acted at last," said Davidson finally. "He's a weak man and he shilly-shallied. He said she was only here for a fortnight anyway, and if she went on to Apia that was under British jurisdiction and had nothing to do with him."

The missionary sprang to his feet and strode across the room.

"It's terrible the way the men who are in authority seek to evade their responsibility. They speak as though evil that was out of sight ceased to be evil. The very existence of that woman is a scandal and it does not help matters to shift it to another of the islands. In the end I had to speak straight from the shoulder."

Davidson's brow lowered, and he protruded his firm chin. He looked fierce and determined.

"What do you mean by that?"

"Our mission is not entirely without influence at Washington. I pointed out to the governor that it wouldn't do him any good if there was a complaint about the way he managed things here."

"When has she got to go?" asked the doctor, after a pause.

"The San Francisco boat is due here from Sydney next Tuesday. She's to sail on that."

That was in five day's time. It was next day, when he was coming back from the hospital where for want of something better to do Macphail spent most of his mornings, that the half-caste stopped him as he was going upstairs.

"Excuse me, Dr. Macphail, Miss Thompson's sick. Will you have a look at her?"

"Certainly."

Horn led him to her room. She was sitting in a chair idly, neither reading nor sewing, staring in front of her. She wore her white dress and the large hat with the flowers on it. Macphail noticed that her skin was yellow and muddy under her powder, and her eyes were heavy.

"I'm sorry to hear you're not well," he said.

"Oh, I ain't sick really. I just said that, because I just had to see you. I've got to clear on a boat that's going to 'Frisco."

She looked at him and he saw that her eyes were suddenly startled. She opened and clenched her hands spasmodically. The trader stood at the door, listening.

"So I understand," said the doctor.

She gave a little gulp.

"I guess it ain't very convenient for me to go to 'Frisco just now. I went to see the governor yesterday afternoon, but I couldn't get to him. I saw the secretary, and he told me I'd got to take that boat and that was all there was to it. I just had to see the governor, so I waited outside his house this morning, and when he come out I spoke to him. He didn't want to speak to me, I'll say, but I wouldn't let him shake me off, and at last he said he hadn't no objection to my staying here till the next boat to Sydney if the Rev. Davidson will stand for it."

She stopped and looked at Dr. Macphail anxiously.

"I don't know exactly what I can do," he said.

"Well, I thought maybe you wouldn't mind asking him. I swear to God I won't start anything here if he'll just only let me stay. I won't go out of the house if that'll suit him. It's no more'n a fortnight."

"I'll ask him."

"He won't stand for it," said Horn. "He'll have you out on Tuesday, so you may as well make up your mind to it."

"Tell him I can get work in Sydney, straight stuff, I mean. 'Tain't asking very much."

"I'll do what I can."

"And come and tell me right away, will you? I can't set down to a thing till I get the dope one way or the other."

It was not an errand that much pleased the doctor, and, characteristically perhaps, he went about it indirectly. He told his wife what Miss Thompson had said to him and asked her to speak to Mrs. Davidson. The missionary's attitude seemed rather arbitrary and it could do no harm if the girl were allowed to stay in Pago-Pago another fortnight. But he was not prepared for the result of his diplomacy. The missionary came to him straightway.

"Mrs. Davidson tells me that Thompson has been speaking to you."

Dr. Macphail, thus directly tackled, had the shy man's resentment at being forced out into the open. He felt his temper rising, and he flushed.

"I don't see that it can make any difference if she goes to Sydney rather than to San Francisco, and so long as she promises to behave while she's here it's dashed hard to persecute her."

The missionary fixed him with his stern eyes.

"Why is she unwilling to go back to San Francisco?"

"I didn't enquire," answered the doctor with some asperity. "And I think one does better to mind one's own business."

Perhaps it was not a very tactful answer.

"The governor has ordered her to be deported by the first boat that leaves the island. He's only done his duty and I will not interfere. Her presence is a peril here."

"I think you're very harsh and tyrannical."

The two ladies looked up at the doctor with some alarm, but they need not have feared a quarrel, for the missionary smiled gently.

"I'm terribly sorry you should think that of me, Dr. Macphail. Believe me, my heart bleeds for that unfortunate woman, but I'm only trying to do my duty."

The doctor made no answer. He looked out of the window sullenly. For once it was not raining and across the bay you saw nestling among the trees the huts of a native village.

"I think I'll take advantage of the rain stopping to go out," he said.

"Please don't bear me malice because I can't accede to your wish," said Davidson, with a melancholy smile. "I respect you very much, doctor, and I should be sorry if you thought ill of me."

"I have no doubt you have a sufficiently good opinion of yourself to bear mine with equanimity," he retorted.

"That's one on me," chuckled Davidson.

When Dr. Macphail, vexed with himself because he had been uncivil to no purpose, went downstairs, Miss Thompson was waiting for him with her door ajar.

"Well," she said, "have you spoken to him?"

"Yes, I'm sorry, he won't do anything," he answered, not looking at her in his embarrassment.

But then he gave her a quick glance, for a sob broke from her. He saw that her face was white with fear. It gave him a shock of dismay. And suddenly he had an idea.

"But don't give up hope yet. I think it's a shame the way they're treating you and I'm going to see the governor myself."

"Now?"

He nodded. Her face brightened.

"Say, that's real good of you. I'm sure he'll let me stay if you speak for me. I just won't do a thing I didn't ought all the time I'm here."

Dr. Macphail hardly knew why he had made up his mind to appeal to the governor. He was perfectly indifferent to Miss Thompson's affairs, but the missionary had irritated him, and with him temper was a smouldering thing. He found the governor at home. He was a large, handsome man, a sailor, with a grey toothbrush moustache; and he wore a spotless uniform of white drill.

"I've come to see you about a woman who's lodging in the same house as we are," he said. "Her name's Thompson."

"I guess I've heard nearly enough about her, Dr. Macphail," said the governor, smiling. "I've given her the order to get out next Tuesday and that's all I can do."

"I wanted to ask you if you couldn't stretch a point and let her stay here till the boat comes in from San Francisco so that she can go to Sydney. I will guarantee her good behavior."

The governor continued to smile, but his eyes grew small and serious.

"I'd be very glad to oblige you, Dr. Macphail, but I've given the order and it must stand."

The doctor put the case as reasonably as he could, but now the governor ceased to smile at all. He listened sullenly, with averted gaze. Macphail saw that he was making no impression.

"I'm sorry to cause any lady inconvenience, but she'll have to sail on Tuesday and that's all there is to it."

"But what difference can it make?"

"Pardon me, doctor, but I don't feel called upon to explain my official actions except to the proper authorities."

Macphail looked at him shrewdly. He remembered Davidson's

hint that he had used threats, and in the governor's attitude he read a singular embarrassment.

"Davidson's a damned busybody," he said hotly.

"Between ourselves, Dr. Macphail, I don't say that I have formed a very favorable opinion of Mr. Davidson, but I am bound to confess that he was within his rights in pointing out to me the danger that the presence of a woman of Miss Thompson's character was to a place like this where a number of enlisted men are stationed among a native population."

He got up and Dr. Macphail was obliged to do so too.

"I must ask you to excuse me. I have an engagement. Please give my respects to Mrs. Macphail."

The doctor left him crest-fallen. He knew that Miss Thompson would be waiting for him, and unwilling to tell her himself that he had failed, he went into the house by the back door and sneaked up the stairs as though he had something to hide.

At supper he was silent and ill-at-ease, but the missionary was jovial and animated. Dr. Macphail thought his eyes rested on him now and then with triumphant good-humour. It struck him suddenly that Davidson knew of his visit to the governor and of its ill success. But how on earth could he have heard of it? There was something sinister about the power of that man. After supper he saw Horn on the verandah and, as though to have a casual word with him, went out.

"She wants to know if you've seen the governor," the trader whispered.

"Yes. He wouldn't do anything. I'm awfully sorry, I can't do anything more."

"I knew he wouldn't. They daren't go against the missionaries."

"What are you talking about?" said Davidson affably, coming out to join them.

"I was just saying there was no chance of your getting over to Apia for at least another week," said the trader glibly.

He left them, and the two men returned into the parlour. Mr. Davidson devoted one hour after each meal to recreation. Presently a timid knock was heard at the door.

"Come in," said Mrs. Davidson, in her sharp voice.

The door was not opened. She got up and opened it. They saw Miss Thompson standing at the threshold. But the change in her appearance was extraordinary. This was no longer the flaunting hussy who had jeered at them in the road, but a broken, frightened woman. Her hair, as a rule so elaborately arranged, was tumbling untidily over her neck. She wore bedroom slippers and a skirt and blouse. They were unfresh and bedraggled. She stood at the door with the tears streaming down her face and did not dare to enter.

"What do you want?" said Mrs. Davidson harshly.

"May I speak to Mr. Davidson?" she said in a choking voice.

The missionary rose and went towards her.

"Come right in, Miss Thompson," he said in cordial tones. "What can I do for you?"

She entered the room.

"Say, I'm sorry for what I said to you the other day an' for—for everythin' else. I guess I was a bit lit up. I beg pardon."

"Oh, it was nothing. I guess my back's broad enough to bear a few hard words."

She stepped towards him with a movement that was horribly cringing.

"You've got me beat. I'm all in. You won't make me go back to 'Frisco?"

His genial manner vanished and his voice grew on a sudden hard and stern.

"Why don't you want to go back there?"

She cowered before him.

"I guess my people live there. I don't want them to see me like this. I'll go anywhere else you say."

"Why don't you want to go back to San Francisco?"

"I've told you."

He leaned forward, staring at her, and his great, shining eyes seemed to try to bore into her soul. He gave a sudden gasp.

"The penitentiary."

She screamed, and then she fell at his feet, clasping his legs.

"Don't send me back there. I swear to you before God I'll be a good woman. I'll give all this up."

She burst into a torrent of confused supplication and the tears coursed down her painted cheeks. He leaned over her and, lifting her face, forced her to look at him.

"Is that it, the penitentiary?"

"I beat it before they could get me," she gasped. "If the bulls grab me it's three years for mine."

He let go his hold of her and she fell in a heap on the floor, sobbing bitterly. Dr. Macphail stood up.

"This alters the whole thing," he said. "You can't make her go back when you know this. Give her another chance. She wants to turn over a new leaf."

"I'm going to give her the finest chance she's ever had. If she repents let her accept her punishment."

She misunderstood the words and looked up. There was a gleam of hope in her heavy eyes.

"You'll let me go?"

"No. You shall sail for San Francisco on Tuesday."

She gave a groan of horror and then burst into low, hoarse shrieks which sounded hardly human, and she beat her head passionately on the ground. Dr. Macphail sprang to her and lifted her up.

"Come on, you mustn't do that. You'd better go to your room and lie down. I'll get you something."

He raised her to her feet and partly dragging her, partly carrying her, got her downstairs. He was furious with Mrs. Davidson and with his wife because they made no effort to help. The half-caste was standing on the landing and with his assistance he managed to get her on the bed. She was moaning and crying. She was almost insensible. He gave her a hypodermic injection. He was hot and exhausted when he went upstairs again.

"I've got her to lie down."

The two women and Davidson were in the same position as when he had left them. They could not have moved or spoken since he went.

"I was waiting for you," said Davidson, in a strange, distant voice. "I want you all to pray with me for the soul of our erring sister."

He took the Bible off a shelf, and sat down at the table at which they had supped. It had not been cleared, and he pushed the tea-pot out of the way. In a powerful voice, resonant and deep, he read to them the chapter in which is narrated the meeting of Jesus Christ with the woman taken in adultery.

"Now kneel with me and let us pray for the soul of our dear sister, Sadie Thompson."

He burst into a long, passionate prayer in which he implored God to have mercy on the sinful woman. Mrs. Macphail and Mrs. Davidson knelt with covered eyes. The doctor, taken by surprise, awkward and sheepish, knelt too. The missionary's prayer had a savage eloquence. He was extraordinarily moved, and as he spoke the tears ran down his cheeks. Outside, the pitiless rain fell, fell steadily, with a fierce malignity that was all too human.

At last he stopped. He paused for a moment and said:

"We will now repeat the Lord's prayer."

They said it and then, following him, they rose from their knees. Mrs. Davidson's face was pale and restful. She was comforted and at peace, but the Macphails felt suddenly bashful. They did not know which way to look.

"I'll just go down and see how she is now," said Dr. Macphail.

When he knocked at her door it was opened for him by Horn. Miss Thompson was in a rocking-chair, sobbing quietly.

"What are you doing there?" exclaimed Macphail. "I told you to lie down."

"I can't lie down. I want to see Mr. Davidson."

"My poor child, what do you think is the good of it? You'll never move him."

"He said he'd come if I sent for him."

Macphail motioned to the trader.

"Go and fetch him."

He waited with her in silence while the trader went upstairs. Davidson came in.

"Excuse me for asking you to come here," she said, looking at him sombrely.

"I was expecting you to send for me. I knew the Lord would answer my prayer."

They stared at one another for a moment and then she looked away. She kept her eyes averted when she spoke.

"I've been a bad woman. I want to repent."

"Thank God! Thank God! He has heard our prayers."

He turned to the two men.

"Leave me alone with her. Tell Mrs. Davidson that our prayers have been answered."

They went out and closed the door behind them.

"Gee whizz," said the trader.

That night Dr. Macphail could not get to sleep till late, and when he heard the missionary come upstairs he looked at his watch. It was two o'clock. But even then he did not go to bed at once, for through the wooden partition that separated their rooms he heard him praying aloud, till he himself, exhausted, fell asleep.

When he saw him next morning he was surprised at his appearance. He was paler than ever, tired, but his eyes shone with an inhuman fire. It looked as though he were filled with an overwhelming joy.

"I want you to go down presently and see Sadie," he said. "I can't hope that her body is better, but her soul—her soul is transformed."

The doctor was feeling wan and nervous.

"You were with her very late last night," he said.

"Yes, she couldn't bear to have me leave her."

"You look as pleased as Punch," the doctor said irritably.

Davidson's eyes shone with ecstasy.

"A great mercy has been vouchsafed me. Last night I was privileged to bring a lost soul to the loving arms of Jesus."

Miss Thompson was again in the rocking chair. The bed had not been made. The room was in disorder. She had not troubled to dress herself, but wore a dirty dressing-gown, and her hair was tied in a sluttish knot. She had given her face a dab with a wet towel, but it was all swollen and creased with crying. She looked a drab.

She raised her eyes dully when the doctor came in. She was cowed and broken.

"Where's Mr. Davidson?" she asked.

"He'll come presently if you want him," answered Macphail acidly. "I came here to see how you were."

"Oh, I guess I'm O.K. You needn't worry about that."

"Have you had anything to eat?"

"Horn brought me some coffee."

She looked anxiously at the door.

"D'you think he'll come down soon? I feel as if it wasn't so terrible when he's with me."

"Are you still going on Tuesday?"

"Yes, he says I've got to go. Please tell him to come right along. You can't do me any good. He's the only one as can help me now."

"Very well," said Dr. Macphail.

During the next three days the missionary spent almost all his time with Sadie Thompson. He joined the others only to have his meals. Dr. Macphail noticed that he hardly ate.

"He's wearing himself out," said Mrs. Davidson pitifully. "He'll have a breakdown if he doesn't take care, but he won't spare himself."

She herself was white and pale. She told Mrs. Macphail that she had no sleep. When the missionary came upstairs from Miss Thompson he prayed till he was exhausted, but even then he did not sleep for long. After an hour or two he got up and dressed himself, and went for a tramp along the bay. He had strange dreams.

"This morning he told me that he'd been dreaming about the mountains of Nebraska," said Mrs. Davidson.

"That's curious," said Dr. Macphail.

He remembered seeing them from the windows of the train when he crossed America. They were like huge mole-hills, rounded and smooth, and they rose from the plain abruptly. Dr. Macphail remembered how it struck him that they were like a woman's breasts.

Davidson's restlessness was intolerable even to himself. But he was buoyed up by a wonderful exhilaration. He was tearing out by the roots the last vestiges of sin that lurked in the hidden corners of that poor woman's heart. He read with her and prayed with her.

"It's wonderful," he said to them one day at supper. "It's a true rebirth. Her soul, which was black as night, is now pure and white like the new-fallen snow. I am humble and afraid. Her remorse for all her sins is beautiful. I am not worthy to touch the hem of her garment."

"Have you the heart to send her back to San Francisco?" said the doctor. "Three years in an American prison. I should have thought you might have saved her from that?"

"Ah, but don't you see? It's necessary. Do you think my heart doesn't bleed for her? I love her as I love my wife and my sister. All the time that she is in prison I shall suffer all the pain that she suffers."

"Bunkum," cried the doctor impatiently.

"You don't understand because you're blind. She's sinned, and she must suffer. I know what she'll endure. She'll be starved and tortured and humiliated. I want her to accept the punishment of man as a sacrifice to God. I want her to accept it joyfully. She has an opportunity which is offered to very few of us. God is very good and very merciful."

Davidson's voice trembled with excitement. He could hardly articulate the words that tumbled passionately from his lips.

"All day I pray with her and when I leave her I pray again, I pray with all my might and main, so that Jesus may grant her this great mercy. I want to put in her heart the passionate desire to be punished so that at the end, even if I offered to let her go, she would refuse. I want her to feel that the bitter punishment of prison is the thank-offering that she places at the feet of our Blessed Lord, who gave his life for her."

The days passed slowly. The whole household, intent on the wretched, tortured woman downstairs, lived in a state of unnatural excitement. She was like a victim that was being prepared for the savage rites of a bloody idolatry. Her terror numbed her. She could not bear to let Davidson out of her sight; it was only when he was with her that she had courage, and she hung upon him with a slavish dependence. She cried a great deal, and she read the Bible, and prayed. Sometimes she was exhausted and apathetic. Then she did indeed look forward to her ordeal, for it seemed to offer an escape, direct and concrete, from the anguish she was enduring. She could not bear much longer the vague terrors which now assailed her. With her sins she had put aside all personal vanity, and she slopped about her room, unkempt and dishevelled, in her tawdry dressing-gown. She had not taken off her night-dress for four days, nor put on stockings. Her room was littered and untidy. Meanwhile the rain fell with a cruel persistence. You felt that the heavens must at last be empty of water, but still it poured down, straight and heavy, with a maddening iteration, on the iron roof. Everything was damp and clammy. There was mildew on the walls and on the boots that stood on the floor. Through the sleepless nights the mosquitoes droned their angry chant.

"If it would only stop raining for a single day it wouldn't be so sad," said Dr. Macphail.

They all looked forward to the Tuesday when the boat for San Francisco was to arrive from Sydney. The strain was intolerable. So far as Dr. Macphail was concerned, his pity and his resentment were alike extinguished by his desire to be rid of the unfortunate woman. The inevitable must be accepted. He felt he would breathe more freely when the ship had sailed. Sadie Thompson was to be escorted on board by a clerk in the governor's office. This person called on the Monday evening and told Miss Thompson to be prepared at eleven in the morning. Davidson was with her.

"I'll see that everything is ready. I mean to come on board with her myself."

Miss Thompson did not speak.

When Dr. Macphail blew out his candle and crawled cautiously under his mosquito curtains, he gave a sigh of relief.

"Well, thank God that's over. By this time to-morrow she'll be gone."

"Mrs. Davidson will be glad too. She says he's wearing himself to a shadow," said Mrs. Macphail. "She's a different woman."

"Who?"

"Sadie. I should never have thought it possible. It makes one humble."

Dr. Macphail did not answer, and presently he fell asleep. He was tired out, and he slept more soundly than usual.

He was awakened in the morning by a hand placed on his arm, and, starting up, saw Horn by the side of his bed. The trader put his finger on his mouth to prevent any exclamation from Dr. Macphail and beckoned him to come. As a rule he wore shabby ducks, but now he was barefoot and wore only the *lava-lava* of the natives. He looked suddenly savage, and Dr. Macphail, getting out of bed, saw that he was heavily tattooed. Horn made him a sign to come on to the verandah. Dr. Macphail got out of bed and followed the trader out.

"Don't make a noise," he whispered. "You're wanted. Put on a coat and some shoes. Quick."

Dr. Macphail's first thought was that something had happened to Miss Thompson.

"What is it? Shall I bring my instruments?"

"Hurry, please, hurry."

Dr. Macphail crept back into the bedroom, put on a waterproof over his pyjamas, and a pair of rubber-soled shoes. He rejoined the trader, and together they tiptoed down the stairs. The door leading out to the road was open and at it were standing half a dozen natives.

"What is it?" repeated the doctor.

"Come along with me," said Horn.

He walked out and the doctor followed him. The natives came after them in a little bunch. They crossed the road and came on to the beach. The doctor saw a group of natives standing round some object at the water's edge. They hurried along, a couple of dozen yards perhaps, and the natives opened up as the doctor came up. The trader pushed him forwards. Then he saw, lying half in the water and half out, a dreadful object, the body of Davidson. Dr. Macphail bent down—he was not a man to lose his head in an emergency—and turned the body over. The throat was cut from ear to ear, and in the right hand was still the razor with which the deed was done.

"He's quite cold," said the doctor. "He must have been dead some time."

"One of the boys saw him lying there on his way to work just now and came and told me. Do you think he did it himself?"

"Yes. Someone ought to go for the police."

Horn said something in the native tongue, and two youths started off.

"We must leave him here till they come," said the doctor.

"They mustn't take him into my house. I won't have him in my house."

"You'll do what the authorities say," replied the doctor sharply. "In point of fact I expect they'll take him to the mortuary."

They stood waiting where they were. The trader took a cigarette from a fold in his *lava-lava* and gave one to Dr. Macphail. They smoked while they stared at the corpse. Dr. Macphail could not understand.

"Why do you think he did it?" asked Horn.

The doctor shrugged his shoulders. In a little while native police came along, under the charge of a marine, with a stretcher, and immediately afterwards a couple of naval officers and a naval doctor. They managed everything in a businesslike manner.

"What about the wife?" said one of the officers.

"Now that you've come I'll go back to the house and get some things on. I'll see that it's broken to her. She'd better not see him till he's been fixed up a little."

"I guess that's right," said the naval doctor.

When Dr. Macphail went back he found his wife nearly dressed.

"Mrs. Davidson's in a dreadful state about her husband," she said to him as soon as he appeared. "He hasn't been to bed all night. She heard him leave Miss Thompson's room at two, but he went out. If he's been walking about since then he'll be absolutely dead."

Dr. Macphail told her what had happened and asked her to break the news to Mrs. Davidson.

"But why did he do it?" she asked, horror-stricken.

"I don't know."

"But I can't. I can't."

"You must."

She gave him a frightened look and went out. He heard her go into Mrs. Davidson's room. He waited a minute to gather himself together and then began to shave and wash. When he was dressed he sat down on the bed and waited for his wife. At last she came.

"She wants to see him," she said.

"They've taken him to the mortuary. We'd better go down with her. How did she take it?"

"I think she's stunned. She didn't cry. But she's trembling like a leaf."

"We'd better go at once."

When they knocked at her door Mrs. Davidson came out. She was very pale, but dry-eyed. To the doctor she seemed unnaturally composed. No word was exchanged, and they set out in silence down the road. When they arrived at the mortuary Mrs. Davidson spoke.

"Let me go in and see him alone."

They stood aside. A native opened a door for her and closed it behind her. They sat down and waited. One or two white men came and talked to them in undertones. Dr. Macphail told them again what he knew of the tragedy. At last the door was quietly opened and Mrs. Davidson came out. Silence fell upon them.

"I'm ready to go back now," she said.

Her voice was hard and steady. Dr. Macphail could not understand the look in her eyes. Her pale face was very stern. They walked back slowly, never saying a word, and at last they came round the bend on the other side of which stood their house. Mrs. Davidson gave a gasp, and for a moment they stopped still. An incredible sound assaulted their ears. The gramophone which had been silent for so long was playing, playing ragtime loud and harsh.

"What's that?" cried Mrs. Macphail with horror.

"Let's go on," said Mrs. Davidson.

They walked up the steps and entered the hall. Miss Thompson was standing at her door, chatting with a sailor. A sudden change had taken place in her. She was no longer the cowed drudge of the last days. She was dressed in all her finery, in her white dress, with the shiny boots over which her fat legs bulged in her cotton stockings; her hair was elaborately arranged; and she wore that enormous hat covered with gaudy flowers. Her face was painted, her eyebrows were boldly black, and her lips were scarlet. She held herself erect. She was the flaunting queen that they had known at first. As they came in she broke into a loud, jeering laugh; and then, when Mrs. Davidson involuntarily stopped, she collected the spittle in her mouth and spat. Mrs. Davidson cowered back, and two red spots rose suddenly to her cheeks. Then, covering her face with her hands, she broke away and ran quickly up the stairs. Dr. Macphail was outraged. He pushed past the woman into her room.

"What the devil are you doing?" he cried. "Stop that damned machine."

He went up to it and tore the record off. She turned on him.

"Say, doc, you can that stuff with me. What the hell are you doin' in my room?"

"What do you mean?" he cried. "What d'you mean?"

She gathered herself together. No one could describe the scorn of her expression or the contemptuous hatred she put into her answer.

"You men! You filthy, dirty pigs! You're all the same, all of you. Pigs! Pigs!"

Dr. Macphail gasped. He understood.

The Blue Hotel

Stephen Crane
(1871–1900)

*The youngest of fourteen children born to a clergyman
and his wife, Stephen Crane spent his adolescent years in
the New Jersey and New York areas. In his early teens he
worked during the summers for his brother's news agency;
at age sixteen he was contributing to a column written by
his mother and ghost writing for two of his brothers who
were correspondents for the New York* Tribune. *During
his one semester at Syracuse University in 1891, Crane
wrote the first draft of* Maggie: A Girl of the Streets.
*Even after rewriting the novel, Crane was unable to find a
publisher who would accept it: his manuscript was "too
honest." Determined to publish* Maggie, *Crane borrowed
money from one of his brothers for a private printing, but
it went unsold. However, Crane soon completed* The Red
Badge of Courage, *which appeared in serial form in the
Philadelphia* Press *in 1894. With its publication as a book
in the following year, Crane's merit as a writer was widely
recognized and he quickly became a national celebrity.*

*Working as a foreign correspondent in 1896, Crane was
shipwrecked on route to Cuba; his ordeal at sea later in-
spired* The Open Boat and Other Tales of Adventure
*(1898). He went to Greece in 1897 to cover the Greco-
Turkish War, and during most of the next year was in Cuba
reporting the Spanish-American War. In 1899 Crane and his
wife settled in Sussex, England, where they lavishly entertained countless guests, among them many prominent
authors. Although suffering from tuberculosis, Crane continued to write steadily;* The Monster and Other Stories
*(1899), which includes "The Blue Hotel," was published
shortly before his death, and several of his works appeared
posthumously.*

I

The Palace Hotel at Fort Romper was painted a light blue, a shade that is on the legs of a kind of heron, causing the bird to declare its position against any background. The Palace Hotel, then, was always screaming and howling in a way that made the dazzling winter landscape of Nebraska seem only a grey swampish hush. It stood alone on the prairie, and when the snow was falling the town two hundred yards away was not visible. But when the traveller alighted at the railway station he was obliged to pass the Palace Hotel before he could come upon the company of low clapboard houses which composed Fort Romper, and it was not to be thought that any traveller could pass the Palace Hotel without looking at it. Pat Scully, the proprietor, had proved himself a master of strategy when he chose his paints. It is true that on clear days, when the great transcontinental expresses, long lines of swaying Pullmans, swept through Fort Romper, passengers were overcome at the sight, and the cult that knows the brown-reds and the subdivisions of the dark greens of the East expressed shame, pity, horror, in a laugh. But to the citizens of this prairie town and to the people who would naturally stop there, Pat Scully had performed a feat. With this opulence and splendour, these creeds, classes, egotisms, that streamed through Romper on the rails day after day, they had no colour in common.

As if the displayed delights of such a blue hotel were not sufficiently enticing, it was Scully's habit to go every morning and evening to meet the leisurely trains that stopped at Romper and work his seductions upon any man that he might see wavering, gripsack in hand.

One morning, when a snow-crusted engine dragged its long string of freight cars and its one passenger coach to the station, Scully performed the marvel of catching three men. One was a shaky and quick-eyed Swede, with a great shining cheap valise; one was a tall bronzed cowboy, who was on his way to a ranch near the Dakota line; one was a silent little man from the East, who didn't look it, and didn't announce it. Scully practically made them prisoners. He was so nimble and merry and kindly that each probably felt it would be the height of brutality to try to escape.

THE BLUE HOTEL From the Perennial Library edition of *Great Short Works of Stephen Crane,* Harper & Row, Publishers, Inc.

They trudged off over the creaking board sidewalks in the wake of the eager little Irishman. He wore a heavy fur cap squeezed tightly down on his head. It caused his two red ears to stick out stiffly, as if they were made of tin.

At last, Scully, elaborately, with boisterous hospitality, conducted them through the portals of the blue hotel. The room which they entered was small. It seemed to be merely a proper temple for an enormous stove, which, in the centre, was humming with godlike violence. At various points on its surface the iron had become luminous and glowed yellow from the heat. Beside the stove Scully's son Johnnie was playing High-Five with an old farmer who had whiskers both grey and sandy. They were quarrelling. Frequently the old farmer turned his face toward a box of sawdust—coloured brown from tobacco juice—that was behind the stove, and spat with an air of great impatience and irritation. With a loud flourish of words Scully destroyed the game of cards, and bustled his son upstairs with part of the baggage of the new guests. He himself conducted them to three basins of the coldest water in the world. The cowboy and the Easterner burnished themselves fiery red with this water, until it seemed to be some kind of metal-polish. The Swede, however, merely dipped his fingers gingerly and with trepidation. It was notable that throughout this series of small ceremonies the three travellers were made to feel that Scully was very benevolent. He was conferring great favours upon them. He handed the towel from one to another with an air of philanthropic impulse.

Afterward they went to the first room, and, sitting about the stove, listened to Scully's officious clamour at his daughters, who were preparing the midday meal. They reflected in the silence of experienced men who tread carefully amid new people. Nevertheless, the old farmer, stationary, invincible in his chair near the warmest part of the stove, turned his face from the sawdust-box frequently and addressed a glowing commonplace to the strangers. Usually he was answered in short but adequate sentences by either the cowboy or the Easterner. The Swede said nothing. He seemed to be occupied in making furtive estimates of each man in the room. One might have thought that he had the sense of silly suspicion which comes to guilt. He resembled a badly frightened man.

Later, at dinner, he spoke a little, addressing his conversation entirely to Scully. He volunteered that he had come from New York, where for ten years he had worked as a tailor. These facts seemed to strike Scully as fascinating, and afterward he volunteered that he had lived at Romper for fourteen years. The Swede asked about the crops and the price of labour. He seemed barely to listen to Scully's extended replies. His eyes continued to rove from man to man.

Finally, with a laugh and a wink, he said that some of these Western communities were very dangerous; and after his statement he straightened his legs under the table, tilted his head, and laughed again, loudly. It was plain that the demonstration had no meaning to the others. They looked at him wondering and in silence.

II

As the men trooped heavily back into the front room, the two little windows presented views of a turmoiling sea of snow. The huge arms of the wind were making attempts—mighty, circular, futile—to embrace the flakes as they sped. A gate-post like a still man with a blanched face stood aghast amid this profligate fury. In a hearty voice Scully announced the presence of a blizzard. The guests of the blue hotel, lighting their pipes, assented with grunts of lazy masculine contentment. No island of the sea could be exempt in the degree of this little room with its humming stove. Johnnie, son of Scully, in a tone which defined his opinion of his ability as a card-player, challenged the old farmer of both grey and sandy whiskers to a game of High-Five. The farmer agreed with a contemptuous and bitter scoff. They sat close to the stove, and squared their knees under a wide board. The cowboy and the Easterner watched the game with interest. The Swede remained near the window, aloof, but with a countenance that showed signs of an inexplicable excitement.

The play of Johnnie and the grey-beard was suddenly ended by another quarrel. The old man arose while casting a look of heated scorn at his adversary. He slowly buttoned his coat, and then stalked with fabulous dignity from the room. In the discreet silence of all other men the Swede laughed. His laughter rang somehow childish. Men by this time had begun to look at him askance, as if they wished to inquire what ailed him.

A new game was formed jocosely. The cowboy volunteered to become the partner of Johnnie, and they all then turned to ask the Swede to throw in his lot with the little Easterner. He asked some questions about the game, and, learning that it wore many names, and that he had played it when it was under an alias, he accepted the invitation. He strode toward the men nervously, as if he expected to be assaulted. Finally, seated, he gazed from face to face and laughed shrilly. This laugh was so strange that the Easterner looked up quickly, the cowboy sat intent and with his mouth open, and Johnnie paused, holding the cards with still fingers.

Afterward there was a short silence. Then Johnnie said, "Well, let's get at it. Come on now!" They pulled their chairs forward until their knees were bunched under the board. They began to play, and their interest in the game caused the others to forget the manner of the Swede.

The cowboy was a board-whacker. Each time that he held superior cards he whanged them, one by one, with exceeding force, down upon the improvised table, and took the tricks with a glowing air of prowess and pride that sent thrills of indignation into the hearts of his opponents. A game with a board-whacker in it is sure to become intense. The countenances of the Easterner and the Swede were miserable whenever the cowboy thundered down his aces and kings, while Johnnie, his eyes gleaming with joy, chuckled and chuckled.

Because of the absorbing play none considered the strange ways of the Swede. They paid strict heed to the game. Finally, during a lull caused by a new deal, the Swede suddenly addressed Johnnie: "I suppose there have been a good many men killed in this room." The jaws of the others dropped and they looked at him.

"What in hell are you talking about?" said Johnnie.

The Swede laughed again his blatant laugh, full of a kind of false courage and defiance. "Oh, you know what I mean all right," he answered.

"I'm a liar if I do!" Johnnie protested. The card was halted, and the men stared at the Swede. Johnnie evidently felt that as the son of the proprietor he should make a direct inquiry. "Now, what might you be drivin' at, mister?" he asked. The Swede winked at him. It was a wink full of cunning. His fingers shook on the edge of the board. "Oh, maybe you think I have been to nowheres. Maybe you think I'm a tenderfoot?"

"I don't know nothin' about you," answered Johnnie, "and I don't give a damn where you've been. All I got to say is that I don't know what you're driving at. There hain't never been nobody killed in this room."

The cowboy, who had been steadily gazing at the Swede, then spoke: "What's wrong with you, mister?"

Apparently it seemed to the Swede that he was formidably menaced. He shivered and turned white near the corners of his mouth. He sent an appealing glance in the direction of the little Easterner. During these moments he did not forget to wear his air of advanced pot-valour. "They say they don't know what I mean," he remarked mockingly to the Easterner.

The latter answered after prolonged and cautious reflection. "I don't understand you," he said, impassively.

The Swede made a movement then which announced that he thought he had encountered treachery from the only quarter where he had expected sympathy, if not help. "Oh, I see you are all against me. I see ———"

The cowboy was in a state of deep stupefaction. "Say," he cried, as he tumbled the deck violently down upon the board, "say, what are you gittin' at, hey?"

The Swede sprang up with the celerity of a man escaping from a snake on the floor. "I don't want to fight!" he shouted. "I don't want to fight!"

The cowboy stretched his long legs indolently and deliberately. His hands were in his pockets. He spat into the sawdust-box. "Well, who the hell thought you did?" he inquired.

The Swede backed rapidly toward a corner of the room. His hands were out protectingly in front of his chest, but he was making an obvious struggle to control his fright. "Gentlemen," he quavered, "I suppose I am going to be killed before I can leave this house! I suppose I am going to be killed before I can leave this house!" In his eyes was the dying-swan look. Through the windows could be seen the snow turning blue in the shadow of dusk. The wind tore at the house, and some loose thing beat regularly against the clapboards like a spirit tapping.

A door opened, and Scully himself entered. He paused in surprise as he noted the tragic attitude of the Swede. Then he said, "What's the matter here?"

The Swede answered him swiftly and eagerly: "These men are going to kill me."

"Kill you!" ejaculated Scully. "Kill you! What are you talkin'?"

The Swede made the gesture of a martyr.

Scully wheeled sternly upon his son. "What is this, Johnnie?"

The lad had grown sullen. "Damned if I know," he answered. "I can't make no sense to it." He began to shuffle the cards, fluttering them together with an angry snap. "He says a good many men have been killed in this room, or something like that. And he says he's goin' to be killed here too. I don't know what ails him. He's crazy, I shouldn't wonder."

Scully then looked for an explanation to the cowboy, but the cowboy simply shrugged his shoulders.

"Kill you?" said Scully again to the Swede. "Kill you? Man, you're off your nut."

"Oh, I know," burst out the Swede. "I know what will happen. Yes, I'm crazy—yes. Yes, of course, I'm crazy—yes. But I know one thing ———" There was a sort of sweat and misery and terror upon his face. "I know I won't get out of here alive."

The cowboy drew a deep breath, as if his mind was passing into the last stages of dissolution. "Well, I'm doggoned," he whispered to himself.

Scully wheeled suddenly and faced his son. "You've been troublin' this man!"

Johnnie's voice was loud with its burden of grievance. "Why, good Gawd, I ain't done nothin' to 'im."

The Swede broke in. "Gentlemen, do not disturb yourselves. I will leave this house. I will go away, because"—he accused them dramatically with his glance—"because I do not want to be killed."

Scully was furious with his son. "Will you tell me what is the matter, you young divil? What's the matter, anyhow? Speak out!"

"Blame it!" cried Johnnie in despair, "don't I tell you I don't know? He—he says we want to kill him, and that's all I know. I can't tell what ails him."

The Swede continued to repeat: "Never mind, Mr. Scully; never mind. I will leave this house. I will go away, because I do not wish to be killed. Yes, of course, I am crazy—yes. But I know one thing! I will go away. I will leave this house. Never mind, Mr. Scully; never mind. I will go away."

"You will not go 'way," said Scully. "You will not go 'way until I hear the reason of this business. If anybody has troubled you I will take care of him. This is my house. You are under my roof, and I will not allow any peaceable man to be troubled here." He cast a terrible eye upon Johnnie, the cowboy, and the Easterner.

"Never mind, Mr. Scully; never mind. I will go away. I do not wish to be killed." The Swede moved toward the door which opened upon the stairs. It was evidently his intention to go at once for his baggage.

"No, no," shouted Scully peremptorily; but the white-faced man slid by him and disappeared. "Now," said Scully severely, "what does this mane?"

Johnnie and the cowboy cried together: "Why, we didn't do nothin' to 'im!"

Scully's eyes were cold. "No," he said, "you didn't?"

Johnnie swore a deep oath. "Why, this is the wildest loon I ever see. We didn't do nothin' at all. We were jest sittin' here playin' cards, and he ——"

The father suddenly spoke to the Easterner. "Mr. Blanc," he asked, "what has these boys been doin'?"

The Easterner reflected again. "I didn't see anything wrong at all," he said at last, slowly.

Scully began to howl. "But what does it mane?" He stared ferociously at his son. "I have a mind to lather you for this, me boy."

Johnnie was frantic. "Well, what have I done?" he bawled at his father.

III

"I think you are tongue-tied," said Scully finally to his son, the cowboy, and the Easterner; and at the end of his scornful sentence he left the room.

Upstairs the Swede was swiftly fastening the straps of his great valise. Once his back happened to be half turned toward the door, and, hearing a noise there, he wheeled and sprang up, uttering a loud cry. Scully's wrinkled visage showed grimly in the light of the small lamp he carried. This yellow effulgence, streaming upward, coloured only his prominent features, and left his eyes, for instance, in mysterious shadow. He resembled a murderer.

"Man! man!" he exclaimed, "have you gone daffy?"

"Oh, no! Oh, no!" rejoined the other. "There are people in this world who know pretty nearly as much as you do—understand?"

For a moment they stood gazing at each other. Upon the Swede's deathly pale cheeks were two spots brightly crimson and sharply edged, as if they had been carefully painted. Scully placed the light on the table and sat himself on the edge of the bed. He spoke ruminatively. "By cracky, I never heard of such a thing in my life. It's a complete muddle. I can't, for the soul of me, think how you ever got this idea into your head." Presently he lifted his eyes and asked: "And did you sure think they were going to kill you?"

The Swede scanned the old man as if he wished to see into his mind. "I did," he said at last. He obviously suspected that this answer might precipitate an outbreak. As he pulled on a strap his whole arm shook, the elbow wavering like a bit of paper.

Scully banged his hand impressively on the footboard of the bed. "Why, man, we're goin' to have a line of ilitric street-cars in this town next spring."

" 'Alineofelectricstreet-cars,' " repeated the Swede, stupidly.

"And," said Scully, "there's a new railroad goin' to be built down from Broken Arm to here. Not to mintion the four churches and the smashin' big brick schoolhouse. Then there's the big factory, too. Why, in two years Romper'll be a met-tro-*pol*-is."

Having finished the preparation of his baggage, the Swede straightened himself. "Mr. Scully," he said, with sudden hardihood, "how much do I owe you?"

"You don't owe me anythin'," said the old man, angrily.

"Yes, I do," retorted the Swede. He took seventy-five cents from his pocket and tendered it to Scully; but the latter snapped his fingers in disdainful refusal. However, it happened that they both stood gazing in a strange fashion at three silver pieces on the Swede's open palm.

"I'll not take your money," said Scully at last. "Not after what's been goin' on here." Then a plan seemed to strike him. "Here," he cried, picking up his lamp and moving toward the door. "Here! Come with me a minute."

"No," said the Swede, in overwhelming alarm.

"Yes," urged the old man. "Come on! I want you to come and see a picter—just across the hall—in my room."

The Swede must have concluded that his hour was come. His jaw dropped and his teeth showed like a dead man's. He ultimately followed Scully across the corridor, but he had the step of one hung in chains.

Scully flashed the light high on the wall of his own chamber. There was revealed a ridiculous photograph of a little girl. She was leaning against a balustrade of gorgeous decoration, and the formidable bang to her hair was prominent. The figure was as graceful as an upright sled-stake, and, withal, it was the hue of lead. "There," said Scully, tenderly, "that's the picter of my little girl that died. Her name was Carrie. She had the purtiest hair you ever saw! I was that fond of her, she———"

Turning then, he saw that the Swede was not contemplating the picture at all, but, instead, was keeping keen watch on the gloom in the rear.

"Look, man!" cried Scully, heartily. "That's the picter of my little gal that died. Her name was Carrie. And then here's the picter of my oldest boy, Michael. He's a lawyer in Lincoln, an' doin' well. I gave that boy a grand eddication, and I'm glad for it now. He's a fine boy. Look at 'im now. Ain't he bold as blazes, him there in Lincoln, an honoured an' respicted gintleman! An honoured and respicted gintleman," concluded Scully with a flourish. And, so saying, he smote the Swede jovially on the back.

The Swede faintly smiled.

"Now," said the old man, "there's only one more thing." He dropped suddenly to the floor and thrust his head beneath the bed. The Swede could hear his muffled voice. "I'd keep it under me piller if it wasn't for that boy Johnnie. Then there there's the old woman——Where is it now? I never put it twice in the same place. Ah, now come out with you!"

Presently he backed clumsily from under the bed, dragging with him an old coat rolled into a bundle. "I've fetched him," he muttered. Kneeling on the floor, he unrolled the coat and extracted from its heart a large yellow-brown whisky-bottle.

His first manoeuvre was to hold the bottle up to the light. Reassured, apparently, that nobody had been tampering with it, he thrust it with a generous movement toward the Swede.

The weak-kneed Swede was about to eagerly clutch this element of strength, but he suddenly jerked his hand away and cast a look of horror upon Scully.

"Drink," said the old man affectionately. He had risen to his feet, and now stood facing the Swede.

There was a silence. Then again Scully said: "Drink!"

The Swede laughed wildly. He grabbed the bottle, put it to his mouth; and as his lips curled absurdly around the opening and his throat worked, he kept his glance, burning with hatred, upon the old man's face.

IV

After the departure of Scully the three men, with the cardboard still upon their knees, preserved for a long time an astonished silence. Then Johnnie said: "That's the doddangedest Swede I ever see."

"He ain't no Swede," said the cowboy, scornfully.

"Well, what is he then?" cried Johnnie. "What is he then?"

"It's my opinion," replied the cowboy deliberately, "he's some kind of a Dutchman." It was a venerable custom of the country to entitle as Swedes all light-haired men who spoke with a heavy tongue. In consequence the idea of the cowboy was not without its daring. "Yes, sir," he repeated. "It's my opinion this feller is some kind of a Dutchman."

"Well, he says he's a Swede, anyhow," muttered Johnnie, sulkily. He turned to the Easterner: "What do you think, Mr. Blanc?"

"Oh, I don't know," replied the Easterner.

"Well, what do you think makes him act that way?" asked the cowboy.

"Why, he's frightened." The Easterner knocked his pipe against a rim of the stove. "He's clear frightened out of his boots."

"What at?" cried Johnnie and the cowboy together.

The Easterner reflected over his answer.

"What at?" cried the others again.

"Oh, I don't know, but it seems to me this man has been reading dime novels, and he thinks he's right out in the middle of it —the shootin' and stabbin' and all."

"But," said the cowboy, deeply scandalized, "this ain't Wyoming, ner none of them places. This is Nebrasker."

"Yes," added Johnnie, "an' why don't he wait till he gits *out West?*"

The travelled Easterner laughed. "It isn't different there even —not in these days. But he thinks he's right in the middle of hell."

Johnnie and the cowboy mused long.

"It's awfully funny," remarked Johnnie at last.

"Yes," said the cowboy. "This is a queer game. I hope we don't git snowed in, because then we'd have to stand this here man bein' around with us all the time. That wouldn't be no good."

"I wish pop would throw him out," said Johnnie.

Presently they heard a loud stamping on the stairs, accompanied by ringing jokes in the voice of old Scully, and laughter, evidently from the Swede. The men around the stove stared vacantly at each other. "Gosh!" said the cowboy. The door flew open, and old Scully, flushed and anecdotal, came into the room. He was jabbering at the Swede, who followed him, laughing bravely. It was the entry of two roisterers from a banquet hall.

"Come now," said Scully sharply to the three seated men, "move up and give us a chance at the stove." The cowboy and the Easterner obediently sidled their chairs to make room for the new-comers. Johnnie, however, simply arranged himself in a more indolent attitude, and then remained motionless.

"Come! Git over, there," said Scully.

"Plenty of room on the other side of the stove," said Johnnie.

"Do you think we want to sit in the draught?" roared the father.

But the Swede here interposed with a grandeur of confidence. "No, no. Let the boy sit where he likes," he cried in a bullying voice to the father.

"All right! All right!" said Scully, deferentially. The cowboy and the Easterner exchanged glances of wonder.

The five chairs were formed in a crescent about one side of the stove. The Swede began to talk; he talked arrogantly, profanely, angrily. Johnnie, the cowboy, and the Easterner maintained a morose silence, while old Scully appeared to be receptive and eager, breaking in constantly with sympathetic ejaculations.

Finally the Swede announced that he was thirsty. He moved in his chair, and said that he would go for a drink of water.

"I'll git it for you," cried Scully at once.

"No," said the Swede, contemptuously. "I'll get it for myself." He arose and stalked with the air of an owner off into the executive parts of the hotel.

As soon as the Swede was out of hearing Scully sprang to his feet and whispered intensely to the others: "Upstairs he thought I was tryin' to poison 'im."

"Say," said Johnnie, "this makes me sick. Why don't you throw 'im out in the snow?"

"Why, he's all right now," declared Scully. "It was only that he was from the East, and he thought this was a tough place. That's all. He's all right now."

The cowboy looked with admiration upon the Easterner. "You were straight," he said. "You were on to that there Dutchman." ·

"Well," said Johnnie to his father, "he may be all right now, but I don't see it. Other time he was scared, but now he's too fresh."

Scully's speech was always a combination of Irish brogue and idiom, Western twang and idiom, and scraps of curiously formal diction taken from the story-books and newspapers. He now hurled a strange mass of language at the head of his son. "What do I keep? What do I keep? What do I keep?" he demanded, in a voice of thunder. He slapped his knee impressively, to indicate that he himself was going to make reply, and that all should heed. "I keep a hotel," he shouted. "A hotel, do you mind? A guest under my roof has sacred privileges. He is to be intimidated by none. Not one word shall he hear that would prijudice him in favour of goin' away. I'll not have it. There's no place in this here town where they can say they iver took in a guest of mine because he was afraid to stay here." He wheeled suddenly upon the cowboy and the Easterner. "Am I right?"

"Yes, Mr. Scully," said the cowboy, "I think you're right."

"Yes, Mr. Scully," said the Easterner, "I think you're right."

V

At six-o'clock supper, the Swede fizzed like a fire-wheel. He sometimes seemed on the point of bursting into riotous song, and in all his madness he was encouraged by old Scully. The Easterner was encased in reserve; the cowboy sat in wide-mouthed amazement, forgetting to eat, while Johnnie wrathily demolished great plates of food. The daughters of the house, when they were obliged to replenish the biscuits, approached as warily as Indians, and, having succeeded in their purpose, fled with ill-concealed trepidation. The Swede domineered the whole feast, he gave it the appearance of a cruel bacchanal. He seemed to have grown suddenly taller; he gazed, brutally disdainful, into every face. His voice rang through the room. Once he jabbed out harpoon-fashion with his fork to pinion a biscuit, the weapon nearly impaled the hand of the Easterner, which had been stretched quietly out for the same biscuit.

After supper, as the men fled toward the other room, the Swede smote Scully ruthlessly on the shoulder. "Well, old boy, that was a good, square meal." Johnnie looked hopefully at his father; he knew that shoulder was tender from an old fall; and, indeed, it appeared for a moment as if Scully was going to flame out over the matter, but in the end he smiled a sickly smile and remained silent. The others understood from his manner that he was admitting his responsibility for the Swede's new view-point.

Johnnie, however, addressed his parent in an aside. "Why don't you license somebody to kick you downstairs?" Scully scowled darkly by way of reply.

When they were gathered about the stove, the Swede insisted on another game of High-Five. Scully gently deprecated the plan at first, but the Swede turned a wolfish glare upon him. The old man subsided, and the Swede canvassed the others. In his tone there was always a great threat. The cowboy and the Easterner both remarked indifferently that they would play. Scully said that he would presently have to go to meet the 6.58 train, and so the Swede turned menacingly upon Johnnie. For a moment their glances crossed like blades, and then Johnnie smiled and said, "Yes, I'll play."

They formed a square, with the little board on their knees. The Easterner and the Swede were again partners. As the play went on, it was noticeable that the cowboy was not board-whacking as usual. Meanwhile, Scully, near the lamp, had put on his spectacles and, with an appearance curiously like an old priest, was reading a newspaper. In time he went out to meet the 6.58 train, and, despite his precautions, a gust of polar wind whirled into the room as he opened the door. Besides scattering the cards, it chilled the players to the marrow. The Swede cursed frightfully. When Scully returned, his entrance disturbed a cosy and friendly scene. The Swede again cursed. But presently they were once more intent, their heads bent forward and their hands moving swiftly. The Swede had adopted the fashion of board-whacking.

Scully took up his paper and for a long time remained immersed in matters which were extraordinarily remote from him. The lamp burned badly, and once he stopped to adjust the wick. The newspaper, as he turned from page to page, rustled with a slow and comfortable sound. Then suddenly he heard three terrible words: "You are cheatin'!"

Such scenes often prove that there can be little of dramatic import in environment. Any room can present a tragic front; any room can be comic. This little den was now hideous as a torture-chamber. The new faces of the men themselves had changed it upon the instant. The Swede held a huge fist in front of Johnnie's face, while the latter looked steadily over it into the blazing orbs of his accuser. The Easterner had grown pallid; the cowboy's jaw had dropped in that expression of bovine amazement which was one of his important mannerisms. After the three words, the first sound in the room was made by Scully's paper as it floated forgotten to his feet. His spectacles had also fallen from his nose, but by a clutch he had saved them in air. His hand, grasping the spectacles, now remained poised awkwardly and near his shoulder. He stared at the card-players.

Probably the silence was while a second elapsed. Then, if the floor had been suddenly twitched out from under the men they could not have moved quicker. The five had projected themselves headlong toward a common point. It happened that Johnnie, in rising to hurl himself upon the Swede, had stumbled slightly because of his curiously instinctive care for the cards and the board. The loss of the moment allowed time for the arrival of Scully, and also allowed the cowboy time to give the Swede a great push which sent him staggering back. The men found tongue together, and hoarse shouts of rage, appeal, or fear burst from every throat. The cowboy pushed and jostled feverishly at the Swede, and the Easterner and Scully clung wildly to Johnnie; but through the smoky air, above the swaying bodies of the peace-compellers, the eyes of the two warriors ever sought each other in glances of challenge that were at once hot and steely.

Of course the board had been overturned, and now the whole company of cards was scattered over the floor, where the boots of the men trampled the fat and painted kings and queens as they gazed with their silly eyes at the war that was waging above them.

Scully's voice was dominating the yells. "Stop now! Stop, I say! Stop, now——"

Johnnie, as he struggled to burst through the rank formed by Scully and the Easterner, was crying, "Well, he says I cheated! He says I cheated! I won't allow no man to say I cheated! If he says I cheated, he's a —— ——!"

The cowboy was telling the Swede, "Quit, now! Quit, d'ye hear ——"

The screams of the Swede never ceased: "He did cheat! I saw him! I saw him——"

As for the Easterner, he was importuning in a voice that was not heeded: "Wait a moment, can't you? Oh, wait a moment. What's the good of a fight over a game of cards? Wait a moment ——"

In this tumult no complete sentences were clear. "Cheat"——

"Quit"—"He says"—these fragments pierced the uproar and rang out sharply. It was remarkable that, whereas Scully undoubtedly made the most noise, he was the least heard of any of the riotous band.

Then suddenly there was a great cessation. It was as if each man had paused for breath; and although the room was still lighted with the anger of men, it could be seen that there was no danger of immediate conflict, and at once Johnnie, shouldering his way forward, almost succeeded in confronting the Swede. "What did you say I cheated for? What did you say I cheated for? I don't cheat, and I won't let no man say I do!"

The Swede said, "I saw you! I saw you!"

"Well," cried Johnnie, "I'll fight any man what says I cheat!"

"No, you won't," said the cowboy. "Not here."

"Ah, be still, can't you?" said Scully, coming between them.

The quiet was sufficient to allow the Easterner's voice to be heard. He was repeating, "Oh, wait a moment, can't you? What's the good of a fight over a game of cards? Wait a moment!"

Johnnie, his red face appearing above his father's shoulder, hailed the Swede again. "Did you say I cheated?"

The Swede showed his teeth. "Yes."

"Then," said Johnnie, "we must fight."

"Yes, fight," roared the Swede. He was like a demoniac. "Yes, fight! I'll show you what kind of a man I am! I'll show you who you want to fight! Maybe you think I can't fight! Maybe you think I can't! I'll show you, you skin, you card-sharp! Yes, you cheated! You cheated! You cheated!"

"Well, let's go at it, then, mister," said Johnnie, coolly.

The cowboy's brow was beaded with sweat from his efforts in intercepting all sorts of raids. He turned in despair to Scully. "What are you goin' to do now?"

A change had come over the Celtic visage of the old man. He now seemed all eagerness; his eyes glowed.

"We'll let them fight," he answered stalwartly. "I can't put up with it any longer. I've stood this damned Swede till I'm sick. We'll let them fight."

VI

The men prepared to go out of doors. The Easterner was so nervous that he had great difficulty in getting his arms into the sleeves of his new leather coat. As the cowboy drew his fur cap down over his ears his hands trembled. In fact, Johnnie and old Scully were the only ones who displayed no agitation. These preliminaries were conducted without words.

Scully threw open the door. "Well, come on," he said. Instantly, a terrific wind caused the flame of the lamp to struggle at its wick, while a puff of black smoke sprang from the chimney-top. The stove was in mid-current of the blast, and its voice swelled to equal the roar of the storm. Some of the scarred and bedabbled cards were caught up from the floor and dashed helplessly against the further wall. The men lowered their heads and plunged into the tempest as into a sea.

No snow was falling, but great whirls and clouds of flakes, swept up from the ground by the frantic winds, were streaming southward with the speed of bullets. The covered land was blue with the sheen of an unearthly satin, and there was no other hue save where, at the low, black railway station—which seemed incredibly distant—one light gleamed like a tiny jewel. As the men floundered into a thigh-deep drift, it was known that the Swede was bawling out something. Scully went to him, put a hand on his shoulder, and projected an ear. "What's that you say?" he shouted.

"I say," bawled the Swede again, "I won't stand much show against this gang. I know you'll all pitch on me."

Scully smote him reproachfully on the arm. "Tut, man!" he yelled. The wind tore the words from Scully's lips and scattered them far alee.

"You are all a gang of——" boomed the Swede, but the storm also seized the remainder of this sentence.

Immediately turning their backs upon the wind, the men had swung around a corner to the sheltered side of the hotel. It was the function of the little house to preserve here, amid this great devastation of snow, an irregular V-shape of heavily encrusted grass, which crackled beneath the feet. One could imagine the great drifts piled against the windward side. When the party reached the comparative peace of this spot it was found that the Swede was still bellowing.

"Oh, I know what kind of a thing this is! I know you'll all pitch on me. I can't lick you all!"

Scully turned upon him panther-fashion. "You'll not have to whip all of us. You'll have to whip my son Johnnie. An' the man what troubles you durin' that time will have me to dale with."

The arrangements were swiftly made. The two men faced each other, obedient to the harsh commands of Scully, whose face, in the subtly luminous gloom, could be seen set in the austere impersonal lines that are pictured on the countenances of the Roman veterans. The Easterner's teeth were chattering, and he was hopping up and down like a mechanical toy. The cowboy stood rock-like.

The contestants had not stripped off any clothing. Each was in his ordinary attire. Their fists were up, and they eyed each other in a calm that had the elements of leonine cruelty in it.

During this pause, the Easterner's mind, like a film, took lasting impressions of three men—the iron-nerved master of the ceremony; the Swede, pale, motionless, terrible; and Johnnie, serene yet ferocious, brutish yet heroic. The entire prelude had in it a tragedy greater than the tragedy of action, and this aspect was accentuated by the long, mellow cry of the blizzard, as it sped the tumbling and wailing flakes into the black abyss of the south.

"Now!" said Scully.

The two combatants leaped forward and crashed together like bullocks. There was heard the cushioned sound of blows, and of a curse squeezing out from between the tight teeth of one.

As for the spectators, the Easterner's pent-up breath exploded from him with a pop of relief, absolute relief from the tension of the preliminaries. The cowboy bounded into the air with a yowl. Scully was immovable as from supreme amazement and fear at the fury of the fight which he himself had permitted and arranged.

For a time the encounter in the darkness was such a perplexity of flying arms that it presented no more detail than would a swiftly revolving wheel. Occasionally a face, as if illumined by a flash of light, would shine out, ghastly and marked with pink spots. A moment later, the men might have been known as shadows, if it were not for the involuntary utterance of oaths that came from them in whispers.

Suddenly a holocaust of warlike desire caught the cowboy, and he bolted forward with the speed of a broncho. "Go it, Johnnie! go it! Kill him! Kill him!"

Scully confronted him. "Kape back," he said; and by his glance the cowboy could tell that this man was Johnnie's father.

To the Easterner there was a monotony of unchangeable fighting that was an abomination. This confused mingling was eternal to his sense, which was concentrated in a longing for the end, the priceless end. Once the fighters lurched near him, and as he scrambled hastily backward he heard them breathe like men on the rack.

"Kill him, Johnnie! Kill him! Kill him! Kill him!" The cowboy's face was contorted like one of those agony masks in museums.

"Keep still," said Scully, icily.

Then there was a sudden loud grunt, incomplete, cut short, and Johnnie's body swung away from the Swede and fell with sickening heaviness to the grass. The cowboy was barely in time to prevent the mad Swede from flinging himself upon his prone adversary. "No, you don't," said the cowboy, interposing an arm. "Wait a second."

Scully was at his son's side. "Johnnie! Johnnie, me boy!" His voice had a quality of melancholy tenderness. "Johnnie! Can you go on with it?" He looked anxiously down into the bloody, pulpy face of his son.

There was a moment of silence, and then Johnnie answered in his ordinary voice, "Yes, I—it—yes."

Assisted by his father he struggled to his feet. "Wait a bit now till you git your wind," said the old man.

A few paces away the cowboy was lecturing the Swede. "No, you don't! Wait a second!"

The Easterner was plucking at Scully's sleeve. "Oh, this is enough," he pleaded. "This is enough! Let it go as it stands. This is enough!"

"Bill," said Scully, "git out of the road." The cowboy stepped aside. "Now." The combatants were actuated by a new caution as they advanced toward collision. They glared at each other, and then the Swede aimed a lightening blow that carried with it his entire weight. Johnnie was evidently half stupid from weakness, but he miraculously dodged, and his fist sent the over-balanced Swede sprawling.

The cowboy, Scully, and the Easterner burst into a cheer that was like the chorus of triumphant soldiery, but before its conclusion the Swede had scuffled agilely to his feet and come in berserk abandon at his foe. There was another perplexity of flying arms, and Johnnie's body again swung away and fell, even as a bundle might fall from a roof. The Swede instantly staggered to a little wind-waved tree and leaned upon it, breathing like an engine, while his savage and flame-lit eyes roamed from face to face as the men bent over Johnnie. There was a splendour of isolation in his situation at this time which the Easterner felt once when, lifting his eyes from the man on the ground, he beheld that mysterious and lonely figure, waiting.

"Are you any good yet, Johnnie?" asked Scully in a broken voice.

The son gasped and opened his eyes languidly. After a moment he answered, "No—I ain't—any good—any—more." Then, from shame and bodily ill, he began to weep, the tears furrowing down through the blood-stains on his face. "He was too—too—too heavy for me."

Scully straightened and adressed the waiting figure. "Stranger," he said, evenly, "it's all up with our side." Then his voice changed into that vibrant huskiness which is commonly the tone of the most simple and deadly announcements. "Johnnie is whipped."

Without replying, the victor moved off on the route to the front door of the hotel.

The cowboy was formulating new and unspellable blasphemies. The Easterner was startled to find that they were out in a wind that seemed to come direct from the shadowed arctic floes. He heard again the wail of the snow as it was flung to its grave in the south. He knew now that all this time the cold had been sinking into him deeper and deeper, and he wondered that he had not perished. He felt indifferent to the condition of the vanquished man.

"Johnnie can you walk?" asked Scully.

"Did I hurt—hurt him any?" asked the son.

"Can you walk, boy? Can you walk?"

Johnnie's voice was suddenly strong. There was a robust impatience in it. "I asked you whether I hurt him any!"

"Yes, yes, Johnnie," answered the cowboy, consolingly; "he's hurt a good deal."

They raised him from the ground, and as soon as he was on his feet he went tottering off, rebuffing all attempts at assistance. When the party rounded the corner they were fairly blinded by the pelting of the snow. It burned their faces like fire. The cowboy carried Johnnie through the drift to the door. As they entered, some cards again rose from the floor and beat against the wall.

The Easterner rushed to the stove. He was so profoundly chilled that he almost dared to embrace the glowing iron. The Swede was not in the room. Johnnie sank into a chair and, folding his arms on his knees, buried his face in them. Scully, warming one foot and then the other at a rim of the stove, muttered to himself with Celtic mournfulness. The cowboy had removed his fur cap, and with a dazed and rueful air he was running one hand through his tousled locks. From overhead they could hear the creaking of boards, as the Swede tramped here and there in his room.

The sad quiet was broken by the sudden flinging open of a door that led toward the kitchen. It was instantly followed by an inrush of women. They precipitated themselves upon Johnnie amid a chorus of lamentation. Before they carried their prey off to the kitchen, there to be bathed and harangued with that mixture of sympathy and abuse which is a feat of their sex, the mother straightened herself and fixed old Scully with an eye of stern reproach. "Shame be upon you, Patrick Scully!" she cried. "Your own son, too. Shame be upon you!"

"There, now! Be quiet, now!" said the old man, weakly.

"Shame be upon you, Patrick Scully!" The girls, rallying to this slogan, sniffed disdainfully in the direction of those trembling accomplices, the cowboy and the Easterner. Presently they bore Johnnie away, and left the three men to dismal reflection.

VII

"I'd like to fight this here Dutchman myself," said the cowboy, breaking a long silence.

Scully wagged his head sadly. "No, that wouldn't do. It wouldn't be right. It wouldn't be right."

"Well, why wouldn't it?" argued the cowboy. "I don't see no harm in it."

"No," answered Scully, with mournful heroism. "It wouldn't be right. It was Johnnie's fight, and now we mustn't whip the man just because he whipped Johnnie."

"Yes, that's true enough," said the cowboy; "but—he better not get fresh with me, because I couldn't stand no more of it."

"You'll not say a word to him," commanded Scully, and even then they heard the tread of the Swede on the stairs. His entrance was made theatric. He swept the door back with a bang and swaggered to the middle of the room. No one looked at him. "Well," he cried, insolently, at Scully, "I s'pose you'll tell me now how much I owe you?"

The old man remained stolid. "You don't owe me nothin'."

"Huh!" said the Swede, "huh! Don't owe 'im nothin'."

The cowboy addressed the Swede. "Stranger, I don't see how you come to be so gay around here."

Old Scully was instantly alert. "Stop!" he shouted, holding his hand forth, fingers upward. "Bill, you shut up!"

The cowboy spat carelessly into the sawdust-box. "I didn't say a word, did I?" he asked.

"Mr. Scully," called the Swede, "how much do I owe you?" It was seen that he was attired for departure, and that he had his valise in his hand.

"You don't owe me nothin'," repeated Scully in the same imperturbable way.

"Huh!" said the Swede. "I guess you're right. I guess if it was any way at all, you'd owe me somethin'. That's what I guess." He turned to the cowboy. " 'Kill him! Kill him! Kill him!' " he mimicked, and then guffawed victoriously. " 'Kill him!' " He was convulsed with ironical humour.

But he might have been jeering the dead. The three men were immovable and silent, staring with glassy eyes at the stove.

The Swede opened the door and passed into the storm, giving one derisive glance backward at the still group.

As soon as the door was closed, Scully and the cowboy leaped to their feet and began to curse. They trampled to and fro, waving their arms and smashing into the air with their fists. "Oh, but that was a hard minute!" wailed Scully. "That was a hard minute! Him there leerin' and scoffin'! One bang at his nose was worth forty dollars to me that minute! How did you stand it, Bill?"

"How did I stand it?" cried the cowboy in a quivering voice. "How did I stand it? Oh!"

The old man burst into a sudden brogue. "I'd loike to take that Swade," he wailed, "and hould 'im down on a shtone flure and bate 'im to a jelly wid a shtick!"

The cowboy groaned in sympathy. "I'd like to git him by the neck and ha-ammer him"—he brought his hand down on a chair with a noise like a pistol-shot—"hammer that there Dutchman until he couldn't tell himself from a dead coyote!"

"I'd bate 'im until he———"

"I'd show *him* some things———."

And then together they raised a yearning, fanatic cry—"Oh-o-oh! if we only could———"

"Yes!"

"Yes!"

"And then I'd———"

"O-o-oh!"

VIII

The Swede, tightly gripping his valise, tacked across the face of the storm as if he carried sails. He was following a line of little naked, gasping trees which, he knew, must mark the way of the road. His face, fresh from the pounding of Johnnie's fists, felt more pleasure than pain in the wind and the driving snow. A number of square shapes loomed upon him finally, and he knew them as the houses of the main body of the town. He found a street and made travel along it, leaning heavily upon the wind whenever, at a corner, a terrific blast caught him.

He might have been in a deserted village. We picture the world as thick with conquering and elate humanity, but here, with the bugles of the tempest pealing, it was hard to imagine a peopled earth. One viewed the existence of man then as a marvel, and conceded a glamour of wonder to these lice which were caused to cling to a whirling, fire-smitten, ice-locked, disease-stricken, space-lost bulb. The conceit of man was explained by this storm to be the very engine of life. One was a coxcomb not to die in it. However, the Swede found a saloon.

In front of it an indomitable red light was burning, and the snowflakes were made blood-colour as they flew through the circumscribed territory of the lamp's shining. The Swede pushed open the door of the saloon and entered. A sanded expanse was before him, and at the end of it four men sat about a table drinking. Down one side of the room extended a radiant bar, and its guardian was leaning upon his elbows listening to the talk of the men at the table. The Swede dropped his valise upon the floor and, smiling fraternally upon the barkeeper, said, "Gimme some whisky, will you?" The man placed a bottle, a whisky-glass, and a glass of ice-thick water upon the bar. The Swede poured himself an abnormal portion of whisky and drank it in three gulps. "Pretty bad night," remarked the bartender, indifferently. He was making the pretension of blindness which is usually a distinction of his class; but it could have been seen that he was furtively studying the half-erased blood-stains on the face of the Swede. "Bad night," he said again.

"Oh, it's good enough for me," replied the Swede, hardily, as he poured himself some more whisky. The barkeeper took his coin and manoeuvred it through its reception by the highly nickelled cash-machine. A bell rang; a card labelled "20 cts." had appeared.

"No," continued the Swede, "this isn't too bad weather. It's good enough for me."

"So?" murmured the barkeeper, languidly.

The copious drams made the Swede's eyes swim, and he breathed a trifle heavier. "Yes, I like this weather. I like it. It suits me." It was apparently his design to impart a deep significance to these words.

"So?" murmured the bartender again. He turned to gaze dreamily at the scroll-like birds and bird-like scrolls which had been drawn with soap upon the mirrors in back of the bar.

"Well, I guess I'll take another drink," said the Swede, presently. "Have something?"

"No, thanks; I'm not drinkin'," answered the bartender. Afterward he asked, "How did you hurt your face?"

The Swede immediately began to boast loudly. "Why, in a fight. I thumped the soul out of a man down here at Scully's hotel."

The interest of the four men at the table was at last aroused.

"Who was it?" said one.

"Johnnie Scully," blustered the Swede. "Son of the man what runs it. He will be pretty near dead for some weeks, I can tell you. I made a nice thing of him, I did. He couldn't get up. They carried him in the house. Have a drink?"

Instantly the men in some subtle way encased themselves in reserve. "No, thanks," said one. The group was of curious formation. Two were prominent local business men; one was the district attorney; and one was a professional gambler of the kind known as "square." But a scrutiny of the group would not have enabled an observer to pick the gambler from the men of more reputable pursuits. He was, in fact, a man so delicate in manner, when among people of fair class, and so judicious in his choice of victims, that in the strictly masculine part of the town's life he had come to be explicitly trusted and admired. People called him a thoroughbred. The fear and contempt with which his craft was regarded were undoubtedly the reason why his quiet dignity shone conspicuous above the quiet dignity of men who might be merely hatters, billiard-markers, or grocery clerks. Beyond an occasional unwary traveller who came by rail, this gambler was supposed to prey solely upon reckless and senile farmers, who, when flush with good crops, drove into town in all the pride and confidence of an absolutely invulnerable stupidity. Hearing at times in circuitous fashion of the despoilment of such a farmer, the important men of Romper invariably laughed in contempt of the victim, and if they thought of the wolf at all, it was with a kind of pride at the knowledge that he would never dare think of attacking their wisdom and courage. Besides, it was popular that this gambler had a real wife and two real children in a neat cottage in a suburb, where he led an exemplary home life; and when any one even suggested a discrepancy in his character, the crowd immediately vociferated descriptions of this virtuous family circle. Then men who led exemplary home lives, and men who did not lead exemplary home lives, all subsided in a bunch, remarking that there was nothing more to be said.

However, when a restriction was placed upon him—as, for instance, when a strong clique of members of the new Pollywog Club refused to permit him, even as a spectator, to appear in the rooms of the organization—the candour and gentleness with which he accepted the judgment disarmed many of his foes and made his friends more desperately partisan. He invariably distinguished between himself and a respectable Romper man so quickly and frankly that his manner actually appeared to be a continual broadcast compliment.

And one must not forget to declare the fundamental fact of his entire position in Romper. It is irrefutable that in all affairs outside his business, in all matters that occur eternally and commonly between man and man, this thieving card-player was so generous, so just, so moral, that, in a contest, he could have put to flight the consciences of nine tenths of the citizens of Romper.

And so it happened that he was seated in this saloon with the two prominent local merchants and the district attorney.

The Swede continued to drink raw whisky, meanwhile babbling at the barkeeper and trying to induce him to indulge in potations. "Come on. Have a drink. Come on. What—no? Well, have a little one, then. By gawd, I've whipped a man to-night, and I want to celebrate. I whipped him good, too. Gentlemen," the Swede cried to the men at the table, "have a drink?"

"Ssh!" said the barkeeper.

The group at the table, although furtively attentive, had been pretending to be deep in talk, but now a man lifted his eyes toward the Swede and said, shortly, "Thanks. We don't want any more."

At this reply the Swede ruffled out his chest like a rooster. "Well," he exploded, "it seems I can't get anybody to drink with me in this town. Seems so, don't it? Well!"

"Ssh!" said the barkeeper.

"Say," snarled the Swede, "don't you try to shut me up. I won't have it. I'm a gentleman, and I want people to drink with me. And I want 'em to drink with me now. *Now*—do you understand?" He rapped the bar with his knuckles.

Years of experience had calloused the bartender. He merely grew sulky. "I hear you," he answered.

"Well," cried the Swede, "listen hard then. See those men over there? Well, they're going to drink with me, and don't you forget it. Now you watch."

"Hi!" yelled the barkeeper, "this won't do!"

"Why won't it?" demanded the Swede. He stalked over to the table, and by chance laid his hand upon the shoulder of the gambler. "How about this?" he asked wrathfully. "I asked you to drink with me."

The gambler simply twisted his head and spoke over his shoulder. "My friend, I don't know you."

"Oh, hell!" answered the Swede, "come and have a drink."

"Now, my boy," advised the gambler, kindly, "take your hand off my shoulder and go 'way and mind your own business." He was a little, slim man, and it seemed strange to hear him use this tone of heroic patronage to the burly Swede. The other men at the table said nothing.

"What! You won't drink with me, you little dude? I'll make you, then! I'll make you!" The Swede had grasped the gambler frenziedly at the throat, and was dragging him from his chair. The other men sprang up. The barkeeper dashed around the corner of his bar. There was a great tumult, and then was seen a long blade in the hand of the gambler. It shot forward, and a human body, this citadel of virtue, wisdom, power, was pierced as easily as if it had been a melon. The Swede fell with a cry of supreme astonishment.

The prominent merchants and the district attorney must have at once tumbled out of the place backward. The bartender found himself hanging limply to the arm of a chair and gazing into the eyes of a murderer.

"Henry," said the latter, as he wiped his knife on one of the towels that hung beneath the bar rail, "you tell 'em where to find me. I'll be home, waiting for 'em." Then he vanished. A moment afterward the barkeeper was in the street dinning through the storm for help and, moreover, companionship.

The corpse of the Swede, alone in the saloon, had its eyes fixed upon a dreadful legend that dwelt atop of the cash-machine: "This registers the amount of your purchase."

IX

Months later, the cowboy was frying pork over the stove of a little ranch near the Dakota line, when there was a quick thud of hoofs outside, and presently the Easterner entered with the letters and the papers.

"Well," said the Easterner at once, "the chap that killed the Swede has got three years. Wasn't much, was it?"

"He has? Three years?" The cowboy poised his pan of pork, while he ruminated upon the news. "Three years. That ain't much."

"No. It was a light sentence," replied the Easterner as he unbuckled his spurs. "Seems there was a good deal of sympathy for him in Romper."

"If the bartender had been any good," observed the cowboy, thoughtfully, "he would have gone in and cracked that there Dutchman on the head with a bottle in the beginnin' of it and stopped all this here murderin'."

"Yes, a thousand things might have happened," said the Easterner, tartly.

The cowboy returned his pan of pork to the fire, but his philosophy continued. "It's funny, ain't it? If he hadn't said Johnnie was cheatin' he'd be alive this minute. He was an awful fool. Game played for fun, too. Not for money. I believe he was crazy."

"I feel sorry for that gambler," said the Easterner.

"Oh, so do I," said the cowboy. "He don't deserve none of it for killin' who he did."

"The Swede might not have been killed if everything had been square."

"Might not have been killed?" exclaimed the cowboy. "Everythin' square? Why, when he said that Johnnie was cheatin' and acted like such a jackass? And then in the saloon he fairly walked up to git hurt?" With these arguments the cowboy browbeat the Easterner and reduced him to rage.

"You're a fool!" cried the Easterner, viciously. "You're a bigger jackass than the Swede by a million majority. Now let me tell you one thing. Let me tell you something. Listen! Johnnie *was* cheating!"

" 'Johnnie'," said the cowboy, blankly. There was a minute of silence, and then he said, robustly. "Why, no. The game was only for fun."

"Fun or not," said the Easterner, "Johnnie was cheating. I saw him. I know it. I saw him. And I refused to stand up and be a man. I let the Swede fight it out alone. And you—you were simply puffing around the place and wanting to fight. And then old Scully himself! We are all in it! This poor gambler isn't even a noun. He is kind of an adverb. Every sin is the result of a collaboration. We, five of us, have collaborated in the murder of this Swede. Usually there are from a dozen to forty women really involved in every murder, but in this case it seems to be only five men—you, I, Johnnie, old Scully; and that fool of an unfortunate gambler came merely as a culmination, the apex of a human movement, and gets all the punishment."

The cowboy, injured and rebellious, cried out blindly into this fog of mysterious theory: "Well, I didn't do anythin', did I?"

Man and nature

To Build a Fire

Jack London
(1876–1916)

*Born in San Francisco, Jack London was the son of Flora
Wellman and W. H. Chaney, who was a linguist and as-
trologer. Soon after his birth, his mother married John
London, a widower with several children of his own.
London worked constantly during his adolescence in order
to help his stepfather support the family. He had two
paper routes on weekdays, worked on an ice wagon Saturdays, and set pins in a bowling alley at night. After his
stepfather was severely injured in a train accident, London
began to work ten to twenty hours a day in a cannery. By
the time he was little more than twenty, London had also
bummed his way around the country, became an expert
sailor, tried his hand as an oyster pirate, sailed to Japan and
the coast of Siberia, and won a writing contest sponsored
by the San Francisco* Call—*all the while reading more
books than most college graduates.*

*London's breakthrough as a professional writer came
when* The Black Cat, *a well-known Eastern magazine, accepted one of his stories for publication, and in 1900 he
achieved national fame with the publication of* The Son of
the Wolf, *his first short-story collection. London soon became internationally popular with the publication of such
novels as* The Call of the Wild (*1903*), The Sea Wolf
(*1904*), White Fang (*1906*), The Iron Heel (*1907*) and
The Valley of the Moon (*1913*).

Day had broken cold and gray, exceedingly cold and gray, when the man turned aside from the main Yukon trail and climbed the high earthbank where a dim and little traveled trail led eastward through the fat spruce timberland. It was a steep bank, and he paused for breath at the top, excusing the act to himself by looking at his watch. It was nine o'clock. There was no sun nor hint of sun, though there was not a cloud in the sky. It was a clear day, and yet there seemed an intangible pall over the face of things, a subtle gloom that made the day dark, and that was due to the absence of sun. This fact did not worry the man. He was used to the lack of sun. It had been days since he had seen the sun, and he knew that a few more days must pass before that cheerful orb, due south, would just peep above the skyline and dip immediately from view.

The man flung a look back along the way he had come. The Yukon lay a mile wide and hidden under three feet of ice. On top of this ice were as many feet of snow. It was all pure white, rolling in gentle undulations where the ice jams of the freeze-up had formed. North and south, as far as his eye could see, it was unbroken white, save for a dark hairline that curved and twisted from around the spruce-covered island to the south, and that curved and twisted away into the north, where it disappeared behind another spruce-covered island. This dark hairline was the trail—the main trail—that led south five hundred miles to the Chilcoot Pass, Dyea, and salt water; and that led north seventy miles to Dawson, and still on to the north a thousand miles to Nulato, and finally to St. Michael on Bering Sea, a thousand miles and half a thousand more.

But all this—that mysterious, far-reaching hairline trail, the absence of sun from the sky, the tremendous cold, and the strangeness and weirdness of it all—made no impression on the man. It was not because he was long used to it. He was a newcomer in the land, a *chechaquo,* and this was his first winter. The trouble with him was that he was without imagination. He was quick and alert in the things of life, but only in the things, and not in the significances. Fifty degrees below zero meant eighty-odd degrees of frost. Such fact impressed him as being cold and uncomfortable, and that was all. It did not lead him to meditate upon his frailty as a creature of temperature, and upon man's frailty in general, able only to live within certain narrow limits of heat and cold; and from there on it did not lead him to the conjectural field of immortality

TO BUILD A FIRE   Reprinted by permission of Irving Shepard, Jack London Ranch, Glen Ellen, California.

and man's place in the universe. Fifty degrees below zero stood for a bite of frost that hurt and that must be guarded against by the use of mittens, ear flaps, warm moccasins, and thick socks. Fifty degrees below zero was to him just precisely fifty degrees below zero. That there should be anything more to it than that was a thought that never entered his head.

As he turned to go on, he spat speculatively. There was a sharp, explosive crackle that startled him. He spat again. And again, in the air, before it could fall to the snow, the spittle crackled. He knew that at fifty below spittle crackled on the snow, but this spittle had crackled in the air. Undoubtedly it was colder than fifty below—how much colder he did not know. But the temperature did not matter. He was bound for the old claim on the left fork of Henderson Creek, where the boys were already. They had come over across the divide from the Indian Creek country, while he had come the roundabout way to take a look at the possibilities of getting out logs in the spring from the islands in the Yukon. He would be in to camp by six o'clock; a bit after dark, it was true, but the boys would be there, a fire would be going, and a hot supper would be ready. As for lunch, he pressed his hand against the protruding bundle under his jacket. It was also under his shirt, wrapped up in a handkerchief and lying against the naked skin. It was the only way to keep the biscuits from freezing. He smiled agreeably to himself as he thought of those biscuits, each cut open and sopped in bacon grease, and each enclosing a generous slice of fried bacon.

He plunged in among the big spruce trees. The trail was faint. A foot of snow had fallen since the last sled had passed over, and he was glad he was without a sled, traveling light. In fact, he carried nothing but the lunch wrapped in the handkerchief. He was surprised, however, at the cold. It certainly was cold, he concluded, as he rubbed his numb nose and cheekbones with his mittened hand. He was a warm-whiskered man, but the hair on his face did not protect the high cheekbones and the eager nose that thrust itself aggressively into the frosty air.

At the man's heels trotted a dog, a big native husky, the proper wolf dog, gray-coated and without any visible or temperamental difference from its brother, the wild wolf. The animal was depressed by the tremendous cold. It knew that it was no time for traveling. Its instinct told it a truer tale than was told to the man by the man's judgment. In reality, it was not merely colder than fifty below zero; it was colder than sixty below, than seventy below. It was seventy-five below zero. Since the freezing point is thirty-two above zero, it meant that one hundred and seven degrees of frost obtained. The dog did not know anything about thermometers. Possibly in its brain there was no sharp consciousness of a condition of very cold such as was in the man's brain. But the brute had its instinct. It experienced a vague but menacing apprehension that subdued it and made it slink along at the man's heels, and that made it question eagerly every unwonted movement of the man as if expecting him to go into camp or to seek shelter somewhere and build a fire. The dog had learned fire, and it wanted fire, or else to burrow under the snow and cuddle its warmth away from the air.

The frozen moisture of its breathing had settled on its fur in a fine powder of frost, and especially were its jowls, muzzle, and eyelashes whitened by its crystaled breath. The man's red beard and mustache were likewise frosted, but more solidly, the deposit taking the form of ice and increasing with every warm, moist breath he exhaled. Also, the man was chewing tobacco, and the muzzle of ice held his lips so rigidly that he was unable to clear his chin when he expelled the juice. The result was that a crystal beard of the color and solidity of amber was increasing its length on his chin. If he fell down it would shatter itself, like glass, into brittle fragments. But he did not mind the appendage. It was the penalty all tobacco chewers paid in that country, and he had been out before in two cold snaps. They had not been so cold as this, he knew, but by the spirit thermometer at Sixty Mile he knew they had been registered at fifty below and at fifty-five.

He held on through the level stretch of woods for several miles, crossed a wide flat of niggerheads, and dropped down a bank to the frozen bed of a small stream. This was Henderson Creek, and he knew he was ten miles from the forks. He looked at his watch. It was ten o'clock. He was making four miles an hour, and he calculated that he would arrive at the forks at half-past twelve. He decided to celebrate that event by eating his lunch there.

The dog dropped in again at his heels, with a tail drooping discouragement, as the man swung along the creek bed. The furrow of the old sled trail was plainly visible, but a dozen inches of snow covered the marks of the last runners. In a month no man had come up or down that silent creek. The man held steadily on. He was not much given to thinking, and just then particularly he had nothing to think about save that he would eat lunch at the forks and that at six o'clock he would be in camp with the boys. There was nobody to talk to; and, had there been, speech would have been impossible because of the ice muzzle on his mouth. So he continued monotonously to chew tobacco and to increase the length of his amber beard.

Once in a while the thought reiterated itself that it was very cold and that he had never experienced such cold. As he walked along he rubbed his cheekbones and nose with the back of his mittened hand. He did this automatically, now and again changing hands. But rub as he would, the instant he stopped his cheekbones went numb, and the following instant the end of his nose went numb. He was sure to frost his cheeks; he knew that, and experienced a pang of regret that he had not devised a nose strap of the sort Bud wore in cold snaps. Such a strap passed across the cheeks, as well, and saved them. But it didn't matter much, after all. What were frosted cheeks? A bit painful, that was all; they were never serious.

Empty as a man's mind was of thoughts, he was keenly observant, and he noticed the changes in the creek, the curves and bends and timber jams, and always he sharply noted where he placed his feet. Once, coming around a bend, he shied abruptly, like a startled horse, curved away from the place where he had been walking, and retreated several paces back along the trail. The creek he knew was frozen clear to the bottom—no creek could contain water in that arctic winter—but he knew also that there were springs that bubbled out from the hillsides and ran along under the snow and on top the ice of the creek. He knew that the coldest snaps never froze these springs, and he knew likewise their danger. They were traps. They hid pools of water under the snow that might be three inches deep, or three feet. Sometimes a skin of ice half an inch thick covered them, and in turn was covered by the snow. Sometimes there were alternate layers of water and ice skin, so that when one broke through he kept on breaking through for a while, sometimes wetting himself to the waist.

That was why he had shied in such panic. He had felt the give under his feet and heard the crackle of a snow-hidden ice skin. And to get his feet wet in such a temperature meant trouble and danger. At the very least it meant delay, for he would be forced to stop and build a fire, and under its protection to bare his feet while he dried his socks and moccasins. He stood and studied the creek bed and its banks, and decided that the flow of water came from the right. He reflected awhile, rubbing his nose and cheeks, then skirted to the left, stepping gingerly and testing the footing for each step. Once clear of the danger, he took a fresh chew of tobacco and swung along at his four-mile gait.

In the course of the next two hours he came upon several similar traps. Usually the snow above the hidden pools had a sunken, candied appearance that advertised the danger. Once again, however, he had a close call; and once, suspecting danger, he compelled the dog to go in front. The dog did not want to go. It hung back until the man shoved it forward, and then it went quickly across the white, unbroken surface. Suddenly it broke through, floundered to one side, and got away to firmer footing. It had wet its forefeet and legs, and almost immediately the water that clung to it turned to ice. It made quick efforts to lick the ice off its legs, then dropped down in the snow and began to bite out the ice that had formed between the toes. This was a matter of instinct. To permit the ice to remain would mean sore feet. It did not know this. It merely obeyed the mysterious prompting that arose from the deep crypts of its being. But the man knew, having achieved a judgment on the subject, and he removed the mitten from his right hand and helped tear out the ice-particles. He did not expose his fingers more than a minute, and was astonished at the swift numbness that smote them. It certainly was cold. He pulled on the mitten hastily, and beat the hand savagely across his chest.

At twelve o'clock the day was at its brightest. Yet the sun was too far south on its winter journey to clear the horizon. The bulge of the earth intervened between it and Henderson Creek, where the man walked under a clear sky at noon and cast no shadow. At half-past twelve, to the minute, he arrived at the forks of the creek. He was pleased at the speed he had made. If he kept it up, he would certainly be with the boys by six. He unbuttoned his jacket and shirt and drew forth his lunch. The action consumed no more than a quarter of a minute, yet in that brief moment the numbness laid hold of the exposed fingers. He did not put the mitten on, but, instead, struck the fingers a dozen sharp smashes against his leg. Then he sat down on a snow-covered log to eat. The sting that followed upon the striking of his fingers against his leg ceased so quickly that he was startled. He had had no chance to take a bite of biscuit. He struck the fingers repeatedly and returned them to the mitten, baring the other hand for the purpose of eating. He tried to take a mouthful, but the ice muzzle prevented. He had forgotten to build a fire and thaw out. He chuckled at his foolishness, and as he chuckled he noted the numbness creeping into the exposed fingers. Also, he noted that the stinging which had first come to his toes when he sat down was already passing away. He wondered whether the toes were warm or numb. He moved them inside the moccasins and decided that they were numb.

He pulled the mitten on hurriedly and stood up. He was a bit frightened. He stamped up and down until the stinging returned into the feet. It certainly was cold, was his thought. That man from Sulphur Creek had spoken the truth when telling how cold it sometimes got in the country. And he had laughed at him at the time! That showed one must not be too sure of things. There was no mistake about it, it *was* cold. He strode up and down, stamping his feet and threshing his arms, until reassured by the returning warmth. Then he got out matches and proceeded to make a fire.

From the undergrowth, where high water of the previous spring had lodged a supply of seasoned twigs, he got his firewood. Working carefully from a small beginning, he soon had a roaring fire, over which he thawed the ice from his face and in the protection of which he ate his biscuits. For the moment the cold of space was outwitted. The dog took satisfaction in the fire, stretching out close enough for warmth and far enough away to escape being singed.

When the man had finished, he filled his pipe and took his comfortable time over a smoke. Then he pulled on his mittens, settled the earflaps of his cap firmly about his ears, and took the creek trail up the left fork. The dog was disappointed and yearned back toward the fire. This man did not know cold. Possibly all the generations of his ancestry had been ignorant of cold, of real cold, of cold one hundred and seven degrees below freezing point. But the dog knew; all its ancestry knew, and it had inherited the knowledge. And it knew that it was not good to walk abroad in such fearful cold. It was the time to lie snug in a hole in the snow and wait for a curtain of cloud to be drawn across the face of outer space whence this cold came. On the other hand, there was no keen intimacy between the dog and the man. The one was the toil slave of the other, and the only caresses it had ever received were the caresses of the whiplash and of harsh and menacing throat sounds that threatened the whiplash. So the dog made no effort to communicate its apprehension to the man. It was not concerned in the welfare of the man; it was for its own sake that it yearned back toward the fire. But the man whistled, and spoke to it with the sound of whiplashes, and the dog swung in at the man's heels and followed after.

The man took a chew of tobacco and proceeded to start a new amber beard. Also, his moist breath quickly powdered with white his mustache, eyebrows, and lashes. There did not seem to be so many springs on the left fork of the Henderson, and for half an hour the man saw no signs of any. And then it happened. At a place where there were no signs, where the soft, unbroken snow seemed to advertise solidity beneath, the man broke through. It was not deep. He wet himself halfway to the knees before he floundered out to the firm crust.

He was angry, and cursed his luck aloud. He had hoped to get into camp with the boys at six o'clock, and this would delay him an hour, for he would have to build a fire and dry out his footgear. This was imperative at that low temperature—he knew that much; and he turned aside to the bank, which he climbed. On top, tangled in the underbrush about the trunks of several small spruce trees, was a high-water deposit of dry firewood—sticks and twigs, principally, but also larger portions of seasoned branches and fine, dry, last year's grasses. He threw down several large pieces on top of the snow. This served for a foundation and prevented the young flame from drowning itself in the snow it otherwise would melt. The flame he got by touching a match to a small shred of birch bark that he took from his pocket. This burned even more readily than paper. Placing it on the foundation, he fed the young flame, with wisps of dry grass and with the tiniest dry twigs.

He worked slowly and carefully, keenly aware of his danger. Gradually, as the flame grew stronger, he increased the size of the twigs with which he fed it. He squatted in the snow, pulling the twigs out from their entanglement in the brush and feeding directly to the flame. He know there must be no failure. When it is seventy-five below zero, a man must not fail in his first attempt to build a fire—that is, if his feet are wet. If his feet are dry, and he fails, he can run along the trail for a half a mile and restore his circulation. But the circulation of wet and freezing feet cannot be restored by running when it is seventy-five below. No matter how fast he runs, the wet feet will freeze the harder.

All this the man knew. The old-timer on Sulphur Creek had told him about it the previous fall, and now he was appreciating the advice. Already all sensation had gone out of his feet. To build the fire he had been forced to remove his mittens, and the fingers had quickly gone numb. His pace of four miles an hour had kept his heart pumping blood to the surface of his body and to all the extremities. But the instant he stopped, the action of the pump eased down. The cold of space smote the unprotected tip of the planet, and he, being on that unprotected tip, received the full force of the blow. The blood of his body recoiled before it. The blood was alive, like the dog, and like the dog it wanted to hide away and cover itself up from the fearful cold. So long as he walked four miles an hour, he pumped that blood, willy-nilly, to the surface; but now it ebbed away and sank down into the re-cesses of his body. The extremities were the first to feel its ab-scence. His wet feet froze the faster, and his exposed fingers numbed the faster, though they had not yet begun to freeze. Nose and cheeks were already freezing, while the skin of all his body chilled as it lost its blood.

But he was safe. Toes and nose and cheeks would be only touched by the frost, for the fire was beginning to burn with strength. He was feeding it with twigs the size of his finger. In another minute he would be able to fed it with branches the size of his wrist, and then he could remove his wet foot-gear, and, while it dried, he could keep his naked feet warm by the fire, rubbing them at first, of course, with snow. The fire was a success. He was safe. He remembered the advice of the old-timer on Sulphur Creek, and smiled. The old-timer had been very serious in laying down the law that no man must travel alone in the Klondike after fifty below. Well, there he was; he had had the accident; he was alone; and he had saved himself. Those old-timers were rather womanish, some of them, he thought. All a man had to do was to keep his head, and he was all right. Any man who was a man could travel alone. But it was surprising, the rapidity with which his cheeks and nose were freezing. And he had not thought his fingers could go lifeless in so short a time. Lifeless they were, for he could scarcely make them move together to grip a twig, and they seemed remote from his body and from him. When he touched a twig, he had to look and see whether or not he had hold of it. The wires were pretty well down between him and his finger ends.

All of which counted for little. There was the fire, snapping and crackling and promising life with every dancing flame. He started to untie his moccasins. They were coated with ice; the thick German socks were like sheaths of iron halfway to the knees; and the moccasin strings were like rods of steel all twisted and knotted as by some conflagration. For a moment he tugged with his numb fingers, then, realizing the folly of it, he drew his sheath knife.

But before he could cut the strings, it happened. It was his own fault or, rather, his mistake. He should not have built the fire under the spruce tree. He should have built it in the open. But it had been easier to pull the twigs from the brush and drop them directly on the fire. Now the tree under which he had done this carried a weight of snow on its boughs. No wind had blown for weeks, and each bough was fully freighted. Each time he had pulled a twig he had communicated a slight agitation to the tree— an imperceptible agitation, so far as he was concerned, but an agitation sufficient to bring about the disaster. High up in the tree one bough capsized its load of snow. This fell on the boughs beneath, capsizing them. This process continued, spreading out and involving the whole tree. It grew like an avalanche, and it descended without warning upon the man and the fire, and the fire was blotted out! Where it had burned was a mantle of fresh and disordered snow.

The man was shocked. It was as though he had just heard his own sentence of death. For a moment he sat and stared at the spot where the fire had been. Then he grew very calm. Perhaps the old-timer on Sulphur Creek was right. If he only had a trail mate he would have been in no danger now. The trail mate could have built the fire. Well, it was up to him to build the fire over again, and this second time there must be no failure. Even if he succeeded, he would most likely lose some toes. His feet must be badly frozen by now, and there would be some time before the second fire was ready.

Such were his thoughts, but he did not sit and think them. He was busy all the time they were passing through his mind. He made a new foundation for a fire, this time in the open, where no treacherous tree could blot it out. Next, he gathered dry grasses and tiny twigs from the high-water flotsam. He could not bring his fingers together to pull them out, but he was able to gather them by the handful. In this way he got many rotten twigs and bits of green moss that were undesirable, but it was the best he could do. He worked methodically, even collecting an armful of the larger branches to be used later when the fire gathered strength. And all the while the dog sat and watched him, a certain yearning wistfulness in its eyes, for it looked upon him as the fire provider, and the fire was slow in coming.

When all was ready, the man reached in his pocket for a second piece of birch bark. He knew the bark was there, and, though he could not feel it with his fingers, he could hear its crisp rustling as he fumbled for it. Try as he would, he could not clutch hold of it. And all the time, in his consciousness, was the knowledge that each instant his feet were freezing. This thought tended to put him in a panic, but he fought against it and kept calm. He pulled on his mittens with his teeth, and threshed his arms back and forth, beating his hands with all his might against his sides. He did this sitting down, and he stood up to do it; and all the while the dog sat in the snow, its wolf brush of a tail curled around warmly over its forefeet, its sharp wolf ears pricked forward intently as it watched the man. And the man, as he beat and threshed with his arms and hands, felt a great surge of envy as he regarded the creature that was warm and secure in its natural covering.

After a time he was aware of the first faraway signals of sensation in his beaten fingers. The faint tingling grew stronger till it evolved into a stinging ache that was excruciating, but which the man hailed with satisfaction. He stripped the mitten from his right hand and fetched forth the birch bark. The exposed fingers were quickly going numb again. Next he brought out his bunch of sulphur matches. But the tremendous cold had already driven the life out of his fingers. In his effort to separate one match from the others, the whole bunch fell in the snow. He tried to pick it out of the snow, but failed. The dead fingers could neither touch nor clutch. He was very careful. He drove the thought of his freezing feet, and nose, and cheeks, out of his mind, devoting his whole soul to the matches. He watched, using the sense of vision in place of that of touch, and when he saw his fingers on each side of the bunch, he closed them—that is, he willed to close them, for the wires were down, and the fingers did not obey. He pulled the mitten on the right hand, and beat it fiercely against his knee. Then, with both mittened hands, he scooped the bunch of matches, along with much snow, into his lap. Yet he was no better off.

After some manipulation he managed to get the bunch between the heels of his mittened hands. In this fashion he carried it to his mouth. The ice crackled and snapped when by a violent effort he opened his mouth. He drew the lower jaw in, curled the upper lip out of the way, and scraped the bunch with his upper teeth in order to separate a match. He succeeded in getting one, which he dropped on his lap. He was no better off. He could not pick it up. Then he devised a way. He picked it up in his teeth and scratched it on his leg. Twenty times he scratched before he succeeded in lighting it. As it flamed he held it with his teeth to the birch bark. But the burning brimstone went up his nostrils and into his lungs, causing him to cough spasmodically. The match fell into the snow and went out.

The old-timer on Sulphur Creek was right, he thought in the moment of controlled despair that ensued: after fifty below, a man should travel with a parner. He beat his hands, but failed in exciting any sensation. Suddenly he bared both hands, removing the mittens with his teeth. He caught the whole bunch between the heels of his hands. His arm muscles not being frozen enabled him to press the hand heels tightly against the matches. Then he scratched the bunch along his leg. It flared into flame, seventy sulphur matches at once! There was no wind to blow them out. He kept his head to one side to escape the strangling fumes, and held the blazing bunch to the birch bark. As he so held it, he became aware of sensation in his hand. His flesh was burning. He could smell it. Deep down below the surface he could feel it. The sensation developed into pain that grew acute. And still he endured it, holding the flame of the matches clumsily to the bark that would not light readily because his own burning hands were in the way, absorbing most of the flame.

At last, when he could endure no more, he jerked his hands apart. The blazing matches fell sizzling into the snow, but the birch bark was alight. He began laying dry grasses and the tiniest twigs on the flame. He could not pick and choose, for he had to lift the fuel between the heels of his hands. Small pieces of rotten wood and green moss clung to the twigs, and he bit them off as well as he could with his teeth. He cherished the flame carefully and awkwardly. It meant life, and it must not perish. The withdrawal of blood from the surface of his body now made him begin to shiver, and he grew more awkward. A large piece of green moss fell squarely on the little fire. He tried to poke it out with his fingers, but his shivering frame make him poke too far, and he disrupted the nucleus of the little fire, the burning grasses and tiny twigs separating and scattering. He tried to poke them together again, but in spite of the tenseness of the effort, his shivering got away with him, and the twigs were hopelessly scattered. Each twig gushed a puff of smoke and went out. The fire provider had failed. As he looked apathetically about him, his eyes chanced on the dog, sitting across the ruins of the fire from him, in the snow, making restless, hunching movements, slightly lifting one forefoot and then the other, shifting its weight back and forth on them with wistful eagerness.

The sight of the dog put a wild idea into his head. He remembered the tale of the man, caught in a blizzard, who killed a steer and crawled inside the carcass, and so was saved. He would kill the dog and bury his hands in the warm body until the numbness went out of them. Then he could build another fire. He spoke to the dog, calling it to him; but in his voice was a strange note of fear that frightened the animal, who had never known the man to speak in such way before. Something was the matter, and its suspicious nature sensed danger—it knew not what danger, but somewhere, somehow, in its brain arose an apprehension of the man. It flattened its ears down at the sound of the man's voice, and its restless, hunching movements and the liftings and shiftings of its forefeet became more pronounced; but it would not come to the man. He got on his hands and knees and crawled toward the dog. This unusual posture again excited suspicion, and the animal sidled mincingly away.

The man sat up in the snow for a moment and struggled for calmness. Then he pulled on his mittens, by means of his teeth, and got upon his feet. He glanced down at first in order to assure himself that he was really standing up, for the absence of sensation in his feet left him unrelated to the earth. His erect position in itself started to drive the webs of suspicion from the dog's mind; and when he spoke peremptorily, with the sound of whiplashes in his voice, the dog rendered its customary allegiance and came to him. As it came within reaching distance, the man lost his control. His arms flashed out to the dog, and he experienced genuine surprise when he discovered that his hands could not clutch, that there was neither bend nor feeling in the fingers. He had forgotten for the moment that they were frozen and that they were freezing more and more. All this happened quickly, and before the animal could get away, he encircled its body with his arms. He sat down in the snow, and in this fashion held the dog, while it snarled and whined and struggled.

But it was all he could do, hold its body encircled in his arms and sit there. He realized that he could not kill the dog. There was no way to do it. With his helpless hands he could neither draw nor hold his sheath knife nor throttle the animal. He released it, and it plunged wildly away, with tail between its legs, and still snarling. It halted forty feet away and surveyed him curiously, with ears sharply pricked forward. The man looked down at his hands in order to locate them, and found them hanging on the ends of his arms. It struck him as curious that one should have to use his eyes in order to find out where his hands were. He began threshing his arms back and forth, beating the mittened hands against his sides. He did this for five minutes, violently, and his heart pumped enough blood up to the surface to put a stop to his shivering. But no sensation was aroused in the hands. He had an impression that they hung like weights on the ends of his arms, but when he tried to run the impression down, he could not find it.

A certain fear of death, dull and oppressive, came to him. This fear quickly became poignant as he realized that it was no longer a mere matter of freezing his fingers and toes, or of losing his hands and feet, but that it was a matter of life and death with the chances against him. This threw him into a panic, and he turned and ran up the creek bed along the old, dim trail. The dog joined in behind and kept up with him. He ran blindly, without intention, in fear such as he had never known in his life. Slowly, as he plowed and floundered through the snow, he began to see things again—the banks of the creek, the old timber jams, the leafless aspens, and the sky. The running made him feel better. He did not shiver. Maybe, if he ran on, his feet would thaw out; and anyway, if he ran far enough, he would reach camp and the boys. Without doubt he would lose some fingers and toes and some of his face; but the boys would take care of him, and save the rest of him when he got there. And at the same time there was another thought in his mind that said he would never get to the camp and the boys; that it was too many miles away, that the freezing had too great a start on him, and that he would soon be stiff and dead. This thought he kept in the background and refused to consider. Sometimes it pushed itself forward and demanded to be heard, but he thrust it back and strove to think of other things.

It struck him as curious that he could run at all on feet so frozen that he could not feel them when they struck the earth and took the weight of his body. He seemed to himself to skim along above the surface, and to have no connection with the earth. Somewhere he had once seen a winged Mercury, and he wondered if Mercury felt as he felt when skimming over the earth.

His theory of running until he reached camp and the boys had one flaw in it: he lacked the endurance. Several times he stumbled, and finally he tottered, crumpled up, and fell. When he tried to rise, he failed. He must sit and rest, he decided, and next time he would merely walk and keep on going. As he sat and regained his breath, he noted that he was feeling quite warm and comfortable. He was not shivering, and it even seemed that a warm glow had come to his chest and trunk. And yet, when he touched his nose or cheeks, there was no sensation. Running would not thaw them out. Nor would it thaw out his hands and feet. Then the thought came to him that the frozen portions of his body must be extending. He tried to keep this thought down, to forget it, to think of something else; he was aware of the panicky feeling that it caused, and he was afraid of the panic. But the thought asserted itself, and persisted, until it produced a vision of his body totally frozen. This was too much, and he made another wild run along the trail. Once he slowed down to a walk, but the thought of the freezing extending itself made him run again.

And all the time the dog ran with him, at his heels. When he fell down a second time, it curled its tail over its forefeet and sat in front of him, facing him, curiously eager and intent. The warmth and security of the animal angered him, and he cursed it till it flattened down its ears appeasingly. This time the shivering came more quickly upon the man. He was losing in his battle with the frost. It was creeping into his body from all sides. The thought of it drove him on, but he ran no more than a hundred feet, when he staggered and pitched headlong. It was his last panic. When he had recovered his breath and control, he sat up and entertained in his mind the conception of meeting death with dignity. However, the conception did not come to him in such terms. His idea of it was that he had been making a fool of himself, running around like a chicken with its head cut off—such was the simile that occurred to him. Well, he was bound to freeze anyway, and he might as well take it decently. With the new-found peace of mind came the first glimmerings of drowsiness. A good idea, he thought, to sleep off to death. It was like taking an anesthetic. Freezing was not so bad as people thought. There were lots worse ways to die.

He pictured the boys finding his body next day. Suddenly he found himself with them, coming along the trail and looking for himself. And, still with them, he came around a turn in the trail and found himself lying in the snow. He did not belong with himself any more, for even then he was out of himself, standing with the boys and looking at himself in the snow. It certainly was cold, was his thought. When he got back to the States he could tell the folks what real cold was. He drifted on from this to a vision of the old-timer on Sulphur Creek. He could see him quite clearly, warm and comfortable and smoking a pipe.

"You were right, old hoss; you were right," the man mumbled to the old-timer of Sulphur Creek.

Then the man drowsed off into what seemed to him the most comfortable and satisfying sleep he had ever known. The dog sat facing him and waiting. The brief day drew to a close in a long, slow twilight. There were no signs of a fire to be made, and, besides, never in the dog's experience had it known a man to sit like that in the snow and make no fire. As the twilight drew on, its eager yearning for the fire mastered it, and with a great lifting and shifting of forefeet, it whined softly, then flattened its ears down in anticipation of being chidden by the man. But the man remained silent. Later, the dog whined loudly. And still later it crept close to the man and caught the scent of death. This made the animal bristle and back away. A little longer it delayed, howling under the stars that leaped and danced and shone brightly in the cold sky. Then it turned and trotted up the trail in the direction of the camp it knew, where were the other food providers and fire providers.

The Ledge

Lawrence Sargent Hall
(b. 1915)

Lawrence Sargent Hall was born in Haverhill, Massachu-
setts. He graduated in 1936 from Bowdoin College in
Brunswick, Maine, and received a doctorate from Yale in
1941. After teaching briefly at Ohio University, Hall
joined the United States Naval Reserve. A teacher of
English and history at the United States Naval Academy
during 1942 and 1943, he was later assigned to sea duty
and obtained the rank of Lieutenant Commander. In 1946
Hall returned to Bowdoin College as assistant professor;
he has since become Chapman Professor of English and
Chairman of the English Department. Hall is a scholar,
novelist, and short-story writer who has published such
diverse works as Hawthorne: Critic of Society (*1943*), *a*
scholarly study; Stowaway (*1961*), *a novel which won the*
Faulkner Award; and "The Ledge," which won the O.
Henry Memorial Award for 1960.

On Christmas morning before sunup the fisherman embraced his warm wife and left his close bed. She did not want him to go. It was Christmas morning. He was a big, raw man, with too much strength, whose delight in winter was to hunt the sea ducks that flew in to feed by the outer ledges, bare at low tide.

As his bare feet touched the cold floor and the frosty air struck his nude flesh, he might have changed his mind in the dark of this special day. It was a home day, which made it seem natural to think of the outer ledges merely as some place he had shot ducks in the past. But he had promised his son, thirteen, and his nephew, fifteen, who came from inland. That was why he had given them his present of an automatic shotgun each the night before, on Christmas Eve. Rough man though he was known to be, and no spoiler of boys, he kept his promises when he understood what they meant. And to the boys, as to him, home meant where you came for rest after you had had your Christmas fill of action and excitement.

His legs astride, his arms raised, the fisherman stretched as high as he could in the dim privacy of his bedroom. Above the snug murmur of his wife's protest he heard the wind in the pines and knew it was easterly as the boys had hoped and he had surmised the night before. Conditions would be ideal, and when they were, anybody ought to take advantage of them. The birds would be flying. The boys would get a man's sport their first time outside on the ledges.

His son at thirteen, small but steady and experienced, was fierce to grow up in hunting, to graduate from sheltered waters and the blinds along the shores of the inner bay. His nephew at fifteen, an overgrown farm boy, had a farm boy's love of the sea, though he could not swim a stroke and was often sick in choppy weather. That was the reason his father, the fisherman's brother, was a farmer and chose to sleep in on the holiday morning at his brother's house. Many of the ones the farmer had grown up with were regularly seasick and could not swim, but they were unafraid of the water. They could not have dreamed of being anything but fishermen. The fisherman himself could swim like a seal and was never sick, and he would sooner die than be anything else.

He dressed in the cold and dark, and woke the boys gruffly. They tumbled out of bed, their instincts instantly awake while their thoughts still fumbled slumbrously. The fisherman's wife in the adjacent bedroom heard them apparently trying to find their clothes, mumbling sleepily and happily to each other, while her husband went down to the hot kitchen to fry eggs—sunny-side up, she knew, because that was how they all liked them.

Always in the winter she hated to have them go outside, the weather was so treacherous and there were so few others out in case of trouble. To the fisherman these were no more than woman's fears, to be taken for granted and laughed off. When they were first married they fought miserably every fall because she was after him constantly to put up his boat until spring. The fishing was all outside in winter, and though prices were high the storms made the rate of attrition high on gear. Nevertheless he did well. So she could do nothing with him.

People thought him a hard man, and gave him the reputation of being all out for himself because he was inclined to brag and be disdainful. If it was true, and his own brother was one of those who strongly felt it was, they lived better than others, and his brother had small right to criticize. There had been times when in her loneliness she had yearned to leave him for another man. But it would have been dangerous. So over the years she had learned to shut her mind to his hard-driving, and take what comfort she might from his unsympathetic competence. Only once or twice, perhaps, had she gone so far as to dwell guiltily on what it would be like to be a widow.

The thought that her boy, possibly because he was small, would not be insensitive like his father, and the rattle of dishes and smell of frying bacon downstairs in the kitchen shut off from the rest of the chilly house, restored the cozy feeling she had had before she was alone in bed. She heard them after a while go out and shut the back door.

Under her window she heard the snow grind drily beneath their boots, and her husband's sharp, exasperated commands to the boys. She shivered slightly in the envelope of her own warmth. She listened to the noise of her son and nephew talking elatedly. Twice she caught the glimmer of their lights on the white ceiling above the window as they went down the path to the shore. There would be frost on the skiff and freezing suds at the water's edge. She herself used to go gunning when she was younger; now, it seemed to her, anyone going out like that on Christmas morning had to be incurably male. They would none of them think about her until they returned and piled the birds they had shot on top of the sink for her to dress.

Ripping into the quiet pre-dawn cold she heard the hot snarl of the outboard taking them out to the boat. It died as abruptly as it had burst into life. Two or three or four or five minutes later the big engine broke into a warm reassuring roar. He had the best of equipment, and he kept it in the best of condition. She closed her eyes. It would not be too long before the others would be up for Christmas. The summer drone of the exhaust deepened. Then gradually it faded in the wind until it was lost at sea, or she slept.

The engine had started immediately in spite of the temperature. This put the fisherman in a good mood. He was proud of his boat. Together he and the two boys heaved the skiff and outboard onto the stern and secured it athwartships. His son went forward along the deck, iridescent in the ray of the light the nephew shone through the windshield, and cast the mooring pennant loose into darkness. The fisherman swung to starboard, glanced at his compass, and headed seaward down the obscure bay.

There would be just enough visibility by the time they reached the headland to navigate the crooked channel between the islands. It was the only nasty stretch of water. The fisherman had done it often in the fog or at night—he always swore he could go anywhere in the bay blindfolded—but there was no sense in taking chances if you didn't have to. From the mouth of the channel he could lay a straight course for Brown Cow Island, anchor the boat out of sight behind it, and from the skiff set their tollers off Devil's Hump three hundred yards to seaward. By then the tide would be clearing the ledge and they could land and be ready to shoot around half-tide.

It was early, it was Christmas, and it was farther out than most hunters cared to go in this season of the closing year, so that he felt sure no one would be taking possession ahead of them. He had shot thousands of ducks there in his day. The Hump was by far the best hunting. Only thing was you had to plan for the right conditions because you didn't have too much time. About four hours was all, and you had to get it before three in the afternoon when the birds left and went out to sea ahead of nightfall.

They had it figured exactly right for today. The ledge would not be going under until after the gunning was over, and they would be home for supper in good season. With a little luck the boys would have a skiff-load of birds to show for their first time outside. Well beyond the legal limit, which was no matter. You took what you could get in this life, or the next man made out and you didn't.

The fisherman had never failed to make out gunning from Devil's Hump. And this trip, he had a hunch, would be above ordinary. The easterly wind would come up just stiff enough, the tide was right, and it was going to storm by tomorrow morning so the birds would be moving. Things were perfect.

The old fierceness was in his bones. Keeping a weather eye to the murk out front and a hand on the wheel, he reached over and cuffed both boys playfully as they stood together close to the heat of the exhaust pipe running up through the center of the house. They poked back at him and shouted above the drumming engine, making bets as they always did on who would shoot the most birds. This trip they had the thrill of new guns, the best money could buy, and a man's hunting ground. The black retriever wagged at them and barked. He was too old and arthritic to be allowed in December water, but he was jaunty anyway at being brought along.

Groping in his pocket for his pipe the fisherman suddenly had his high spirits rocked by the discovery that he had left his tobacco at home. He swore. Anticipation of a day out with nothing to smoke made him incredulous. He searched his clothes, and then he searched them again, unable to believe the tobacco was not somewhere. When the boys inquired what was wrong he spoke angrily to them, blaming them for being in some devious way at fault. They were instantly crestfallen and willing to put back after the tobacco, though they could appreciate what it meant only through his irritation. But he bitterly refused. That would throw everything out of phase. He was a man who did things the way he set out to do.

He clamped his pipe between his teeth, and twice more during the next few minutes he ransacked his clothes in disbelief. He was no stoic. For one relaxed moment he considered putting about and gunning somewhere nearer home. Instead he held his course and sucked the empty pipe, consoling himself with the reflection that at least he had whiskey enough if it got too uncomfortable on the ledge. Peremptorily he made the boys check to make certain the bottle was really in the knapsack with the lunches where he thought he had taken care to put it. When they reassured him he despised his fate a little less.

The fisherman's judgment was as usual accurate. By the time they were abreast of the headland there was sufficient light so that he could wind his way among the reefs without slackening speed. At last he turned his bow toward open ocean, and as the winter dawn filtered upward through long layers of smoky cloud on the eastern rim his spirits rose again with it.

He opened the throttle, steadied on his course, and settled down to the two hour run. The wind was stronger but seemed less cold coming from the sea. The boys had withdrawn from the fisherman and were talking together while they watched the sky through the windows. The boat churned solidly through a light chop, flinging spray off her flaring bow. Astern the headland thinned rapidly till it lay like a blackened sill on the grey water. No other boats were abroad.

The boys fondled their new guns, sighted along the barrels, worked the mechanisms, compared notes, boasted, and gave each other contradictory advice. The fisherman got their attention once and pointed at the horizon. They peered through the windows and saw what looked like a black scum floating on top of gently agitated water. It wheeled and tilted, rippled, curled, then rose, strung itself out and became a huge raft of ducks escaping over the sea. A good sign.

The boys rushed out and leaned over the washboards in the wind and spray to see the flock curl below the horizon. Then they went and hovered around the hot engine, bewailing their lot. If only they had been already set out and waiting. Maybe these ducks would be crazy enough to return later and be slaughtered. Ducks were known to be foolish.

In due course and right on schedule they anchored at mid-morning in the lee of Brown Cow Island. They put the skiff overboard and loaded it with guns, knapsacks, and tollers. The boys showed their eagerness by being clumsy. The fisherman showed his in bad temper and abuse which they silently accepted in the absorbed tolerance of being boys. No doubt they laid it to lack of tobacco.

By outboard they rounded the island and pointed due east in the direction of a ridge of foam which could be seen whitening the surface three hundred yards away. They set the decoys in a broad, straddling vee opening wide into the ocean. The fisherman warned them not to get their hands wet, and when they did he made them carry on with red and painful fingers, in order to teach them. Once the last toller was bobbing among his fellows, brisk and alluring, they got their numbed fingers inside their oilskins and hugged their warm crotches. In the meantime the fisherman had turned the skiff toward the patch of foam where as if by magic, like a black glossy rib of earth, the ledge had broken through the belly of the sea.

Carefully they inhabited their slippery nub of the North American continent, while the unresting Atlantic swelled and swirled as it had for eons around the indomitable edges. They hauled the skiff after them, established themselves as comfortably as they could in a shallow sump on top, lay on their sides a foot or so above the water, and waited, guns in hand.

In time the fisherman took a thermos bottle from the knapsack and they drank steaming coffee, and waited for the nodding decoys to lure in the first flight to the rock. Eventually the boys got hungry and restless. The fisherman let them open the picnic lunch and eat one sandwich apiece, which they both shared with the dog. Having no tobacco the fisherman himself would not eat.

Actually the day was relatively mild, and they were warm enough at present in their woollen clothes and socks underneath oilskins and hip boots. After a while, however, the boys began to feel cramped. Their nerves were agonized by inactivity. The nephew complained and was severely told by the fisherman—who pointed to the dog, crouched unmoving except for his white-rimmed eyes—that part of doing a man's hunting was learning how to wait. But he was beginning to have misgivings of his own. This could be one of those days where all the right conditions masked an incalculable flaw.

If the fisherman had been alone, as he often was, stopping off when the necessary coincidence of tide and time occurred on his way home from hauling trawls, and had plenty of tobacco, he would not have fidgeted. The boys' being nervous made him nervous. He growled at them again. When it came it was likely to come all at once, and then in a few moments be over. He warned them not to slack off, never to slack off, to be always ready. Under his rebuke they kept their tortured peace, though they could not help shifting and twisting until he lost what patience he had left and bullied them into lying still. A duck could see an eyelid twitch. If the dog could go without moving so could they.

"Here it comes!" the fisherman said tersely at last.

The boys quivered with quick relief. The flock came in downwind, quartering slightly, myriad, black, and swift.

"Beautiful——" breathed the fisherman's son.

"All right," said the fisherman, intense and precise. "Aim at singles in the thickest part of the flock. Wait for me to fire and then don't stop shooting till your gun's empty." He rolled up onto his left elbow and spread his legs to brace himself. The flock bore down, arrowy and vibrant, then a hundred yards beyond the decoys it veered off.

"They're going away!" the boys cried, sighting in.

"Not yet!" snapped the fisherman. "They're coming round."

The flock changed shape, folded over itself, and drove into the wind in a tight arc. "Thousands——" the boys hissed through their teeth. All at once a whistling storm of black and white broke over the decoys.

"Now!" the fisherman shouted. "Perfect!" And he opened fire at the flock just as it hung suspended in momentary chaos above the tollers. The three pulled at their triggers and the birds splashed into the water, until the last report went off unheard, the last smoking shell flew unheeded over their shoulders, and the last of the routed flock scattered diminishing, diminishing, diminishing in every direction.

Exultantly the boys dropped their guns, jumped up and scrambled for the skiff.

"I'll handle that skiff!" the fisherman shouted at them. They stopped. Gripping the painter and balancing himself he eased the skiff into the water stern first and held the bow hard against the side of the rock shelf the skiff rested on. "You stay here," he said to his nephew. "No sense in all three of us going in the boat."

The boy on the reef gazed at the grey water rising and falling hypnotically along the glistening edge. It had dropped about a foot since their arrival. "I want to go with you," he said in a sullen tone, his eyes on the steaming eddies.

"You want to do what I tell you if you want to gun with me," answered the fisherman harshly. The boy couldn't swim, and he wasn't going to have him climbing in and out of the skiff any more than necessary. Besides he was too big.

The fisherman took his son in the skiff and cruised round and round among the decoys picking up dead birds. Meanwhile the other boy stared unmoving after them from the highest part of the ledge. Before they had quite finished gathering the dead birds, the fisherman cut the outboard and dropped to his knees in the skiff. "Down!" he yelled. "Get down!" About a dozen birds came tolling in. "Shoot—shoot!" his son hollered from the bottom of the boat to the boy on the ledge.

The dog, who had been running back and forth whining, sank to his belly, his muzzle on his forepaws. But the boy on the ledge never stirred. The ducks took late alarm at the skiff, swerved aside and into the air, passing with a whirr no more than fifty feet over the head of the boy, who remained on the ledge like a statue, without his gun, watching the two crouching in the boat.

The fisherman's son climbed onto the ledge and held the painter. The bottom of the skiff was covered with feathery black and white bodies with feet upturned and necks lolling. He was jubilant. "We got twenty-seven!" he told his cousin. "How's that? Nine apiece. Boy——" he added, "what a cool Christmas!"

The fisherman pulled the skiff onto its shelf and all three went and lay down again in anticipation of the next flight. The son, reloading, patted his shotgun affectionately. "I'm going to get me ten next time," he said. Then asked his cousin, "Whatsamatter—didn't you see the strays?"

"Yeah," the boy said.

"How come you didn't shoot at 'em?"

"Didn't feel like it," replied the boy, still with a trace of sullenness.

"You stupid or something?" The fisherman's son was astounded. "What a highlander!" But the fisherman, though he said nothing, knew that the older boy had had an attack of ledge fever.

"Cripes!" his son kept at it. "I'd at least of tried."

"Shut up," the fisherman finally told him, "and leave him be."

At slack water three more flocks came in, one right after the other, and when it was over, the skiff was half full of clean, dead birds. During the subsequent lull they broke out for lunch and ate it all and finished the hot coffee. For a while the fisherman sucked away on his cold pipe. Then he had himself a swig of whiskey.

The boys passed the time contentedly jabbering about who shot the most—there were ninety-two all told—which of their friends they would show the biggest ones to, how many each could eat at a meal provided they didn't have to eat any vegetables. Now and then they heard sporadic distant gunfire on the mainland, at its nearest point about two miles to the north. Once far off they saw a fishing boat making in the direction of home.

At length the fisherman got a hand inside his oilskins and produced his watch.

"Do we have to go now?" asked his son.

"Not just yet," he replied. "Pretty soon." Everything had been perfect. As good as he had ever had it. Because he was getting tired of the boys' chatter he got up, heavily in his hip boots, and stretched. The tide had turned and was coming in, the sky was more ashen, and the wind had freshened enough so that whitecaps were beginning to blossom. It would be a good hour before they had to leave the ledge and pick up the tollers. However, he guessed they would leave a little early. On account of the rising wind he doubted there would be much more shooting. He stepped carefully along the back of the ledge, to work his kinks out. It was also getting a little colder.

The whiskey had begun to warm him, but he was unprepared for the sudden blaze that flashed upward inside him from belly to head. He was standing looking at the shelf where the skiff was. Only the foolish skiff was not there!

For the second time that day the fisherman felt the deep vacuity of disbelief. He gaped, seeing nothing but the flat shelf of rock. He whirled, started toward the boys, slipped, recovered himself, fetched a complete circle, and stared at the unimaginably empty shelf. Its emptiness made him feel as if everything he had done that day so far, his life so far, he had dreamed. What could have happened? The tide was still nearly a foot below. There had been no sea to speak of. The skiff could hardly have slid off by itself. For the life of him, consciously careful as he inveterately was, he could not now remember hauling it up the last time. Perhaps in the heat of hunting, he had left it to the boy. Perhaps he could not remember which was the last time.

"Christ—" he exclaimed loudly, without realizing it because he was so entranced by the invisible event.

"What's wrong, Dad?" asked his son, getting to his feet.

The fisherman went blind with uncontainable rage. "Get back down there where you belong!" he screamed. He scarcely noticed the boy sink back in amazement. In a frenzy he ran along the ledge thinking the skiff might have been drawn up at another place, though he knew better. There was no other place.

He stumbled, half falling, back to the boys who were gawking at him in consternation, as though he had gone insane. "God damn it!" he yelled savagely, grabbing both of them and yanking them to their knees. "Get on your feet!"

"What's wrong?" his son repeated in a stifled voice.

"Never mind what's wrong," he snarled. "Look for the skiff—it's adrift!" When they peered around he gripped their shoulders, brutally facing them about. "Downwind—" He slammed his fist against his thigh. "Jesus!" he cried, struck to madness at their stupidity.

At last he sighted the skiff himself, magically bobbing along the grim sea like a toller, a quarter of a mile to leeward on a direct course for home. The impulse to strip himself naked was succeeded instantly by a queer calm. He simply sat down on the ledge and forgot everything except the marvellous mystery.

As his awareness partially returned he glanced toward the boys. They were still observing the skiff speechlessly. Then he was gazing into the clear young eyes of his son.

"Dad," asked the boy steadily, "what do we do now?"

That brought the fisherman upright. "The first thing we have to do," he heard himself saying with infinite tenderness as if he were making love, "is think."

"Could you swim it?" asked his son.

He shook his head and smiled at them. They smiled quickly back, too quickly. "A hundred yards maybe, in this water. I wish I could," he added. It was the most intimate and pitiful thing he had ever said. He walked in circles round them, trying to break the stall his mind was left in.

He gauged the level of the water. To the eye it was quite stationary, six inches from the shelf at this second. The fisherman did not have to mark it on the side of the rock against the passing of time to prove to his reason that it was rising, always rising. Already it was over the brink of reason, beyond the margins of thought—a senseless measurement. No sense to it.

All his life the fisherman had tried to lick the element of time, by getting up earlier and going to bed later, owning a faster boat, planning more than the day would hold, and tackling just one other job before the deadline fell. If, as on rare occasions he had the grand illusion, he ever really had beaten the game, he would need to call on all his reserves of practice and cunning now.

He sized up the scant but unforgivable three hundred yards to Brown Cow Island. Another hundred yards behind it his boat rode at anchor, where, had he been aboard, he could have cut in a fathometer to plumb the profound and occult seas, or a ship-to-shore radio on which in an interminably short time he would have heard his wife's voice talking to him over the air about homecoming.

"Couldn't we wave something so somebody would see us?" his nephew suggested.

The fisherman spun round. "Load your guns!" he ordered. They loaded as if the air had suddenly gone frantic with birds. "I'll fire once and count to five. Then you fire. Count to five. That way they won't just think it's only somebody gunning ducks. We'll keep doing that."

"We've only got just two-and-a-half boxes left," said his son.

The fisherman nodded, understanding that from beginning to end their situation was purely mathematical, like the ticking of the alarm clock in his silent bedroom. Then he fired. The dog, who had been keeping watch over the decoys, leaped forward and yelped in confusion. They all counted off, fired the first five rounds by threes, and reloaded. The fisherman scanned first the horizon, then the contracting borders of the ledge, which was the sole place the water appeared to be climbing. Soon it would be over the shelf.

They counted off and fired the second five rounds. "We'll hold off a while on the last one," the fisherman told the boys. He sat down and pondered what a trivial thing was a skiff. This one he and the boy had knocked together in a day. Was a gun, manufactured for killing.

His son tallied up the remaining shells, grouping them symmetrically in threes on the rock when the wet box fell apart. "Two short," he announced. They reloaded and laid the guns on their knees.

Behind thickening clouds they could not see the sun going down. The water, coming up, was growing blacker. The fisherman thought he might have told his wife they would be home before dark since it was Christmas day. He realized he had forgotten about its being any particular day. The tide would not be high until two hours after sunset. When they did not get in by nightfall, and could not be raised by radio, she might send somebody to hunt for them right away. He rejected this arithmetic immediately, with a sickening shock, recollecting it was a two-and-a-half hour. run at best. Then it occurred to him that she might send somebody on the mainland who was nearer. She would think he had engine trouble.

He rose and searched the shoreline, barely visible. Then his glance dropped to the toy shoreline at the edges of the reef. The shrinking ledge, so sinister from a boat, grew dearer minute by minute as though the whole wide world he gazed on from horizon to horizon balanced on its contracting rim. He checked the water level and found the shelf awash.

Some of what went through his mind the fisherman told to the boys. They accepted it without comment. If he caught their eyes they looked away to spare him or because they were not yet old enough to face what they saw. Mostly they watched the rising water. The fisherman was unable to initiate a word of encouragement. He wanted one of them to ask him whether somebody would reach them ahead of the tide. He would have found it possible to say yes. But they did not inquire.

The fisherman was not sure how much, at their age, they were able to imagine. Both of them had seen from the docks drowned bodies put ashore out of boats. Sometimes they grasped things, and sometimes not. He supposed they might be longing for the comfort of their mothers, and was astonished, as much as he was capable of any astonishment except the supreme one, to discover himself wishing he had not left his wife's dark, close, naked bed that morning.

"Is it time to shoot now?" asked his nephew.

"Pretty soon," he said, as if he were putting off making good on a promise. "Not yet."

His own boy cried softly for a brief moment, like a man, his face averted in an effort neither to give nor show pain.

"Before school starts," the fisherman said, wonderfully detached, "we'll go to town and I'll buy you boys anything you want."

With great difficulty, in a dull tone as though he did not in the least desire it, his son said after a pause, "I'd like one of those new thirty-horse outboards."

"All right," said the fisherman. And to his nephew, "How about you?"

The nephew shook his head desolately. "I don't want anything," he said.

After another pause the fisherman's son said, "Yes he does, Dad. He wants one too."

"All right—" the fisherman said again, and said no more.

The dog whined in uncertainty and licked the boys' faces where they sat together. Each threw an arm over his back and hugged him. Three strays flew in and sat companionably down among the stiff-necked decoys. The dog crouched, obedient to his training. The boys observed them listlessly. Presently, sensing something untoward, the ducks took off, splashing the wave tops with feet and wingtips, into the dusky waste.

The sea began to make up in the mounting wind, and the wind bore a new and deathly chill. The fisherman, scouring the somber, dwindling shadow of the mainland for a sign, hoped it would not snow. But it did. First a few flakes, then a flurry, then storming past horizontally. The fisherman took one long, bewildered look at Brown Cow Island three hundred yards dead to leeward, and got to his feet.

Then it shut in, as if what was happening on the ledge was too private even for the last wan light of the expiring day.

"Last round," the fisherman said austerely.

The boys rose and shouldered their tacit guns. The fisherman fired into the flying snow. He counted methodically to five. His son fired and counted. His nephew. All three fired and counted. Four rounds.

"You've got one left, Dad," his son said.

The fisherman hesitated another second, then he fired the final shell. Its pathetic report, like the spat of a popgun, whipped away on the wind and was instantly blanketed in falling snow.

Night fell all in a moment to meet the ascending sea. They were now barely able to make one another out through driving snowflakes, dim as ghosts in their yellow oilskins. The fisherman heard a sea break and glanced down where his feet were. They seemed to be wound in a snowy sheet. Gently he took the boys by the shoulders and pushed them in front of him, feeling with his feet along the shallow sump to the place where it triangulated into a sharp crevice at the highest point of the ledge. "Face ahead," he told them. "Put the guns down."

"I'd like to hold mine, Dad," begged his son.

"Put it down," said the fisherman. "The tide won't hurt it. Now brace your feet against both sides and stay there."

They felt the dog, who was pitch black, running up and down in perplexity between their straddled legs. "Dad," said his son, "what about the pooch?"

If he had called the dog by name it would have been too personal. The fisherman would have wept. As it was he had all he could do to keep from laughing. He bent his knees, and when he touched the dog hoisted him under one arm. The dog's belly was soaking wet.

So they waited, marooned in their consciousness, surrounded by a monstrous tidal space which was slowly, slowly closing them out. In this space the periwinkle beneath the fisherman's boots was king. While hovering airborne in his mind he had an inward glimpse of his house as curiously separate, like a June mirage.

Snow, rocks, seas, wind the fisherman had lived by all his life. Now he thought he had never comprehended what they were, and he hated them. Though they had not changed. He was deadly chilled. He set out to ask the boys if they were cold. There was no sense. He thought of the whiskey, and sidled backward, still holding the awkward dog, till he located the bottle under water with his toe. He picked it up squeamishly as though afraid of getting his sleeve wet, worked his way forward and bent over his son. "Drink it," he said, holding the bottle against the boy's ribs. The boy tipped his head back, drank, coughed hotly, then vomited.

"I can't," he told his father wretchedly.

"Try—try—" the fisherman pleaded, as if it meant the difference between life and death.

The boy obediently drank, and again he vomited hotly. He shook his head against his father's chest and passed the bottle forward to his cousin, who drank and vomited also. Passing the bottle back, the boys dropped it in the frigid water between them.

When the waves reached his knees the fisherman set the warm dog loose and said to his son, "Turn around and get up on my shoulders." The boy obeyed. The fisherman opened his oilskin jacket and twisted his hands behind him through his suspenders, clamping the boy's booted ankles with his elbows.

"What about the dog?" the boy asked.

"He'll make his own way all right," the fisherman said. "He can take the cold water." His knees were trembling. Every instinct shrieked for gymnastics. He ground his teeth and braced like a colossus against the sides of the submerged crevice.

The dog, having lived faithfully as though one of them for eleven years, swam a few minutes in and out around the fisherman's legs, not knowing what was happening, and left them without a whimper. He would swim and swim at random by himself, round and round in the blinding night, and when he had swum routinely through the paralyzing water all he could, he would simply, in one incomprehensible moment, drown. Almost the fisherman, waiting out infinity, envied him his pattern.

Freezing seas swept by, flooding inexorably up and up as the earth sank away imperceptibly beneath them. The boy called out once to his cousin. There was no answer. The fisherman, marvelling on a terror without voice, was dumbly glad when the boy did not call again. His own boots were long full of water. With no sensation left in his straddling legs he dared not move them. So long as the seas came sidewise against his hips, and then sidewise against his shoulders, he might balance—no telling how long. The upper half of him was what felt frozen. His legs, disengaged from his nerves and his will, he came to regard quite scientifically. They were the absurd, precarious axis around which reeled the surged universal tumult. The waves would come on and on; he could not visualize how many tossing reinforcements lurked in the night beyond—inexhaustible numbers, and he wept in supernatural fury at each because it was higher, till he transcended hate and took them, swaying like a convert, one by one as they lunged against him and away aimlessly into their own undisputed, wild realm.

From his hips upward the fisherman stretched to his utmost as a man does whose spirit reaches out of dead sleep. The boy's head, none too high, must be at least seven feet above the ledge. Though growing larger every minute, it was a small light life. The fisherman meant to hold it there, if need be, through a thousand tides.

By and by the boy, slumped on the head of his father, asked, "Is it over your boots, dad?"

"Not yet," the fisherman said. Then through his teeth he added, "If I fall—kick your boots off—swim for it—downwind—to the island. . . ."

"You. . . ?" the boy finally asked.

The fisherman nodded against the boy's belly. "—Won't see each other," he said.

The boy did for the fisherman the greatest thing that can be done. He may have been too young for perfect terror, but he was old enough to know there were things beyond the power of any man. All he could do he did, by trusting his father to do all he could, and asking nothing more.

The fisherman, rocked to his soul by a sea, held his eyes shut upon the interminable night.

"Is it time now?" the boy said.

The fisherman could hardly speak. "Not yet," he said. "Not just yet. . . ."

As the land mass pivoted toward sunlight the day after Christmas, a tiny fleet of small craft converged off shore like iron filings to a magnet. At daybreak they found the skiff floating unscathed off the headland, half full of ducks and snow. The shooting *had* been good, as someone hearing on the nearby mainland the previous afternoon had supposed. Two hours afterward they found the unharmed boat adrift five miles at sea. At high noon they found the fisherman at ebb tide, his right boot jammed cruelly into a glacial crevice of the ledge beside three shotguns, his hands tangled behind him in his suspenders, and under his right elbow a rubber boot with a sock and a live starfish in it. After dragging unlit depths all day for the boys, they towed the fisherman home in his own boat at sundown, and in the frost of evening, mute with discovering purgatory, laid him on his wharf for his wife to see.

She, somehow, standing on the dock as in her frequent dream, gazing at the fisherman pure as crystal on the icy boards, a small rubber boot still frozen under one clenched arm, saw him exaggerated beyond remorse or grief, absolved of his mortality.

The
way
life
is

The Patented Gate and the Mean Hamburger

Robert Penn Warren
(b. 1905)

Robert Penn Warren was born in Guthrie, Kentucky and grew up in the South, which is the setting for most of his fictional works. After graduating from Vanderbilt University in 1925, he studied at the University of California, Berkeley, and Yale University, and, from 1928 to 1930, attended Oxford University as a Rhodes Scholar. A novelist, poet, playwright, and critic, Warren has taught courses in the various forms of writing at such universities as Southwestern, Vanderbilt, Louisiana State, and Yale. In 1947 his novel All the King's Men (1946) *won him the Pulitzer Prize in fiction; and, in 1958 for* Promises: Poems, 1954–1956 (1957), *he received both the National Book Award and the Pulitzer Prize in poetry.*

Among Warren's other major works are John Brown: The Making of a Martyr (1929), Thirty-Six Poems (1935), The Circus in the Attic, and Other Short Stories (1948), Selected Poems: New and Old, 1923–1966 (1966), Incarnations: Poems, 1966–1968 (1968); *and the novels* Night Rider (1939), At Heaven's Gate (1943), World Enough and Time (1950), Band of Angels (1955), The Flood: A Romance for Our Time (1964), *and* Meet Me in the Green Glen (1971).

You have seen him a thousand times. You have seen him standing on the street corner on Saturday afternoon, in the little county-seat towns. He wears blue jean pants, or overalls washed to a pale pastel blue like the color of sky after a shower in spring, but because it is Saturday he has on a wool coat, an old one, perhaps the coat left from the suit he got married in a long time back. His long wrist bones hang out from the sleeves of the coat, the tendons showing along the bone like the dry twist of grapevine still corded on the stove-length of a hickory sapling you would find in his wood box beside his cookstove among the split chunks of gum and red oak. The big hands, with the knotted, cracked joints and the square, horn-thick nails, hang loose off the wrist bone like clumsy, home-made tools hung on the wall of a shed after work. If it is summer, he wears a straw hat with a wide brim, the straw fraying loose around the edge. If it is winter, he wears a felt hat, black once, but now weathered with streaks of dark gray and dull purple in the sunlight. His face is long and bony, the jawbone long under the drawn-in cheeks. The flesh along the jawbone is nicked in a couple of places where the unaccustomed razor has been drawn over the leather-coarse skin. A tiny bit of blood crusts brown where the nick is. The color of the face is red, a dull red like the red clay mud or clay dust which clings to the bottom of his pants and to the cast-iron-looking brogans on his feet, or a red like the color of a piece of hewed cedar which has been left in the weather. The face does not look alive. It seems to be molded from the clay or hewed from the cedar. When the jaw moves, once, with its deliberate, massive motion on the quid of tobacco, you are still not convinced. That motion is but the cunning triumph of a mechanism concealed within.

But you see the eyes. You see that the eyes are alive. They are pale blue or gray, set back under the deep brows and thorny eyebrows. They are not wide, but are squinched up like eyes accustomed to wind or sun or to measuring the stroke of the ax or to fixing the object over the rifle sights. When you pass, you see that the eyes are alive and are warily and dispassionately estimating you from the ambush of the thorny brows. Then you pass on, and he stands there in that stillness which is his gift.

With him may be standing two or three others like himself, but they are still, too. They do not talk. The young men, who will be like these men when they get to be fifty or sixty, are down at the

THE PATENTED GATE AND THE MEAN HAMBURGER   Copyright, 1947, by Robert Penn Warren. Reprinted from his volume *The Circus in the Attic, and Other Stories* by permission of Harcourt Brace Jovanovich, Inc.

beer parlor, carousing and laughing with a high, whickering laugh. But the men on the corner are long past all that. They are past many things. They have endured and will endure in their silence and wisdom. They will stand on the street corner and reject the world which passes under their level gaze as a rabble passes under the guns of a rocky citadel around whose base a slatternly town has assembled.

I had seen Jeff York a thousand times, or near, standing like that on the street corner in town, while the people flowed past him, under the distant and wary and dispassionate eyes in ambush. He would be waiting for his wife and the three towheaded children who were walking around the town looking into store windows and at the people. After a while they would come back to him, and then, wordlessly, he would lead them to the store where they always did their trading. He would go first, marching with a steady bent-kneed stride, setting the cast-iron brogans down deliberately on the cement; then his wife, a small woman with covert, sidewise, curious glances for the world, would follow, and behind her the towheads bunched together in a dazed, glory-struck way. In the store, when their turn came, Jeff York would move to the counter, accept the clerk's greeting, and then bend down from his height to catch the widespread directions of his wife. He would straighten up and say, "Gimmie a sack of flahr, if'n you please." Then when the sack of flour had been brought, he would lean again to his wife for the next item. When the stuff had all been bought and paid for with the grease-thick, wadded dollar bills which he took from an old leather coin purse with a metal catch to it, he would heave it all together into his arms and march out, his wife and towheads behind him and his eyes fixed level over the heads of the crowd. He would march down the street and around to the hitching lot where the wagons were, and put his stuff into his wagon and cover it with an old quilt to wait till he got ready to drive out to his place.

For Jeff York had a place. That was what made him different from the other men who looked like him and with whom he stood on the street corner on Saturday afternoon. They were croppers, but he, Jeff York, had a place. But he stood with them because his father had stood with their fathers and his grandfathers with their grandfathers, or with men like their fathers and grandfathers, in other towns, in settlements in the mountains, in towns beyond the mountains. They were the great-great-great-grandsons of men who, half woodsmen and half farmers, had been shoved into the sand hills, into the limestone hills, into the barrens, two hundred, two hundred and fifty years before and had learned there the way to grabble a life out of the sand and the stone. And when the soil had leached away into the sand or burnt off the stone, they went on west, walking with the bent-kneed stride over the mountains, their eyes squinching warily in the gaunt faces, the rifle over the crooked arm, hunting a new place.

But there was a curse on them. They only knew the life they knew, and that life did not belong to the fat bottom lands, where the cane was head-tall, and to the grassy meadows and the rich swale. So they passed those places by and hunted for the place which was like home and where they could pick up the old life, with the same feel in the bones and the squirrel's bark sounding the same after first light. They had walked a long way, to the sand hills of Alabama, to the red country of North Mississippi and Louisiana, to the Barrens of Tennessee, to the Knobs of Kentucky and the scrub country of West Kentucky, to the Ozarks. Some of them had stopped in Cobb County, Tennessee, in the hilly eastern part of the county, and had built their cabins and dug up the ground for the corn patch. But the land had washed away there, too, and in the end they had come down out of the high land into the bottoms—for half of Cobb County is a rich, swelling country —where the corn was good and the tobacco unfurled a leaf like a yard of green velvet and the white houses stood among the cedars and tulip trees and maples. But they were not to live in the white houses with the limestone chimneys set strong at the end of each gable. No, they were to live in the shacks on the back of the farms, or in cabins not much different from the cabins they had once lived in two hundred years before over the mountains or, later, in the hills of Cobb County. But the shacks and the cabins now stood on somebody else's ground, and the curse which they had brought with them over the mountain trail, more precious than the bullet mold or grandma's quilt, the curse which was the very feeling in the bones and the habit in the hand, had come full circle.

Jeff York was one of those men, but he had broken the curse. It had taken him more than thirty years to do it, from the time when he was nothing but a big boy until he was fifty. It had taken him from sun to sun, year in and year out, and all the sweat in his body, and all the power of rejection he could muster, until the very act of rejection had become a kind of pleasure, a dark, secret, savage dissipation, like an obsessing vice. But those years had given him his place, sixty acres with a house and barn.

When he bought the place, it was not very good. The land was run-down from years of neglect and abuse. But Jeff York put brush in the gullies to stop the wash and planted clover on the run-down fields. He mended the fences, rod by rod. He patched the roof on the little house and propped up the porch, buying the lumber and shingles almost piece by piece and one by one as he could spare the sweat-bright and grease-slick quarters and half-dollars out of his leather purse. Then he painted the house. He painted it white, for he knew that that was the color you painted a house sitting back from the road with its couple of maples, beyond the clover field.

Last, he put up the gate. It was a patented gate, the kind you can ride up to and open by pulling on a pull rope without getting off your horse or out of your buggy or wagon. It had a high pair of posts, well braced and with a high crossbar between, and the bars for the opening mechanism extending on each side. It was painted white, too. Jeff was even prouder of the gate than he was of the place. Lewis Simmons, who lived next to Jeff's place, swore he had seen Jeff come out after dark on a mule and ride in and out of that gate, back and forth, just for the pleasure of pulling on the rope and making the mechanism work. The gate was the seal Jeff York had put on all the years of sweat and rejection. He could sit on his porch on a Sunday afternoon in summer, before milking time, and look down the rise, down the winding dirt track, to the white gate beyond the clover, and know what he needed to know about all the years passed.

Meanwhile Jeff York had married and had had the three tow-heads. His wife was twenty years or so younger than he, a small, dark woman, who walked with her head bowed a little and from that humble and unprovoking posture stole sidewise, secret glances at the world from eyes which were brown or black—you never could tell which because you never remembered having looked her straight in the eye—and which were surprisingly bright in that sidewise, secret flicker, like the eyes of a small, cunning bird which surprise you from the brush. When they came to town she moved along the street, with a child in her arms or later with the three trailing behind her, and stole her looks at the world. She wore a calico dress, dun-colored, which hung loose to conceal whatever shape her thin body had, and in winter over the dress a brown wool coat with a scrap of fur at the collar which looked like some tattered growth of fungus feeding on old wood. She wore black high-heeled shoes, slippers of some kind, which she kept polished and which surprised you under that dress and coat. In the slippers she moved with a slightly limping, stealthy gait, almost sliding them along the pavement, as though she had not fully mastered the complicated trick required to use them properly. You knew that she wore them only when she came to town, that she carried them wrapped up in a piece of newspaper until their wagon had reached the first house on the outskirts of town, and that, on the way back, at the same point, she would take them off and wrap them up again and hold the bundle in her lap until she got home. If the weather happened to be bad, or if it was winter, she would have a pair of old brogans under the wagon seat.

It was not that Jeff York was a hard man and kept his wife in clothes that were as bad as those worn by the poorest of the women of the croppers. In fact, some of the cropper women, poor or not, black or white, managed to buy dresses with some color in them and proper hats, and went to the moving picture show on Saturday afternoon. But Jeff still owed a little money on his place, less than two hundred dollars, which he had had to borrow to rebuild his barn after it was struck by lightning. He had, in fact, never been entirely out of debt. He had lost a mule which had got out on the highway and been hit by a truck. That had set him back. One of his towheads had been sickly for a couple of winters. He had not been in deep, but he was not a man, with all those years of rejection behind him, to forget the meaning of those years. He was good enough to his family. Nobody ever said the contrary. But he was good to them in terms of all the years he had lived through. He did what he could afford. He bought the towheads a ten-cent bag of colored candy every Saturday afternoon for them to suck on during the ride home in the wagon, and the last thing before they left town, he always took the lot of them over to the dog-wagon to get hamburgers and orange pop.

The towheads were crazy about hamburgers. And so was his wife, for that matter. You could tell it, even if she didn't say anything, for she would lift her bowed-forward head a little, and her face would brighten, and she would run her tongue out to wet her lips just as the plate with the hamburger would be set on the counter before her. But all those folks, like Jeff York and his family, like hamburgers, with pickle and onions and mustard and tomato catsup, the whole works. It is something different. They stay out in the country and eat hog-meat, when they can get it, and greens and corn bread and potatoes, and nothing but a pinch of salt to brighten it on the tongue, and when they get to town and get hold of beef and wheat bread and all the stuff to jack up the flavor, they have to swallow to keep the mouth from flooding before they even take the first bite.

So the last thing every Saturday, Jeff York would take his family over to Slick Hardin's *Dew Drop Inn Diner* and give them the treat. The diner was built like a railway coach, but it was set on a concrete foundation on a lot just off the main street of town. At each end the concrete was painted to show wheels. Slick Hardin kept the grass just in front of the place pretty well mowed and one or two summers he even had a couple of flower beds in the middle of that shirttail-size lawn. Slick had a good business. For a few years he had been a prelim fighter over in Nashville and had got his name in the papers a few times. So he was a kind of hero, with the air of romance about him. He had been born, however, right in town and, as soon as he had found out he wasn't ever going to be good enough to be a real fighter, he had come back home and started the dogwagon, the first one ever in town. He was a slick-skinned fellow, about thirty-five, prematurely bald, with his head slick all over. He had big eyes, pale blue and slick looking like agates. When he said something that he thought smart, he would roll his eyes around, slick in his head like marbles, to see who was laughing. Then he'd wink. He had done very well with his business, for despite the fact that he had picked up city ways and a lot of city talk, he still remembered enough to deal with the country people, and they were the ones who brought the dimes in. People who lived right there in town, except for school kids in the afternoon and the young toughs from the pool room or men on the night shift down at the railroad, didn't often get around to the dogwagon.

Slick Hardin was perhaps trying to be smart when he said what he did to Mrs. York. Perhaps he had forgotten, just for that moment, that people like Jeff York and his wife didn't like to be kidded, at least not in that way. He said what he did, and then grinned and rolled his eyes around to see if some of the other people present were thinking it was funny.

Mrs. York was sitting on a stool in front of the counter, flanked on one side by Jeff York and on the other by the three towheads. She had just sat down to wait for the hamburger—there were several orders in ahead of the York order—and had been watching in her sidewise fashion every move of Slick Hardin's hands as he patted the pink meat onto the hot slab and wiped the split buns over the greasy iron to make them ready to receive it. She always watched him like that, and when the hamburger was set before her she would wet her lips with her tongue.

That day Slick set the hamburger down in front of Mrs. York, and said, "Anybody likes hamburger much as you, Mrs. York, ought to git him a hamburger stand."

Mrs. York flushed up, and didn't say anything, staring at her plate. Slick rolled his eyes to see how it was going over, and somebody down the counter snickered. Slick looked back at the Yorks, and if he had not been so encouraged by the snicker he might, when he saw Jeff York's face, have hesitated before going on with his kidding. People like Jeff York are touchous, and they are especially touchous about the womenfolks, and you do not make jokes with or about their womenfolks unless it is perfectly plain that the joke is a very special kind of friendly joke. The snicker down the counter had defined the joke as not entirely friendly. Jeff was looking at Slick, and something was growing slowly in that hewed-cedar face, and back in the gray eyes in the ambush of thorny brows.

But Slick did not notice. The snicker had encouraged him, and so he said, "Yeah, if I liked them hamburgers much as you, I'd buy me a hamburger stand. Fact, I'm selling this one. You want to buy it?"

There was another snicker, louder, and Jeff York, whose hamburger had been about half way to his mouth for another bite, laid it down deliberately on his plate. But whatever might have happened at that moment did not happen. It did not happen because Mrs. York lifted her flushed face, looked straight at Slick Hardin, swallowed hard to get down a piece of the hamburger or to master her nerve, and said in a sharp, strained voice, "You sellen this place?"

There was complete silence. Nobody had expected her to say anything. The chances were she had never said a word in that diner in the couple of hundred times she had been in it. She had come in with Jeff York and, when a stool had come vacant, had sat down, and Jeff had said, "Gimme five hamburgers, if'n you please, and make 'em well done, and five bottles of orange pop." Then, after the eating was over, he had always laid down seventy-five cents on the counter—that is, after there were five hamburger-eaters in the family—and walked out, putting his brogans down slow, and his wife and kids following without a word. But now she spoke up and asked the question, in that strained, artificial voice, and everybody, including her husband, looked at her with surprise.

As soon as he could take it in, Slick Hardin replied, "Yeah, I'm selling it."

She swallowed hard again, but this time it could not have been hamburger, and demanded, "What you asken fer hit?"

Slick looked at her in the new silence, half shrugged, a little contemptuously, and said, "Fourteen hundred and fifty dollars."

She looked back at him, while the blood ebbed from her face. "Hit's a lot of money," she said in a flat tone, and returned her gaze to the hamburger on her plate.

"Lady," Slick said defensively, "I got that much money tied up here. Look at that there stove. It is a *Heat Master* and they cost. Them coffee urns, now. Money can't buy no better. And this here lot, lady, the diner sets on. Anybody knows I got that much money tied up here. I got more. This lot cost me more'n . . ." He suddenly realized that she was not listening to him. And he must have realized, too, that she didn't have a dime in the world and couldn't buy his diner, and that he was making a fool of himself, defending his price. He stopped abruptly, shrugged his shoulders, and then swung his wide gaze down the counter to pick out somebody to wink to.

But before he got the wink off, Jeff York had said, "Mr. Hardin."

Slick looked at him and asked, "Yeah?"

"She didn't mean no harm," Jeff York said. "She didn't mean to be messen in yore business."

Slick shrugged. "Ain't no skin off my nose," he said. "Ain't no secret I'm selling out. My price ain't no secret neither."

Mrs. York bowed her head over her plate. She was chewing a mouthful of her hamburger with a slow, abstracted motion of her jaw, and you knew that it was flavorless on her tongue.

That was, of course, on a Saturday. On Thursday afternoon of the next week Slick was in the diner alone. It was the slack time, right in the middle of the afternoon. Slick, as he told it later, was wiping off the stove and wasn't noticing. He was sort of whistling to himself, he said. He had a way of whistling soft through his teeth. But he wasn't whistling loud, he said, not so loud he wouldn't have heard the door open or the steps if she hadn't come gum-shoeing in on him to stand there waiting in the middle of the floor until he turned round and was so surprised he nearly had heart failure. He had thought he was there alone, and there she was, watching every move he was making, like a cat watching a goldfish swim in a bowl.

"Howdy-do," he said, when he got his breath back.

"This place still fer sale?" she asked him.

"Yeah, lady," he said.

"What you asken fer hit?"

"Lady, I done told you," Slick replied, "fourteen hundred and fifty dollars."

"Hit's a heap of money," she said.

Slick started to tell her how much money he had tied up there, but before he had got going, she had turned and slipped out of the door.

"Yeah," Slick said later to the men who came into the diner, "me like a fool starting to tell her how much money I got tied up here when I knowed she didn't have a dime. That woman's crazy. She must walked that five or six miles in here just to ask me something she already knowed the answer to. And then turned right round and walked out. But I am selling me this place. I'm tired of slinging hash to them hicks. I got me some connections over in Nashville and I'm gonna open me a place over there. A cigar stand and about three pool tables and maybe some beer. I'll have me a sort of club in the back. You know, membership cards to git in, where the boys will play a little game. Just sociable. I got good connections over in Nashville. I'm selling this place. But that woman, she ain't got a dime. She ain't gonna buy it."

But she did.

On Saturday Jeff York led his family over to the diner. They ate hamburgers without a word and marched out. After they had gone, Slick said, "Looks like she ain't going to make the invest-mint. Gonna buy a block of bank stock instead." Then he rolled his eyes, located a brother down the counter, and winked.

It was almost the end of the next week before it happened. What had been going on inside the white house out on Jeff York's place nobody knew or was to know. Perhaps she just starved him out, just not doing the cooking or burning everything. Perhaps she just quit attending to the children properly and he had to come back tired from work and take care of them. Perhaps she just lay in bed at night and talked and talked to him, asking him to buy it, nagging him all night long, while he would fall asleep and then wake up with a start to hear her voice still going on. Or perhaps she just turned her face away from him and wouldn't let him touch her. He was a lot older than she, and she was probably the only woman he had ever had. He had been too ridden by his dream and his passion for rejection during all the years before to lay even a finger on a woman. So she had him there. Because he was a lot older and because he had never had another woman. But perhaps she used none of these methods. She was a small, dark, cunning woman, with a sidewise look from her lowered face, and she could have thought up ways of her own, no doubt.

Whatever she thought up, it worked. On Friday morning Jeff York went to the bank. He wanted to mortgage his place, he told Todd Sullivan, the president. He wanted fourteen hundred and fifty dollars, he said. Todd Sullivan would not let him have it. He already owed the bank one hundred and sixty dollars and the best he could get on a mortgage was eleven hundred dollars. That was in 1935 and then farmland wasn't worth much and half the land in the country was mortgaged anyway. Jeff York sat in the chair by Todd Sullivan's desk and didn't say anything. Eleven hundred dollars would not do him any good. Take off the hundred and sixty he owed and it wouldn't be but a little over nine hundred dollars clear to him. He sat there quietly for a minute, apparently turning that fact over in his head. Then Todd Sullivan asked him, "How much you say you need?"

Jeff York told him.

"What you want it for?" Todd Sullivan asked.

He told him that.

"I tell you," Todd Sullivan said, "I don't want to stand in the way of a man bettering himself. Never did. That diner ought to be a good proposition, all right, and I don't want to stand in your way if you want to come to town and better yourself. It will be a step up from that farm for you, and I like a man has got ambition. The bank can't lend you the money, not on that piece of property. But I tell you what I'll do. I'll buy your place. I got me some walking horses I'm keeping out on my father's place. But I could use me a little place of my own. For my horses. I'll give you seventeen hundred for it. Cash."

Jeff York did not say anything to that. He looked slow at Todd Sullivan as though he did not understand.

"Seventeen hundred," the banker repeated. "That's a good figure. For these times."

Jeff was not looking at him now. He was looking out the window, across the alleyway—Todd Sullivan's office was in the back of the bank. The banker, telling about it later when the doings of Jeff York had become for a moment a matter of interest, said, "I thought he hadn't even heard me. He looked like he was half asleep or something. I coughed to sort of wake him up. You know the way you do. I didn't want to rush him. You can't rush those people, you know. But I couldn't sit there all day. I had offered him a fair price."

It was, as a matter of fact, a fair price for the times, when the bottom was out of everything in the section.

Jeff York took it. He took the seventeen hundred dollars and bought the dogwagon with it, and rented a little house on the edge of town and moved in with his wife and the towheads. The first day after they got settled, Jeff York and his wife went over to the diner to get instructions from Slick about running the place. He showed Mrs. York all about how to work the coffee machine and the stove, and how to make up the sandwiches, and how to clean the place up after herself. She fried up hamburgers for all of them, herself, her husband, and Slick Hardin, for practice, and they ate the hamburgers while a couple of hangers-on watched them. "Lady," Slick said, for he had money in his pocket and was heading out for Nashville on the seven o'clock train that night, and was feeling expansive, "lady, you sure fling a mean hamburger."

He wiped the last crumbs and mustard off his lips, got his valise from behind the door, and said, "Lady, git in there and pitch. I hope you make a million hamburgers." Then he stepped out into the bright fall sunshine and walked away whistling up the street, whistling through his teeth and rolling his eyes as though there were somebody to wink to. That was the last anybody in town ever saw of Slick Hardin.

The next day, Jeff York worked all day at the diner. He was scrubbing up the place inside and cleaning up the trash which had accumulated behind it. He burned all the trash. Then he gave the place a good coat of paint outside, white paint. That took him two days. Then he touched up the counter inside with varnish. He straightened up the sign out front, which had begun to sag a little. He had that place looking spick and span.

Then on the fifth day after they got settled—it was Sunday—he took a walk in the country. It was along toward sun when he started out, not late, as a matter of fact, for by October the days are shortening up. He walked out the Curtisville pike and out the cut-off leading to his farm. When he entered the cut-off, about a mile from his own place, it was still light enough for the Bowdoins, who had a filling station at the corner, to see him plain when he passed.

The next time anybody saw him was on Monday morning about six o'clock. A man taking milk into town saw him. He was hanging from the main cross bar of the white patented gate. He had jumped off the gate. But he had propped the thing open so there wouldn't be any chance of clambering back up on it if his neck didn't break when he jumped and he should happen to change his mind.

But that was an unnecessary precaution, as it developed. Dr. Stauffer said that his neck was broken very clean. "A man who can break a neck as clean as that could make a living at it," Dr. Stauffer said. And added, "If he's damned sure it ain't ever his own neck."

Mrs. York was much cut up by her husband's death. People were sympathetic and helpful, and out of a mixture of sympathy and curiosity she got a good starting trade at the diner. And the trade kept right on. She got so she didn't hang her head and look sidewise at you and the world. She would look straight at you. She got so she could walk in high heels without giving the impression that it was a trick she was learning. She wasn't a bad-looking woman, as a matter of fact, once she had caught on how to fix herself up a little. The railroad men and the pool hall gang liked to hang out there and kid with her. Also, they said, she flung a mean hamburger.

The Language of Men

Norman Mailer
(b. 1923)

Norman Mailer was born in Long Branch, New Jersey. When he was four years old, his family moved to Brooklyn, New York, where he graduated from Boys High School in 1939. Mailer then went to Harvard to study aeronautical engineering but soon became more interested in writing. "The Greatest Thing in the World," one of the numerous short stories he wrote as an undergraduate, won Story *magazine's college contest for 1941. After graduating from college in 1943, Mailer entered the Army and served in the Philippines and Japan. His novel about the war,* The Naked and the Dead, *was published in 1948 and won wide critical acclaim.*

Some years ago Mailer began writing, producing, and acting in films, whose subjects have ranged from politics to pornography. Mailer ran for mayor of New York City in 1969, proposing that it should be made the fifty-first state and that every neighborhood should exercise self-determination: he lost the election to John Lindsay. In 1971, the furor that surrounds Mailer increased when he published The Prisoner of Sex, *his controversial view of the Women's Liberation movement. Among his other works are* The Deer Park (*1955*), *a book about Hollywood celebrities;* Advertisements for Myself (*1959*), *a confessional autobiography;* An American Dream (*1964*), *a disturbing view of American life in the early sixties;* Why Are We in Vietnam? (*1967*); Miami and the Siege of Chicago: An Informal History of the Republican and Democratic Conventions of 1968 (*1968*); and* Of a Fire on the Moon (*1970*).

In the beginning, Sanford Carter was ashamed of becoming an Army cook. This was not from snobbery, at least not from snobbery of the most direct sort. During the two and a half years Carter had been in the Army he had come to hate cooks more and more. They existed for him as a symbol of all that was corrupt, overbearing, stupid, and privileged in Army life. The image which came to mind was a fat cook with an enormous sandwich in one hand, and a bottle of beer in the other, sweat pouring down a porcine face, foot on a flour barrel, shouting at the K.P.'s, "Hurry up, you men, I ain't got all day." More than once in those two and a half years, driven to exasperation, Carter had been on the verge of throwing his food into a cook's face as he passed on the serving line. His anger often derived from nothing: the set of a pair of fat lips, the casual heavy thump of the serving spoon into his plate, or the resentful conviction that the cook was not serving him enough. Since life in the Army was in most aspects a marriage, this rage over apparently harmless details was not a sign of unbalance. Every soldier found some particular habit of the Army spouse impossible to support.

Yet Sanford Carter became a cook and, to elaborate the irony, did better as a cook than he had done as anything else. In a few months he rose from a Private to a first cook with the rank of Sergeant, Technician. After the fact, it was easy to understand. He had suffered through all his Army career from an excess of eagerness. He had cared too much, he had wanted to do well, and so he had often been tense at moments when he would better have been relaxed. He was very young, twenty-one, had lived the comparatively gentle life of a middle-class boy, and needed some success in the Army to prove to himself that he was not completely worthless.

In succession, he had failed as a surveyor in Field Artillery, a clerk in an Infantry headquarters, a telephone wireman, and finally a rifleman. When the war ended, and his regiment went to Japan, Carter was still a rifleman; he had been a rifleman for eight months. What was more to the point, he had been in the platoon as long as any of its members; the skilled hard-bitten nucleus of veterans who had run his squad had gone home one by one, and it seemed to him that through seniority he was entitled to at least a corporal's rating. Through seniority he was so entitled, but on no other ground. Whenever responsibility had been handed to him,

THE LANGUAGE OF MEN   Reprinted by permission of G. P. Putnam's Sons from *Advertisements for Myself* by Norman Mailer. Copyright © 1959 by Norman Mailer.

he had discharged it miserably, tensely, overconscientiously. He had always asked too many questions, he had worried the task too severely, he had conveyed his nervousness to the men he was supposed to lead. Since he was also sensitive enough and proud enough never to curry favor with the noncoms in the platoons, he was in no position to sit in on their occasional discussions about who was to succeed them. In a vacuum of ignorance, he had allowed himself to dream that he would be given a squad to lead, and his hurt was sharp when the squad was given to a replacement who had joined the platoon months after him.

The war was over, Carter had a bride in the States (he had lived with her for only two months), he was lonely, he was obsessed with going home. As one week dragged into the next, and the regiment, the company, and his own platoon continued the same sort of training which they had been doing ever since he had entered the Army, he thought he would snap. There were months to wait until he would be discharged and meanwhile it was intolerable to him to be taught for the fifth time the nomenclature of the machine gun, to stand a retreat parade three evenings a week. He wanted some niche where he could lick his wounds, some Army job with so many hours of work and so many hours of complete freedom, where he could be alone by himself. He hated the Army, the huge Army which had proved to him that he was good at no work, and incapable of succeeding at anything. He wrote long, aching letters to his wife, he talked less and less to the men around him and he was close to violent attacks of anger during the most casual phases of training—during close-order drill or cleaning his rifle for inspection. He knew that if he did not find his niche it was possible that he would crack.

So he took an opening in the kitchen. It promised him nothing except a day of work, and a day of leisure which would be completely at his disposal. He found that he liked it. He was given at first the job of baking the bread for the company, and every other night he worked till early in the morning, kneading and shaping his fifty-pound mix of dough. At two or three he would be done, and for his work there would be the tangible reward of fifty loaves of bread, all fresh from the oven, all clean and smelling of fertile accomplished creativity. He had the rare and therefore intensely satisfying emotion of seeing at the end of an Army chore the product of his labor.

A month after he became cook the regiment was disbanded, and those men who did not have enough points to go home were sent to other outfits. Carter ended at an ordnance company in another Japanese city. He had by now given up all thought of getting a noncom's rating before he was discharged, and was merely content to work each alternate day. He took his work for granted and so he succeeded at it. He had begun as a baker in the new company kitchen; before long he was the first cook. It all happened quickly. One cook went home on points, another caught a skin disease, a third was transferred from the kitchen after contracting a venereal infection. On the shift which Carter worked there were left only himself and a man who was illiterate. Carter was put nominally in charge, and was soon actively in charge. He looked up each menu in an Army recipe book, collected the items, combined them in the order indicated, and after the proper time had elapsed, took them from the stove. His product tasted neither better nor worse than the product of all other Army cooks. But the mess sergeant was impressed. Carter had filled a gap. The next time ratings were given out Carter jumped at a bound from Private to Sergeant T/4.

On the surface he was happy; beneath the surface he was overjoyed. It took him several weeks to realize how grateful and delighted he felt. The promotion coincided with his assignment to a detachment working in a small seaport up the coast. Carter arrived there to discover that he was in charge of cooking for thirty men, and would act as mess sergeant. There was another cook, and there were four permanent Japanese K.P.'s, all of them good workers. He still cooked every other day, but there was always time between meals to take a break of at least an hour and often two; he shared a room with the other cook and lived in comparative privacy for the first time in several years; the seaport was beautiful; there was only one officer, and he left the men alone; supplies were plentiful due to a clerical error which assigned rations for forty men rather than thirty; and in general everything was fine. The niche had become a sinecure.

This was the happiest period of Carter's life in the Army. He came to like his Japanese K.P.'s. He studied their language, he visited their homes, he gave them gifts of food from time to time. They worshiped him because he was kind to them and generous, because he never shouted, because his good humor bubbled over into games, and made the work of the kitchen seem pleasant. All the while he grew in confidence. He was not a big man, but his body filled out from the heavy work; he was likely to sing a great deal, he cracked jokes with the men on the chow line. The kitchen became his property, it became his domain, and since it was a warm room, filled with sunlight, he came to take pleasure in the very sight of it. Before long his good humor expanded into a series of efforts to improve the food. He began to take little pains and make little extra efforts which would have been impossible if he had been obliged to cook for more than thirty men. In the morning he would serve the men fresh eggs scrambled or fried to their desire in fresh butter. Instead of cooking sixty eggs in one large pot he cooked two eggs at a time in a frying pan, turning them to the taste of each soldier. He baked like a housewife satisfying her young husband; at lunch and dinner there was pie or cake, and often both. He went to great lengths. He taught the K.P.'s how to make the toast come out right. He traded excess food for spices in Japanese stores. He rubbed paprika and garlic on the chickens. He even made pastries to cover such staples as corn beef hash and meat and vegetable stew.

It all seemed to be wasted. In the beginning the men might have noticed these improvements, but after a period they took them for granted. It did not matter how he worked to satisfy them; they trudged through the chow line with their heads down, nodding coolly at him, and they ate without comment. He would hang around the tables after the meal, noticing how much they consumed, and what they discarded; he would wait for compliments, but the soldiers seemed indifferent. They seemed to eat without tasting the food. In their faces he saw mirrored the distaste with which he had once stared at cooks.

The honeymoon was ended. The pleasure he took in the kitchen and himself curdled. He became aware again of his painful desire to please people, to discharge responsibility, to be a man. When he had been a child, tears had come into his eyes at a cross word, and he had lived in an atmosphere where his smallest accomplishment was warmly praised. He was the sort of young man, he often thought bitterly, who was accustomed to the attention and the protection of women. He would have thrown away all he possessed— the love of his wife, the love of his mother, the benefits of his education, the assured financial security of entering his father's business—if he had been able just once to dig a ditch as well as the most ignorant farmer.

Instead, he was back in the painful unprotected days of his first entrance into the Army. Once again the most casual actions became the most painful, the events which were most to be taken for granted grew into the most significant, and the feeding of the men at each meal turned progressively more unbearable.

So Sanford Carter came full circle. If he had once hated the cooks, he now hated the troops. At mealtimes his face soured into the belligerent scowl with which he had once believed cooks to be born. And to himself he muttered the age-old laments of the housewife: how little they appreciated what he did.

Finally there was an explosion. He was approached one day by Corporal Taylor, and he had come to hate Taylor, because Taylor was the natural leader of the detachment and kept the other men endlessly amused with his jokes. Taylor had the ability to present himself as inefficient, shiftless, and incapable, in such a manner as to convey that really the opposite was true. He had the lightest touch, he had the greatest facility, he could charm a geisha in two minutes and obtain anything he wanted from a supply sergeant in five. Carter envied him, envied his grace, his charmed indifference; then grew to hate him.

Taylor teased Carter about the cooking, and he had the knack of knowing where to put the knife. "Hey, Carter," he would shout across the mess hall while breakfast was being served, "you turned my eggs twice, and I asked for them raw." The men would shout with laughter. Somehow Taylor had succeeded in conveying all of the situation, or so it seemed to Carter, insinuating everything, how Carter worked and how it meant nothing, how Carter labored to gain their affection and earned their contempt. Carter would scowl, Carter would answer in a rough voice, "Next time I'll crack them over your head." "You crack 'em, I'll eat 'em," Taylor would pipe back, "but just don't put your fingers in 'em." And there would be another laugh. He hated the sight of Taylor.

It was Taylor who came to him to get the salad oil. About twenty of the soldiers were going to have a fish fry at the geisha house; they had bought the fish at the local market, but they could not buy oil, so Taylor was sent as the deputy to Carter. He was charming to Carter, he complimented him on the meal, he clapped him on the back, he dissolved Carter to warmth, to private delight in the attention, and the thought that he had misjudged Taylor. Then Taylor asked for the oil.

Carter was sick with anger. Twenty men out of the thirty in the detachment were going on the fish fry. It meant only that Carter was considered one of the ten undesirables. It was something he had known, but the proof of knowledge is always more painful than the acquisition of it. If he had been alone his eyes would have clouded. And he was outraged at Taylor's deception. He could imagine Taylor saying ten minutes later, "You should have seen the grease job I gave to Carter. I'm dumb, but man, he's dumber."

Carter was close enough to giving him the oil. He had a sense of what it would mean to refuse Taylor, he was on the very edge of mild acquiescence. But he also had a sense of how he would despise himself afterward.

"No," he said abruptly, his teeth gritted, "you can't have it."

"What do you mean we can't have it?"

"I won't give it to you." Carter could almost feel the rage which Taylor generated at being refused.

"You won't give away a lousy five gallons of oil to a bunch of G.I.'s having a party?"

"I'm sick and tired," Carter began.

"So am I." Taylor walked away.

Carter knew he would pay for it. He left the K.P.'s and went to change his sweat-soaked work shirt, and as he passed the large dormitory in which most of the detachment slept he could hear Taylor's high-pitched voice. Carter did not bother to take off his shirt. He returned instead to the kitchen, and listened to the sound of men going back and forth through the hall and of a man shouting with rage. That was Hobbs, a Southerner, a big man with a big bellowing voice.

There was a formal knock on the kitchen door. Taylor came in. His face was pale and his eyes showed a cold satisfaction. "Carter," he said, "the men want to see you in the big room."

Carter heard his voice answer huskily. "If they want to see me, they can come into the kitchen."

He knew he would conduct himself with more courage in his own kitchen than anywhere else. "I'll be here for a while."

Taylor closed the door, and Carter picked up a writing board to which was clamped the menu for the following day. Then he made a pretense of examining the food supplies in the pantry closet. It was his habit to check the stocks before deciding what to serve the next day, but on this night his eyes ranged thoughtlessly over the canned goods. In a corner were seven five-gallon tins of salad oil, easily enough cooking oil to last a month. Carter came out of the pantry and shut the door behind him.

He kept his head down and pretended to be writing the menu when the soldiers came in. Somehow there were even more of them than he had expected. Out of the twenty men who were going to the party, all but two or three had crowded through the door.

Carter took his time, looked up slowly. "You men want to see me?" he asked flatly.

They were angry. For the first time in his life he faced the hostile expressions of many men. It was the most painful and anxious moment he had ever known.

"Taylor says you won't give us the oil," someone burst out.

"That's right, I won't," said Carter. He tapped his pencil against the scratchboard, tapping it slowly and, he hoped, with an appearance of calm.

"What a stink deal," said Porfirio, a little Cuban whom Carter had always considered his friend.

Hobbs, the big Southerner, stared down at Carter. "Would you mind telling the men why you've decided not to give us the oil?" he asked quietly.

" 'Cause I'm blowed if I'm going to cater to you men. I've catered enough," Carter said. His voice was close to cracking with the outrage he had suppressed for so long, and he knew that if he continued he might cry. "I'm the acting mess sergeant," he said as coldly as he could, "and I decide what goes out of this kitchen." He stared at each one in turn, trying to stare them down, feeling mired in the rut of his own failure. They would never have dared this approach to another mess sergeant.

"What crud," someone muttered.

"You won't give a lousy five-gallon can of oil for a G.I. party," Hobbs said more loudly.

"I won't. That's definite. You men can get out of here."

"Why, you lousy little snot," Hobbs burst out, "how many five-gallon cans of oil have you sold on the black market?"

"I've never sold any," Carter might have been slapped with the flat of a sword. He told himself bitterly, numbly, that this was the reward he received for being perhaps the single honest cook in the whole United States Army. And he even had time to wonder at the obscure prejudice which had kept him from selling food for his own profit.

"Man, I've seen you take it out," Hobbs exclaimed. "I've seen you take it to the market."

"I took food to trade for spices," Carter said hotly.

There was an ugly snicker from the men.

"I don't mind if a cook sells," Hobbs said, "every man has his own deal in this Army. But a cook ought to give a little food to a G.I. if he wants it."

"Tell him," someone said.

"It's bull," Taylor screeched. "I've seen Carter take butter, eggs, every damn thing to the market."

Their faces were red, they circled him.

"I never sold a thing," Carter said doggedly.

"And I'm telling you," Hobbs said, "that you're a two-bit crook. You been raiding that kitchen, and that's why you don't give to us now."

Carter knew there was only one way he could possibly answer if he hoped to live among these men again. "That's a goddam lie," Carter said to Hobbs. He laid down the scratchboard, he flipped his pencil slowly and deliberately to one corner of the room, and with his heart aching he lunged toward Hobbs. He had no hope of beating him. He merely intended to fight until he was pounded unconscious, advancing the pain and bruises he would collect as collateral for his self-respect.

To his indescribable relief Porfirio darted between them, held them apart with the pleased ferocity of a small man breaking up a fight. "Now, stop this! Now, stop this!" he cried out.

Carter allowed himself to be pushed back, and he knew that he had gained a point. He even glimpsed a solution with some honor.

He shrugged violently to free himself from Porfirio. He was in a rage, and yet it was a rage he could have ended at any instant. "All right, you men," he swore, "I'll give you the oil, but now that we're at it, I'm going to tell you a thing or two." His face red, his body perspiring, he was in the pantry and out again with a five gallon tin. "Here," he said, "you better have a good fish fry, 'cause it's the last good meal you're going to have for quite a while. I'm sick of trying to please you. You think I have to work—" he was about to say, my fingers to the bone—"well, I don't. From now on, you'll see what chow in the Army is supposed to be like." He was almost hysterical. "Take that oil. Have your fish fry." The fact that they wanted to cook for themselves was the greatest insult of all. "Tomorrow I'll give you real Army cooking."

His voice was so intense that they backed away from him. "Get out of this kitchen," he said. "None of you has any business here."

They filed out quietly, and they looked a little sheepish.

Carter felt weary, he felt ashamed of himself, he knew he had not meant what he said. But half an hour later, when he left the kitchen and passed the large dormitory, he heard shouts of raucous laughter, and he heard his name mentioned and then more laughter.

He slept badly that night, he was awake at four, he was in the kitchen by five, and stood there white-faced and nervous, waiting for the K.P.'s to arrive. Breakfast that morning landed on the men like a lead bomb. Carter rummaged in the back of the pantry and found a tin of dehydrated eggs covered with dust, memento of a time when fresh eggs were never on the ration list. The K.P.'s looked at him in amazement as he stirred the lumpy powder into a pan of water. While it was still half-dissolved he put it on the fire. While it was still wet, he took it off. The coffee was cold, the toast was burned, the oatmeal stuck to the pot. The men dipped forks into their food, took cautious sips of their coffee, and spoke in whispers. Sullenness drifted like vapors through the kitchen.

At noontime Carter opened cans of meat-and-vegetable stew. He dumped them into a pan and heated them slightly. He served the stew with burned string beans and dehydrated potatoes which tasted like straw. For dessert the men had a single lukewarm canned peach and cold coffee.

So the meals continued. For three days Carter cooked slop, and suffered even more than the men. When mealtime came he left the chow line to the K.P.'s and sat in his room, perspiring with shame, determined not to yield and sick with the determination.

Carter won. On the fourth day a delegation of men came to see him. They told him that indeed they had appreciated his cooking in the past, they told him that they were sorry they had hurt his feelings, they listened to his remonstrances, they listened to his grievances, and with delight Carter forgave them. That night, for supper, the detachment celebrated. There was roast chicken with stuffing, lemon meringue pie and chocolate cake. The coffee burned their lips. More than half the men made it a point to compliment Carter on the meal.

In the weeks which followed the compliments diminished, but they never stopped completely. Carter became ashamed at last. He realized the men were trying to humor him, and he wished to tell them it was no longer necessary.

Harmony settled over the kitchen. Carter even became friends with Hobbs, the big Southerner. Hobbs approached him one day, and in the manner of a farmer talked obliquely for an hour. He spoke about his father, he spoke about his girl friends, he alluded indirectly to the night they had almost fought, and finally with the courtesy of a Southerner he said to Carter, "You know, I'm sorry about shooting off my mouth. You were right to want to fight me, and if you're still mad I'll fight you to give you the satisfaction, although I just as soon would not."

"No, I don't want to fight with you now," Carter said warmly. They smiled at each other. They were friends.

Carter knew he had gained Hobbs' respect. Hobbs respected him because he had been willing to fight. That made sense to a man like Hobbs. Carter liked him so much at this moment that he wished the friendship to be more intimate.

"You know," he said to Hobbs, "it's a funny thing. You know I really never did sell anything on the black market. Not that I'm proud of it, but I just didn't."

Hobbs frowned. He seemed to be saying that Carter did not have to lie. "I don't hold it against a man," Hobbs said, "if he makes a little money in something that's his own proper work. Hell, I sell gas from the motor pool. It's just I also give gas if one of the G.I.'s wants to take the jeep out for a joy ride, kind of."

"No, but I never did sell anything." Carter had to explain. "If I ever had sold on the black market, I would have given the salad oil without question."

Hobbs frowned again, and Carter realized he still did not believe him. Carter did not want to lose the friendship which was forming. He thought he could save it only by some further admission. "You know," he said again, "remember when Porfirio broke up our fight? I was awful glad when I didn't have to fight you." Carter laughed, expecting Hobbs to laugh with him, but a shadow passed across Hobbs' face.

"Funny way of putting it," Hobbs said.

He was always friendly thereafter, but Carter knew that Hobbs would never consider him a friend. Carter thought about it often, and began to wonder about the things which made him different. He was no longer so worried about becoming a man; he felt that to an extent he had become one. But in his heart he wondered if he would ever learn the language of men.

The Wall

Jean-Paul Sartre
(b. 1905)

*Born in Paris, Jean-Paul Sartre received his early school-
ing at the* Lycée de la Rochelle *in western France and later
attended the* Lycée Henry IV *in Paris. In 1925 he entered
the* Ecole Normale Supérieure *where, in 1929, he passed
the* agrégation *in philosophy, equivalent to the doctorate
given in this country. During the next several years Sartre
taught in various schools, traveled, and studied in Germany
under Edmund Husserl and Martin Heidegger. He also
began to study the writings of Sören Kierkegaard, the nine-
teenth-century Danish philosopher generally regarded as
the forerunner of existentialism, the philosophy with which
Sartre is associated. Sartre's first novel,* La Nausée (Nausea), *was published in 1938, and was soon followed by*
Le Mur (The Wall), *a collection of short stories.*

*During World War II, Sartre became a leader in the
French Resistence and also contributed essays to such
underground publications as* Les Lettres Françaises *and*
Combat. *His first play* Les Mouches (The Flies) *was produced during this period. After the war, Sartre's writings
won him an international reputation and helped popularize
existentialist philosophy. His works include* L'Etre et le
Néant (Being and Nothingness), *1943;* L'Age de raison
(The Age of Reason), *1945;* Huis clos (No Exit), *1944;
and* Les Mains sales (Dirty Hands), *1948.*

They pushed us into a large white room and my eyes began to blink because the light hurt them. Then I saw a table and four fellows seated at the table, civilians, looking at some papers. The other prisoners were herded together at one end and we were obliged to cross the entire room to join them. There were several I knew, and others who must have been foreigners. The two in front of me were blond with round heads. They looked alike. I imagine they were French. The smaller one kept pulling at his trousers, out of nervousness.

This lasted about three hours. I was dog-tired and my head was empty. But the room was well-heated, which struck me as rather agreeable; we had not stopped shivering for twenty-four hours. The guards led the prisoners in one after the other in front of the table. Then the four fellows asked them their names and what they did. Most of the time that was all—or perhaps from time to time they would ask such questions as: "Did you help sabotage the munitions?" or, "Where were you on the morning of the ninth and what were you doing?" They didn't even listen to the replies, or at least they didn't seem to. They just remained silent for a moment and looked straight ahead, then they began to write. They asked Tom if it was true he had served in the International Brigade. Tom couldn't say he hadn't because of the papers they had found in his jacket. They didn't ask Juan anything, but after he told them his name, they wrote for a long while.

"It's my brother José who's the anarchist," Juan said. "You know perfectly well he's not here now. I don't belong to any party. I never did take part in politics." They didn't answer.

Then Juan said, "I didn't do anything. And I'm not going to pay for what the others did."

His lips were trembling. A guard told him to stop talking and led him away. It was my turn.

"Your name is Pablo Ibbieta?"

I said yes.

The fellow looked at his papers and said, "Where is Ramon Gris?"

"I don't know."

"You hid him in your house from the sixth to the nineteenth."

"I did not."

They continued to write for a moment and the guards led me

THE WALL   Copyright 1945 by Random House, Inc. Reprinted from *Bedside Book of Famous French Stories,* by Belle Becker and Robert N. Linscott, by permission of New Directions Publishing Corporation and Random House, Inc.

away. In the hall, Tom and Juan were waiting between two guards. We started walking. Tom asked one of the guards, "Was that just the preliminary questioning, or was that the trial?" "That was the trial," the guard said. "So now what? What are they going to do with us?" The guard answered drily, "The verdict will be told to you in your cell."

In reality, our cell was one of the cellars of the hospital. It was terribly cold there because it was very drafty. We had been shivering all night long and it had hardly been any better during the day. I had spent the preceding five days in a cellar in the archbishop's palace, a sort of dungeon that must have dated back to the Middle Ages. There were lots of prisoners and not much room, so they housed them just anywhere. But I was not homesick for my dungeon. I hadn't been cold there, but I had been alone, and that gets to be irritating. In the cellar I had company. Juan didn't say a word; he was afraid, and besides, he was too young to have anything to say. But Tom was a good talker and knew Spanish well.

In the cellar there were a bench and four straw mattresses. When they led us back we sat down and waited in silence. After a while Tom said, "Our goose is cooked."

"I think so too," I said. "But I don't believe they'll do anything to the kid."

Tom said, "They haven't got anything on him. He's the brother of the fellow who's fighting, and that's all."

I looked at Juan. He didn't seem to have heard.

Tom continued, "You know what they do in Saragossa? They lay the guys across the road and then they drive over them with trucks. It was a Moroccan deserter who told us that. They say it's just to save ammunition."

I said, "Well, it doesn't save gasoline."

I was irritated with Tom; he shouldn't have said that.

He went on, "There are officers walking up and down the roads with their hands in their pockets, smoking, and they see that it's done right. Do you think they'd put 'em out of their misery? Like hell they do. They just let 'em holler. Sometimes as long as an hour. The Moroccan said the first time he almost puked."

"I don't believe they do that here," I said, "unless they really are short of ammunition."

The daylight came in through four air vents and a round opening that had been cut in the ceiling, to the left, and which opened directly onto the sky. It was through this hole, which was ordinarily closed by means of a trapdoor, that they unloaded coal into the cellar. Directly under the hole, there was a big pile of coal dust; it had been intended for heating the hospital, but at the beginning of the war they had evacuated the patients and the coal had stayed there unused; it even got rained on from time to time, when they forgot to close the trapdoor.

Tom started to shiver. "God damn it," he said, "I'm shivering. There, it is starting again."

He rose and began to do gymnastic exercises. At each movement, his shirt opened and showed his white, hairy chest. He lay down on his back, lifted his legs in the air and began to do the scissors movement. I watched his big buttocks tremble. Tom was tough, but he had too much fat on him. I kept thinking that soon bullets and bayonet points would sink into that mass of tender flesh as though it were a pat of butter.

I wasn't exactly cold, but I couldn't feel my shoulders or my arms. From time to time, I had the impression that something was missing and I began to look around for my jacket. Then I would suddenly remember they hadn't given me a jacket. It was rather awkward. They had taken our clothes to give them to their own soldiers and had left us only our shirts and these cotton trousers the hospital patients wore in mid-summer. After a moment, Tom got up and sat down beside me, breathless.

"Did you get warmed up?"

"Damn it, no. But I'm all out of breath."

Around eight o'clock in the evening, a Major came in with two falangists.

"What are the names of those three over there?" he asked the guard.

"Steinbock, Ibbieta and Mirbal," said the guard.

The Major put on his glasses and examined his list.

"Steinbock—Steinbock. . . . Here it is. You are condemned to death. You'll be shot tomorrow morning."

He looked at his list again.

"The other two, also," he said.

"That's not possible," said Juan. "Not me."

The Major looked at him with surprise. "What's your name?"

"Juan Mirbal."

"Well, your name is here," said the Major, "and you're condemned to death."

"I didn't do anything," said Juan.

The Major shrugged his shoulders and turned toward Tom and me.

"You are both Basque?"

"No, nobody's Basque."

He appeared exasperated.

"I was told there were three Basques. I'm not going to waste my time running after them. I suppose you don't want a priest?"

We didn't even answer.

Then he said, "A Belgian doctor will be around in a little while. He has permission to stay with you all night."

He gave a military salute and left.

"What did I tell you?" Tom said. "We're in for something swell."

"Yes," I said. "It's a damned shame for the kid."

I said that to be fair, but I really didn't like the kid. His face was too refined and it was disfigured by fear and suffering, which had twisted all his features. Three days ago, he was just a kid with a kind of affected manner some people like. But now he looked like an aging fairy, and I thought to myself he would never be young again, even if they let him go. It wouldn't have been a bad thing to show him a little pity, but pity makes me sick, and besides, I couldn't stand him. He hadn't said anything more, but he had turned gray. His face and hands were gray. He sat down again and stared, round-eyed, at the ground. Tom was good-hearted and tried to take him by the arm, but the kid drew himself away violently and made an ugly face. "Leave him alone," I said quietly. "Can't you see he's going to start to bawl?" Tom obeyed regretfully. He would have liked to console the kid; that would have kept him occupied and he wouldn't have been tempted to think about himself. But it got on my nerves. I had never thought about death, for the reason that the question had never come up. But now it had come up, and there was nothing else to do but think about it.

Tom started talking. "Say, did you ever bump anybody off?" he asked me. I didn't answer. He started to explain to me that he had bumped off six fellows since August. He hadn't yet realized what we were in for, and I saw clearly he didn't *want* to realize it. I myself hadn't quite taken it in. I wondered if it hurt very much. I thought about the bullets; I imagined their fiery hail going through my body. All that was beside the real question; but I was calm, we had all night in which to realize it. After a while Tom stopped talking and I looked at him out of the corner of my eye. I saw that he, too, had turned gray and that he looked pretty miserable. I said to myself, "It's starting." It was almost dark, a dull light filtered through the air vents across the coal pile and made a big spot under the sky. Through the hole in the ceiling I could already see a star. The night was going to be clear and cold.

The door opened and two guards entered. They were followed by a blond man in a tan uniform. He greeted us.

"I'm the doctor," he said. "I've been authorized to give you any assistance you may require in these painful circumstances."

He had an agreeable, cultivated voice.

I said to him, "What are you going to do here?"

"Whatever you want to do. I shall do everything in my power to lighten these few hours."

"Why did you come to us? There are lots of others: the hospital's full of them."

"I was sent here," he answered vaguely. "You'd probably like to smoke, wouldn't you?" he added suddenly. "I've got some cigarettes and even some cigars."

He passed around some English cigarettes and some *puros,* but we refused them. I looked him straight in the eye and he appeared uncomfortable.

"You didn't come here out of compassion," I said to him. "In fact, I know who you are. I saw you with some fascists in the barracks yard the day I was arrested."

I was about to continue, when all at once something happened to me which surprised me: the presence of this doctor had suddenly ceased to interest me. Usually, when I've got hold of a man I don't let go. But somehow the desire to speak had left me. I shrugged my shoulders and turned away. A little later, I looked up and saw he was watching me with an air of curiosity. The guards had sat down on one of the mattresses. Pedro, the tall thin one, was twiddling his thumbs, while the other one shook his head occasionally to keep from falling asleep.

"Do you want some light?" Pedro suddenly asked the doctor. The other fellow nodded, "Yes." I think he was not overintelligent, but doubtless he was not malicious. As I looked at his big, cold, blue eyes, it seemed to me the worst thing about him was his lack of imagination. Pedro went out and came back with an oil lamp which he set on the corner of the bench. It gave a poor light, but it was better than nothing; the night before we had been left in the dark. For a long while I stared at the circle of light the lamp threw on the ceiling. I was fascinated. Then, suddenly, I came to, the light circle paled, and I felt as if I were being crushed under an enormous weight. It wasn't the thought of death, and it wasn't fear; it was something anonymous. My cheeks were burning hot and my head ached.

I roused myself and looked at my two companions. Tom had his head in his hands and only the fat, white nape of his neck was visible. Juan was by far the worst off; his mouth was wide open and his nostrils were trembling. The doctor came over to him and touched him on the shoulder, as though to comfort him; but his eyes remained cold. Then I saw the Belgian slide his hand furtively down Juan's arm to his wrist. Indifferent, Juan let himself be handled. Then, as though absent-mindedly, the Belgian laid three fingers over his wrist; at the same time, he drew away somewhat and managed to turn his back to me. But I leaned over backward and saw him take out his watch and look at it a moment before relinquishing the boy's wrist. After a moment, he let the inert hand fall and went and leaned against the wall. Then, as if he had suddenly remembered something very important that had to be noted down immediately, he took a notebook from his pocket and wrote a few lines in it. "The son-of-a-bitch," I thought angrily. "He better not come and feel my pulse; I'll give him a punch in his dirty jaw."

He didn't come near me, but I felt he was looking at me. I raised my head and looked back at him. In an impersonal voice, he said, "Don't you think it's frightfully cold here?"

He looked purple with cold.

"I'm not cold," I answered him.

He kept looking at me with a hard expression. Suddenly I understood, and I lifted my hands to my face. I was covered with sweat. Here, in this cellar, in mid-winter, right in a draft, I was sweating. I ran my fingers through my hair, which was stiff with sweat; at the same time, I realized my shirt was damp and sticking to my skin. I had been streaming with perspiration for an hour, at least, and had felt nothing. But this fact hadn't escaped that Belgian swine. He had seen the drops rolling down my face and had said to himself that it showed an almost pathological terror; and he himself had felt normal and proud of it because he was cold. I wanted to get up and go punch his face in, but I had hardly started to make a move before my shame and anger had disappeared. I dropped back onto the bench with indifference.

I was content to rub my neck with my handkerchief because now I felt the sweat dripping from my hair onto the nape of my neck and that was disagreeable. I soon gave up rubbing myself, however, for it didn't do any good; my handkerchief was already wringing wet and I was still sweating. My buttocks, too, were sweating, and my damp trousers stuck to the bench.

Suddenly, Juan said, "You're a doctor, aren't you?"

"Yes," said the Belgian.

"Do people suffer—very long?"

"Oh! When. . . ? No, no," said the Belgian, in a paternal voice, "it's quickly over."

His manner was as reassuring as if he had been answering a paying patient.

"But I. . . . Somebody told me—they often have to fire two volleys."

"Sometimes," said the Belgian, raising his head, "it just happens that the first volley doesn't hit any of the vital organs."

"So then they have to reload their guns and aim all over again?"

Juan thought for a moment, then added hoarsely, "But that takes time!"

He was terribly afraid of suffering. He couldn't think about anything else, but that went with his age. As for me, I hardly thought about it any more and it certainly was not fear of suffering that made me perspire.

I rose and walked toward the pile of coal dust. Tom gave a start and looked at me with a look of hate. I irritated him because my shoes squeaked. I wondered if my face was as putty-colored as his. Then I noticed that he, too, was sweating. The sky was magnificent; no light at all came into our dark corner and I had only to lift my head to see the Big Bear. But it didn't look the way it had looked before. Two days ago, from my cell in the archbishop's palace, I could see a big patch of sky and each time of day brought back a different memory. In the morning, when the sky was a deep blue, and light, I thought of beaches along the Atlantic; at noon, I could see the sun, and I remembered a bar in Seville where I used to drink manzanilla and eat anchovies and olives; in the afternoon, I was in the shade, and I thought of the deep shadow which covers half of the arena while the other half gleams in the sunlight: it really gave me a pang to see the whole earth reflected in the sky like that. Now, however, no matter how much I looked up in the air, the sky no longer recalled anything. I liked it better that way. I came back and sat down next to Tom. There was a long silence.

Then Tom began to talk in a low voice. He had to keep talking, otherwise he lost his way in his own thoughts. I believe he was talking to me, but he didn't look at me. No doubt he was afraid to look at me, because I was gray and sweating. We were both alike and worse than mirrors for each other. He looked at the Belgian, the only one who was alive.

"Say, do you understand? I don't."

Then I, too, began to talk in a low voice. I was watching the Belgian.

"Understand what? What's the matter?"

"Something's going to happen to us that I don't understand."

There was a strange odor about Tom. It seemed to me that I was more sensitive to odors than ordinarily. With a sneer, I said, "You'll understand, later."

"That's not so sure," he said stubbornly. "I'm willing to be courageous, but at least I ought to know. . . . Listen, they're going to take us out into the courtyard. All right. The fellows will be standing in line in front of us. How many of them will there be?"

"Oh, I don't know. Five, or eight. Not more."

"That's enough. Let's say there'll be eight of them. Somebody will shout 'Shoulder arms!' and I'll see the eight rifles aimed at me. I'm sure I'm going to feel like going through the wall. I'll push against the wall as hard as I can with my back, and the wall won't give in. The way it is in a nightmare. . . . I can imagine all that. Ah, if you only knew how well I can imagine it!"

"Skip it!" I said. "I can imagine it too."

"It must hurt like the devil. You know they aim at your eyes and mouth so as to disfigure you," he added maliciously. "I can feel the wounds already. For the last hour I've been having pains in my head and neck. Not real pains—it's worse still. They're the pains I'll feel tomorrow morning. And after that, then what?"

I understood perfectly well what he meant, but I didn't want to seem to understand. As for the pains, I, too, felt them all through my body, like a lot of little gashes. I couldn't get used to them, but I was like him, I didn't think they were very important.

"After that," I said roughly, "you'll be eating daisies."

He started talking to himself, not taking his eyes off the Belgian, who didn't seem to be listening to him. I knew what he had come for, and that what we were thinking didn't interest him. He had come to look at our bodies, our bodies which were dying alive.

"It's like in a nightmare," said Tom. "You want to think of something, you keep having the impression you've got it, that you're going to understand, and then it slips away from you, it eludes you and it's gone again. I say to myself, afterwards, there won't be anything. But I don't really understand what that means. There are moments when I almost do—and then it's gone again. I start to think of the pains, the bullets, the noise of the shooting. I am a materialist, I swear it; and I'm not going crazy, either. But there's something wrong. I see my own corpse. That's not hard, but it's *I* who see it, with *my* eyes. I'll have to get to the point where I think—where I think I won't see anything more. I won't hear anything more, and the world will go on for the others. We're not made to think that way, Pablo. Believe me, I've stayed awake all night waiting for something. But this is not the same thing. This will grab us from behind, Pablo, and we won't be ready for it."

"Shut up," I said. "Do you want me to call a father confessor?"

He didn't answer. I had already noticed that he had a tendency to prophesy and call me "Pablo" in a kind of pale voice. I didn't like that very much, but it seems all the Irish are like that. I had a vague impression that he smelled of urine. Actually, I didn't like Tom very much, and I didn't see why, just because we were going to die together, I should like him any better. There are certain fellows with whom it would be different—with Ramon Gris, for instance. But between Tom and Juan, I felt alone. In fact, I liked it better that way. With Ramon I might have grown soft. But I felt terribly hard at that moment, and I wanted to stay hard.

Tom kept on muttering, in a kind of absent-minded way. He was certainly talking to keep from thinking. Naturally, I agreed with him, and I could have said everything he was saying. It's not *natural* to die. And since I was going to die, nothing seemed natural any more: neither the coal pile, nor the bench, nor Pedro's dirty old face. Only it was disagreeable for me to think the same things Tom thought. And I knew perfectly well that all night long, within five minutes of each other, we would keep on thinking things at the same time, sweating or shivering at the same time. I looked at him sideways and, for the first time, he seemed strange to me. He had death written on his face. My pride was wounded. For twenty-four hours I had lived side by side with Tom, I had listened to him, I had talked to him, and I knew we had nothing in common. And now we were as alike as twin brothers, simply because we were going to die together. Tom took my hand without looking at me.

"Pablo, I wonder. . . . I wonder if it's true that we just cease to exist."

I drew my hand away.

"Look between your feet, you dirty dog."

There was a puddle between his feet and water was dripping from his trousers.

"What's the matter?" he said frightened.

"You're wetting your pants," I said to him.

"It's not true," he said furiously. "I can't be . . . I don't feel anything."

The Belgian had come closer to him. With an air of false concern, he asked, "Aren't you feeling well?"

Tom didn't answer. The Belgian looked at the puddle without comment.

"I don't know what that is," Tom said savagely, "but I'm not afraid. I swear to you, I'm not afraid."

The Belgian made no answer. Tom rose and went to the corner. He came back, buttoning his fly, and sat down, without a word. The Belgian was taking notes.

We were watching the doctor. Juan was watching him too. All three of us were watching him because he was alive. He had the gestures of a living person, the interests of a living person; he was shivering in this cellar the way living people shiver; he had an obedient, well-fed body. We, on the other hand, didn't feel our bodies any more—not the same way, in any case. I felt like touching my trousers, but I didn't dare to. I looked at the Belgian, well-planted on his two legs, master of his muscles—and able to plan for tomorrow. We were like three shadows deprived of blood; we were watching him and sucking his life like vampires.

Finally he came over to Juan. Was he going to lay his hand on the nape of Juan's neck for some professional reason, or had he obeyed a charitable impulse? If he had acted out of charity, it was the one and only time during the whole night. He fondled Juan's head and the nape of his neck. The kid let him do it, without taking his eyes off him. Then, suddenly, he took hold of the doctor's hand and looked at it in a funny way. He held the Belgian's hand between his own two hands and there was nothing pleasing about them, those two gray paws squeezing that fat red hand. I sensed what was going to happen and Tom must have sensed it, too. But all the Belgian saw was emotion, and he smiled paternally. After a moment, the kid lifted the big red paw to his mouth and started to bite it. The Belgian drew back quickly and stumbled toward the wall. For a second, he looked at us with horror. He must have suddenly understood that we were not men like himself. I began to laugh, and one of the guards started up. The other had fallen asleep with his eyes wide open, showing only the whites.

I felt tired and over-excited at the same time. I didn't want to think any more about what was going to happen at dawn—about death. It didn't make any sense, and I never got beyond just words, or emptiness. But whenever I tried to think about something else I saw the barrels of rifles aimed at me. I must have lived through my execution twenty times in succession; one time I thought it was the real thing; I must have dozed off for a moment. They were dragging me toward the wall and I was resisting; I was imploring their pardon. I woke with a start and looked at the Belgian. I was afraid I had cried out in my sleep. But he was smoothing his mustache; he hadn't noticed anything. If I had wanted to, I believe I could have slept for a while. I had been awake for the last forty-eight hours, and I was worn out. But I didn't want to lose two hours of life. They would have had to come and wake me at dawn. I would have followed them, drunk with sleep, and I would have gone off without so much as "Gosh!" I didn't want it that way, I didn't want to die like an animal. I wanted to understand. Besides, I was afraid of having nightmares. I got up and began to walk up and down and, so as to think about something else, I began to think about my past life. Memories crowded in on me, helter-skelter. Some were good and some were bad—at least that was how I had thought of them *before*. There were faces and happenings. I saw the face of a little *novilero* who had gotten himself horned during the *Feria,* in Valencia. I saw the face of one of my uncles, of Ramon Gris. I remembered all kinds of things that had happened: how I had been on strike for three months in 1926, and had almost died of hunger. I recalled a night I had spent on a bench in Granada; I hadn't eaten for three days, I was nearly wild, I didn't want to give up the sponge. I had to smile. With what eagerness I had run after happiness, and women, and liberty! And to what end? I had wanted to liberate Spain, I admired Py Margall, I had belonged to the anarchist movement. I had spoken at public meetings. I took everything as seriously as if I had been immortal.

At that time I had the impression that I had my whole life before me, and I thought to myself, "It's all a god-damned lie." Now it wasn't worth anything because it was finished. I wondered how I had ever been able to go out and have a good time with girls. I wouldn't have lifted my little finger if I had ever imagined that I would die like this. I saw my life before me, finished, closed, like a bag, and yet what was inside was not finished. For a moment I tried to appraise it. I would have liked to say to myself, "It's been a good life." But it couldn't be appraised, it was only an outline. I had spent my time writing checks on eternity, and had understood nothing. Now, I didn't miss anything. There were a lot of things I might have missed: the taste of manzanilla, for instance, or the swims I used to take in summer in a little creek near Cadiz. But death had taken the charm out of everything.

Suddenly the Belgian had a wonderful idea.

"My friends," he said to us, "if you want me to—and providing the military authorities give their consent—I could undertake to deliver a word or some token from you to your loved ones. . . ."

Tom growled, "I haven't got anybody."

I didn't answer. Tom waited for a moment, then he looked at me with curiosity. "Aren't you going to send any message to Concha?"

"No."

I hated that sort of sentimental conspiracy. Of course, it was my fault, since I had mentioned Concha the night before, and I should have kept my mouth shut. I had been with her for a year. Even as late as last night, I would have cut my arm off with a hatchet just to see her again for five minutes. That was why I had mentioned her. I couldn't help it. Now I didn't care any more about seeing her. I hadn't anything more to say to her. I didn't even want to hold her in my arms. I loathed my body because it had turned gray and was sweating—and I wasn't even sure that I didn't loathe hers too. Concha would cry when she heard about my death; for months she would have no more interest in life. But still it was I who was going to die. I thought of her beautiful, loving eyes. When she looked at me something went from her to me. But I thought to myself that it was all over; if she looked at me *now* her gaze would not leave her eyes, it would not reach out to me. I was alone.

Tom too, was alone, but not the same way. He was seated astride his chair and had begun to look at the bench with a sort of smile, with surprise, even. He reached out his hand and touched the wood cautiously, as though he were afraid of breaking something, then he drew his hand back hurriedly, and shivered. I wouldn't have amused myself touching that bench, if I had been Tom, that was just some more Irish play-acting. But somehow it seemed to me too that the different objects had something funny about them. They seemed to have grown paler, less massive than before. I had only to look at the bench, the lamp or the pile of coal dust to feel I was going to die. Naturally, I couldn't think clearly about my death, but I saw it everywhere, even on the different objects, the way they had withdrawn and kept their distance, tactfully, like people talking at the bedside of a dying person. It was *his own death* Tom had just touched on the bench.

In the state I was in, if they had come and told me I could go home quietly, that my life would be saved, it would have left me cold. A few hours, or a few years of waiting are all the same, when you've lost the illusion of being eternal. Nothing mattered to me any more. In a way, I was calm. But it was a horrible kind of calm—because of my body. My body—I saw with its eyes and I heard with its ears, but it was no longer I. It sweat and trembled independently, and I didn't recognize it any longer. I was obliged to touch it and look at it to know what was happening to it, just as if it had been someone else's body. At times I still felt it. I felt a slipping, a sort of headlong plunging, as in a falling airplane, or else I heard my heart beating. But this didn't give me confidence. In fact, everything that came from my body had something damned dubious about it. Most of the time it was silent, it stayed put and I didn't feel anything other than a sort of heaviness, a loathsome presence against me. I had the impression of being bound to an enormous vermin.

The Belgian took out his watch and looked at it.

"It's half-past three," he said.

The son-of-a-bitch! He must have done it on purpose. Tom jumped up. We hadn't yet realized the time was passing. The night surrounded us like a formless, dark mass; I didn't even remember it had started.

Juan started to shout. Wringing his hands, he implored, "I don't want to die! I don't want to die!"

He ran the whole length of the cellar with his arms in the air, then he dropped down onto one of the mattresses, sobbing. Tom looked at him with dismal eyes and didn't even try to console him any more. The fact was, it was no use; the kid made more noise than we did, but he was less affected, really. He was like a sick person who defends himself against his malady with a high fever. When there's not even any fever left, it's much more serious.

He was crying. I could tell he felt sorry for himself; he was thinking about death. For one second, one single second, I too felt like crying, crying out of pity for myself. But just the contrary happened. I took one look at the kid, saw his thin, sobbing shoulders, and I felt I was inhuman. I couldn't feel pity either for these others or for myself. I said to myself, "I want to die decently."

Tom had gotten up and was standing just under the round opening looking out for the first signs of daylight. I was determined, I wanted to die decently, and I only thought about that. But underneath, ever since the doctor had told us the time, I felt time slipping, flowing by, one drop at a time.

It was still dark when I heard Tom's voice.

"Do you hear them?"

"Yes."

People were walking in the courtyard.

"What the hell are they doing? After all, they can't shoot in the dark."

After a moment, we didn't hear anything more. I said to Tom, "There's the daylight."

Pedro got up yawning, and came and blew out the lamp. He turned to the man beside him. "It's hellish cold."

The cellar had grown gray. We could hear shots at a distance.

"It's about to start," I said to Tom. "That must be in the back courtyard."

Tom asked the doctor to give him a cigarette. I didn't want any; I didn't want either cigarettes or alcohol. From that moment on, the shooting didn't stop.

"Can you take it in?" Tom said.

He started to add something, then he stopped and began to watch the door. The door opened and a lieutenant came in with four soldiers. Tom dropped his cigarette.

"Steinbock?"

Tom didn't answer. Pedro pointed him out.

"Juan Mirbal?"

"He's the one on the mattress."

"Stand up," said the Lieutenant.

Juan didn't move. Two soldiers took hold of him by the armpits and stood him up on his feet. But as soon as they let go of him he fell down.

The soldiers hesitated a moment.

"He's not the first one to get sick," said the Lieutenant. "You'll have to carry him, the two of you. We'll arrange things when we get there." He turned to Tom. "All right, come along."

Tom left between two soldiers. Two other soldiers followed, carrying the kid by his arms and legs. He was not unconscious; his eyes were wide open and tears were rolling down his cheeks. When I started to go out, the Lieutenant stopped me.

"Are you Ibbieta?"

"Yes."

"You wait here. They'll come and get you later on."

They left. The Belgian and the two jailers left too, and I was alone. I didn't understand what had happened to me, but I would have liked it better if they had ended it all right away. I heard the volleys at almost regular intervals; at each one, I shuddered. I felt like howling and tearing my hair. But instead, I gritted my teeth and pushed my hands deep into my pockets, because I wanted to stay decent.

An hour later, they came to fetch me and took me up to the first floor in a little room which smelt of cigar smoke and was so hot it seemed to me suffocating. Here there were two officers sitting in comfortable chairs, smoking, with papers spread out on their knees.

"Your name is Ibbieta?"

"Yes."

"Where is Ramon Gris?"

"I don't know."

The man who questioned me was small and stocky. He had hard eyes behind his glasses.

"Come nearer," he said to me.

I went nearer. He rose and took me by the arms, looking at me in a way calculated to make me go through the floor. At the same time he pinched my arms with all his might. He didn't mean to hurt me; it was quite a game; he wanted to dominate me. He also seemed to think it was necessary to blow his fetid breath right into my face. We stood like that for a moment, only I felt more like laughing than anything else. It takes a lot more than that to intimidate a man who's about to die: it didn't work. He pushed me away violently and sat down again.

"It's your life or his," he said. "You'll be allowed to go free if you tell us where he is."

After all, these two bedizened fellows with their riding crops and boots were just men who were going to die one day. A little later than I, perhaps, but not a great deal. And there they were, looking for names among their papers, running after other men in order to put them in prison or do away with them entirely. They had their opinions on the future of Spain and on other subjects. Their petty activities seemed to me to be offensive and ludicrous. I could no longer put myself in their place. I had the impression they were crazy.

The little fat fellow kept looking at me, tapping his boots with his riding crop. All his gestures were calculated to make him appear like a spirited, ferocious animal.

"Well? Do you understand?"

"I don't know where Gris," I said. "I thought he was in Madrid."

The other officer lifted his pale hand indolently. This indolence was also calculated. I saw through all their little tricks, and I was dumbfounded that men should still exist who took pleasure in that kind of thing.

"You have fifteen minutes to think it over," he said slowly. "Take him to the linen-room, and bring him back here in fifteen minutes. If he continues to refuse, he'll be executed at once."

They knew what they were doing. I had spent the night waiting. After that, they had made me wait another hour in the cellar, while they shot Tom and Juan, and now they locked me in the linen-room. They must have arranged the whole thing the night before. They figured that sooner or later people's nerves wear out and they hoped to get me that way.

They made a big mistake. In the linen-room I sat down on a ladder because I felt very weak, and I began to think things over. Not their proposition, however. Naturally I knew where Gris was. He was hiding in his cousins' house, about two miles outside of the city. I knew, too, that I would not reveal his hiding place, unless they tortured me (but they didn't seem to be considering that). All that was definitely settled and didn't interest me in the least. Only I would have liked to understand the reasons for my own conduct. I would rather die than betray Gris. Why? I no longer liked Ramon Gris. My friendship for him had died shortly before dawn along with my love for Concha, along with my own desire to live. Of course I still admired him—he was hard. But it was not for that reason that I was willing to die in his place; his life was no more valuable than mine. No life was of any value. A man was going to be stood up against a wall and fired at till he dropped dead. It didn't make any difference whether it was I or Gris or somebody else. I knew perfectly well he was more useful to the Spanish cause than I was, but I didn't give a God damn about Spain or anarchy, either; nothing had any importance now. And yet, there I was. I could save my skin by betraying Gris and

I refused to do it. It seemed more ludicrous to me than anything else; it was stubbornness.

I thought to myself, "Am I hardheaded!" And I was seized with a strange sort of cheerfulness.

They came to fetch me and took me back to the two officers. A rat darted out under our feet and that amused me. I turned to one of the falangists and said to him, "Did you see that rat?"

He made no reply. He was gloomy, and took himself very seriously. As for me, I felt like laughing, but I restrained myself because I was afraid that if I started, I wouldn't be able to stop. The falangist wore mustaches. I kept after him, "You ought to cut off those mustaches, you fool."

I was amused by the fact that he let hair grow all over his face while he was still alive. He gave me a kind of half-hearted kick, and I shut up.

"Well," said the fat officer, "have you thought things over?"

I looked at them with curiosity, like insects of a very rare species.

"I know where he is," I said. "He's hiding in the cemetery. Either in one of the vaults, or in the gravediggers' shack."

I said that just to make fools of them. I wanted to see them get up and fasten their belts and bustle about giving orders.

They jumped to their feet.

"Fine. Moles, go ask Lieutenant Lopez for fifteen men. And as for you," the little fat fellow said to me, "if you've told the truth, I don't go back on my word. But you'll pay for this, if you're pulling our leg."

They left noisily and I waited in peace, still guarded by the falangists. From time to time I smiled at the thought of the face they were going to make. I felt dull and malicious. I could see them lifting up the gravestones, or opening the doors of the vaults one by one. I saw the whole situation as though I were another person: the prisoner determined to play the hero, the solemn falangists with their mustaches and the men in uniform running around among the graves. It was irresistibly funny.

After half an hour, the little fat fellow came back alone. I thought he had come to give the order to execute me. The others must have stayed in the cemetery.

The officer looked at me. He didn't look at all foolish.

"Take him out in the big courtyard with the others," he said. "When military operations are over, a regular tribunal will decide his case."

I thought I must have misunderstood.

"So they're not—they're not going to shoot me?" I asked.

"Not now, in any case. Afterwards, that doesn't concern me."

I still didn't understand.

"But why?" I said to him.

He shrugged his shoulders without replying, and the soldiers led me away. In the big courtyard there were a hundred or so prisoners, women, children and a few old men. I started to walk around the grass plot in the middle. I felt absolutely idiotic. At noon we were fed in the dining hall. Two or three fellows spoke to me. I must have known them, but I didn't answer. I didn't even know where I was.

Toward evening, about ten new prisoners were pushed into the courtyard. I recognized Garcia, the baker.

He said to me, "Lucky dog! I didn't expect to find you alive."

"They condemned me to death," I said, "and then they changed their minds. I don't know why."

"I was arrested at two o'clock," Garcia said.

"What for?"

Garcia took no part in politics.

"I don't know," he said. "They arrest everybody who doesn't think the way they do."

He lowered his voice.

"They got Gris."

I began to tremble.

"When?"

"This morning. He acted like a damned fool. He left his cousins' house Tuesday because of a disagreement. There were any number of fellows who would have hidden him, but he didn't want to be indebted to anybody any more. He said, 'I would have hidden at Ibbieta's, but since they've got him, I'll go hide in the cemetery.'"

"In the cemetery?"

"Yes. It was the god-damnedest thing. Naturally they passed by there this morning; that had to happen. They found him in the gravediggers' shack. They opened fire at him and they finished him off."

"In the cemetery!"

Everything went around in circles, and when I came to I was sitting on the ground. I laughed so hard the tears came to my eyes.

The Portable Phonograph

Walter Van Tilburg Clark
(1909–1971)

Clark earned a bachelor's degree and a master's degree at the University of Nevada, where his father was president from 1917 to 1937, a second master's degree at the University of Vermont, and a doctorate at Colgate University. After teaching for ten years in New York, he moved back to the West, where he taught at various colleges and universities, including the University of Montana, San Francisco State College, and the University of Nevada.

Clark is considered a western writer: he grew up in the West, spent most of his adult life there, and used a western setting in most of his writings. Thus, in this respect, "The Portable Phonograph" is atypical of Clark's major works. His most famous work, The Ox-Bow Incident *(1940), studies the psychological aspects of a lynching in Nevada's cattle country. In* The Track of the Cat *(1949), a much longer novel, Clark creates an atmosphere of almost palpable terror and malignity as he describes the stalking of a marauding mountain lion during a blizzard in the Sierras. Most of his best short stories are collected in* The Watchful Gods and Other Stories *(1950).*

The red, sunset, with narrow, black cloud strips like threats across it, lay on the curved horizon of the prairie. The air was still and cold, and in it settled the mute darkness and greater cold of night. High in the air there was wind, for through the veil of the dusk the clouds could be seen gliding rapidly south and changing shapes. A queer sensation of torment, of two-sided, unpredictable nature, arose from the stillness of the earth air beneath the violence of the upper air. Out of the sunset, through the dead, matted grass and isolated weed stalks of the prairie, crept the narrow and deeply rutted remains of a road. In the road, in places, there were crusts of shallow, brittle ice. There were little islands of an old oiled pavement in the road too, but most of it was mud, now frozen rigid. The frozen mud still bore the toothed impress of great tanks, and a wanderer on the neighboring undulations might have stumbled, in this light, into large, partially filled-in and weed-grown cavities, their banks channelled and beginning to spread into badlands. These pits were such as might have been made by falling meteors, but they were not. They were the scars of gigantic bombs, their rawness already made a little natural by rain, seed, and time. Along the road, there were rakish remnants of fence. There was also, just visible, one portion of tangled and multiple barbed wire still erect, behind which was a shelving ditch with small caves, now very quiet and empty, at intervals in its back wall. Otherwise there was no structure or remnant of a structure visible over the dome of the darkling earth, but only, in sheltered hollows, the darker shadows of young trees trying again.

Under the wuthering arch of the high wind a V of wild geese fled south. The rush of their pinions sounded briefly, and the faint, plaintive notes of their expeditionary talk. Then they left a still greater vacancy. There was the smell and expectation of snow, as there is likely to be when the wild geese fly south. From the remote distance, towards the red sky, came faintly the protracted howl and quick yap-yap of a prairie wolf.

North of the road perhaps a hundred yards, lay the parallel and deeply intrenched course of a small creek, lined with leafless alders and willows. The creek was already silent under ice. Into the bank above it was dug a sort of cell, with a single opening, like the mouth of a mine tunnel. Within the cell there was a little red of fire, which showed dully through the opening, like a reflection or a deception of the imagination. The light came from the chary burning of four blocks of poorly aged peat, which gave off a petty warmth and much acrid smoke. But the precious remnants of wood, old fence posts and timbers from the long-deserted dug-outs, had to be saved for the real cold, for the time when a man's breath blew white, the moisture in his nostrils stiffened at once when he stepped out, and the expansive blizzards paraded for days over the vast open, swirling and settling and thickening, till the dawn of the cleared day when the sky was thin blue-green and the terrible cold, in which a man could not live for three hours un-warmed, lay over the uniformly drifted swell of the plain.

Around the smoldering peat, four men were seated cross-legged. Behind them, traversed by their shadows, was the earth bench, with two old and dirty army blankets, where the owner of the cell slept. In a niche in the opposite wall were a few tin utensils which caught the glint of the coals. The host was rewrapping in a piece of daubed burlap four fine, leather-bound books. He worked slowly and very carefully, and at last tied the bundle securely with a piece of grass-woven cord. The other three looked intently upon the process, as if a great significance lay in it. As the host tied the cord, he spoke. He was an old man, his long, matted beard and hair gray to nearly white. The shadows made his brows and cheek-bones appear gnarled, his eyes and cheeks deeply sunken. His big hands, rough with frost and swollen by rheumatism, were awk-ward but gentle at their task. He was like a prehistoric priest per-forming a fateful ceremonial rite. Also his voice had in it a suitable quality of deep, reverent despair, yet perhaps at the moment, a sharpness of selfish satisfaction.

'When I perceived what was happening,' he said, 'I told myself, "It is the end. I cannot take much; I will take these." '

'Perhaps I was impractical,' he continued. 'But for myself, I do not regret, and what do we know of those who will come after us? We are the doddering remnant of a race of mechanical fools. I have saved what I love; the soul of what was good in us is here; perhaps the new ones will make a strong enough beginning not to fall behind when they become clever.'

He rose with slow pain and placed the wrapped volumes in the niche with his utensils. The others watched him with the same ritualistic gaze.

'Shakespeare, the Bible, *Moby Dick,* the *Divine Comedy,*' one of them said softly. 'You might have done worse, much worse.'

'You will have a little soul left until you die,' said another harshly. 'That is more than is true of us. My brain becomes thick, like my hands.' He held the big, battered hands, with their black nails, in the glow to be seen.

'I want paper to write on,' he said. 'And there is none.'

The fourth man said nothing. He sat in the shadow farthest

from the fire, and sometimes his body jerked in its rags from the cold. Although he was still young, he was sick and coughed often. Writing implied a greater future than he now felt able to consider.

The old man seated himself laboriously, and reached out, groaning at the movement, to put another block of peat on the fire. With bowed heads and averted eyes, his three guests acknowledged his magnanimity.

'We thank you, Doctor Jenkins, for the reading,' said the man who had named the books.

They seemed then to be waiting for something. Doctor Jenkins understood, but was loath to comply. In an ordinary moment he would have said nothing. But the words of *The Tempest,* which he had been reading, and the religious attention of the three made this an unusual occasion.

'You wish to hear the phonograph,' he said grudgingly.

The two middle-aged men stared into the fire, unable to formulate and expose the enormity of their desire.

The young man, however, said anxiously, between suppressed coughs, 'Oh, please,' like an excited child.

The old man rose again in his difficult way, and went to the back of the cell. He returned and placed tenderly upon the packed floor, where the firelight might fall upon it, an old portable phonograph in a black case. He smoothed the top with his hand, and then opened it. The lovely green-felt-covered disk became visible.

'I have been using thorns as needles,' he said. 'But tonight, because we have a musician among us'—he bent his head to the young man, almost invisible in the shadow—'I will use a steel needle. There are only three left.'

The two middle-aged men stared at him in speechless adoration. The one with the big hands, who wanted to write, moved his lips, but the whisper was not audible.

'Oh, don't!' cried the young man, as if he were hurt. 'The thorns will do beautifully.'

'No,' the old man said. 'I have become accustomed to the thorns, but they are not really good. For you, my young friend, we will have good music tonight.'

'After all,' he added generously, and beginning to wind the phonograph, which creaked, 'they can't last forever.'

'No, nor we,' the man who needed to write said harshly. 'The needle, by all means.'

'Oh, thanks,' said the young man. 'Thanks,' he said again in a low, excited voice, and then stifled his coughing with a bowed head.

'The records, though,' said the old man when he had finished winding, 'are a different matter. Already they are very worn. I do not play them more than once a week. One, once a week, that is what I allow myself.

'More than a week I cannot stand it; not to hear them,' he apologized.

'No, how could you?' cried the young man. 'And with them here like this.'

'A man can stand anything,' said the man who wanted to write, in his harsh, antagonistic voice.

'Please, the music,' said the young man.

'Only the one,' said the old man. 'In the long run, we will remember more that way.'

He had a dozen records with luxuriant gold and red seals. Even in that light the others could see that the threads of the records were becoming worn. Slowly he read out the titles, and the tremendous, dead names of the composers and the artists and the orchestras. The three worked upon the names in their minds, carefully. It was difficult to select from such a wealth what they would at once most like to remember. Finally, the man who wanted to write named Gershwin's 'New York.'

'Oh, no!' cried the sick young man, and then could say nothing more because he had to cough. The others understood him, and the harsh man withdrew his selection and waited for the musician to choose.

The musician begged Doctor Jenkins to read the titles again, very slowly, so that he could remember the sounds. While they were read, he lay back against the wall, his eyes closed, his thin, horny hand pulling at his light beard, and listened to the voices and the orchestras and the single instruments in his mind.

When the reading was done he spoke despairingly. 'I have forgotten,' he complained; 'I cannot hear them clearly.'

'There are things missing,' he explained.

'I know,' said Doctor Jenkins. 'I thought that I knew all of Shelley by heart. I should have brought Shelley.'

'That's more soul than we can use,' said the harsh man. '*Moby Dick* is better.'

'By God, we can understand that,' he emphasized.

The Doctor nodded.

'Still,' said the man who had admired the books, 'we need the absolute if we are to keep a grasp on anything.'

'Anything but these sticks and peat clods and rabbit snares,' he said bitterly.

'Shelley desired an ultimate absolute,' said the harsh man. 'It's too much,' he said. 'It's no good; no earthly good.'

The musician selected a Debussy nocturne. The others considered and approved. They rose to their knees to watch the Doctor prepare for the playing, so that they appeared to be actually in an attitude of worship. The peat glow showed the thinness of their bearded faces, and the deep lines in them, and revealed the condition of their garments. The other two continued to kneel as the old man carefully lowered the needle onto the spinning disk, but the musician suddenly drew back against the wall again, with his knees up, and buried his face in his hands.

At the first notes of the piano the listeners were startled. They stared at each other. Even the musician lifted his head in amazement, but then quickly bowed it again, strainingly, as if he were suffering from a pain he might not be able to endure. They were all listening deeply, without movement. The wet, blue-green notes tinkled forth from the old machine, and were individual, delectable presences in the cell. The individual, delectable presences swept into a sudden tide of unbearably beautiful dissonance, and then continued fully the swelling and ebbing of that tide, the dissonant inpourings, and the resolutions, and the diminishments, and the little, quiet wavelets of interlude lapping between. Every sound was piercing and singularly sweet. In all the men except the musician, there occurred rapid sequences of tragically heightened recollection. He heard nothing but what was there. At the final, whispering disappearance, but moving quietly so that the others would not hear him and look at him, he let his head fall back in agony, as if it were drawn there by the hair, and clenched the fingers of one hand over his teeth. He sat that way while the others were silent, and until they began to breathe again normally. His drawn-up legs were trembling violently.

Quickly Doctor Jenkins lifted the needle off, to save it and not to spoil the recollection with scraping. When he had stopped the whirling of the sacred disk, he courteously left the phonograph open and by the fire, in sight.

The others, however, understood. The musician rose last, but then abruptly, and went quickly out at the door without saying anything. The others stopped at the door and gave their thanks in low voices. The Doctor nodded magnificently.

'Come again,' he invited, 'in a week. We will have the "New York." '

When the two had gone together, out towards the rimed road, he stood in the entrance, peering and listening. At first, there was only the resonant boom of the wind overhead, and then far over the dome of the dead, dark plain, the wolf cry lamenting. In the rifts of clouds the Doctor saw four stars flying. It impressed the Doctor that one of them had just been obscured by the beginning of a flying cloud at the very moment he heard what he had been listening for, a sound of suppressed coughing. It was not near-by, however. He believed that down against the pale alders he could see the moving shadow.

With nervous hands he lowered the piece of canvas which served as his door, and pegged it at the bottom. Then quickly and quietly, looking at the piece of canvas frequently, he slipped the records into the case, snapped the lid shut, and carried the phonograph to his couch. There, pausing often to stare at the canvas and listen, he dug earth from the wall and disclosed a piece of board. Behind this there was a deep hole in the wall, into which he put the phonograph. After a moment's consideration, he went over and reached down his bundle of books and inserted it also. Then, guardedly, he once more sealed up the hole with the board and the earth. He also changed his blankets, and the grass-stuffed sack which served as a pillow, so that he could lie facing the entrance. After carefully placing two more blocks of peat upon the fire, he stood for a long time watching the stretched canvas, but it seemed to billow naturally with the first gusts of a lowering wind. At last he prayed, and got in under his blankets, and closed his smoke-smarting eyes. On the inside of the bed, next the wall, he could feel with his hand, the comfortable piece of lead pipe.

Plumbing the depths

La Lupa

Giovanni Verga
(1840–1922)

Born in 1840 into a family of established landowners in the Sicilian city of Catania, Giovanni Verga was educated primarily by private tutors. Long resolved on becoming a writer, Verga went to Florence in 1865 where he be- friended members of a literary circle and continued to write; in 1871 he moved to Milan. For almost fifteen years he remained in northern Italy writing romanzi (*novels of "elegance and adultery," as Verga styled them*). *They usually centered on the psychological burdens endured by the upper class and were written in Tuscan, the language of the educated Florentines. Although he was a popular writer while he lived in the North, Verga did not fully de- velop his talents until he returned to Sicily and began to write, in standard Italian, about the fishermen and peasants he had known as a child. Between 1880 and 1883 he pub- lished three of his most famous books:* Vita dei campi (Cavalleria Rusticana and Other Stories) *in which "La Lupa"`appears;* I Malavoglia (The House by the Medlar Tree); *and* Novelle rusticane (Little Novels of Sicily). Mastro Don Gesualdo, *his final major work, was completed in 1889. After that year, Verga mainly wrote plays based on his short stories, including one derived from "La Lupa."*

She was tall, and thin; but she had the firm, vigorous bosom of a brown woman, though she was no longer young. Her face was pale, as though she had the malaria always on her, and in her pallor two great dark eyes, and fresh, red lips, that seemed to eat you.

In the village they called her *la Lupa,* because she had never had enough—of anything. The women crossed themselves when they saw her go by, alone like a roving she-dog, with that ranging, suspicious motion of a hungry wolf. She bled their sons and their husbands dry in a twinkling, with those red lips of hers, and she had merely to look at them with her great evil eyes, to have them running after her skirts, even if they'd been kneeling at the altar of Saint Agrippina. Fortunately, *la Lupa* never entered the church, neither at Easter nor at Christmas, nor to hear Mass, nor to confess.—Fra Angiolino, of Santa Maria di Jesu, who had been a true servant of God, had lost his soul because of her.

Maricchia, poor thing, was a good girl and a nice girl, and she wept in secret because she was *la Lupa's* daughter, and nobody would take her in marriage, although she had her marriage-chest full of linen, and her piece of fertile land in the sun, as good as any other girl in the village.

Then one day *la Lupa* fell in love with a handsome lad who'd just come back from serving as a soldier, and was cutting the hay alongside her in the closes belonging to the lawyer: but really what you'd call falling in love, feeling your body burn under your stuff bodice, and suffering, when you stared into his eyes, the thirst that you suffer in the hot hours of June, away in the burning plains. But he went on mowing quietly, with his nose bent over his swath, and he said to her: "Why, what's wrong with you, Mrs. Pina?"— In the immense fields, where only the grasshoppers crackled into flight, when the sun beat down like lead, *la Lupa* gathered armful after armful together, tied sheaf after sheaf, without ever wearying, without straightening her back for a moment, without putting her lips to the flask, so that she could keep at Nanni's heels, as he mowed and mowed, and asked her from time to time: "Why, what do you want, Mrs. Pina?"

One evening she told him, while the men were dozing in the stackyard, tired from the long day, and the dogs were howling away in the vast, dark, open country: "You! I want you! Thou'rt

LA LUPA   Translated by D. H. Lawrence. Reprinted from *Cavalleria Rusticana and Other Stories,* by Giovanni Verga, by permission of Laurence Pollinger Ltd. and the Estate of the late Mrs. Frieda Lawrence.

handsome as the day, and sweet as honey to me. I want thee, lad!"

"Ah! I'd rather have your daughter, who's a filly," replied Nanni, laughing.

La Lupa clutched her hands in her hair, and tore her temples, without saying a word, and went away, and was seen no more in the yard. But in October she saw Nanni again, when they were getting the oil out of the olives, because he worked next her house, and the screeching of the oil-press didn't let her sleep at night.

"Take the sack of olives," she said to her daughter, "and come with me."

Nanni was throwing the olives under the millstone with the shovel, in the dark chamber like a cave, where the olives were ground and pressed, and he kept shouting *Ohee!* to the mule, so it shouldn't stop.

"Do you want my daughter Maricchia?" Mrs. Pina asked him.

"What are you giving your daughter Maricchia?" replied Nanni.

"She has what her father left, and I'll give her my house into the bargain; it's enough for me if you'll leave me a corner in the kitchen, where I can spread myself a bit of a straw mattress to sleep on."

"All right! If it's like that, we can talk about it at Christmas," said Nanni.

Nanni was all greasy and grimy with the oil and the olives set to ferment, and Maricchia didn't want him at any price; but her mother seized her by the hair, at home in front of the fireplace, and said to her between her teeth:

"If thou doesn't take him, I'll lay thee out!"

La Lupa was almost ill, and the folks were saying that the devil turns hermit when he gets old. She no longer went roving round; she no longer sat in the doorway, with those eyes of one possessed. Her son-in-law, when she fixed on him those eyes of hers, would start laughing, and draw out from his breast the bit of Madonna's dress, to cross himself. Maricchia stayed at home nursing the children, and her mother went to the fields, to work with the men, just like a man, weeding, hoeing, tending the cattle, pruning the vines, whether in the north-east wind or the east winds of January, or in the hot, stifling African wind of August, when the mules let their heads hang in dead weight, and the men slept face downwards under the wall, on the north side. *Between vesper bell and the night-bell's sound, when no good woman goes roving round,* Mrs. Pina was the only soul to be seen wandering through the countryside, on the ever-burning stones of the little roads, through the parched stubble of the immense fields, which lost themselves in the sultry haze of the distance, far off, far off, towards misty Etna, where the sky weighed down upon the horizon, in the afternoon heat.

"Wake up!" said *la Lupa* to Nanni, who was asleep in the ditch, under the dusty hedge, with his arms round his head. "Wake up! I've brought thee some wine to cool thy throat."

Nanni opened his eyes wide like a disturbed child, half-awake, seeing her erect above him, pale, with her arrogant bosom, and her eyes black as coals, and he stretched out his hand gropingly, to keep her off.

"No! No good woman goes roving round between vespers and night," sobbed Nanni, pressing his face down again in the dry grass of the ditch-bottom, away from her, clutching his hair with his hands. "Go away! Go away! Don't you come into the stackyard again!"

She did indeed go away, *la Lupa,* but fastening up again the coils of her superb black hair, staring straight in front of her, as she stepped over the hot stubble, with eyes black as coals.

And she came back into the stackyard time and again, and Nanni no longer said anything; and when she was late coming, in the hour between evensong and night, he went to the top of the white, deserted little road to look for her, with sweat on his forehead;—and afterwards, he clutched his hair in his hand, and repeated the same thing every time: "Go away! Go away! Don't you come into the stackyard again!"

Maricchia wept night and day; and she glared at her mother with eyes that burned with tears and jealousy; like a young she-wolf herself now, when she saw her coming in from the fields, every time silent and pallid.

"Vile woman!" she said to her. "Vile, vile mother!"

"Be quiet!"

"Thief! Thief that you are!"

"Be quiet!"

"I'll go to the Sergeant, I will."

"Then go!"

And she did go, finally, with her child in her arms, went fearless and without shedding a tear, like a madwoman, because now she also was in love with that husband of hers, whom they'd forced her to accept, greasy and grimy from the olives set to ferment.

The Sergeant went for Nanni, and threatened him with gaol and the gallows. Nanni began to sob and to tear his hair; he denied nothing, he didn't try to excuse himself.—"It's the temptation," he said. "It's the temptation of hell!" and he threw himself at the feet of the Sergeant, begging to be sent to gaol.

"For pity's sake, Sergeant, get me out of this hell! Have me hung, or send me to prison; but don't let me see her again, never, never!"

"No!" replied *la Lupa* to the Sergeant. "I kept myself a corner in the kitchen, to sleep in, when I gave her my house for her dowry. The house is mine. I won't be turned out."

A little while later, Nanni got a kick in the chest from a mule, and was likely to die; but the parish priest wouldn't bring the Host to him, unless *la Lupa* left the house. *La Lupa* departed, and then her son-in-law could prepare himself to depart also, like a good Christian; he confessed, and took the communion with such evident signs of repentance and contrition that all the neighbours and the busybodies wept round the bed of the dying man.

And better for him if he had died that time, before the devil came back to tempt him and to get a grip on his body and his soul, when he was well.

"Leave me alone!" he said to *la Lupa*. "For God's sake, leave me in peace! I've been face to face with death. Poor Maricchia is only driven wild. Now all the place knows about it. If I never see you again, it's better for you and for me."

And he would have liked to tear his eyes out so as not to see again those eyes of *la Lupa,* which, when they fixed themselves upon his, made him lose both body and soul. He didn't know what to do, to get free from the spell she put on him. He paid for Masses for the souls in Purgatory, and he went for help to the priest and to the Sergeant. At Easter he went to confession, and he publicly performed the penance of crawling on his belly and licking the stones of the sacred threshold before the church for a length of six feet.

After that, when *la Lupa* came back to tempt him:

"Hark here!" he said. "Don't you come again into the stackyard; because if you keep on coming after me, as sure as God's above I'll kill you."

"Kill me, then," replied *la Lupa*. "It doesn't matter to me; I'm not going to live without thee."

He, when he perceived her in the distance, amid the fields of green young wheat, he left off hoeing the vines, and went to take the axe from the elm-tree. *La Lupa* saw him advancing towards her, pale and wild-eyed, with the axe glittering in the sun, but she did not hesitate in her step, nor lower her eyes, but kept on her way to meet him, with her hands full of red poppies, and consuming him with her black eyes.

"Ah! Curse your soul!" stammered Nanni.

The World
the Children Made

Ray Bradbury
(b. 1920)

At the age of seven, Ray Bradbury listened eagerly as his aunt read aloud from Edgar Allan Poe and the Oz books; at age eight, he delighted in the Buck Rogers comic strip. During the next few years "Tarzan," the magazine Amazing Stories, *and "Flash Gordon" sustained his passion for fantasy and the fabulous world of the future. As a teenager, Bradbury began to write and illustrate his own stories, and vowed that his work would some day appear in* Best American Short Stories. *He published his first story when he was nineteen and, by age twenty-one, had become a popular science-fiction writer. Since then, his work has continuously been successful, appearing at first in such publications as* Weird Tales, Amazing Stories, Astonishing, *and* Captain Future *and accepted in later years by* American Mercury, Charm, Mademoiselle, *and* Colliers. *At twenty-six, he realized his adolescent ambition when his story "The Big Black and White Game" was included in* The Best American Short Stories of 1946. *Bradbury has published several collections of short stories, among them* Dark Carnival (1947), The Martian Chronicles (1950), The Illustrated Man (1951), *and* The Golden Apples of the Sun (1953). *He is the author of* Farenheit 451 (1953), *and wrote the scenario for a movie version of* Moby Dick.

"**G**eorge, I wish you'd look at the nursery."

"What's wrong with it?"

"I don't know."

"Well, then."

"I just want you to look at it, is all, or call a psychologist in to look at it."

"What would a psychologist want with a nursery?"

"You know very well what he'd want." His wife paused in the middle of the kitchen and watched the stove busy humming to itself, making supper for four. "It's just that the nursery is different now than it was."

"All right, let's have a look."

They walked down the hall of their sound-proofed Happylife Home, which had cost them thirty thousand dollars installed, this house which clothed and fed and rocked them to sleep and played and sang and was good to them. Their approach sensitized a switch somewhere and the nursery light flicked on when they came within ten feet of it. Similarly, behind them in the halls lights went on and off as they left them behind, with a soft automaticity.

"Well," said George Hadley.

They stood on the thatched floor of the nursery. It was forty feet across by forty feet long and thirty feet high; it had cost half again as much as the rest of the house. "But nothing's too good for our children," George had said.

The nursery was silent. It was empty as a jungle glade at hot high noon. The walls were blank and two-dimensional. Now, as George and Lydia Hadley stood in the center of the room, the walls began to purr and recede into crystalline distance, it seemed, and presently an African veld appeared in three dimensions, on all sides, in color, reproduced to the final pebble and bit of straw. The ceiling above them became a deep sky with a hot yellow sun.

George Hadley felt the perspiration start on his brow. "Let's get out of this sun," he said. "This is a little too real. But I don't see anything wrong."

"Wait a moment; you'll see," said his wife.

Now the hidden odorophonics were beginning to blow a wind of odor at the two people in the middle of the baked veldland. The hot straw smell of lion grass, the cool green smell of the hidden water hole, the great rusty smell of animals, the smell of dust like a red paprika in the hot air. And now the sounds—the thump of distant antelope feet on grassy sod, the papery rustling of vultures. A shadow passed through the sky. The shadow flickered on George Hadley's upturned, sweating face.

"Filthy creatures," he heard his wife say.

"The vultures."

"You see, there are the lions, far over that way. Now they're on their way to the water hole. They've just been eating," said Lydia. "I don't know what."

"Some animal." George Hadley put his hand up to shield off the burning light from his squinted eyes. "A zebra or a baby giraffe maybe."

"Are you sure?" His wife sounded peculiarly tense.

"No, it's a little late to be sure," he said, amused. "Nothing over there I can see but cleaned bone, and the vultures dropping for what's left."

"Did you hear that scream?" she asked.

"No."

"About a minute ago?"

"Sorry, no."

The lions were coming. And again, George Hadley was filled with admiration for the mechanical genius who had conceived this room. A miracle of efficiency selling for an absurdly low price. Every home should have one. Oh, occasionally they frightened you with their clinical accuracy, they startled you, they gave you a twinge, but most of the time what fun for everyone, not only your own son and daughter but for yourself. When you felt like a quick jaunt to a foreign land, a quick change of scenery—well, here it was.

And here were the lions now, fifteen feet away—so real, so feverishly and startlingly real that you could feel the prickling fur on your hand, and your mouth was stuffed with the dusty upholstery smell of their heated pelts, and the yellow of them was in your eyes like the yellow of an exquisite French tapestry, the yellow of lions and summer grass, and the sound of the matted lion lungs exhaling on the silent noontide, and the smell of meat from the panting, dripping mouths.

The lions stood looking at George and Lydia Hadley with terrible green-yellow eyes.

"Watch out!" screamed Lydia.

The lions came running at them. Lydia bolted and ran. Instinctively, George sprang after her. Outside, in the hall, with the door slammed, he was laughing and she was crying, and they both stood appalled at the other's reaction.

"George!"

"Lydia! Oh, my dear poor sweet Lydia!"

"They almost got us!"

"Walls, Lydia, remember; crystal walls, that's all they are. Oh, they look real, I must admit; Africa in your parlor, but it's all dimensional superreactionary, supersensitive color film and mental-tape film behind glass screens. It's all odorophonics and sonics, Lydia. Here's my handkerchief."

"I'm afraid." She came to him and put her body against him and cried steadily. "Did you see? Did you feel? It's too real."

"Now, Lydia—"

"You've got to tell Wendy and Peter not to read any more on Africa."

"Of course, of course." He patted her.

"Promise?"

"Sure."

"And lock the nursery for a few days until I get my nerves settled."

"You know how difficult Peter is about that. When I punished him a month ago by locking the nursery for even a few hours, the tantrum he threw. And Wendy too. They live for the nursery."

"It's got to be locked, that's all there is to it."

"All right." Reluctantly he locked the huge door. "You've been working too hard. You need a rest."

"I don't know, I don't know," she said, blowing her nose and sitting down in a chair that immediately began to rock and comfort her. "Maybe I don't have enough to do. Maybe I have time to think too much. Why don't we shut the whole house off for a few days and take a vacation?"

"You mean you want to fry my eggs for me?"

"Yes." She nodded.

"And darn my socks?"

"Yes." A frantic, watery-eyed nodding.

"And sweep the house?"

"Yes, yes; oh, yes!"

"But I thought that's why we bought this house—so we wouldn't have to do anything?"

"That's just it. I feel like I don't belong here. The house is wife and mother now, and nursemaid. Can I compete with an African veld? Can I give a bath and scrub to the children as efficiently or quickly as the automatic scrub bath can? I cannot. And it isn't just me. It's you. You've been awfully nervous lately."

"I suppose I have been smoking too much."

"You look as if you didn't know what to do with yourself in this house, either. You smoke a little more every morning and drink a little more every afternoon and need a little more sedative every night. You're beginning to feel unnecessary too."

"Am I?" He paused and tried to feel into himself to see what was really there.

"Oh, George!" She looked beyond him at the nursery door. "Those lions can't get out of there, can they?"

He looked at the door and saw it tremble as if something had jumped against it from the other side.

"Of course not," he said.

At dinner they ate alone, for Wendy and Peter were at a special plastic carnival across town and had televised home to say they'd be late, to go ahead eating. So George Hadley, bemused, sat watching the dining-room table produce warm dishes of food from its mechanical interior.

"We forgot the ketchup," he said.

"Sorry," said a small voice within the table, and ketchup appeared.

As for the nursery, thought George Hadley, it wouldn't hurt for the children to be locked out of it a while. Too much of anything wasn't good for anyone. And it was clearly indicated that the children had been spending a little too much time on Africa. That sun. He could feel it on his neck, still, like a hot paw. And the lions. And the smell of blood. Remarkable how the nursery caught the telepathic emanations of the children's minds and created life to fill their every desire. The children thought lions, and there were lions. The children thought zebras, and there were zebras. Sun, sun. Giraffes, giraffes. Death, and death.

Death thoughts. They were awfully young, Wendy and Peter, for death thoughts. Or no, you were never too young, really. Long before you knew what death was you were wishing it on someone else. When you were two years old you were shooting people with cap pistols.

But this—the long hot African veld, the awful death in the jaws of a lion. And repeated again and again.

"Where are you going?"

He didn't answer Lydia. Preoccupied, he let the lights glow softly on ahead of him, extinguish behind him as he padded to the nursery door. He listened against it. Far away, a lion roared.

He unlocked the door and opened it. Just before he stepped inside, he heard a faraway scream. And then another roar from the lions, which subsided quickly. He stepped into Africa. How many times in the last year had be opened this door and found Wonderland, Alice, the Mock Turtle, or Aladdin and his magic lamp. But now, this yellow hot Africa, this bake oven with murder in the heat. Perhaps Lydia was right. Perhaps they needed a little vacation from this fantasy which was growing a bit too real for ten-year-old children. It was all right to exercise one's mind with gymnastic fantasies, but when the lively child mind settled on one pattern—It seemed that at a distance, for the past month, he had heard lions roaring and smelled their strong odor seeping as far away as his study door. But, being busy, he had paid it no attention.

George Hadley stood on the African grassland alone. The lions looked up from their feeding, watching him. The only flaw to the illusion was the open door through which he could see his wife, far down the dark hall, like a framed picture, eating abstractedly.

"Go away," he said to the lions.

They did not go.

He knew the principle of the room exactly. You sent out your thoughts. Whatever you thought would appear.

"Let's have the Emerald City of Oz!" he snapped.

The veldland remained, the lions remained.

"Come on, room! I demand Oz!"

Nothing happened.

"Oz!"

He went back to dinner. "The fool room's out of order," he said. "It won't respond."

"Or—"

"Or what?"

"Or it can't change," said Lydia, "because the children have thought about Africa and lions and killing so many days that the room's in a rut."

"Could be."

"Or Peter's set it to remain that way."

"Set it?"

"He may have got into the machinery and fixed something."

"Peter doesn't know machinery."

"He's a wise one for ten; that I.Q. of his—"

"Nevertheless—"

"Hello, Mom. . . . Hello, Dad."

The Hadleys turned. Wendy and Peter were coming in the front door, cheeks like peppermint candy, eyes like bright blue agate marbles, a smell of ozone on their jumps from their trip in the helicopter.

"You're just in time for supper," said both parents.

"We're full of strawberry ice cream and hot dogs," said the children, holding hands. "But we'll sit and watch."

"Yes, come tell us about the nursery," said George Hadley.

The brother and sister blinked at him and then at each other. "Nursery?"

"All about Africa and everything," said the father, with false joviality.

"I don't understand," said Peter.

"Your mother and I were just traveling through Africa with rod and reel; Tom Swift and his Electric Lion," said George Hadley.

"There's no Africa in the nursery," said Peter simply.

"Oh, come now; we know better."

"I don't remember any Africa," said Peter to Wendy. "Do you?"

"No."

"Run see and come tell."

She obeyed.

"Wendy, come back here!" said George Hadley, but she was gone. Too late, he realized he had forgotten to lock the nursery door after his last inspection.

"Wendy'll look and come tell us," said Peter.

"She doesn't have to tell me. I've seen it."

"I'm sure you're mistaken, Father."

"I'm not, Peter. Come along, now."

But Wendy was back. "It's not Africa," she said breathlessly.

"We'll see about this," said George Hadley, and they all walked down the hall together and opened the nursery door.

There was a green, lovely forest, a lovely river, a purple mountain. The African veldland was gone. The lions were gone. Only Rima was here now, singing a song so beautiful that it brought tears to their eyes.

George Hadley looked in at the changed scene. "Go to bed," he said to the children.

They opened their mouths.

"You heard me," he said.

They went off to the air closet, where a window sucked them like brown leaves up the flue to their slumber rooms.

George Hadley walked through the singing glade and picked up something that lay in the corner near where the lions had been. He walked slowly back to his wife.

"What is that?" she asked.

"An old wallet of mine," he said.

He showed it to her. The smell of hot grass was on it and the smell of a lion. There were drops of saliva on it, it had been chewed, and there were blood smears on both sides.

He closed the nursery door and locked it.

In the middle of the night he was still awake and he knew his wife was awake. "Do you think Wendy changed it?" she said at last in the dark room.

"Of course."

"Made it from a veld into a forest and put Rima there instead of lions?"

"Yes."

"Why?"

"I don't know. But it's staying locked until I find out."

"How did your wallet get there?"

"It was part of the game, I suppose."

"What's going on?"

"I don't know anything," he said, "except that I'm beginning to be sorry we bought that room for the children. If the children are neurotic at all, a room like that——"

"It's supposed to help them work off their neuroses in a healthful way."

"I'm starting to wonder." He stared at the ceiling.

"We've given the children everything they ever wanted. Is this our reward—secrecy, disobedience?"

"They've been acting funny ever since you forbade them to take the Rocket to New York a few months ago."

"They're not old enough to do that alone, I explained."

"Nevertheless, I've noticed they're decidedly cool toward us since."

"I think I'll have David McClean come tomorrow morning to have a look at Africa."

"But it's not Africa now; it's Green Mansions country and Rima."

"I have a feeling it'll be Africa again before then."

A moment later they heard the screams. Two screams. Two people screaming from downstairs. And then a roar of lions.

"Wendy and Peter aren't in their rooms," said his wife.

He lay in his bed with his beating heart. "No," he said. "They've broken into the nursery."

"Those screams—they sound familiar."

"Do they?"

"Yes, awfully."

And although their beds tried very hard, the two adults couldn't be rocked asleep for another hour. A smell of cats was in the night air.

"Father?" said Peter.

"Yes." George Hadley glanced up from breakfast.

Peter looked at his shoes. He never looked at his father any more, nor at his mother. "You aren't going to lock up the nursery for good, are you?"

"That all depends."

"On what?" snapped Peter.

"On you and your sister. If you intersperse this Africa with a little variety—oh, Sweden perhaps, or Denmark or China."

"What's wrong with Africa, Father?"

"Oh, so now you admit you have been conjuring up Africa, do you?"

"I wouldn't want the nursery locked up," said Peter coldly. "Ever."

"Matter of fact, we're thinking of turning the whole house off for about a month. Live sort of a carefree one-for-all existence."

"That sounds dreadful! Would I have to tie my own shoes instead of letting the shoe tier do it? And brush my own teeth and comb my hair and give myself a bath?"

"It would be fun for a change, don't you think?"

"No, it would be horrid. I didn't like it when you took out the picture painter last month."

"That's because I wanted you to learn to paint all by yourself, son."

"I don't want to do anything but look and listen and smell. What else is there to do?"

"All right, go play in Africa."

"Will you shut off the house sometime soon?"

"We're considering it."

"I don't think you'd better consider it any more, Father."

"I won't have any threats from my son!"

"Very well." Peter strolled off to the nursery.

"Am I on time?" said David McClean.

"Breakfast?" asked George Hadley.

"Thanks, had some. What's the trouble?"

"David, you're a psychologist."

"I should hope so."

"Well, then, have a look at our nursery. You saw it a year ago when you dropped by. Did you notice anything peculiar about it then?"

"Can't say I did. The usual violences, a tendency toward a slight paranoia here or there, usual in children because they feel persecuted by parents constantly, but oh, really nothing."

They walked down the hall. "I locked the nursery up," explained the father, "and the children broke into it during the night. I let them stay so they could form the patterns for you to see."

There was a terrible screaming from the nursery.

"There it is," said George Hadley. "See what you make of it."

They walked in on the children without rapping. The screams had faded. The lions were feeding.

"Run outside a moment, children," said George Hadley. . . . "No, don't change the mental combination. Leave the walls as they are. Get!"

With the children gone, the two men stood studying the lions clustered at a distance, eating with great relish whatever it was they had caught.

"I wish I knew what it was," said George Hadley. "Sometimes I can almost see. Do you think if I brought high-powered glasses here and—"

"Hardly." He turned to study all four walls. "How long has this been going on?"

"A little over a month."

"It certainly doesn't feel good."

"I want facts, not feelings."

"My dear George, a psychologist never saw a fact in his life. He only hears about feelings, vague things. This doesn't feel good, I tell you. Trust my hunches and my instincts. I have a nose for something bad. This is very bad. My advice to you is to have the whole room torn down and your children brought to me every day for the next year for treatment."

"Is it that bad?"

"I'm afraid so. One of the original uses of these nurseries was so that we could study the patterns left on the walls by the child's mind, study at our leisure, and help the child. In this case however, the room has become a channel toward . . . destructive thoughts, instead of a release away from them."

"Didn't you sense this before?"

"I sensed only that you had spoiled your children more than most. And now you're letting them down in some way. What way?"

"I wouldn't let them go to New York."

"What else?"

"I've taken away a few machines from the house and threatened them, a month ago, with closing up the nursery unless they did their homework. I did close it for a few days to show I meant business."

"Ah-ha!"

"Does that mean anything?"

"Everything. Where before they had a Santa Claus, now they have a Scrooge. Children prefer Santas. You've let this room and this house replace you and your wife in your children's affections. This room is their mother and father, far more important in their lives than their real parents. And now you come along and want to shut it off. No wonder there's hatred here. You can feel it coming out of the sky. Feel that sun. George, you'll have to change your life. Like too many others, you've built it around creature comforts. Why, you'd starve tomorrow if something went wrong in your kitchen. You wouldn't know how to tap an egg. Nevertheless, turn everything off. Start new. It'll take time. But we'll make good children out of bad in a year; wait and see."

"But won't the shock be too much for the children, shutting the room up abruptly for good?"

"I don't want them going any deeper into this, that's all."

The lions were finished with their red feast. The lions were standing on the edge of the clearing, watching the two men.

"Now *I'm* feeling persecuted," said McClean. "Let's get out of here. I never have cared for these rooms. Make me nervous."

"The lions look real, don't they?" said George Hadley. "I don't suppose there's any way—"

"What?"

"—that they could *become* real?"

"Not that I know."

"Some flaw in the machinery, a tampering or something?"

"No."

They went to the door.

"I don't imagine the room will like being turned off," said the father.

"Nothing ever likes to die, even a room."

"I wonder if it hates me for wanting to swich it off?"

"Paranoia is thick around here today," said David McClean. "You can follow it like a spoor. Hello." He bent and picked up a bloody scarf. "This yours?"

"No." George Hadley's face was rigid. "It belongs to Lydia."

They went to the fuse box together and threw the switch that killed the nursery.

The two children were in hysterics. They screamed and pranced and threw things. They sobbed and swore and jumped at the furniture.

"George," said Lydia Hadley, "turn on the nursery, just for a few moments. You can't be so abrupt."

"No."

"You can't be so cruel."

"Lydia, it's off, and it stays off. And the whole house dies as of here and now. The more I see of the mess we've put ourselves in, the more it sickens me. We've been contemplating our mechanical, electronic navels for too long. Lord, how we need a breath of honest air!"

And he marched about the house turning off the voice clocks, the stoves, the heaters, the shoe shiners, the shoe lacers, the body scrubbers and swabbers and massagers, and every other machine he could put his hand to.

The house was full of dead bodies, it seemed. It felt like a mechanical cemetery. So silent. None of the humming hidden energy of machines waiting to function at the tap of a button.

"Don't let them do it!" wailed Peter at the ceiling, as if he were talking to the house, the nursery. "Don't let Father kill everything!" He turned to his father. "Oh, I hate you!"

"Insults won't get you anywhere."

"I wish you were dead!"

"We were, for a long while. Now we're really going to start living. Instead of being handled and massaged, we're going to live."

Wendy was still crying, and Peter joined her again. "Just a moment! Just one moment! Just another moment of nursery!" they wailed.

"Oh, George," said the wife, "it can't hurt."

"All right, all right, if they'll only just shut up. One minute, mind you, and then off forever."

"Daddy, Daddy, Daddy!" sang the children, smiling with wet faces.

"And then we're going on a vacation. David McClean is coming back in half an hour to help us move out and get to the airport. I'm going to dress. . . . You turn the nursery on for a minute, Lydia—just a minute, mind you."

And the three of them went babbling off while he let himself be vacuumed upstairs through the air flue and set about dressing himself. A minute later Lydia appeared.

"I'll be glad when we get away," she sighed.

"Did you leave them in the nursery?"

"I wanted to dress too. Oh, that horrid Africa. What can they see in it?"

"Well, in five minutes we'll be on our way to Iowa. Lord, how did we ever get in this house? What prompted us to buy a nightmare?"

"Pride, money, foolishness."

"I think we'd better get downstairs before those kids get engrossed with those beasts again."

Just then they heard the children calling, "Daddy, Mommy, come quick, quick!"

They went downstairs on the air flue and ran down the hall. The children were nowhere in sight. "Wendy? Peter!"

They ran into the nursery. The veldland was empty, save for the lions waiting, looking at them. "Peter, Wendy?"

The door slammed.

"Wendy, Peter!"

George Hadley and his wife whirled and ran back to the door.

"Open the door!" cried George Hadley, trying the knob. "Why, they've locked it from the outside! . . . Peter!" He beat at the door. "Open up!"

He heard Peter's voice outside, against the door.

"Don't let them switch off the nursery and the house," he was saying.

Mr. and Mrs. George Hadley beat at the door. "Now, don't be ridiculous, children. It's time to go. Mr. McClean'll be here in a minute and—"

And then they heard the sounds.

The lions on three sides of them, in the yellow veld grass, padding through the dry straw, rumbling and roaring in their throats. The lions.

Mr. Hadley looked at his wife, and they turned and looked back at the beasts, which rustled slowly forward, crouching, tails stiff. Mr. and Mrs. Hadley screamed. And suddenly they realized why those other screams had sounded familiar.

"Well, here I am," said David McClean in the nursery doorway. "Oh, hello." He stared at the two children seated in the center of the open glade, eating a little picnic lunch. Beyond them was the water hole and the yellow veldland; above was the hot sun. He began to perspire. "Where are your father and mother?"

The children looked up and smiled. "Oh, they'll be here directly."

"Good, we must get going." At a distance, Mr. McClean saw the lions fighting and clawing, and then quieting down to feed in silence under the shady trees. He squinted at the lions with his hand up to his eyes. Now the lions were done feeding. They came down to the water hole to drink.

A shadow flickered over Mr. McClean's hot face. Many shadows flickered. The vultures were dropping down the blazing sky.

"A cup of tea?" asked Wendy in the silence.

The Cove

Gina Berriault
(b. 1929)

Gina Berriault was born in California and has spent most of her life in various northern cities of that state. Aside from one year as Visiting Lecturer in the Writer's Workshop at the University of Iowa, she has worked primarily as a free-lance writer. Her short stories have been published in such magazines as Esquire, Harper's Bazaar, Paris Review, and Saturday Evening Post. In 1956 Gina Berriault won the Paris Review-Aga Kahn prize in fiction, and in both 1958 and 1960 her work appeared in O. Henry Award Prize Stories. Her longer works include the novels The Descent (1960) and Conference of Victims (1962), and a collection of short stories, The Mistress (1965).

Sometimes the realtor's listings book will fall open to the photographs of homes not within the means of the couple on the other side of the desk, and the wife will put out her hand, almost instinctively, to see what is beyond them. Of the several properties, the couple will pause longest over a particular house on the leeward side of the island. The woman will wish aloud that they could afford it, laughing, sighing, drooping, indecorous in a time that calls for reserve, while the husband will nod and agree robustly, even goddammning. They select, after the usual excursions with the realtor to several houses within the city and on its ex-

THE COVE Reprinted by permission of Gina Berriault. First published in Esquire Magazine.

panding edge, a house not much different from the one back home. The property that they coveted is shown only to those fortunate families for whom every hour is opportune. Persons who sometimes roam through houses they cannot afford in order to impress the realtor, or—though they have not met him before—vindictively waste his time, never venture onto the verdant grounds and across the threshold of that property. It is much too ideal to violate with one's lack of promise or even with that vindictiveness against the realtor that asks no reason for itself. Whoever might have in mind to dare an excursion is deterred by what might be suspicion on the part of the realtor: although everything is amiable and potential as they sit around his desk, elbows almost touching, knees almost touching, hands touching over maps and matches, a gulf suddenly divides him and them.

The realtor unlocked the wrought-iron gate, swung it open and stepped aside, waiting until all the members of the family had passed into the garden. Following at a discreet distance in order not to interfere with their breathtaking entry into a domain certain to be theirs and free of intruders such as himself, he bowed his head to choose the next key from the green leather case in the palm of his hand—both case and keys given him by the owner. The father went first along the path, his index finger held by the youngest of the four children, a girl of two who was walking clumsily on her toes. They were followed by the two boys, one twelve, the other nine, both lean, both wearing tan knee shorts and white pullovers edged thinly with red. The eldest, a girl of sixteen, strolled behind the boys, the wide pleats of her short white skirt parting and closing. The mother, young in spite of the number of her children, was the last of the procession except for the realtor who was, respectfully, not a part of it, following the mother by a yard, observing as if against his will how the flowers in the cloth of her dress vibrated with the movements of her body and with their own disputing colors. In the center of the emerald dusk of fern and bamboo and flowering shrubs, the father paused and so the rest paused. The garden was filled with a humming that seemed to emanate from its own exuberance until it became apparent that the sound was the sea's constant humming rising up through the density of mountain stone. Two myna birds flew up from a lichee tree in the garden, flapping over the road and settling in a breadfruit tree high on the upper slope.

The realtor unlocked the heavy teak door, found that it stuck, and pushed, his brow against it. The members of the family fanned out across the large room toward the wall of sliding glass that gave them an immense view of the sea. The realtor slid open one segment of the glass and they walked out across the terrace and over to the stone wall, and all, leaning there, gazed out on the masses of land to each side, tremendous green shoulders of earth that seemed to recede and swell in the hot light; gazed down on the vertical, winding stone stairs and, at its foot, far down, the cove. Black, volcanic rocks edged the cove, molding it into the shape of a three-quarter moon. The sea broke on the barricading reef and, after heaving and swelling on the inward side of the reef, swept almost languidly across the cove, breaking again.

The realtor took the liberty of leaning his elbows on the wall, along with the rest of them. The soft, ascending wind pressed his shirt—so white it shone in the sun—against his chest. For a few moments the shirt beat against his chest as if stirred by the beat of his heart, then the wind continued up and his shirt hung loosely again, unstirring. He was neither tall nor short, neither fat nor lean, but this averageness was like a happy medium he had attained by his own efforts. The surface of his face was receptive of all reasonable requests. Under the surface, as if it were a matter of modesty, lay a look of gratification for pleasures granted to past clients, and because this look was not outward it precluded any wondering about what might lie under. Consequently, in the eyes of the father, who was a shrewd man and who considered shrewdness a virtue, the realtor was a simple man, lacking shrewdness. The realtor was silent while they gazed down, musing and exclaiming, as if even one word might be an intrusion as intolerable as an uninvited guest down with them in that pricelessly private cove.

When they began to enter back into the house to inspect the rooms, the realtor walked by the side of the father, pointing out the stoutness of the beams, the solidity of the teak floors, the lavish use of marble. Servants were no problem, he told them, although he would advise them not to inquire at the village. They might find someone there, but someone unreliable who would prefer to reside in the village and come to work in the morning, if that someone felt so inclined. In his office was a list of servants with references, and one couple—Japanese—he heartily recommended. The realtor did not accompany the father and older children down to the cove. He remained up in the house, strolling from room to room with the mother and the little girl and waiting with them in the garden for the others to climb up.

The father returned carrying the coat of his dark mainland suit over his shoulder. His tie hung over the other shoulder, blown back by the warm wind down in the cove. The two boys refused to sit down, though they were panting from the climb. They stood shifting weight from one foot to the other, excited, tossing their hair from their brows. Their tennis shoes and white socks were wet and sand laced their bare legs. Although, with other clients, the realtor, by habit, strained to hear low conversations going on across a room from him or in the back of his station wagon, in order, later, to contradict spontaneously as if he had not heard the criticism or adverse speculating, and although he often used a contemptuous indifference to jolt the obsequious into action and the hostile into a recognition of the value of his time, with this family he was almost deaf, almost mute. While they were gathered again in the garden, the realtor thumbed through a black leather notebook, inquiring if they might care to see another house, closer to the city, with pool and an acre of garden, or a large apartment, a condominium, with a spectacular view. The father, still exhilarated from the descent and his exploration of the cove, suspected that this reminding of other places was a strategy to rouse the family to a desperate desire for this one. He smiled tolerantly, clapped his elder son around the shoulders, and moved toward the gate. The realtor followed the family, swinging the gate closed and locking it while they stood by the road, gazing up at the rest of the land above or gazing out to sea, familiarizing themselves with the spot.

By early June the family had moved in. Canvas chairs and chaise lounges colored the terrace and in the cove a small rowboat rigged with a yellow sail resembled a floating flower. Children called to one another up and down the stairs, their voices always on the verge of echoing, and sometimes a brightly colored garment or towel lay for a night and part of the next day on the steps or on the sand and, seen from above, the fallen cloth claimed that region for the family. Lichee shells, like dry, brown, paper-thin cups, and their large, black, shiny pits lay scattered on the terrace, the soft, sweet, translucent fruit sucked from the pits with exaggerated smacking sounds by the two boys and the younger girl. The fragrance of plumeria and pikake drifted down to the cove and the scent of the sea rose, permeating the rooms of the house. At certain times of the day, early morning and late evening, the water in the cove was like a giant, dark, narcissist's mirror overhung by the mingled scents. Four cousins, ranging in age from seven to eleven, came over by plane from the mainland in July. They came all together, although from two families, the older ones in charge of the two younger. They were met at the island airport by the entire family. It was already early evening by the time the children got down into the cove. The sons and elder daughter of the host family ventured out farther toward the reef than their cousins who, adrift for the first time in the sea, were awed by the gradual loss of the others to the dusk and distance and by the eeriness of their containment in that large stone bowl that seemed to shrink when they dropped their heads back and gazed up at the great shoulders of earth and, far up yet only halfway up, the lighted house that hung in the green, darkening mass.

The realtor passed the house once, with him in his station wagon an executive of a hotel chain who was interested in acreage on the island. The client was talking incessantly, and the realtor did not glance out to find the foliage and the gate that marked the property until they had passed it by a mile.

On days that were oppressively warm, the damp heat, the metallic, lifeless shining of the waters, the steaming garden, and the land mass on which the house was perched, all seemed to comprise an initiation. They were more conscious than ever that they dwelled on an island. On more pleasant days it had begun to be as habitually under their feet as the continent they had been born to. Now the heat loosed the moorings of the island and of the memory, and the continent itself seemed to have been no more solidly in place than the island. The children swam in the morning and again in the afternoon, played cards and other games under the three large umbrellas on the sand, and indolently amused themselves in the house. The mother took her dips in the morning before anyone was up. The air was already warm and the sun bright, but a diffident presence was with her: a coolness that she was certain she would not have found had her family accompanied her. The father swam in the afternoon with the children. Each parent had a time that favored him.

After his swim, the father lay prone on the sand, his feet toward the land, his head toward the sea. He closed his eyes, hearing the water, the barking of the small grey poodle running back and forth in the shallows, and the voices of the smaller children under the umbrellas. He lifted his head from his arms to face the other way, glancing out to the figures borne high on the serene, incoming swell. Three were more or less in a row, the fourth, his elder son, was at a farther distance, treading water. He laid his head down again and did not see the boy tossed into the air. One of the younger boys on the sand saw and laughed at what he thought was his cousin's amazing antic. His son's scream came to the father in two ways: it came over the water and it came through the sand, reverberating against his body. The boy was in the same spot, his arms raised. A few yards from the boy a dark fin detached itself from the dark, swarming spots that plagued the father's vision in the intense light, circled the boy, and disappeared. The boy disappeared with it, lost like the fin in the glittering air and water.

Their excitement in the water deafened the rest of the children to the terror in the cry. The father running into the water was a common sight to them, and their abiding in the water for so many more hours of the day gave them, as usual, a secret sense of their superior adaptability. The great, dark body gliding past them and around and beneath them sent them to shore as clumsily and eccentrically as if they had never learned to swim. The children under the umbrellas huddled down on their haunches, facing the sea or facing the cliffs, screaming the name of the creature. The father felt the shark pass under him and glimpsed it, and his own body seemed to dissolve, as if that languidly, monstrously gliding creature destroyed him without touching him. Way above the cove a child was climbing the steps, screaming up to the house the same word as the children below, and stumbling on the dog that ran up before him and stopped and ran up farther, barking all the way.

The daughter, with the help of the older boys, pushed the small dinghy across the sand and out into the water. Alone, to leave room in the boat for her father and brother, she rowed out to the place where her father was diving and waited there, the boat rocking and tugging away from her oars. She watched for the fin and for the large, dark body again, sighting neither within the great bowl of water, luminous, clear, except for the spreading and separating patch of blood a yard from the boat. The father rose and dove again, rose and clung to the side of the boat, and the sound of his breath was the sound of their terror as they drifted, rocked by the water and by the boat's own rocking. When he had rested for a few minutes he dove again and when he rose he lifted up to her the body of the boy. Her thin arms straining, she held to the body against the tug and drag of the water while her father swung himself up into the boat; then together they drew the body up.

The realtor unlocked the gate and stepped aside to permit the family to precede him. The family crossed the garden, the children, a small boy and a girl, maneuvering around and between their parents in order to lead the way. Not all of the family were present. Two of the older children were in boarding school and a third child was in college. Rain had fallen only a few minutes before; steam was rising along the roof and a glittering was going on in the shade of the garden. A few doves were stirring in the trees. When the realtor moved toward the house the parents followed without lingering. The realtor spoke very little as he led the way out onto the terrace and back through the rooms, as if words were unnecessary since it was obvious that the property was to belong to this family. The mother was confused by the certainty. Before marriage she had been a hungry actress, and the years of her marriage—only the two younger children were hers—had not overcome her mistrust of certainty. She felt the need to catch the eye of the realtor and, even if her glance appeared to be flirtatious, convey to him her desire to comply. He did not meet her eyes but, his head bowed as if in solemn understanding, he moved away to lead the family farther.

Just for fun— and sanity

Heartburn

Hortense Calisher
(*b. 1911*)

Hortense Calisher grew up in New York City and has lived there most of her life. After graduating from Barnard College in New York in 1932, she worked as an "investigator" for the Department of Public Welfare. She has since taught English at Barnard College, The State University of Iowa, and Sarah Lawrence College and presently teaches writing at Columbia University and the City College of New York. Although several of her stories had appeared earlier in The New Yorker, *Hortense Calisher became known as a professional writer in 1951 with the publication of her short-story collection* In the Absence of Angels. *Since then she has published a number of novels, including* False Entry (*1961*), Textures of Life (*1963*), Journal from Ellipsia (*1965*), The Railway Police and the Last Trolley Ride (*1966*), *and* The New Yorkers (*1969*); *she has also contributed short stories, articles, and reviews to such publications as* The New Yorker, Harper's, Harper's Bazaar, Mademoiselle, *the* Reporter, *the New York* Times, *and* The American Scholar.

The light, gritty wind of a spring morning blew in on the doctor's shining, cleared desk, and on the tall buttonhook of a man who leaned agitatedly toward him.

"I have some kind of small animal lodged in my chest," said the man. He coughed, a slight, hollow apologia to his ailment, and sank back in his chair.

"Animal?" said the doctor, after a pause which had the unfortunate quality of comment. His voice, however, was practiced, deft, colored only with the careful suspension of judgment.

"Probably a form of newt or toad," answered the man, speaking with clipped distaste, as if he would disassociate himself from the idea as far as possible. His face quirked with sad foreknowledge. "Of course, you don't believe me."

The doctor looked at him noncommittally. Paraphrased, an old refrain of the poker table leapt erratically in his mind. "Nits" —no—"newts and gnats and one-eyed jacks," he thought. But already the anecdote was shaping itself, trim and perfect, for display at the clinic luncheon table. "Go on," he said.

"Why won't any of you come right out and say what you think!" the man said angrily. Then he flushed, not hectically, the doctor noted, but with the well-bred embarrassment of the normally reserved. "Sorry. I didn't mean to be rude."

"You've already had an examination?" The doctor was a neurologist, and most of his patients were referrals.

"My family doctor. I live up in Boston."

"Did you tell him—er. . . ?" The doctor sought gingerly for a phrase.

One corner of the man's mouth lifted, as if he had watched others in the same dilemma. "I went through the routine first. Fluoroscope, metabolism, cardiograph. Even gastroscopy." He spoke, the doctor noted, with the regrettable glibness of the patient who has shopped around.

"And—the findings?" said the doctor, already sure of the answer.

The man leaned forward, holding the doctor's glance with his own. A faint smile riffled his mouth. "Positive."

"Positive!"

"Well," said the man, "machines have to be interpreted after all, don't they?" He attempted a shrug, but the quick eye of the doctor saw that the movement masked a slight contortion within his tweed suit, as if the man writhed away from himself but concealed it quickly, as one masks a hiccup with a cough. "A curious flutter in the cardiograph, a strange variation in the metabolism, an alien shadow under the fluoroscope." He coughed again and put a genteel hand over his mouth, but this time the doctor saw it clearly—the slight, cringing motion.

"You see," added the man, his eyes helpless and apologetic above the polite covering hand. "It's alive. It *travels*."

"Yes. Yes, of course," said the doctor, soothingly now. In his mind hung the word, ovoid and perfect as a drop of water about to fall. Obsession. A beautiful case. He thought again of the luncheon table.

"What did your doctor recommend?" he said.

"A place with more resources, like the Mayo Clinic. It was then that I told him I knew what it was, as I've told you. And how I acquired it." The visitor paused. "Then, of course, he was forced to pretend to believe me."

"Forced?" said the doctor.

"Well," said the visitor, "actually, I think he did believe me. People tend to believe anything these days. All this mass media information gives them the habit. It takes a strong individual to disbelieve evidence."

The doctor was confused and annoyed. Well, "What then?" he said peremptorily, ready to rise from his desk in dismissal.

Again came the fleeting bodily grimace and the quick cough. "He—er . . . he gave me a prescription."

The doctor raised his eyebrows, in a gesture he was swift to retract as unprofessional.

"For heartburn, I think it was," added his visitor demurely.

Tipping back in his chair, the doctor tapped a pencil on the edge of the desk. "Did he suggest you seek help—on another level?"

"Many have suggested it," said the man.

"But I'm not a psychiatrist!" said the doctor irritably.

"Oh, I know that. You see, I came to you because I had the luck to hear one of your lectures at the Academy. The one on 'Overemphasis on the Non-somatic Causes of Nervous Disorder.' It takes a strong man to go against the tide like that. A disbeliever. And that's what I sorely need." The visitor shuddered, this time letting the *frisson* pass uncontrolled. "You see," he added, thrusting his clasped hands forward on the desk, and looking ruefully at the doctor, as if he would cushion him against his next remark, "you see—I am a psychiatrist."

The doctor sat still in his chair.

"Ah, I can't help knowing what you are thinking," said the man. "I would think the same. A streamlined version of the Napoléonic delusion." He reached into his breast pocket, drew out a wallet, and fanned papers from it on the desk.

"Never mind. I believe you!" said the doctor hastily.

"Already?" said the man sadly.

Reddening, the doctor hastily looked over the collection of letters, cards of membership in professional societies, licenses, and so on—very much the same sort of thing he himself would have had to amass, had he been under the same necessity of proving his identity. Sanity, of course, was another matter. The documents were all issued to Dr. Curtis Retz at a Boston address. Stolen, possibly, but something in the man's manner, in fact everything in it except his unfortunate hallucination, made the doctor think otherwise. Poor guy, he thought. Occupational fatigue, perhaps. But what a form! The Boston variant, possibly. "Suppose you start from the beginning," he said benevolently.

"If you can spare the time . . ."

"I have no more appointments until lunch." And what a lunch that'll be, the doctor thought, already cherishing the pop-eyed scene—Travis the clinic's director (that plethoric Nestor), and young Gruenberg (all of whose cases were unique), his hairy nostrils dilated for once in a *mise-en-scène* which he did not dominate.

Holding his hands pressed formally against his chest, almost in the attitude of one of the minor placatory figures in a *Pietà,* the visitor went on. "I have the usual private practice," he said, "and clinic affiliations. As a favor to an old friend of mine, headmaster of a boys' school nearby, I've acted as guidance consultant there for some years. The school caters to boys of above average intelligence and is run along progressive lines. Nothing's ever cropped up except run-of-the-mill adolescent problems, colored a little, perhaps, by the type of parents who tend to send their children to a school like that—people who are—well—one might say, almost tediously aware of their commitments as parents."

The doctor grunted. He was that kind of parent himself.

"Shortly after the second term began, the head asked me to come down. He was worried over a sharp drop of morale which seemed to extend over the whole school—general inattention in classes, excited note-passing, nightly disturbances in the dorms—all pointing, he had thought at first, to the existence of some fancier than usual form of hazing, or to one of those secret societies, sometimes laughable, sometimes with overtones of the corrupt, with which all schools are familiar. Except for one thing. One after the other, a long list of boys had been sent to the infirmary by the various teachers who presided in the dining room. Each of the boys had shown a marked debility, and what the resident doctor called 'All the stigmata of pure fright. Complete unwillingness to confide.' Each of the boys pleaded stubbornly for his own release, and a few broke out of their own accord. The interesting thing was that each child did recover shortly after his own release, and it was only after this that another boy was seen to fall ill. No two were afflicted at the same time."

"Check the food?" said the doctor.

"All done before I got there. According to my friend, all the trouble seemed to have started with the advent of one boy, John Hallowell, a kid of about fifteen, who had come to the school late in the term with a history of having run away from four other schools. Records at these classed him as very bright, but made oblique references to 'personality difficulties' which were not defined. My friend's school, ordinarily pretty independent, had taken the boy at the insistence of old Simon Hallowell, the boy's uncle, who is a trustee. His brother, the boy's father, is well known for his marital exploits which have nourished the tabloids for years. The mother lives mostly in France and South America. One of these perennial dryads, apparently, with a youthfulness maintained by money and a yearly immersion in the fountains of American plastic surgery. Only time she sees the boy . . . Well, you can imagine. What the feature articles call a Broken Home."

The doctor shifted in his chair and lit a cigarette.

"I won't keep you much longer," said the visitor. "I saw the boy." A violent fit of coughing interrupted him. This time his curious writhing motion went frankly unconcealed. He got up from his chair and stood at the window, gripping the sill and breathing heavily until he had regained control, and went on, one hand pulling unconsciously at his collar. "Or, at least, I think I saw him. On my way to visit him in his room I bumped into a tall red-headed boy in a football sweater, hurrying down the hall with a windbreaker and a poncho slung over his shoulder. I asked for Hallowell's room; he jerked a thumb over his shoulder at the door just behind him, and continued past me. It never occurred to me . . . I was expecting some adenoidal gangler with acne . . . or one of these sinister little angel faces, full of neurotic sensibility.

"The room was empty. Except for its finicky neatness, and a rather large amount of livestock, there was nothing unusual about it. The school, according to the current trend, is run like a farm, with the boys doing the chores, and pets are encouraged. There was a tank with a couple of turtles near the window, beside it another, full of newts, and in one corner a large cage of well-tended, brisk white mice. Glass cases, with carefully mounted series of lepidoptera and hymenoptera, showing the metamorphic stages, hung on the walls, and on a drawing board there was a daintily executed study of Branchippus, the 'fairy shrimp.'

"While I paced the room, trying to look as if I wasn't prying, a greenish little wretch, holding himself together as if he had an imaginary shawl draped around him, slunk into the half-dark room and squeaked 'Hallowell?' When he saw me he started to duck, but I detained him and found that he had had an appointment with Hallowell too. When it was clear, from his description, that Hallowell must have been the redhead I'd seen leaving, the poor urchin burst into tears.

" 'I'll never get rid of it now!' he wailed. From then on it wasn't hard to get the whole maudlin story. It seems that shortly after Hallowell's arrival at school he acquired a reputation for unusual proficiency with animals and for out-of-the-way lore which would impress the ingenuous. He circulated the rumor that he could swallow small animals and regurgitate them at will. No one actually saw him swallow anything, but it seems that in some mumbo-jumbo with another boy who had shown cynicism about the whole thing, it was claimed that Hallowell had, well, divested himself of something, and passed it on to the other boy, with the statement that the latter would only be able to get rid of his cargo when he in turn found a boy who would disbelieve *him*."

The visitor paused, calmer now, and leaving the window sat down again in the chair opposite the doctor, regarding him with such fixity that the doctor shifted uneasily, with the apprehension of one who is about to be asked for a loan.

"My mind turned to the elementary sort of thing we've all done at times. You know, circle of kids in the dark, piece of cooked cauliflower passed from hand to hand with the statement that the stuff is fresh brains of some neophyte who hadn't taken his initiation seriously. My young informer, Moulton his name was, swore however that this hysteria (for of course, that's what I thought it) was passed on singly, from boy to boy, without any such séances. He'd been home to visit his family, who are missionaries on leave, and had been infected by his roommate on his return to school, unaware that by this time the whole school had protectively turned believers, en masse. His own terror came, not only from his conviction that he was possessed, but from his inability to find anybody who would take his dare. And so he'd finally come to Hallowell. . . .

"By this time the room was getting really dark and I snapped on the light to get a better look at Moulton. Except for an occasional shudder, like a bodily tic, which I took to be the aftereffects of hard crying, he looked like a healthy enough boy who'd been scared out of his wits. I remember that a neat little monograph was already forming itself in my mind, a group study on mass psychosis, perhaps, with effective anthropological references to certain savage tribes whose dances include a rite known as 'eating evil.'

"The kid was looking at me. 'Do you believe me?' he said suddenly. 'Sir?' he added, with a naive cunning which tickled me.

" 'Of course,' I said, patting his shoulder absently. 'In a way.'

"His shoulder slumped under my hand. I felt its tremor, direct misery palpitating between my fingers.

" 'I thought . . . maybe for a man . . . it wouldn't be . . .' His voice trailed off.

" 'Be the same? . . . I don't know,' I said slowly, for of course, I was answering, not his actual question, but the overtone of some cockcrow of meaning that evaded me.

"He raised his head and petitioned me silently with his eyes. Was it guile, or simplicity, in his look, and was it for conviction, or the lack of it, that he arraigned me? I don't know. I've gone back over what I did then, again and again, using all my own knowledge of the mechanics of decision, and I know that it wasn't just sympathy, or a pragmatic reversal of therapy, but something intimately important for me, that made me shout with all my strength—'Of course I don't believe you!'

"Moulton, his face contorted, fell forward on me so suddenly that I stumbled backwards, sending the tank of newts crashing to the floor. Supporting him with my arms, I hung on to him while he heaved, face downwards. At the same time I felt a tickling, sliding sensation in my own ear, and an inordinate desire to follow it with my finger, but both my hands were busy. It wasn't a minute 'til I'd gotten him onto the couch, where he drooped, a little white about the mouth, but with that chastened, purified look of the physically relieved, although he hadn't actually upchucked.

"Still watching him, I stooped to clear up the debris, but he bounded from the couch with amazing resilience.

" 'I'll do it,' he said.

" 'Feel better?'

"He nodded, clearly abashed, and we gathered up the remains of the tank in a sort of mutual embarrassment. I can't remember that either of us said a word, and neither of us made more than a half-hearted attempt to search for the scattered pests which had apparently sought crannies in the room. At the door we parted, muttering as formal a goodnight as was possible between a grown man and a small boy. It wasn't until I reached my own room and sat down that I realized, not only my own extraordinary behavior, but that Moulton, standing, as I suddenly recalled, for the first time quite straight, had sent after me a look of pity and speculation.

"Out of habit, I reached into my breast pocket for my pencil, in order to take notes as fresh as possible. And then I felt it . . . a skittering, sidling motion, almost beneath my hand. I opened my jacket and shook myself, thinking that I'd picked up something in the other room . . . but nothing. I sat quite still, gripping the pencil, and after an interval it came again—an inchoate creeping, a twitter of movement almost *lackadaisical,* as of something inching itself lazily along—but this time on my other side. In a frenzy, I peeled off my clothes, inspected myself wildly, and enumerating to myself a reassuring abracadabra of explanation—skipped heartbeat, intercostal pressure of gas—I sat there naked, waiting. And after a moment, it came again, that wandering, aquatic motion, as if something had flipped itself over just enough to make me aware, and then settled itself, this time under the sternum, with a nudge like that of some inconceivable foetus. I jumped up and shook myself again, and as I did so I caught a glimpse of myself in the mirror in the closet door. My face, my own face, was ajar with fright, and I was standing there, hooked over, as if I were wearing an imaginary shawl."

In the silence after his visitor's voice stopped, the doctor sat there in the painful embarrassment of the listener who has played confessor, and whose expected comment is a responsibility he wishes he had evaded. The breeze from the open window fluttered the papers on the desk. Glancing out at the clear, regular façade of the hospital wing opposite, at whose evenly shaded windows the white shapes of orderlies and nurses flickered in consoling routine, the doctor wished petulantly that he had fended off the man and all his papers in the beginning. What right had the man to arraign *him*? Surprised at his own inner vehemence, he pulled himself together. "How long ago?" he said at last.

"Four months."

"And since?"

"It's never stopped." The visitor now seemed brimming with a tentative excitement, like a colleague discussing a mutually puzzling case. "Everything's been tried. Sedatives do obtain some sleep, but that's all. Purgatives. Even emetics." He laughed slightly, almost with pride. "Nothing like that works," he continued, shaking his head with the doting fondness of a patient for some symptom which has confounded the best of them. "It's too cagey for that."

With his use of the word "it," the doctor was propelled back into that shapely sense of reality which had gone admittedly askew during the man's recital. To admit the category of "it," to dip even a slightly co-operative finger in another's fantasy, was to risk one's own equilibrium. Better not to become involved in argument with the possessed, lest one's own apertures of belief be found to have been left ajar.

"I am afraid," the doctor said blandly, "that your case is outside my field."

"As a doctor?" said his visitor. "Or as a man?"

"Let's not discuss me, if you please."

The visitor leaned intently across the desk. "Then you admit that to a certain extent, we *have* been—?"

"Well," said the man disparagingly, "of course, that too is a kind of stand. The commonest, I've found." He sighed, pressing one hand against his collarbone. "I suppose you have a prescription too, or a recommendation. Most of them do."

The doctor did not enjoy being judged. "Why don't you hunt up young Hallowell?" he said, with malice.

"Disappeared. Don't you think I tried?" said his vis-à-vis ruefully. Something furtive, hope, perhaps, spread its guileful corruption over his face. "That means you do give a certain credence—"

"Nothing of the sort!"

"Well then," said his interrogator, turning his palms upward.

The doctor leaned forward, measuring his words with exasperation. "Do you mean you *want* me to tell you you're crazy!"

"In my spot," answered his visitor meekly, "which would you prefer?"

Badgered to the point of commitment, the doctor stared back at his inconvenient Diogenes. Swollen with irritation, he was only half conscious of an uneasy, vestigial twitching of his ear muscles, which contracted now as they sometimes did when he listened to atonal music.

"O.K., O.K. . . !" he shouted suddenly, slapping his hand down on the desk and thrusting his chin forward. "Have it your way then! I don't believe you!"

Rigid, the man looked back at him cataleptically, seeming, for a moment, all eye. Then, his mouth stretching in that medieval grimace, risorial and equivocal, whose mask appears sometimes on one side of the stage, sometimes on the other, he fell forward on the desk, with a long, mewing sigh.

Before the doctor could reach him, he had raised himself on his arms and their foreheads touched. They recoiled, staring downward. Between them on the desk, as if one of its mahogany shadows had become animate, something seemed to move—small, seal-colored, and ambiguous. For a moment it filmed back and forth, arching in a crude, primordial inquiry; then, homing straight for the doctor, whose jaw hung down in a rictus of shock, it disappeared from view.

Sputtering, the doctor beat the air and his own person wildly with his hands, and staggered upward from his chair. The breeze blew hypnotically, and the stranger gazed back at him with such perverse calm that already he felt an assailing doubt of the lightning, untoward event. He fumbled back over his sensations of the minute before, but already piecemeal and chimerical, they eluded him now, as they might forever.

"It's unbelievable," he said weakly.

His visitor put up a warding hand, shaking it fastidiously. *"Au contraire!"* he replied daintily, as though by the use of another language he would remove himself still further from commitment. Reaching forward, he gathered up his papers into a sheaf, and stood up, stretching himself straight with an all-over bodily yawn of physical ease that was like an affront. He looked down at the doctor, one hand fingering his wallet. "No," he said reflectively, "guess not." He tucked the papers away. "Shall we leave it on the basis of—er—professional courtesy?" he inquired delicately.

Choking on the sludge of his rage, the doctor looked back at him, inarticulate.

Moving toward the door, the visitor paused. "After all," he said, "with your connections . . . try to think of it as a temporary inconvenience." Regretfully, happily, he closed the door behind him.

The doctor sat at his desk, humped forward. His hands crept to his chest and crossed. He swallowed, experimentally. He hoped it was rage. He sat there, waiting. He was thinking of the luncheon table.

The Open Window

"Saki" (*H. H. Munro*)
(*1870–1916*)

"Saki," the cupbearer in the Rubáiyát, *is the pseudonym of Hector Hugh Munro. Born in Burma of Scottish parents, Munro was sent to England at an early age, where he was raised by two aunts. In his early twenties he returned and worked briefly with the Burma Military Police; but when the climate of the East proved detrimental to his health, he left again for England. Munro later spent six years in Russia and the Balkans as a foreign correspondent for the* Morning Post. *During this period he wrote and sent to England for publication many of the humorous short stories that are the basis of his literary reputation. When World War I broke out, Munro, like a number of his younger literary compatriots, enlisted as a private, despite several offers of a commission. He was killed in November, 1916, at the battle of Beaumont-Hamel.*

The only work Munro ever published under his own name was The Rise of the Russian Empire (*1900*). *In 1902 a series of whimsical political articles he had written were collected and published as* The Westminster Alice. *His novels and collections of short stories include* Reginald (*1904*), The Chronicles of Clovis (*1912*), The Unbearable Bassington (*1912*), When William Came (*1914*), Beasts and Super-Beasts (*1914*), The Toys of Peace and Other Papers (*1919*), *and* The Square Egg and Other Sketches (*1924*).

"My aunt will be down presently, Mr. Nuttel," said a very self-possessed young lady of fifteen; "in the meantime you must try and put up with me."

Framton Nuttel endeavored to say the correct something which should duly flatter the niece of the moment without unduly discounting the aunt that was to come. Privately he doubted more than ever whether these formal visits on a succession of total strangers would do much towards helping the nerve cure which he was supposed to be undergoing.

"I know how it will be," his sister had said when he was preparing to migrate to this rural retreat; "you will bury yourself down there and not speak to a living soul, and your nerves will be worse than ever from moping. I shall just give you letters of introduction to all the people I know there. Some of them, as far as I can remember, were quite nice."

Framton wondered whether Mrs. Sappleton, the lady to whom he was presenting one of the letters of introduction, came into the nice division.

"Do you know many of the people round here?" asked the niece, when she judged that they had had sufficient silent communion.

"Hardly a soul," said Framton. "My sister was staying here, at the rectory, you know, some four years ago, and she gave me letters of introduction to some of the people here."

He made the last statement in a tone of distinct regret.

"Then you know practically nothing about my aunt?" pursued the self-possessed young lady.

"Only her name and address," admitted the caller. He was wondering whether Mrs. Sappleton was in the married or widowed state. An undefinable something about the room seemed to suggest masculine habitation.

"Her great tragedy happened just three years ago," said the child; "that would be since your sister's time."

"Her tragedy?" asked Framton; somehow in this restful country spot tragedies seemed out of place.

"You may wonder why we keep that window wide open on an October afternoon," said the niece, indicating a large French window that opened on to a lawn.

"It is quite warm for the time of the year," said Framton; "but has that window got anything to do with the tragedy?"

"Out through that window, three years ago to a day, her hus-

THE OPEN WINDOW   From *The Short Stories of Saki* by H. H. Munro. Reprinted by permission of The Viking Press, Inc.

band and her two young brothers went off for their day's shooting. They never came back. In crossing the moor to their favorite snipe-shooting ground they were all three engulfed in a treacherous piece of bog. It had been that dreadful wet summer, you know, and places that were safe in other years gave way suddenly without warning. Their bodies were never recovered. That was the dreadful part of it." Here the child's voice lost its self-possessed note and became falteringly human. "Poor aunt always thinks that they will come back someday, they and the little brown spaniel that was lost with them, and walk in at that window just as they used to do. That is why the window is kept open every evening till it is quite dusk. Poor dear aunt, she has often told me how they went out, her husband with his white waterproof coat over his arm, and Ronnie, her youngest brother, singing 'Bertie, why do you bound?' as he always did to tease her, because she said it got on her nerves. Do you know, sometimes on still, quiet evenings like this, I almost get a creepy feeling that they will all walk in through that window——"

She broke off with a little shudder. It was a relief to Framton when the aunt bustled into the room with a whirl of apologies for being late in making her appearance.

"I hope Vera has been amusing you?" she said.

"She has been very interesting," said Framton.

"I hope you don't mind the open window," said Mrs. Sappleton briskly; "my husband and brothers will be home directly from shooting, and they always come in this way. They've been out for snipe in the marshes today, so they'll make a fine mess over my poor carpets. So like you menfolk, isn't it?"

She rattled on cheerfully about the shooting and the scarcity of birds, and the prospects for duck in the winter. To Framton it was all purely horrible. He made a desperate but only partially successful effort to turn the talk on to a less ghastly topic; he was conscious that his hostess was giving him only a fragment of her attention, and her eyes were constantly straying past him to the open window and the lawn beyond. It was certainly an unfortunate coincidence that he should have paid his visit on this tragic anniversary.

"The doctors agree in ordering me complete rest, an absence of mental excitement, and avoidance of anything in the nature of violent physical exercise," announced Framton, who labored under the tolerably widespread delusion that total strangers and chance acquaintances are hungry for the least detail of one's ailments and infirmities, their cause and cure. "On the matter of diet they are not so much in agreement," he continued.

"No?" said Mrs. Sappleton, in a voice which only replaced a yawn at the last moment. Then she suddenly brightened into alert attention—but not to what Framton was saying.

"Here they are at last!" she cried. "Just in time for tea, and don't they look as if they were muddy up to the eyes!"

Framton shivered slightly and turned towards the niece with a look intended to convey sympathetic comprehension. The child was staring out through the open window with a dazed horror in her eyes. In a chill shock of nameless fear Framton swung round in his seat and looked in the same direction.

In the deepening twilight three figures were walking across the lawn towards the window; they all carried guns under their arms, and one of them was additionally burdened with a white coat hung over his shoulders. A tired brown spaniel kept close at their heels. Noiselessly they neared the house, and then a hoarse young voice chanted out of the dusk: "I said, Bertie, why do you bound?"

Framton grabbed wildly at his stick and hat; the hall door, the gravel drive, and the front gate were dimly noted stages in his headlong retreat. A cyclist coming along the road had to run into the hedge to avoid imminent collision.

"Here we are, my dear," said the bearer of the white mackintosh, coming in through the windows; "fairly muddy, but most of it's dry. Who was that who bolted out as we came up?"

"A most extraordinary man, a Mr. Nuttel," said Mrs. Sappleton; "could only talk about his illnesses, and dashed off without a word of good-by or apology when you arrived. One would think he had seen a ghost."

"I expect it was the spaniel," said the niece calmly; "he told me he had a horror of dogs. He was once hunted into a cemetery somewhere on the banks of the Ganges by a pack of pariah dogs, and had to spend the night in a newly dug grave with the creatures snarling and grinning and foaming just above him. Enough to make anyone lose their nerve."

Romance at short notice was her speciality.

The Catbird Seat

James Thurber
(*1894–1961*)

James Grover Thurber was born in Columbus, Ohio, and graduated from high school there in 1913. He then entered Ohio State University where he wrote for the student newspaper and eventually became the editor of a monthly magazine; in 1918 Thurber left the university without having received a degree. During World War I he worked in Washington, D.C. and in Paris as a code clerk for the State Department. After the war Thurber returned to Columbus, was employed as a reporter for the Columbus Dispatch, *and wrote and directed musical comedies performed at Ohio State University.*

At a cocktail party in 1927 Thurber met author E. B. White, who became a life-long friend and who introduced him to Harold Ross, editor of the newly founded magazine The New Yorker. *Thurber was hired as managing editor of the magazine and, though he soon renounced this managerial position, remained associated with* The New Yorker *as a contributing editor for the rest of his life. In 1929, with E. B. White, Thurber published his first book,* Is Sex Necessary? *His other books include* The Owl in the Attic and Other Perplexities (*1931*); The Seal in the Bedroom and Other Predicaments (*1932*); My Life and Hard Times (*1933*); The Cream of Thurber (*1939*); Men, Women, and Dogs (*1943*); The Thurber Carnival (*1945*); The Thurber Album (*1952*); *and* Thurber's Dogs (*1955*). *The first of Thurber's now celebrated cartoons appeared in* The New Yorker *in 1931.*

Mr. Martin bought the pack of Camels on Monday night in the most crowded cigar store on Broadway. It was theater time and seven or eight men were buying cigarettes. The clerk didn't even glance at Mr. Martin, who put the pack in his overcoat pocket and went out. If any of the staff at F & S had seen him buy the cigarettes, they would have been astonished, for it was generally known that Mr. Martin did not smoke, and never had. No one saw him.

It was just a week to the day since Mr. Martin had decided to rub out Mrs. Ulgine Barrows. The term "rub out" pleased him because it suggested nothing more than the correction of an error —in this case an error of Mr. Fitweiler. Mr. Martin had spent each night of the past week working out his plan and examining it. As he walked home now he went over it again. For the hundredth time he resented the element of imprecision, the margin of guess-work that entered into the business. The project as he had worked it out was casual and bold, the risks were considerable. Something might go wrong anywhere along the line. And therein lay the cunning of his scheme. No one would ever see in it the cautious, painstaking hand of Erwin Martin, head of the filing department at F & S, of whom Mr. Fitweiler had once said, "Man is fallible but Martin isn't." No one would see his hand, that is, unless it were caught in the act.

Sitting in his apartment, drinking a glass of milk, Mr. Martin reviewed his case again Mrs. Ulgine Barrows, as he had every night for seven nights. He began at the beginning. Her quacking voice and braying laugh had first profaned the halls of F & S on March 7, 1941 (Mr. Martin had a head for dates). Old Roberts, the personnel chief, had introduced her as the newly appointed special adviser to the president of the firm, Mr. Fitweiler. The woman had appalled Mr. Martin instantly, but he hadn't shown it. He had given her his dry hand, a look of studious concentration, and a faint smile. "Well," she had said, looking at the papers on his desk, "are you lifting the oxcart out of the ditch?" As Mr. Martin recalled that moment, over his milk, he squirmed slightly. He must keep his mind on her crimes as a special adviser, not on her peccadillos as a personality. This he found difficult to do, in spite of entering an objection and sustaining it. The faults of the woman as a woman kept chattering on in his mind like an unruly witness. She had, for almost two years now, baited him. In the halls, in the

THE CATBIRD SEAT Copyright © 1945 James Thurber. From *The Thurber Carnival,* published by Harper & Row, New York. Originally printed in *The New Yorker.*

elevator, even in his own office, into which she romped now and then like a circus horse, she was constantly shouting these silly questions at him. "Are you lifting the oxcart out of the ditch? Are you tearing up the pea patch? Are you hollering down the rain barrel? Are you scraping around the bottom of the pickle barrel? Are you sitting in the catbird seat?"

It was Joey Hart, one of Mr. Martin's two assistants, who had explained what the gibberish meant. "She must be a Dodger fan," he had said. "Red Barber announces the Dodger games over the radio and he uses those expressions—picked 'em up down South." Joey had gone on to explain one or two. "Tearing up the pea patch" meant going on a rampage; "sitting in the catbird seat" meant sitting pretty, like a batter with three balls and no strikes on him. Mr. Martin dismissed all this with an effort. It had been annoying, it had driven him near to distraction, but he was too solid a man to be moved to murder by anything so childish. It was fortunate, he reflected as he passed on to the important charges against Mrs. Barrows, that he had stood up under it so well. He had maintained always an outward appearance of polite tolerance. "Why, I even believe you like the woman," Miss Paird, his other assistant, had once said to him. He had simply smiled.

A gavel rapped in Mr. Martin's mind and the case proper was resumed. Mrs. Ulgine Barrows stood charged with willful, blatant, and persistent attempts to destroy the efficiency and system of F & S. It was competent, material, and relevant to review her advent and rise to power. Mr. Martin had got the story from Miss Paird, who seemed always able to find things out. According to her, Mrs. Barrows had met Mr. Fitweiler at a party, where she had rescued him from the embraces of a powerfully built drunken man who had mistaken the president of F & S for a famous retired Middle Western football coach. She had led him to a sofa and somehow worked upon him a monstrous magic. The aging gentleman had jumped to the conclusion there and then that this was a woman of singular attainments, equipped to bring out the best in him and in the firm. A week later he had introduced her into F & S as his special adviser. On that day confusion got its foot in the door. After Miss Tyson, Mr. Brundage, and Mr. Bartlett had been fired and Mr. Munson had taken his hat and stalked out, mailing in his resignation later, old Roberts had been emboldened to speak to Mr. Fitweiler. He mentioned that Mr. Munson's department had been "a little disrupted" and hadn't they perhaps better resume the old system there? Mr. Fitweiler had said certainly not. He had the greatest faith in Mrs. Barrows' ideas. "They require a little seasoning, a little seasoning, is all," he had added. Mr. Roberts had given it up. Mr. Martin reviewed in detail all the changes wrought by Mrs. Barrows. She had begun chipping at the cornices of the firm's edifice and now she was swinging at the foundation stones with a pickaxe.

Mr. Martin came now, in his summing up, to the afternoon of Monday, November 2, 1942—just one week ago. On that day, at 3 P.M., Mrs. Barrows had bounced into his office. "Boo!" she had yelled. "Are you scraping around the bottom of the pickle barrel?" Mr. Martin had looked at her from under his green eyeshade, saying nothing. She had begun to wander about the office, taking it in with her great, popping eyes. "Do you really need *all* these filing cabinets?" she had demanded suddenly. Mr. Martin's heart had jumped. "Each of these files," he had said, keeping his voice even, "plays an indispensable part in the system of F & S." She had brayed at him, "Well, don't tear up the pea patch!" and gone to the door. From there she had bawled, "But you sure have got a lot of fine scrap in here!" Mr. Martin could no longer doubt that the finger was on his beloved department. Her pickaxe was on the upswing, poised for the first blow. It had not come yet; he had received no blue memo from the enchanted Mr. Fitweiler bearing nonsensical instructions deriving from the obscene woman. But there was no doubt in Mr. Martin's mind that one would be forthcoming. He must act quickly. Already a precious week had gone by. Mr. Martin stood up in his living room, still holding his milk glass. "Gentlemen of the jury," he said to himself, "I demand the death penalty for this horrible person."

The next day Mr. Martin followed his routine, as usual. He polished his glasses more often and once sharpened an already sharp pencil, but not even Miss Paird noticed. Only once did he catch sight of his victim; she swept past him in the hall with a patronizing "Hi!" At five-thirty he walked home, as usual, and had a glass of milk, as usual. He had never drunk anything stronger in his life—unless you could count ginger ale. The late Sam Schlosser, the S of F & S, had praised Mr. Martin at a staff meeting several years before for his temperate habits. "Our most efficient worker neither drinks nor smokes," he had said. "The results speak for themselves." Mr. Fitweiler had sat by, nodding approval.

Mr. Martin was still thinking about that red-letter day as he walked over to the Schrafft's on Fifth Avenue near Forty-sixth Street. He got there, as he always did, at eight o'clock. He finished his dinner and the financial page of the *Sun* at a quarter to nine, as he always did. It was his custom after dinner to take a walk. This time he walked down Fifth Avenue at a casual pace. His gloved hands felt moist and warm, his forehead cold. He transferred the Camels from his overcoat to a jacket pocket. He wondered, as he did so, if they did not represent an unnecessary note of strain. Mrs. Barrows smoked only Luckies. It was his idea to puff a few puffs on a Camel (after the rubbing-out), stub it out in the ashtray holding her lipstick-stained Luckies, and thus drag a small red herring across the trail. Perhaps it was not a good idea. It would take time. He might even choke, too loudly.

Mr. Martin had never seen the house on West Twelfth Street where Mrs. Barrows lived, but he had a clear enough picture of it. Fortunately, she had bragged to everybody about her ducky first-floor apartment in the perfectly darling three-story red-brick. There would be no doorman or other attendants; just the tenants of the second and third floors. As he walked along, Mr. Martin realized that he would get there before nine-thirty. He had considered walking north on Fifth Avenue from Schrafft's to a point from which it would take him until ten o'clock to reach the house. At that hour people were less likely to be coming in or going out. But the procedure would have made an awkward loop in the straight thread of his casualness, and he had abandoned it. It was impossible to figure when people would be entering or leaving the house, anyway. There was a great risk at any hour. If he ran into anybody, he would simply have to place the rubbing-out of Ulgine Barrows in the inactive file forever. The same thing would hold true if there were someone in her apartment. In that case he would just say that he had been passing by, recognized her charming house and thought to drop in.

It was eighteen minutes after nine when Mr. Martin turned into Twelfth Street. A man passed him, and a man and a woman talking. There was no one within fifty paces when he came to the house, halfway down the block. He was up the steps and in the small vestibule in no time, pressing the bell under the card that said "Mrs. Ulgine Barrows." When the clicking in the lock started, he jumped forward against the door. He got inside fast, closing the door behind him. A bulb in a lantern hung from the hall ceiling on a chain seemed to give a monstrously bright light. There was nobody on the stair, which went up ahead of him along the left wall. A door opened down the hall in the wall on the right. He went toward it swiftly, on tiptoe.

"Well, for God's sake, look who's here!" bawled Mrs. Barrows, and her braying laugh rang out like the report of a shotgun. He rushed past her like a football tackle, bumping her. "Hey, quit shoving!" she said, closing the door behind them. They were in her living room, which seemed to Mr. Martin to be lighted by a hundred lamps. "What's after you?" she said. "You're as jumpy as a goat." He found he was unable to speak. His heart was wheezing in his throat. "I—yes," he finally brought out. She was jab-

bering and laughing as she started to help him off with his coat.
"No, no," he said. "I'll put it here." He took it off and put it on a
chair near the door. "Your hat and gloves, too," she said. "You're
in a lady's house." He put his hat on top of the coat. Mrs. Barrows
seemed larger than he had thought. He kept his gloves on. "I was
passing by," he said. "I recognized—is there anyone here?" She
laughed louder than ever. "No," she said, "we're all alone. You're
as white as a sheet, you funny man. Whatever *has* come over you?
I'll mix you a toddy." She started toward a door across the room.
"Scotch-and-soda be all right? But say, you don't drink, do you?"
She turned and gave him her amused look. Mr. Martin pulled himself together. "Scotch-and-soda will be all right," he heard himself
say. He could hear her laughing in the kitchen.

Mr. Martin looked quickly around the living room for the
weapon. He had counted on finding one there. There were andirons
and a poker and something in a corner that looked like an Indian
club. None of them would do. It couldn't be that way. He began
to pace around. He came to a desk. On it lay a metal paper knife
with an ornate handle. Would it be sharp enough? He reached for
it and knocked over a small brass jar. Stamps spilled out of it and
it fell to the floor with a clatter. "Hey," Mrs. Barrows yelled from
the kitchen, "are you tearing up the pea patch?" Mr. Martin gave
a strange laugh. Picking up the knife, he tried its point against his
left wrist. It was blunt. It wouldn't do.

When Mrs. Barrows reappeared, carrying two highballs, Mr.
Martin, standing there with his gloves on, became acutely conscious of the fantasy he had wrought. Cigarettes in his pocket, a
drink prepared for him—it was all too grossly improbable. It was
more than that; it was impossible. Somewhere in the back of his
mind a vague idea stirred, sprouted. "For heaven's sake, take off
those gloves," said Mrs. Barrows. "I always wear them in the
house," said Mr. Martin. The idea began to bloom, strange and
wonderful. She put the glasses on a coffee table in front of a sofa
and sat on the sofa. "Come over here, you odd little man," she
said. Mr. Martin went over and sat beside her. It was difficult getting a cigarette out of the pack of Camels, but he managed it.
She held a match for him, laughing. "Well," she said, handing him
his drink, "this is perfectly marvelous. You with a drink and a
cigarette."

Mr. Martin puffed, not too awkwardly, and took a gulp of the
highball. "I drink and smoke all the time," he said. He clinked his
glass against hers. "Here's nuts to that old windbag, Fitweiler,"
he said, and gulped again. The stuff tasted awful, but he made no
grimace. "Really, Mr. Martin," she said, her voice and posture

changing, "you are insulting our employer." Mrs. Barrows was now all special adviser to the president. "I am preparing a bomb," said Mr. Martin, "which will blow the old goat higher than hell." He had only had a little of the drink, which was not strong. It couldn't be that. "Do you take dope or something?" Mrs. Barrows asked coldly. "Heroin," said Mr. Martin. "I'll be coked to the gills when I bump that old buzzard off." "Mr. Martin!" she shouted, getting to her feet. "That will be all of that. You must go at once." Mr. Martin took another swallow of his drink. He tapped his cigarette out in the ashtray and put the pack of Camels on the coffee table. Then he got up. She stood glaring at him. He walked over and put on his hat and coat. "Not a word about this," he said, and laid an index finger against his lips. All Mrs. Barrows could bring out was "Really!" Mr. Martin put his hand on the doorknob. "I'm sitting in the catbird seat," he said. He stuck his tongue out at her and left. Nobody saw him go.

Mr. Martin got to his apartment, walking, well before eleven. No one saw him go in. He had two glasses of milk after brushing his teeth, and he felt elated. It wasn't tipsiness, because he hadn't been tipsy. Anyway, the walk had worn off all effects of the whisky. He got in bed and read a magazine for a while. He was asleep before midnight.

Mr. Martin got to the office at eight-thirty the next morning, as usual. At a quarter to nine, Ulgine Barrows, who had never before arrived at work before ten, swept into his office. "I'm reporting to Mr. Fitweiler now!" she shouted. "If he turns you over to the police, it's no more than you deserve!" Mr. Martin gave her a look of shocked surprise. "I beg your pardon?" he said. Mrs. Barrows snorted and bounced out of the room, leaving Miss Paird and Joey Hart staring after her. "What's the matter with that old devil now?" asked Miss Paird. "I have no idea," said Mr. Martin, resuming his work. The other two looked at him and then at each other. Miss Paird got up and went out. She walked slowly past the closed door of Mr. Fitweiler's office. Mrs. Barrows was yelling inside, but she was not braying. Miss Paird could not hear what the woman was saying. She went back to her desk.

Forty-five minutes later, Mrs. Barrows left the president's office and went into her own, shutting the door. It wasn't until half an hour later that Mr. Fitweiler sent for Mr. Martin. The head of the filing department, neat, quiet, attentive, stood in front of the old man's desk. Mr. Fitweiler was pale and nervous. He took his glasses off and twiddled them. He made a small, bruffing sound in his throat. "Martin," he said, "you have been with us more than twenty years." "Twenty-two, sir," said Mr. Martin. "In that time," pursued the president, "your work and your—uh—manner have been exemplary." "I trust so, sir," said Mr. Martin. "I have understood, Martin," said Mr. Fitweiler, "that you have never taken a drink or smoked." "That is correct, sir," said Mr. Martin. "Ah, yes." Mr. Fitweiler polished his glasses. "You may describe what you did after leaving the office yesterday, Martin," he said. Mr. Martin allowed less than a second for his bewildered pause. "Certainly, sir," he said. "I walked home. Then I went to Schrafft's for dinner. Afterward I walked home again. I went to bed early, sir, and read a magazine for a while. I was asleep before eleven." "Ah, yes," said Mr. Fitweiler again. He was silent for a moment, searching for the proper words to say to the head of the filing department. "Mrs. Barrows," he said finally, "Mrs. Barrows has worked hard, Martin, very hard. It grieves me to report that she has suffered a severe breakdown. It has taken the form of a persecution complex accompanied by distressing hallucinations." "I am very sorry, sir," said Mr. Martin. "Mrs. Barrows is under the delusion," continued Mr. Fitweiler, "that you visited her last evening and behaved yourself in an—uh—unseemly manner." He raised his hand to silence Mr. Martin's little pained outcry. "It is the nature of these psychological diseases," Mr. Fitweiler said, "to fix upon the least likely and most innocent party as the—uh—source of persecution. These matters are not for the lay mind to grasp, Martin. I've just had my psychiatrist, Dr. Fitch, on the phone. He would not, of course, commit himself, but he made enough generalizations to substantiate my suspicions. I suggested to Mrs. Barrows when she had completed her—uh—story to me this morning, that she visit Dr. Fitch, for I suspected a condition at once. She flew, I regret to say, into a rage, and demanded—uh—requested that I call you on the carpet. You may not know, Martin, but Mrs. Barrows had planned a reorganization of your department—subject to my approval, of course, subject to my approval. This brought you, rather than anyone else, to her mind—but again that is a phenomenon for Dr. Fitch and not for us. So, Martin, I am afraid Mrs. Barrows' usefulness here is at an end." "I am dreadfully sorry, sir," said Mr. Martin.

It was at this point that the door to the office blew open with the suddenness of a gas-main explosion and Mrs. Barrows catapulted through it. "Is the little rat denying it?" she screamed. "He can't get away with that!" Mr. Martin got up and moved discreetly to a point beside Mr. Fitweiler's chair. "You drank and smoked at my apartment," she bawled at Mr. Martin, "and you know it! You called Mr. Fitweiler an old windbag and said you were going to blow him up when you got coked to the gills on your heroin!" She stopped yelling to catch her breath and a new glint came into her popping eyes. "If you weren't such a drab, ordinary little man," she said, "I'd think you'd planned it all. Sticking your tongue out, saying you were sitting in the catbird seat, because you thought no one would believe me when I told it! My God, it's really too perfect!" She brayed loudly and hysterically, and the fury was on her again. She glared at Mr. Fitweiler. "Can't you see how he has tricked us, you old fool? Can't you see his little game?" But Mr. Fitweiler had been surreptitiously pressing all the buttons under the top of his desk and employees of F & S began pouring into the room. "Stockton," said Mr. Fitweiler, "you and Fishbein will take Mrs. Barrows to her home. Mrs. Powell, you will go with them." Stockton, who had played a little football in high school, blocked Mrs. Barrows as she made for Mr. Martin. It took him and Fishbein together to force her out of the door into the hall, crowded with stenographers and office boys. She was still screaming imprecations at Mr. Martin, tangled and contradictory imprecations. The hubbub finally died out down the corridor.

"I regret that this has happened," said Mr. Fitweiler. "I shall ask you to dismiss it from your mind, Martin." "Yes, sir," said Mr. Martin, anticipating his chief's "That will be all" by moving to the door. "I will dismiss it." He went out and shut the door, and his step was light and quick in the hall. When he entered his department he had slowed down to his customary gait, and he walked quietly across the room to the W20 file, wearing a look of studious concentration.

For
Discussion

Barn Burning

1. What is the central tension in the story, and how is it resolved?
2. What does the Sartoris mansion symbolize to the boy? To Abner Snopes?
3. How is Abner Snopes characterized? Is he entirely malignant and despicable, or does he possess some redeeming qualities?
4. Does Abner Snopes live by a code, and if so, how would you describe that code?
5. How does the point of view through which the story is narrated contribute to the story's richness?

Gold Coast

1. What is Rob like when he begins his stint as a janitor? In what ways has he changed at the end of the story?
2. How is "narrator Rob" different from "janitor Rob"? What is the narrator's attitude toward his younger self?
3. How does our attitude toward Sullivan change in the course of the story? What causes this change?
4. What seems to be the turning point in Rob's relationship with Sullivan? How is their developing relationship indicative of Rob's increasing maturity?

The Short Happy Life of
Francis Macomber

1. What are the different ways in which the title of the story can be interpreted? Which reading appears to most accurately reflect Hemingway's theme?
2. Why does Hemingway describe the lion's feelings?
3. What are the major elements of Wilson's code of behavior?
4. Wilson equates manhood with a rather special sort of physical courage. How valid is this equation?
5. Why is it in Wilson's own interest to assert that Margot deliberately murdered Macomber? Did she?

The Eighty-Yard Run

1. What does "the eighty-yard run" symbolize?
2. What is the significance of the appearance of Diederich? What does he represent?
3. What does the football field and the game of football come to symbolize?
4. Why is Darling's apparent good fortune in being "set up" in business by his father-in-law really his misfortune?
5. Toward the end of the story Darling reflects that "there must have been a point where [Louise] moved up to me, was even with me for a moment, when I could have held her hand, if I'd known, held tight, gone with her." Is there a particular point in the story when he had this chance and failed to recognize or act on it?

Haircut

1. What is the irony in Whitey's statement, "It probably served Jim right, what he got"? What does Whitey think happened to Jim?

2. How would you characterize Jim Kendall? How does your view of him differ from that of Whitey and Kendall's other cronies?
3. Did Kendall get what he deserved? Why?
4. What does Lardner suggest about the motivations and character of the "practical joker"? Do you agree?
5. What seems to be Lardner's view of the typical "small town" resident? Have you had experiences that either support or contradict this view?

Rain

1. How is Mrs. Davidson characterized?
2. How would the Davidsons define a "good" woman, a "moral" person?
3. What is the nature of the Davidsons' Christianity?
4. What is the central tension in Davidson's character that drives him?
5. What details early in the story foreshadow and lend credibility to Davidson's "lapse"?

The Blue Hotel

1. What aspects of the Swede's character are suggested by the brief initial description: "a shaky and quick-eyed Swede, with a great shining cheap valise"?
2. What world view is communicated through the image of men as "lice which were caused to cling to a whirling, fire-smitten, ice-locked, disease-stricken, space-lost bulb"?
3. How many examples of animal imagery can you identify in the story? What is the function of this imagery?
4. What is the atmosphere of the story? How is it created? How does it heighten the probability of the action?
5. What is the purpose of the final portion of the story, the part after the Swede's death?

To Build a Fire

1. What is gained by London's referring to the central character as "the man," instead of giving him a specific name?
2. How does London characterize the central character? What kind of man is he?
3. Why does London devote so much attention to the dog? What is the thematic significance of this second "character"?
4. Does the story have a "universal" theme, one applicable to all men, all places, all times?

The Ledge

1. What parallels do you find between this story and Greek or Shakespearean tragedies you have read?
   a. What is the *hamartia* or "tragic flaw" in the character of the fisherman? Through what specific action (or failure to perform a specific action) does it manifest itself?
   b. What elements in the story suggest the working of fate?
   c. Does the final portion of the story achieve a catharsis? If so, how?
2. The author does not give individual names to any of the characters. Why?
3. Why does the author refrain from describing the death of the fisherman and his son?
4. What Christian symbolism do you find in the story? What does this symbolism contribute to the meaning and effect of the story?
5. Compare and contrast the character of "the man" in "To Build a Fire" with that of "the fisherman" in "The Ledge." What character traits do they share? In what respects are they different?
6. How do the two stories differ in their impact on the reader?
7. What contrasting views of man are communicated through the two stories?

The Patented Gate and the Mean Hamburger

1. What is the central conflict or tension in the story? What values, life styles, and economics are in conflict?
2. In what sense do the two images "patented gate" and "mean hamburger" symbolize this central conflict?
3. How would you describe the theme of the story, the major idea or ideas that it expresses?

The Language of Men

1. What is "the language of men" that Carter has yet to learn?
2. What are the limitations of "the language of men?" What sort of thoughts and emotions cannot be expressed in this language?
3. What definition of manhood or manliness does "the language of men" suggest? Do you find this a valid definition?
4. What kind of person is Carter? Why would this sort of person find it difficult to learn "the language of men?"
5. What is Mailer's attitude toward "the language of men?" toward Carter?

The Wall

1. What does "the wall" symbolize?
2. Early in the story Tom describes the method of execution in Sarogossa. Pablo feels irritated and thinks Tom "shouldn't have said that." Why is Pablo so irritated?
3. Why does Sartre introduce the Belgian doctor and the two bored guards?
4. During the night in the cellar, Pablo loses all desire, including the desire to live. What is the reason?
5. Pablo believes that Juan "made more noise than we did, but he was less affected, really." In what respects is Juan less affected by the impending execution than Pablo?

The Portable Phonograph

1. What is the time, place, and general environment of this story? What atmosphere is created by this setting?
2. What are the major symbols in the story?
3. What types of men are represented by the four characters? What do these characters represent collectively?
4. What is the character of Doctor Jenkins?
5. What does the "comfortable piece of lead pipe" symbolize? What is the thematic significance of Doctor Jenkins' final act?

La Lupa

1. Verga describes *La Lupa's* emotion for Nanni as "really what you'd call falling in love, feeling your body burn under your stuff bodice, and suffering, when you stared into his eyes, the thirst that you suffer in the hot hours of June, away in the burning plains." How does this view of love—burning, suffering, thirsting—differ from the American view of love as found in advertisements, popular novels, soap operas, women's magazines, etc? Which view of love most closely parallels your own?
2. What features of *La Lupa* represent her passionate nature?
3. How do you account for Nanni's ambivalence toward *La Lupa,* his alternating desire and hate?
4. How does *La Lupa* differ from the *Playboy* foldout or the college Homecoming Queen?
5. Does Nanni strike *La Lupa* with the axe at the end of the story? What textual evidence can you cite in support of your opinion?

The World the Children Made

1. How does Bradbury view children—their emotions and impulses? How does his view differ from the popular attitude toward children? Does his view conflict with or agree with your own?

2. You may have read William Golding's *Lord of the Flies,* or seen the movie version of his novel. In what respects is Golding's thesis similar to Bradbury's in this story?
3. How are Peter and Wendy characterized?
4. Can you identify a specific passage in the story that seems to state its theme or central idea?

The Cove

1. The realtor opens the gate with a key selected from a "green leather case" given him, along with the keys, by the owner. In retrospect, what is signified by the owner's having given the realtor "both case and keys"?
2. What biblical myth does the story suggest to you? What are the parallels between the story and the myth? How do these parallels add an extra dimension to the story?
3. The realtor could have mentioned the presence of sharks, and a shark net could have been installed. Viewing the story as realism, why doesn't he warn the family? Viewing the story symbolically, why does he refrain from warning them?
4. Why does the realtor advise the family not to hire servants from the nearby village?
5. What is the impact and significance of the last paragraph of the story?

Heartburn

1. Why has the psychiatrist sought out this particular doctor?
2. Is the doctor a sympathetic or unsympathetic character? What thoughts, particularly, influence our attitude toward him?
3. One motif that runs through the story is the doctor's anticipation of the coming luncheon. Why does he look forward to the luncheon during most of the story? At the end of the story he is again "thinking of the luncheon table." Why is he now looking forward to the luncheon?
4. How could it be argued that the doctor deserves his fate?

The Open Window

1. How is the visitor's name especially appropriate?
2. What details about Nuttel establish his susceptibility to Vera's tale?
3. Why does Vera question Nuttel before launching into her fabrication?
4. What is the purpose of the last sentence in the story?
5. How would the effect of the story differ if it ended with the account of Framton's flight?

The Catbird Seat

1. At what point in the story does the reader become aware of Thurber's ironic attitude? What are some of the details early in the story that establish this tone?
2. How probable is the action or plot of the story?
3. In what respects are both Martin and Mrs. Barrows "type" characters? Or are they caricatures?
4. The story was first published in 1942. Has it become dated in some of its specifics? Would you find a Mr. Martin in a business concern today? A Mrs. Barrows?
5. Does the story have any serious meaning, or is it entirely "just for fun"? Does it suggest any truths about human nature that apply to other types of situations and other types of people?

A
Selected
Bibliography

Barzun, Jacques. *Classic, Romantic and Modern*. Boston, 1961.

Brooks, Cleanth. "Irony and 'Ironic' Poetry." *College English 9* (1948): 231–7.

Chevalier, Hookan M. *The Ironic Temper: Anatole France and his Time*. New York, 1932.

DeMott, Benjamin. "The New Irony: Sickniks and Others." *The American Scholar,* Winter 1961–62, pp. 108–119.

Dyson, A. E. *The Crazy Fabric*. London, 1965.

Glicksberg, Charles I. *The Ironic Vision in Modern Literature*. The Hague, 1969.

Hutchens, Eleanor N. "The Identification of Irony." *ELH* 27 (1960): 352–63.

Kayre, Alexander. *From the Closed World to the Infinite Universe*. New York, 1958.

Kierkegaard, Sören. *The Concept of Irony, with Constant Reference to Socrates*. Translated by Lee M. Capel. London, 1966.

Mueke, D. C. *The Compass of Irony*. London, 1969.

Niebuhr, Reinhold. *The Irony of American History*. New York, 1952.

Sarton, Mary. "The Shield of Irony." *The Nation,* 14 April 1956, pp. 314–16.

Thompson, Alan R. *The Dry Mock, A Study of Irony in Drama*. Berkeley, 1948.

Thomson, J. A. K. *Irony: An Historical Introduction*. London, 1926.

Turner, F. *The Element of Irony in English Literature*. Cambridge, 1926.

Ward, Hoover. "Irony and Absurdity in the Avant-Garde Theatre," *Kenyon Review,* Summer 1960, pp. 436–54.

Wright, Andrew. "Irony and Fiction." *Journal of Aesthetics of Art Criticism* 12 (1953): 111–18.